Copyright © 2021 Britt Andrews

All rights reserved. No part of this publication may be reproduced, distributed, or transmitted in any form or by any means, including photocopying, recording, or other electronic or mechanical methods, without the prior written permission of the publisher, except in the case of brief quotations in book reviews.

The unauthorized reproduction or distribution of a copyrighted work is illegal. Criminal copyright infringement, including infringement without monetary gain, is investigated by the FBI and is punishable by fines and federal imprisonment.

Please purchase only authorized electronic editions and do not participate in, or encourage, the electronic piracy of copyrighted materials. Your support of the author's rights is appreciated.

This book is a work of fiction. Names, characters, places, brands, and incidents are the products of the author's imagination or used fictitiously. Any resemblance to actual events, locales or persons, living or dead, is entirely coincidental.

Cover by: Jodielocks Designs
Developmental and content Editing: Cassie Hurst
Editing By: Aubergine Editing
Proofreading by: Proofs by Polly
Formatting by: Inked Imagination Author Services
Photography by: TalkNerdy2me
Samantha La Mar www.thetalknerdy.com

THE MAGIC OF ETERNITY

EMERALD LAKES BOOK FIVE

BRITT ANDREWS

This one is dedicated to the books and world that gave me my first escape to another world. The story that captivated my seven year old mind and convinced me that magic is real.

For Narnia and for Aslan!

TRIGGER WARNING

Trigger Warning
This is a full-length RH romance, intended for adults 18 and older. It includes MM content, parental abuse, and sexual assault. There are other themes that readers may find triggering. *This is the final book in the Emerald Lakes series*

Saige

Chapter One

Giggles trickled through the air, wrapping around me like ghosts. I couldn't see anyone. *Where is that laughter coming from?*

My vision cleared and I found myself drifting down the hallway in my cottage, heading for the stairs. Creaking floorboards overhead and the tinkling laughter guided me. I was so curious. My fingertips trailed along the banister, and I barely noticed that I couldn't feel the smooth wood against my skin.

"Come on, little princesses. It's time for bed!" Cam's voice announced. I smiled. My feet carried me to the guest room.

"But, Daddy!"

My stomach swooped, and I audibly gasped. That tiny voice.

"No buts. You two got to stay up later than usual tonight and Daddy's tired," Cam told the little girls who I hadn't seen yet.

A fit of giggles had tears pricking my eyes. "Are you going to fall asleep in here with us again, Daddy?"

I peeked through the crack of the door and took in the scene. Cam's massive body was completely dominating a tiny princess bed, and two small girls were pressed against either side of him. Well, more like half laid on top of him, because there wasn't much room. A small nightstand held a night-light that illuminated the space softly, and my eyes eagerly took in the matching princess bed on the other side.

I stepped into the room but nobody reacted. *I have to see them.*

"Will you tell us the story again?" the girl with the same color hair as mine asked. Her face was covered in freckles and she had the cutest little grin. I sat down on the bed opposite them, my mouth hanging open.

The other girl, the one with deep, richly colored brown hair and ice-blue eyes, nodded enthusiastically. "Pleeeease, Daddy? The one with the pretty queen and her kings." My eyes flew to Cam's face. He smiled at the girls, but it didn't meet his eyes. My heart clenched, but I wasn't sure why.

"Anything for my girls," he murmured, kissing each of their heads as they nestled in against his large chest. He pulled a large blanket with a castle and pink dragons up over the three of them, before clearing his throat.

"Once upon a time, there was a beautiful green witch. With long, pretty red hair like you." He kissed the red-haired girl on her head once more. "And a smile just like yours." He tapped the dark-haired girl on her chin, and she laughed, flashing that smile that was exactly like mine. "She was the sweetest, kindest witch in the land. Her magic was a magic of life. Of love. Of sacrifice..."

MY EYES FLEW open and I tried to sit up, but found myself unable to move. Pain flared in my lower back, abdomen, and my head. *Gods, my head.*

"Deep breath, miss. You're okay."

I heard the words, but they were soft over the roaring of my heartbeat in my ears. *Where am I? Hands. There are hands on me.*

"Who..." I croaked, my throat raw and painful.

"Shhh." Something wet pressed against my forehead, and I

groaned in discomfort. The compress felt nice, but my head was throbbing and I couldn't resist letting my eyes flutter shut.

"H–hurts..."

"This will help," a voice said, and seconds later, the pain in my body faded and I let myself free fall back into the darkness.

"Give me an update," a man's voice boomed, and had I been able, I might've flinched. His voice was familiar, yet I couldn't place it with a face.

Footsteps shuffled around me but my eyes were closed. I was just so tired. Couldn't open them.

"Sire. She's been this way for weeks. Nothing has changed," a male voice responded. It was a voice that I'd been hearing more frequently. Whoever he was, he always spoke gently and with kindness. On some level, I felt safe knowing he was here and that I wasn't alone with that other male.

A crash sounded. Glass breaking. Cursing. "Figure out what the fucking problem is!"

Silence.

"I believe she needs her ma—"

The familiar voice cut off, and the sounds of a scuffle drifted through my subconscious state. "Well, that's not happening! Even if I could. It's not... possible," the angry male growled. "Notify me immediately of any changes. She so much as flexes a toe, I am to be informed!"

A door slammed. Someone squeezed my hand gently.

I'm pretty *sure I'm dead.*

Everything is bright. Isn't that what they say? Go toward the light?

Or don't go toward the light? Which one was it? Either way... there's a light.

"Welcome back, miss."

I blinked slowly, and the room started coming into focus. A face materialized over mine, and I gasped, not expecting to see someone so close. The face moved back.

"Sorry. Didn't mean to scare you. I wasn't sure if you were going to wake up," he explained. "Here." A straw met my lips, and I greedily gulped down the water he was offering.

"Where am I?" I asked, taking in the decently-sized room. A comforter and sheets were pulled up over my body. The large bed I was in felt like a cloud. My brow furrowed as I focused on the exposed stone walls and high-beamed ceilings. Familiarity niggled at my brain, and I was frustrated once again that my memory still seemed fucked up.

The side of the bed dipped, drawing my gaze back to the man who had given me water. He was wearing nursing scrubs, his curly blond hair reached his chin, and I noticed the navy blue glasses he was wearing very nearly matched his eye color. This man was probably around my age, maybe slightly younger.

"It's normal not to remember much when you first wake up after being in a coma for so long," he said softly, and my body jerked.

I cleared my throat. "Coma?"

He nodded. "For nearly a month now, miss. Do you remember your name or anything prior to this moment?"

Panicking, I sifted back through my mind. *What's the last thing I remember?* "My name is Saige Wildes." I knew that much.

"Correct. That's good. I need to take some blood. Why don't you think about what you remember while I do that?"

"What's your name?" I asked, curious.

The man smiled kindly. "I'm your doctor. You can just call me Balor, if you wish. I've been with you the entire time, monitoring your vitals and watching you closely." He tied an elastic band around my upper arm, and I closed my eyes as he poked my vein with a needle. What did I remember? "Don't push yourself too much. You'll likely be fairly exhausted for the next few days. There. All done."

I glanced down at the crook of my elbow and saw a trail of red trickle from the small puncture wound. Air whooshed from my lungs. Fighting. Yelling. The glint of a blade. The roar of a panther. The crash of a chandelier. The pain.

"Okay, okay. Breathe, Saige. Deep breaths. In and out." Balor encouraged me, but I couldn't get myself under control.

Bloodstained hands. Asrael. My men. Khol. Laurie. *Oh gods.*

"Babies. Mine. My b–babies!" I wailed, fumbling with the blankets to see if I was still pregnant. *Please, gods. Please, please.* My hands shook as I threw the blankets off, and a sob nearly suffocated me as I looked down.

"You lost a lot of blood." My eyes flew to Balor as he spoke softly, as if he were speaking to a cornered animal. "Hemorrhaged. Likely due to the stress of the situation you were in."

Tears trekked down my cheeks continuously. I found my voice somehow, despite my throat feeling as though it was closing. "And they're..." Fuck. I rolled onto my side and curled myself into a ball. Inhaling deeply, I tried again. "The babies? Are they—" I shook my head. I couldn't get it out.

Balor smiled. "Miraculously, your babies are doing great. Everything looks perfect, Saige."

I knew I wasn't safe. We weren't safe. I couldn't bring myself to ask about *them*. Exhaustion was swarming me now and I couldn't fight it. My eyelids were so heavy.

A rhythmic thwacking sound began and with each clap of noise, it was harder and harder to keep my eyes open. I watched Balor get up and rush to the window. He cursed and slammed the window closed, pulling the curtains a moment later. I didn't miss the grim look on his face, but I didn't have the energy to ask what was happening outside.

THE NEXT TIME I opened my eyes, the room was dark. Night had fallen while I'd slept, and I felt pressure on my bladder. Not seeing anyone, I pushed myself up, dangling my legs over the side of the bed. I hadn't been up in a long time, and I hoped I didn't fall trying to find a bathroom. How had I peed and stuff while I was unconscious? Ugh, they'd probably put a catheter in me.

Inhaling deeply, I pushed myself off the bed, making sure to keep one hand in contact with the mattress just in case. My head swam. From exertion or just being upright after so long... I wasn't sure. *Gods, I really have to pee.* A sharp jab shot through my crotch and I winced. *What the hell was that?* Another jab and I felt a trickle of warmth run down my thighs. *Oh shit.* I shuffled to the door in the corner, sighing in relief when I found a nice bathroom.

Had my water broken? Or had I just pissed myself? The babies seemed to be really active, and I cupped my large belly as I took possibly the longest pee of my life. *I think I peed myself. My unborn child just Chuck Norris'd my bladder so hard I pissed myself.* I snorted as I wiped. *I bet that was Sloane's kid. I'd put money on it.*

Suddenly it was hard to get air into my lungs, like something was lodged in my throat, cutting off my ability to live. *Where are my men?* Visions of the last time I saw them flashed in my head and I pressed a hand over my mouth to cover my sobs. *I don't even know if they're alive.*

The bathroom door handle turned, and I hastily stood, letting my nightgown fall to my knees as the door opened.

"Hello, daughter."

I spun just in time to get most of my vomit into the toilet.

She laughed without humor. More of a sinister chuckle. "I heard you were awake and had to come see for myself. How are my babies doing?"

Leaning against the wall on shaky legs, I slid down as sweat built on my brow. "Fuck. You," I hissed. Laurie moved through the bathroom, tinkering with things on the counter like she didn't have a care in the world. I could see her face in the mirror. *How did she end up like this?* It didn't make any sense. But I found that I really didn't give a shit. Not anymore.

"They're not yours. They will never be yours. A woman like you should've never been allowed to have children," I spat, the words pure venom on my tongue.

She froze, her body unnaturally still. I leaned my head back against the wall and closed my eyes, still feeling a bit shaky after being sick.

"Where are my men?" I whispered the words, my eyes remaining shut. I couldn't even look at her. She made me sick.

Laurie sighed dramatically. "Where Asrael wants them to be."

"I need to see them," I replied, awkwardly getting myself off the ground.

She smiled. Too widely. Too excited. "And you shall. In two days' time."

"What? What do you mean? Are they hurt? Tell me, Laurie!" I screamed, reaching for her. Red was bleeding into my vision as rage overtook my body. Before I could touch her though, she snatched my wrists and squeezed hard enough that I felt the bones grind against one another. My teeth clenched against the flare of discomfort as she leaned in, her face inches from mine.

"You'll see. In two days. Everyone will see what happens to traitors of the crown." She dropped one of my arms, tugging me harshly out of the bathroom. My feet stumbled over the cool stone floor, still not accustomed to walking or supporting the weight of my body.

"Stop!" I screeched, as I tripped and caught myself on the back of a chair. "What the fuck is wrong with you?" I ripped my arm from her grip, my breaths coming in jagged pants now. Laurie sneered, and I couldn't believe this was the woman who had given birth to me.

"You're what's wrong with me. You've been nothing but an inconvenience to me your entire life!" Her eyes flared with pure hatred, making her beautiful face look hideous. Did she think this was breaking news to me? On some biological level, I'd always wanted her attention, a relationship of some sort. For fuck's sake, she was my mother. But the day she killed Guppy had been the day that hope died completely. You don't get to pick who you're born to, but you can certainly choose who your true family is… and this bitch wasn't it.

"Well then, by all means, get the fuck out of my life! If I ever see your face again, it'll be too soon. You're nothing but a power-hungry cunt with the temperament of a toddler." I breathed heavily, using both hands to support myself as I leaned over the chair. "You and Asrael deserve each other. Evil pieces of shit…" My body trembled with white-hot fury toward these two people who had been doing everything in their power to destroy my life.

Laurie chuckled, and tsked in her patronizing way. She'd always made me feel like I was beneath her. Not as smart. Not as thin. Not as beautiful. Then I realized something. She was *jealous*. A laugh bubbled out of my mouth before I could stop it, and then just kept coming. I dropped into the chair and laughed so hard tears fell.

"What's so funny?" she snarled.

I wiped my wet eyes and shook my head. *Maybe I've lost it. I finally lost my damn mind.* "You're jealous of me." My gaze darted up just in time to see her face. Her eyes widened only for a moment before narrowing. If looks could kill… "I don't know how Khol ever tolerated you."

"More like how I ever tolerated him. He likes to pretend he's not just as bad as I am. Make no mistake, that demon is—and always will be—mine. Az knows. We're all connected. Khol can fool the best of them; he's an excellent liar. It's one of my favorite things about him. So deceptive." She sighed and pushed a stray strand of hair behind her ear. She was speaking about him in present tense, and my heart twisted with hope.

"Where is he?"

She looked at her nails for a moment, and my stomach clenched as she grinned smugly. "I suspect he's still in my bed, where I left him. His appetites are just as strong as they were twenty-eight years ago."

"He's alive?" I croaked, ignoring her other words. Tears welled in my eyes because I'd seen the way that blade had pierced his body, the way he'd dropped to the floor, not moving. But if he was alive, then my other men, my loves...

"Very much alive. Insatiable, really."

I glanced up and scoffed. "You're a liar. I won't believe a word out of your mouth. Never again. Khol wouldn't fuck you if you were the last woman on earth."

Laurie shrugged, like it didn't bother her one way or another if I believed her. "Suit yourself." She walked through the room, heading for the door. "Asrael will be by later to see you." I glared at her, seeing a slow, wicked smirk take over her expression. My stomach sank. She was the queen of low blows and underhanded jabs, so I braced myself for whatever she was about to deliver. "As for me, I have some mages to see. Imagine how surprised I was to see the beautiful Fischer in person again. Talk about a mindfuck."

I pushed to my feet. "You stay away from him!"

"What's even more interesting is that he appeared to have been cloned. We want to know how that happened," she mused, her eyes glittering with excitement.

Appeared. Not appears. Where is Faris? I didn't want to beg her, but damn it. Not knowing was killing me.

"Laurie. Just tell me... I need to know," I whispered, clutching my chest.

"I don't give a shit about what you need. Two days!" She spun, throwing the door open and slamming it behind her hard enough that some of the small glass vials on the nightstand fell over.

A sob broke free and I sank to the floor, my body barely registering the coolness of the stone on my bare legs. I tried to open my mind and search for the consciousnesses of the guys, but there was just a black void. I spoke to them all anyway, hoping for a miracle.

'*Please. If you can hear me, know that I'm alive. The babies are alive. I love you, and I'm going to do whatever I have to do to get you back.*'

Fischer

Chapter Two

*E*ndless cold water assaulted my senses. *You're not gonna drown.* Fuck, I hated waterboarding. The cloth was ripped off my face as the chair's front two legs hit the ground. Air whooshed into my lungs greedily, sweet oxygen the only thing I wanted at that moment. Aside from knowing where the hell my woman was.

"Tell us what we want to know, mage," the interrogator snarled, grabbing my hair and tugging my head back so I was forced to look at him. Thinking about Saige and in turn, my brothers, had a delirious sort of laugh bubbling from my lips. I was the interrogator of our team, and I knew what pissed us off. His dark eyes flashed, and I didn't have a chance to get a deep breath before the cloth was thrown back over my face and I was once again suspended backward.

Even as I lay there, not breathing, all I could feel was pure, unfettered rage. I was going to kill all of these motherfuckers. Just when I thought I was going to pass out from lack of air, a vision of me making all of these bastard's brains go boom drifted behind my eyelids and holy fuck, my cock actually stirred. *I'm sicker than I thought.*

Up again. This time, I spat a mouthful of water right in Don's eyes. That was his name. *What a stupid fucking name.* But oh, how enraged he became by my defiance and lack of fear. That's the thing. Once you've died, there's not much left to be worried about. I'd already experienced that. It was horrible, but I got a second chance.

Don wiped his hand over his face in disgust, flinging my spit off his hand with a sharp downward motion. He gave me a predatory smile that, in hindsight, probably should've been alarming. I'd been down here for so long though, I was out of fucks to give.

"I'll be back later. Then we'll talk. I promise you that, mage," he threatened, turning his back on me to leave the room. And so I wasn't prepared when he quickly turned back and swung a fist at me so hard I felt the inside of my cheek filling with blood. The chair toppled, and I was left groaning in an inch-deep puddle of water from our torture sessions.

From there, it could've been minutes, hours, days, weeks? I had no idea, but I was losing my sense of time. There was no light. Pitch black. My arms were screaming from being in the same position for so long. I'd been barely coherent when Asrael's men had tossed me on that wagon with the others. But coherent enough to know that Faris never got on the wagon. Nobody would tell me a thing about the state of my brothers. Or Saige. Or my daughters.

They'd separated us from the get-go. Probably smart on their part. More mind fuckery, not knowing if the others were suffering the same treatment or if they had already been put out of their misery. My jaw clenched. No. I couldn't think like that. I refused to believe that I'd lost any of them. Except for maybe one.

Sloane.

My dragon.

My poor, tortured man. He was under Asrael's spell once more, and my heart broke every single time I thought about how he might be being used. How he would feel out of control in his own mind. With my own affinity, I knew that fate was sometimes

—nearly always—worse than death itself. Not being able to trust yourself, or know whether your thoughts were your own, or if your trauma had grown a body of its own and snatched yours. Like a possession. Only this kind was worse because it wasn't your routine PTSD, no. Asrael was exerting some kind of control over Sloane in conjunction with the trauma he'd already inflicted upon him in that lab.

I should've taken his memories without his consent. The thought twisted my stomach. I'd always sworn I'd never do such a thing—though I already had, which sickened me. Not that long ago, I'd taken all of their memories when I gave my life for theirs.

But we needed Sloane. The first chance I got, I was taking that trauma from his mind, letting those horrible visions slip away into the ether of my subspace because they had no business even being in existence.

A door creaked, pulling my focus from my internal thoughts. Footsteps crept across the ground as the person approached me. My chair was righted, and I groaned deeply as my head swam from the sudden change in position. I blinked several times, trying to get my vision to clear. The room was still dark, but the person had left the door cracked so it provided a tiny amount of visibility.

Someone's hand landed on my thigh, and I tried to jerk away from their unwanted touch. "Fischer," he whispered, and I actually whimpered.

Did I just imagine that?

"Look at me, baby."

Glancing up, his face came into focus and a harsh sob exploded from my chest. "Sloane. Oh gods. Oh gods," I breathed.

His large hand cupped my cheek—the one Don had smashed, and I hissed from the pain. "Let me see." He turned my face slightly so he could look at my face.

"I'm okay. Sloane, untie me. We need to get out of here now. Have you heard anything about the others? Saige? Is she okay?"

The questions were flying from my mouth and I couldn't slow down. I was desperate for information. Any information. He shook his head. "What does that mean? You can't just shake your head!"

"I'm sorry. I haven't heard anything. I snuck in here to see you. I had to see you," he said softly. "I can't stay long."

My brow furrowed. "What do you mean? We need to go. Now, Sloane. Untie me."

"I can't. It'll be worse if I do," he whispered into the dimly lit space. Shadows danced over his face.

I swallowed roughly. I knew he was fucked up. His mind wasn't his own, but I needed him to come back to me. Right now. "Hey. Have you seen any of the others? Heard anything at all? It's making me insane, not knowing."

"I haven't seen anyone in weeks." His hands drifted up my thighs slowly. "I miss you."

"Sloane, focus. I love you. I miss you so much it hurts me, baby. But we can't stay here in this room. They want to know about Faris. How I'm still alive and how he came to be. I haven't told them anything, but I'm worried that if I don't give them something soon, they're going to turn to more drastic measures. I can't help us if I'm stuck here. Untie me," I pleaded.

"Let me make you feel good, if only for this moment," he replied, reaching into my waistband and palming my soft cock. Nausea swirled as he gripped my shaft, tugging at me.

"No. Sloane, stop. I don't— Fuck!" My words died on my tongue when he took me into his mouth. Tears welled because I hadn't felt any kind of touch that wasn't harmful in who knows how long. And here was my man, giving me a connection to my humanity. But I didn't want it. Not only was I filthy, but this wasn't the time.

I groaned as his tongue swirled. "Please, stop."

He didn't. He continued licking me with the fervor of a man

possessed. *Why isn't he stopping?* It was like he was in another world, lost to me.

"Inferno," I whispered.

"It's okay, pet. Just take it," he murmured around the tip of my dick, and my heart picked up speed. Sloane would never ignore my safe word. He'd also told me I wasn't his 'pet' anymore, either.

The man between my legs, with my cock in his mouth—it wasn't Sloane. Fuck. I jerked, trying to get away, but this imposter held the chair still so he could continue his assault on my body.

"Get away from me!" I screamed, my voice hoarse.

"Listen, pet. Just tell them what they want to know and then they'll let you out of here. We can be together." His hand snaked between my cheeks, and tears broke free. I'd never been assaulted like this. My mind was spinning and my traitorous dick was still hard as stone in this man's mouth. A man who wasn't mine. A man who had stolen Sloane's identity.

My thoughts raced as he touched me, and I tried to go to the void in my mind. The place where Faris used to be. If I could get there, I could block this out. I wouldn't have to be present.

Use him back, a voice whispered through the darkness of my psyche. Was it my own subconscious? Maybe if I played this right, I could feed them false information and use it to my advantage. I'd just have to detach myself completely. As I looked down and saw his dark head bobbing, I wondered if it would've been better or worse for me if they hadn't stolen his image to manipulate me. If this was just a rape by a stranger and not someone wearing the face of a man I loved.

It was fucked. The ways my thighs trembled, despite not wanting this. Not wanting him. Whoever he was.

And then there it was. The void. The darkness. I'd never fallen into it as quickly and as determinedly as I did in that moment. Numbness enveloped me and I welcomed every second of it. I felt the sensation of nothingness creep over every facet of my mind, my body, my fucking soul. I just hoped that when all was said and done, I'd be able to pull myself back out again.

"Laurie," I grunted. His mouth released me. Not that I felt it. Not anymore.

"Laurie?" he asked, puzzled, wiping his bottom lip with the back of his hand.

I let my eyes flutter shut, a dark smirk pulling at the corner of my mouth. "You know this; we've talked about it. Promise me you'll stay away from her. It must've been something she did to me. When she killed me. Her magic."

I'd never lead them back to Saige. They clearly had no idea she was the one responsible for bringing me back to life, and splitting me and Faris. And I was going to guarantee that. If they suspected Laurie had something to do with it, they'd go after her, and hopefully leave my woman alone.

"I bet you're right, pet. You're so smart. Such a good, sweet pet." He went back to his work and I felt a complete sense of disassociation. It was like I was actually standing in the corner, watching. Waiting. Observing.

Sometime later, awareness came back to me. I wasn't in the chair anymore; instead, I was strapped to a long table. The fake Sloane was gone, but Don was back, and the last thing I saw was his face before pain exploded in my ankle.

It went on like that for what felt like an eternity, though time was irrelevant to me at this point. Don would torture me. Fake Sloane would soothe me. I'd feed him false intel. When he'd take what wasn't his to take, I'd fantasize about gouging his fucking eyes out, ripping his balls off, and shoving them up Don's ass.

They thought they'd won. That they were stronger than I was. One night, as I lay on that cold table, my broken ankle throbbing with infection, my fingers—most broken now too—screaming in pain, my ass raw from being used over and over... I grinned. I don't know how I knew, but the air was different tonight. Charged. My brain lit up with little bursts of light. Green light.

Then I heard it. Oh sweet gods, I heard her.

'Please. If you can hear me, know that I'm alive. The babies are alive. I love you, and I'm going to do whatever I have to do to get you back.'

Oh, sweetheart. She was alive. The babies. I allowed a single tear to slip out.

We're all doing whatever we have to do to get back to you.

Cam

Chapter Three

One, two, three, four, five, six, seven. Seven. The number of steps I could take from wall to wall in this cell. Back and forth. Seven, fourteen, twenty-one, twenty-eight...

The cell was very dimly lit, with a light that flickered overhead every ten point seven seconds. My hands sank into my wild, filthy hair. How long had it been since I'd had a shower? A growl rumbled in my chest, and I dropped to the floor, doing push-ups until my arms burned with exertion. There were no windows, so I could only guess how much time had passed. My beard was my only clue. It had to have been weeks. And I was starting to lose it.

I dropped down on the flimsy mattress and stared up at the ceiling. That fucking flickering. I'd almost rather be left in total darkness than deal with that shit.

The first few days in here, I'd done nothing but rage. Scream. Each day, the guard would drop off a tray of food and a glass of water, sliding it through a small opening at the bottom of the door. And every day, I threatened that person, whoever it was, with promises of the most gruesome deaths I could imagine.

I ate the food and drank the water though. I continued exercising because the first chance I got, I was going to strike. It didn't matter that I had injuries from the fight, though thankfully nothing had been broken. I was just battered and bruised.

They had my little witch. My fists clenched on my stomach as I thought of her. My pregnant woman... Darker thoughts often tried to infiltrate my mind, like the fact that she may not be pregnant anymore. I'd caught a glimpse of her on the stone floor as we were wheeled out of the throne room. There'd been blood. A lot of blood.

No.

I wouldn't entertain such thoughts. I couldn't. And my brothers. Deep guilt twisted my heart as I thought of Sloane. I should've done more for him after his capture, more to help him move past the trauma he'd endured at the hands of his father and Asrael. He was still under their spell, exactly where they wanted him.

I'd failed to protect my family. Again.

My jaw ticked, and I had the sudden urge to beat the shit out of something. There was nothing in this shithole to punch though. Unless I went after the wall, and I didn't really feel like shattering my fingers.

So many times I'd lain here and called out to my family in my mind, hoping that they would hear me. But my magic seemed to be blocked here in the castle. So if anyone ever heard my voice, I had no way of knowing because I never heard anything back. It didn't stop me from talking to them.

'Baby girl, I miss you. Your perfect face consumes my mind. How are you feeling, baby? Are the girls treating you okay? Wherever you are, I hope to the stars that you're being taken care of and that you're safe. Don't worry about us, pretty baby. We'll find a way to get back to you.

'I was thinking earlier that it's a good thing I have experience with long hair. I'll be useful with my skills when the girls' hair gets longer. Unless they want it short. That's okay, too. But I can teach the guys how to do it. I expect Faris to do some wild shit with their hair. They'll love it.

'My heart aches for you. For my brothers. I'm not giving up though,

little witch. I made you a promise that I'd always protect you, love you. I intend to keep it. The devil himself couldn't stop me from getting to you, baby girl. Just... stay strong for me. For us. I can't wait to kiss your pouty lips to quiet that sassy mouth. I love you.'

I rolled over onto my side and let sleep drag me under.

A SCREAM HAD me flying off the bed. Every nerve in my body buzzed to life. Did I just imagine it? Was I dreaming? I rushed to the door, pressing my ear against it. I hadn't heard much of anything since I'd been in here. Only when the food tray was delivered did I hear any signs of life.

Just as I was about to turn away, another soul-piercing scream filled the air, and goosebumps broke out along my skin. I knew that scream. It wasn't human. It was feline.

"KAI!" I roared, pounding my fists against the solid door. Bagheera's battle cries overtook my senses. *Something's wrong with him.* "DON'T YOU FUCKING HURT HIM!"

My heart pounded in time with my fists. Sweat dripped down my face as I gripped the handle of the door and pulled with all my might. It wasn't budging. Of course it wasn't.

Then the noise just... stopped. *Why has it stopped?* Panic overtook me, my hands shaking in fear of what could possibly be happening outside of this godsforsaken cell.

"Kai! It's Cam! I'm here, brother!" I called out, hoping that he might be able to hear me. *They must be keeping him somewhat nearby. How fucked would that be if we were all in cells right next to each other. So close and yet...*

The sound of the door bolt being released had me stepping back. As badly as I needed to get out of this cell, I wasn't stupid. My training was still ingrained in me. I needed to see who was on the other side before I blindly darted out of here and ran into a knife or the barrel of a gun.

"Gods above, it smells awful in here."

Oh, hell no.

"Hello, Cameron," Laurie announced, like this was some kind of social visit. Her green eyes darted around the small space, her nose wrinkling in disgust.

I crossed my arms and glared at her, noting the door was now closed. *That's fine. They'll have to open it to let her out.*

When I didn't speak, irritation flitted across her face. "What? No greeting for me? We're practically family now, you know. I wanted to tell you—no hard feelings. If you'd like, you can call me Mom. I know you don't have one."

Jesus. This cunt.

I stared at her, my face unmoving. People like her wanted reactions. Drama. Nothing pissed them off more than not reacting to their mind games.

"What? No questions for me? Nothing that you're just dying to know?"

The questions were burning my tongue with how badly I wanted to spit them out, but I knew she wouldn't answer them. Laurie was a bitch of the worst kind. She shrugged in a suit-yourself kind of way and studied me. I would bet money her magic was completely fine, which was the only thing stopping me from lunging forward and snapping her neck.

"You really need a shower. Come on." She walked to the door and pulled it open, disappearing from the cell. *Is she serious right now?* The door remained cracked. "Let's go, Jacobs. You seriously stink."

I bit the inside of my cheek and cautiously approached the door, stepping out into a dimly lit hallway. This was the first time in a very long time I'd seen anything aside from the inside of that damn room. My eyes took in everything. There were doors that ran the length of the hall, doors that matched mine. More cells. Where was Kai?

Breathing the air out here was such a rush that I nearly felt a burst of euphoria as I trailed behind Laurie. She'd glance back every so often to make sure I was still there. I needed to get my thoughts together. It was risky to go off half-cocked without knowing where I was and without having some kind of plan. But if I had a clear shot to take this bitch out, I wouldn't hesitate.

We approached an archway, and I noted the cement floor giving way to tiles. *Guess the bitch really is taking me to a shower.* Here I was, dressed in a pair of boxer briefs I'd been wearing since the day we fucking got here, and she was prancing around like Queen Cunt in a power suit. The clacking of her heels on the smooth floor made my eye twitch, and I had to clench my fists until my knuckles cracked to restrain myself from ripping her head off.

As it was, I had no clue where I was. Obviously Besmet... but where in Besmet? Still in the castle? Or had I been relocated somewhere? I knew I'd heard Kai earlier, so he was here with me. But for all I knew at this moment, everyone else could be in another realm, the next room, or in a damn grave. I was flying blind, so I tamped down my rage.

"There are towels for you on the bench. Soap and other products are in the shower. No razor. You can understand why," Laurie explained smugly, her heels echoing in the shower room. There were maybe five separate stalls, with a long wooden bench that ran the length of the room, reminding me of a pool locker room.

I eyed her suspiciously as I came to a standstill. What angle was she playing here? The showers didn't have curtains, and there wasn't a snowball's chance in hell I was stripping down in front of this woman.

"No need to be shy, Cameron." She winked. I didn't move. "I've already seen what you have under there. You have some pretty metal, but you're not a robot, are you? No, you're all man." Fuck, I had to swallow to prevent myself from gagging. "Don't worry, I'll be waiting right outside for you to finish. That's the only exit from this room and there's absolutely nothing in here that could double as a weapon, so don't bother." She spun and left the room.

This was the problem with being held as a prisoner. Especially during a war. Nothing was ever done without reason. So why now, after so many weeks, was I being let out of that cell? And right after I'd heard Kai? Maybe they wanted to finally talk to me, instead of ignoring me completely.

Not wasting any time, I stepped into the shower stall, turning the water onto the hottest setting. My boxers hit the cool floor, and I fucking groaned when the water pelted my skin. Holding my head beneath the spray, I let the heat and moisture wash the initial layer of grime from my body.

"Fuuuuck."

Never had a shower felt so good in my thirty years. I spotted a dispenser of soap attached to the wall and quickly filled my hands until they overflowed. Then I scrubbed. And scrubbed. And scrubbed. Until my skin was raw and the wall dispenser was nearly empty. I shampooed my hair and my beard, twice, noting the dark water that circled the drain. *Gods, I'd kill for a toothbrush right about now.*

Once I'd put enough conditioner in my hair and beard to hopefully keep me feeling more human until the next shower, I slumped back against the wall, sliding down to my ass. The water was starting to cool, but I couldn't bring myself to get out. Not yet. Water sluiced down my face and torso, and I reveled in the moment. It was cleansing—not just for my body, but my soul. My determination. I hadn't realized how hopeless I'd begun to feel in the last few days.

Maybe this was their goal. Give me this little slice of normalcy before really fucking me up. Anything less than that would actually surprise me. Slowly, I rose from the shower floor and shut the water off. I dried my body at a snail's pace, in no hurry to see Laurie's face again or return to that godsforsaken room. As I wrapped the towel around my waist, I decided right then that if they tried to make me go back in there, I was going to fight like hell. I couldn't go back.

Heavy footfalls reached my ears, and I paused working the brush I'd found through my hair. Whoever these people were, they were moving fairly swiftly and getting closer.

"It didn't work then?" Laurie asked as the footsteps fell silent.

"No. Need to get him to the infirmary quickly. He had to be resuscitated twice before we convinced Az to take him down from the post," a man said grimly.

I heard Laurie hum as if she was thinking. "Very well. Get him to the doctor. Your king will not be pleased if he dies."

Curiosity got the best of me and I quietly approached the wall that blocked my view of them. The hallway was more crowded than I expected; a handful of guards surrounded a stretcher, all focused forward while one acknowledged her orders. The scent of blood hung in the corridor like a plague, and I scanned the body lying unconscious. Their back was flayed wide open. I'd seen a lot of torture in my life, but I'd never seen someone's flesh look so mangled. The poor fucker had to be dead and if he wasn't, he had to be wishing for it.

A guard moved away, and my eyes locked on the injured man's face. *Oh holy fuck. Fuck.* I spun back against the wall, pressing a hand to my mouth to keep myself from vomiting.

No. No. That... I didn't see that right. It can't be him...

My heart thrashed like an animal caged, and I sucked in a ragged breath, trying to be quiet. Time seemed to crawl, though I knew only a couple of seconds had passed. I gripped the brush in my hand so hard that I could feel the plastic begin to give way. I knew what I'd seen. And I knew what needed to be done.

Tears built up but now was not the time. I knew exactly who the man on the stretcher was, but if I gave him a name in my mind, it would break me. I had to break them first. So he would remain a nameless, faceless being in my mind until I completed my mission.

Four guards. Laurie. The man on the stretcher. Four guards. Kill them. Kill them all. Make them bleed.

In a blink, I was flying past Laurie, jabbing the closest guard in the throat with my fist, before flipping the brush and stabbing as hard as I could directly through the eye. I anticipated the guard on my right so kept hold of the brush, pulling it out with a squelch and a spray of blood as I spun. Ducking low, I kicked my leg out as I twirled, knocking my next target clean off his feet.

I didn't give him time to get up. Hell, he barely hit the ground and I was diving over him, relieving him of the wicked looking dagger that was attached to his hip. My hands shot out in front of me as I sailed over top of that piece of shit, rolled smoothly, and forcefully twisted, releasing the dagger with all of the power I could summon.

There wasn't time to wait, and I was moving, chasing the weapon before it sank into the throat of the guard I'd stolen it from. My intention was to snatch it back to end the other two, but they were already on me. One of them was running right for me just as the other attempted a roundhouse kick. My hand snapped out, snatching his foot mid-air, and I grunted as I jerked his ankle in the opposite direction. He rolled with it, doing some sort of wild martial arts move and landing on his feet.

My eyes narrowed. "You guys fucked up." I sounded like a monster. A beast out for no less than the blood of every being in this castle that meant me or my family harm. The other guard who was coming at me with force finally got within striking distance, and I feigned a punch before clotheslining him with my fucking leg. As soon as he hit the ground, I snaked around his neck, my thighs squeezing his throat tight enough to crush his windpipe.

The towel that had been around my hips was now laying beside me, and I heard the wannabe ninja make a snide comment to the other guy about dying with a flaccid cock on his head, as he grabbed hold of my hair. What a bitch. His arms tried to get around my throat but I raised my shoulders, making it impossible for him to get the right angle. If he wanted to strangle me, he was going to have to try something other than pulling my fucking hair.

The man between my legs was losing the battle when a sharp pain exploded in my side. My jaw clenched as I held in a roar, my gaze landing on the guard who'd stabbed me. My hand shot out, wrapping around his wrist. With a growl, I twisted my hips sharply, and a satisfying crunch met my ears. Releasing the now dead male from my thigh grip, I pulled the knife from my side, earning a punch to the face as the stabber tried to get me to release his wrist.

Grunting, I twisted my body and went for his leg. The knife sliced through his Achilles' tendon like butter. Scrambling, I got up, grabbed the damp towel, and wrapped it around his neck as he dropped to his knees. His gasps and the feel of his hot blood pooling around my bare feet gave me fucking power. Fuel. Livid, I pulled on either side of the towel, creating an effective garrote. The fibers of the towel protested under the force, but he'd be dead by the time I ripped this towel in half.

His clawing hands fell limply at his sides, and I knew he was done when he slumped forward, his body lax. Still, I pulled harder, needing to know for sure. Because these men, what they'd done... I couldn't look. I already knew what I'd seen—*who* I'd seen on that stretcher...

Rising to my full height with a grimace, I pressed the towel to the wound in my side, glaring like the devil himself at Laurie. "Get. The. Fuck. Away. From. Him," I snarled. My hair fell in front of my face, and I could feel the blood soaking the towel.

She eyed me, her fingers running through his hair. "You're quite a fighter. Especially for someone of your size."

"I swear to all the stars in the sky, if you don't get your hands off of him in the next two seconds, I'll show you just how fast you can die by these hands, bitch." I was breathing faster now, likely due to the blood loss.

She laughed. She actually fucking laughed at me. Like we were old friends and this was a joke. "Oh, Cameron. And where do you think you're going to go? He's going to the infirmary to be taken care of, and you will be going back to your cell since you've just proven you don't know how to act like a civilized man within the walls of my kingdom!" She screeched the last part, losing her calm. *Gods, she's completely delusional.*

"He's not leaving my sight, and I'm not going back there. Get out of my way," I warned, taking a step closer and coming to a stop next to the guard who had a shiny dagger protruding from his neck.

"Or what? I could take both of you out faster than you could blink. I still have my magic," she gloated, smirking like she'd won something. I couldn't look away as her fingers sank into his dark hair. She had no fucking right!

But she'd given up information earlier, and I planned to exploit that. The towel slipped from my hand and with it, a steady trickle of blood poured from the wound on my side.

"What are you doing?" she asked, the first sign of uncertainty in her tone.

I shrugged. "You said Asrael wouldn't be happy if he didn't make it. I'm going to gamble here that he feels the same about me. About all of us. Needs us for some reason," I panted, trying to suck in a few deep breaths. I leaned over, pressing my hands on my knees. I had to stay awake just a little longer. My fingers wrapped around the hilt of the dagger, and I rose back up with determination coursing through my veins.

"Cameron," Laurie cautioned, letting her hand fall away from the injured man's hair. Fucking finally. "You wouldn't."

I stretched my left arm out in front of me and stared her in the eyes as I brought the dagger to the center of my wrist. "I would. There isn't anything I wouldn't do for my family. For my woman and my brothers. I would kill every fucking being in this castle with a smile on my face if it meant getting them out of here and away from the likes of you."

The kiss of the blade against my wrist stung but I was committed. I wasn't going back there. She'd yield.

Her green eyes widened as blood started dripping to the floor. "Stop. What do you want?"

I hid my smirk behind my hair. "Lead the way to the infirmary. The two of us"—I gestured to the man on the bed—"we stay together from here on out. And if you so much as think about harming him in this way again, I can't begin to explain to you the horrific way I'll fucking kill you. Start walking, cunt."

Laurie swallowed and reached for the bed.

"DO NOT FUCKING TOUCH HIM!" I bellowed, and she jumped. Without touching the stretcher again, she turned and her heels clacked down the hallway. I put the bloody dagger at the end of the bed and began pushing it down the hall, following her. At least I had something to hold me up. I still couldn't look at him. Not yet. Not yet.

"I'm here now and I'm never leaving your side again. We're going to get out of here, I swear it. Stay with me, K. Please, please, stay with me, Alpha."

Kai

Chapter Four

Two hours earlier

"I can't turn into a fucking dragon!"

Asrael's gaze narrowed on my face, his anger a visible wave of emotion within his dark eyes. "Well then, I guess I'll have to try different measures. The guards will be by to collect you soon. I recommend trying to rest. You're going to need it." He slammed the door shut behind him, and I groaned.

I'd been in this interrogation room for hours. I was starving, thirsty as fuck, and sick of being a captive. I hadn't seen daylight in weeks. Fuck, I hadn't seen anyone aside from Asrael and two of his guards since he'd started paying me visits here. They weren't social visits, either.

I pressed my forehead against the cool steel of the table we always sat at. My body was secured to the chair via chains, solid steel an inch thick and magically reinforced. My hands were bound, each one cuffed and locked to the table. Fuckers.

'Why does he think you can become a dragon?' Bagheera rumbled in my mind.

'I have no idea. I don't know how he'd even know I was able to shift into a mouse. That's not information we've ever given him,' I replied,

sorting through the puzzle pieces in my brain and trying to make sense of everything.

After a pause, I asked. I had to know. Despite knowing what the answer would be, I couldn't not ask.

'Have you heard her at all?' I whispered through the mental link in our shared consciousness. I wasn't doing well being separated from Sprout, but my bond knew she was close enough not to cause me to go into a total depressive state. I was pretty sure that when we'd been separated before, it was the distance that caused my stress to become so overwhelming. While I wasn't completely lost to the darkness yet, not knowing the whereabouts or condition of my family was weighing heavier and heavier.

My panther whined at the inquiry, and I thumped my head against the table. *'We have to get information. Somehow. Bagheera, I'm telling you, I can't live like this. I'm not good with isolation. My mind, it's been...'*

Bagheera grumbled. *'I know. I know the things you think in the dark.'*

'She's mine. She's my mate and I failed her. And the cubs, Bagheera. Gods above, mark my words, I will—'

The sound of the door being thrown open cut off our discussion, and the two guards were on me, hauling me up and unhooking my chains. "Where are we going?" I asked, frustrated with all of these unknowns and knowing I wasn't going to get an answer.

They began dragging me to the door and I caught a whiff of what was mine. *She's here. Somewhere.* My eyes flashed, and I felt hair explode from my back as claws broke through my hands. My movements weren't made with any rational thought. A spray of blood hit my face and chest as one of the guards fell to the ground, holding his throat. My forehead found purchase on the other's nose, busting it on contact.

"Why do you smell like my mate? Where is she?" My voice was a mix between my own and Bagheera's. I was in some kind of strange partial shift that I'd never experienced before. The man stared up at me with wide eyes as blood spurted from his nose. Leaning down, I meant to yell and demand information, but the wild cat scream that left my lips shocked even me. It was so fucking loud. The hair on the dude's head blew back from the force, and the stench of urine hit the air. He sobbed as my claws sank into his shoulders.

"Tell me where she is and I'll kill you quickly." My ears pricked as the sound of boots on stone echoed through the hallway. *More guards. Running out of time.* I grabbed the guard by the collar and slammed him back down, fighting the urge to sink my teeth into his neck and rip until he stopped twitching. "Fucking TELL me!"

Coconut. Vanilla. Sunshine. Her scent was infiltrating my senses like a plague. Another one of those feral cat screams exploded from me, and blood trickled from the guard's ears, his eardrums likely having burst.

"E-east." That was all he got out before the other guards were on us. Something pierced my bicep, and I snarled at the dart there, ripping it out and throwing it down.

The guard in front stepped forward. "Come with us willingly. Don't make this harder on yourself."

My breaths were harsh and ragged, my shoulders heaving with the simple task of breathing. I ran my tongue over my teeth. Teeth that were much sharper and longer than normal.

"Where. Is. My. Mate?" Each word was a snarl. A threat. A promise of death. The guards looked confused by my question, and I blinked rapidly, trying to clear my vision. Things were becoming blurry. If I didn't have long, I'd better make it count.

Dropping down on one knee, I let my head hang.

"Come on, we need to get him outside. The king is not in the mood to be kept waiting," someone said, and they started shuffling closer. I waited until their boots came into my line of vision, restraining myself until I felt a hand on my shoulder.

Without a doubt, I moved faster than I ever had before, sedative be damned. I snatched the wrist of the man who was touching me and sank my fangs deep in his arm before jerking my head and shredding all of the arteries there. My legs propelled me through the air as I leaped onto another guard, fulfilling my earlier fantasy of ripping someone's throat out.

A body hit my back and arms snaked around my throat. I threw a punch back over my shoulder, my claws slicing through the man's face without any resistance. I was like fucking Wolverine. The man released me and slumped to the ground, giving me the capability to spin around and locate the fourth guard. He was right behind me, holding up a gun with a smile on his wicked face.

Bloodlust was driving me at that point. There was no stopping my urge for death. I launched myself at him, and he pulled the trigger. The shot hit my stomach in multiple places before I collided with the guard, landing on top of him. Glancing down, I saw at least five darts sticking from my body—the gun must have been similar to a shotgun. I swayed, the sedative moving rapidly through my bloodstream.

"Will get her," I rasped, reaching for the darts but grabbing nothing but air. My limbs were useless. My body slumped over and I hit the ground with a grunt.

Everything faded away. Except that fucking smell. Sunshine.

SUNSHINE WAS what I saw first when my eyes opened. I had to squint against the brightness, especially after having been kept in the dark for so long. So fucking long in the darkness. My eyes watered with emotion. I'd never been so elated to be outside, to feel the open air whipping around my body, filling my lungs, feeding my fucking soul.

"Welcome back, shifter," Asrael said from somewhere behind me. I couldn't tear my eyes from the sky to see where he was. My arms were bound by my wrists above my head, and I was tied to a cross with the back of my body exposed. What the fuck? My eyes trailed down and I realized I was completely naked. My heart began to race, and the murmurs of a crowd swept through my ears.

Slowly, I turned toward the whispers and saw a group of perhaps fifty people, their faces a mixture of disgust, amusement, and on a few, concern.

"This mage is fighting his nature!" Asrael bellowed, and the crowd responded with jeers and sounds of disapproval. "As your king, it is my duty to ensure that every being in my kingdom reaches their true potential! This shifter needs a push, and I'm the man who is going to give it to him!"

The roar of the crowd was deafening. Fear slithered down my spine, no matter how hard I tried to deny it. To be strong and brave. It made me remember something Sloane had told me once. *"Bravery doesn't mean you aren't afraid. Bravery means you accept that fear and let it fuel your purpose. It's okay to be scared. You just can't let that fear rule you, brother. Let it fucking guide you to achieve your goals."*

I was okay. I'd be okay. Whatever Asrael was planning for me, it wasn't death. If that was the case, I would've died that first day I was taken to my cell with a shattered spine and ribcage. But instead, he'd sent healers to fix me up as good as new. I could handle whatever was coming. *I am brave.*

"We'll continue until you shift into the form I *know* you can, or until you pass out." Asrael rounded the cross and stood with his face inches from mine. His dark hair was styled perfectly, the crown on his head glinting in the sun. It was his eyes that glittered the most though. With malice. With lust for pain and anguish and power. "Make no mistake, shifter. We will continue this day after day until you do as I ask. I will heal you only to repeat the process. Don't hold back. You're only hurting yourself at this point."

"Fuck you, bitch."

A smirk appeared on his handsome face at my defiance, and he held his hand out to the side, palm up. A guard stepped up, placing the handle of a whip into his hand. Asrael stepped closer and ran the handle of the weapon down my cheek and over my lips, as lust flared in his eyes that were locked on mine.

"I am going to enjoy breaking you. I just may have to find some time to try another tactic." He leaned in. "Perhaps tonight, when you're laying in bed with your skin flayed open, I'll come for you. I think I'd like the sight of your bloodied back as I fuck you raw."

I spat right in his face, and he recoiled. "Try it, motherfucker. I'll chop your tiny cock off and leave it on the floor for the ants to eat."

He wiped the spit from his cheek, his eyes darkening. Fucking sadistic piece of shit. "Oh yes. I'm really going to enjoy this." He shoved his fingers in his mouth and sucked my spit from them. "Let's begin."

He turned his back on me, holding his arms out wide like he was a god and everyone here worshipped him. The tail of the whip trailed along the ground as he addressed the onlookers. "The record is eighty-two before passing out from my whip. Let's see how many it takes for this powerful shifter to transform into the best version of himself!" Asrael cried, pumping up the crowd. It was barbaric. Archaic. Wrong.

I tried to relax my body. There was nothing I could do to stop what was coming. If I didn't tense, I had hope it wouldn't be as damaging. I was wrong. The crack of the whip flying through the air was all the warning I got—a split second. A blink. And it stole my breath. My body jerked and my jaw clenched, fighting against making any noise.

The second lash landed across my shoulders as the crowd

counted. I closed my eyes and stood as still as possible. *Thwack. Thwack. Thwack.*

"You're fighting who you are." *Thwack.* "I'm going to help you." *Thwack.* "I know it hurts, but achieving greatness doesn't come without pain!" *Thwack.*

My knees were trembling and tears had started streaming down my face. But I wasn't a fucking dragon shifter. Asrael was obsessed with dragons. I didn't know why, and at that point, I didn't give a shit. If I could've, I would've already shifted into a damn dragon just to get the pain to stop.

Thwack.

"Don't fight me, shifter. You just need proper... motivation. Tell me, did you enjoy the scent of your mate on my guard earlier?"

Thwack.

An almighty roar exploded from my body at his words. "You son of a bitch!"

He chuckled. "I heard about your partial shift. I bet that's something you've never been capable of doing before, am I right?"

Thwack.

Sweat ran down my face as my body jerked from the torture. I'd have lost count of where we were if it wasn't for the crowd counting. He hadn't split my skin yet, but if he increased his force, it wouldn't take much at this point.

"You're welcome, by the way. Imagine what you'll be capable of now that you can do such a thing. You became more. You became better!"

Thwack.

"Thirty-six!" the crowd shouted. I was still standing. My ears were ringing, my heartbeat so loud that the shouts and cheers sounded like whispers.

"Shift!" *Thwack.* "Now!" *Thwack.* His pace picked up through the next barrage of lashings and he moved down, hitting the backs of my thighs now. Fucking hell. They just kept coming.

"Your mate wouldn't want you to fight this, shifter!" I growled at the mention of her. "Ah. So you are listening. Good."

Thwack. Sweat poured down my face, mixing with the tears I wasn't able to hold back. I had no idea where we were in the count. I'd blocked it out, picturing my Cub. The way she'd smile at me. *Thwack.* How she loved when I'd make her homemade snacks. *Thwack.* How much she loved me. *Thwack.*

"Shift and I'll allow you to see her." *Thwack.*

'He's a liar,' Bagheera growled in my mind.

'I can't shift anyway! He's going to kill me,' I shouted, anger setting in now. Dangling my woman like that in front of my face—how dare he?

I knew the moment my skin split under the whip. The crowd gasped. And Asrael didn't stop. He was careful not to hit the same spot, forcing me to endure this torture for as long as possible.

"SHIFT!" he roared.

"IT'S IMPOSSIBLE!" I screamed, as he brought the whip down so hard and fast that all I saw was a flash of bright white light behind my eyes.

The crowd was quiet now as he worked. He'd turned his attention to my ass now, leaving no part of my body untouched by his cruel methods. My arms were shaking so badly; it was getting harder to use the binds as a way to help myself remain on my own two feet.

The whip cracked again against my back, this lash the hardest yet, and I screamed. My feet slipped in the puddle of blood beneath me. The heat of the sun rained down on my shoulders as I hung there, trying to find the strength to rise again. The whip never let up.

'Let the darkness claim you. It is the only way this madness will end,' Bagheera pleaded. It wouldn't be hard to give in. The pain

was so visceral at this point that I felt as though I was floating above this scene, looking down at myself.

"You're so strong. Look at you taking my whip so well. We're closing in on one hundred. By far the strongest man I've had on my cross," Asrael praised me. Like this was something to be proud of. He was turned on—I could hear it in his voice and I'd seen it earlier in his eyes. The thought made me fucking sick.

Another lash. More blood. I couldn't stand. I hung limply and hoped I'd pass out soon. I wasn't going to shift like he wanted. It. Wasn't. Possible. I heard him swearing and breathing heavily, felt lash after lash on my skin until everything became too much. Oblivion finally came for me, and I welcomed it.

THE FIRST THING I noticed when I regained consciousness was a thrumming pain across the entire back of my body. I blinked groggily; my mouth was so dry, I would've lunged for a glass of water. Slowly, I tried to move and was halted immediately by a burst of debilitating pain. I couldn't believe that motherfucker had whipped me publicly... and gotten off on it.

I remembered the husky and breathy tone his voice had taken, the more I broke beneath his whip. It was at that moment I felt movement beneath my cheek, and I was horrified when a hand slipped into my hair, caressing my head. My heart was pounding. Jesus, he was actually following through with his threats. A whine slipped out, thanks to a mixture of the pain I was in and the fear of being used like this.

"Kai?"

I was so fucked in the head that I'd started hearing things. Cam's voice. Wouldn't that be a dream come true?

"K, are you awake?"

His voice broke something in me. Tears built in my eyes, for myself, for my family that I'd lost. I sniffled and took a deep breath—leather and fresh rain.

"Cam?" I whimpered softly.

The person beneath me shifted, gently setting my cheek on a pillow. This had to be some kind of dissociation moment. Imagining that he was here like this, my subconscious was clearly trying to protect my mind from a complete break.

A calloused hand cupped my cheek. "Look at me, Kaito."

I clamped my eyes tighter and refused. His thumb rubbed my cheekbone gently, so soft it was just the barest whisper of a caress.

"Why won't you look at me?" he asked, his tone full of pain.

"Because," I whispered, "if I open my eyes and confirm that this is all in my head... I'm done. If I open my eyes and you're not here, I don't want to be here anymore."

Soft lips pressed against my forehead, and I felt the tickle of a beard. "Kai, it's real. I'm really here. I'm not leaving your side for anything, okay?"

"I'd rather keep my eyes closed. If I have to live in this hell, I'd rather stay right here where my mind is being kind to me for once. If I look and you're not here, Cam... Do you understand what I'm saying?" I was so tired. I likely wasn't making any sense. All I knew was I could lie here and keep this fantasy alive until I passed out again.

"Then keep your eyes closed, Alpha. Let me take care of you." I heard someone shuffling around the bed and then water running. Sometime later—I had no concept left of such things—a cool washcloth was laid over my forehead and eyes. A straw was pushed between my lips next, and I drank greedily, begging for more. I drank three cups before I felt my thirst recede.

"I need to put some things on your wounds. I'm so fucking sorry, K. I didn't find you in time. But I'm here now. I'm here." I heard bottles clinking and packaging being opened. "I can't even use magic to lessen this for you. I think that's why you're not healing yet. It's going to hurt, brother—I'm so sorry, but we can't let these get infected. Bite down on this."

A strip of leather was shoved between my teeth. Fuck. The Cam of my imagination was softly crying. He never used to cry. It seemed like none of us did. Until recently...

The first spray of something hit my back, and I screamed, my body bowing automatically.

"I'm so sorry. So fucking sorry. I'll work fast."

And he did. He worked quickly, but it seemed I had wounds from my shoulders to my fucking heels. I was sweating and panting by the time he finished. Something cool hit my skin and I soaked in the amazing sensation—such a contrast to the pain of moments before. It made my head spin. I must have passed out because when I actually opened my eyes again, my face was turned the other direction.

I was shivering, but couldn't even get under a blanket in my current state. Suddenly hearing voices that were a bit muffled, I tried to calm my chattering teeth.

There was Cam's voice again. Oh gods. *Maybe he really is here.* If he was here though, then he wasn't with Saige. I'd much prefer that she had him right now. Hopefully the others were with her at least.

"Get me a gods damn healer!" Cam boomed.

I turned my head slowly. I had to know; I had to see. The sight I saw... I wasn't prepared. Cam was here. Really here. His beard was wild, his hair hastily tied back, and he looked thinner than I'd ever seen him. That would've been hard enough on its own to see.

A woman's voice rose in volume. "Let me tend to his wounds. If someone finds out you're in here, it won't end well—I guarantee you that." My eyes tracked the sound, and there, right on the other side of the glass door was a woman who had never been more deserving of having her throat shredded by my teeth.

Laurie.

And the witch wanted to work some kind of magic on my body? I'd rather die. Hell, I'd probably end up dying if she was allowed any sort of magical freedom over me. We all knew too well what she was capable of. Sneaky fucking bitch.

Cam looked into the room, and our eyes connected. His mouth parted and within seconds, he was kneeling at my bed, taking my hand and holding on for dear life.

"Kai. Fuck, man. I didn't think you were going to wake up, at least not for a while. Jesus, you're burning up. Are you in a lot of pain? I can mix up some of that soothing mist that you liked last time." He stared into my eyes, full of concern and something else. Despair, maybe?

I cleared my throat and wet my dry lips. "Why is she here, Cam?"

The big blond mage sighed. He was exhausted; the dark circles beneath his eyes told no lies. "It's a long story. I'll tell you, but first I need to get you healed, brother. Your wounds are infected, K. You have a high fever and you've been convulsing in your sleep. She doesn't want anyone else coming in here because she's still trying to save face." The doorknob turned, and Cam snarled over his shoulder. "STAY THE FUCK OUT!"

My teeth were chattering again. "Cam. Don't leave me. Please don't leave me."

"Never. I'll never leave you, but it's you who can't leave *me*, K. You're so sick and there's just... There's nothing I can do for you, brother. I'm so sorry." His deep voice cracked and tears rolled down his gaunt cheeks.

"Send her away. I don't want her near us."

Cam nodded at my request. He rose up from his knees, storming over to the door. My eyes widened when I saw the knife he pulled from his back pocket. *What the fuck? Is he going to kill her now? Oh please gods, let me be witness to that.*

The door opened a couple of inches, and he slid his foot into the gap to keep it jammed open. "We don't need your services.

Get out of here and don't come back unless you have a fucking healer. Do not test me, bitch." I gasped when he pressed the knife to his wrist.

"I can't wait til you get what's coming to you," Laurie sneered, and Cam chuckled darkly.

"If anyone has karmic payback coming, I think we both know it has your name all over it. Get. Me. A. Healer. If he dies, so do I."

What the hell is going on?

The door slammed a beat later, and Cam returned the knife to his pocket, rushing back to my side. "What—" I tried to ask, but he hushed me.

"Let me talk, okay? You just rest and listen." He slipped his hand into mine, squeezing hard.

"Okay," I whispered. "Tell me everything."

And he did. Everything he remembered since waking up in a cell without windows and being kept there for weeks without any human interaction. Fuck. It was exactly what they'd done to me. The weird part though was trying to figure out Laurie's angle. Why had she taken him from the cell at all? She never did anything that wasn't calculated.

"But why hasn't she put an end to us being together in here? Why turn a blind eye?" I wondered out loud, watching as Cam's face hardened, determination flaring in his eyes. I suddenly remembered the way he'd held that knife to his wrist, the words he'd said.

"They want us alive. I'm of no use to her if I'm dead," he said firmly, his face taking on a blank expression. I'd never seen Cam like this before. Hardened. The passion that he'd always possessed was missing, and what was left was someone who was doing what he had to do.

"Fucking hell," I cursed. "Don't even think about doing something like that, Cam. We need you. All of us. Our woman..."

He stood abruptly to pace back and forth beside my bed. "Listen, K. We've always said we'd be honest with each other, and I need to do that now."

I blinked slowly, and his form blurred around the edges. "Tell me the truth then, Thunder Daddy."

He didn't smile. His mouth didn't even twitch at the use of the ridiculous nickname. My stomach sank, because whatever he was going to tell me must be pretty bad.

"Your fever is one hundred and six degrees, and it has been for the past six hours. Nothing I do is bringing it down. Your wounds are looking worse by the minute. I don't even understand how you're awake and speaking right now."

"Is that everything? The full disclosure of my situation?" My voice sounded too soft even to my own ears.

Cam pulled a chair up to the bed and took my hand. "If a healer doesn't come... your body won't be able to continue like this. If the infection gets into your bloodstream—"

"Then I'll die," I finished for him so he wouldn't have to say the words. I watched as he glared at the wall, his jaw tight. "But *you* won't." My words caused him to turn his glower on me, and I gave it right back. Because fuck that. "You need to find Saige. The babies. Our brothers. Get out of here and go find them, and leave me. Once you're gone, she'll bring a healer."

Cam looked thunderous as he pinned me beneath his stare. "I know you're feverish and sick as hell, but you can *fuck off* with that nonsense. I'm not leaving you. We stick together." He paused for a moment. "What does Asrael want from you?"

I laughed and then groaned, because oh gods—the pain was unlike anything I'd experienced before. "Wants me to shift into a fucking dragon."

"A dragon? Can you do that?"

I huffed. "No. Not that I've ever tried, but I just know I won't be able to do it. Call it intuition."

Cam considered that information, probably wondering what the obsession with dragons was as far as Asrael was concerned. I could've told him it was pointless to wonder, because I'd done that for the past few weeks and had figured out nothing that'd provide any answers.

"I–I don't feel good," I mumbled as the room spun before my eyes.

"What is it? What can I get you? Let me grab some wat— Oh my fuck!" Cam exclaimed, and he jumped, swiping at his head as if he were under an attack by bees.

"What are you doing?" I blinked rapidly, wondering if I was hallucinating. Something tiny and black flew from Cam's head, landing on the bed. My body jerked in surprise and panic, because what the fuck was that?

"*Messieurs*. Your rescue party has arrived."

Now I really was losing my mind.

"Napoleon?" Cam gasped, sitting back down in the chair and peering down at the mouse who was now perched two inches from my eyes.

"*Oui*. 'Tis I. You've no bloody idea what I've been through. The halls are swarming with fat Persians with the temperaments of mantis shrimp and the snouts of bloodhounds. There's been a mark on my life from the moment I entered this stone-walled hell," Napoleon rambled, his tiny front paws moving a mile a minute.

"Do you hear him?" I asked, looking at Cam who was staring at the mouse in shock.

"He said there are Persians here. Why are there Persians in the demon realm? And how the hell are you here? And how can I even hear you?" Cam demanded, giving Napoleon a suspicious look.

"Persian cats," Napoleon spat and visibly shivered. "Foul beasts. I was not surprised in the slightest when I laid eyes upon the first smushed face I came across. They belong here. Hell cats. As for my new communication skills? All will be revealed." The tiny mouse sat back on his haunches, waving his paws like a magician.

"How did *you* get here though?" I asked him, blinking heavily. My eyes were so tired.

"Rode here with the team, of course. Can you believe that stunt they pulled in the throne room? My warrior's heart bled with the urge to maim, but of course, I am a patient man. I have played the long game, *géant*. Reconnaissance. I would have made myself known sooner, but the cells in which you were being held captive were sealed up tight. So I put my talents to other uses, and I've learned a great many things."

Cam and I looked at each other. Was the hero of this story really a black mouse with the soul of Napoleon Bonaparte? It was looking more and more like yes, yes he was the fucking hero.

"I saw the horror of what you suffered through, *géant*. You are the bravest man I've had the pleasure of serving with and as such, I've made sure to shit all over Asrael's food that gets delivered to his quarters. Works great as he has a love of freshly cracked peppercorn. Blends right in," Napoleon bragged, and winked. Fuckin' winked. I snorted a laugh, unable to stop myself, but I still grimaced when the humor faded.

Napoleon scurried down the bed toward my feet. "*Mon dieu*, I was so excited to see you that I nearly forgot. Daddy of Thunder, please lift me to that vent."

"Daddy. Of. Thunder?" Cam choked out. If I had the strength, I would have been crying tears of laughter.

"'Tis your name, *non*? Hurry now," Napoleon clapped his paws, and Cam obeyed, walking him over to an air vent that was near the ceiling. "Pop the cover off." Cam made quick work of it and Napoleon disappeared inside, reappearing a moment later with a syringe in his mouth.

"What's this?" Cam took the syringe and held it to the light. The liquid within was dark, sparkling with a myriad of colors.

"Raw healing magic mixed with melted down Nox stone. Stab him with it so we can get the fuck out of here."

"You're sure, Napoleon?" I inquired, though at this point I'd be willing to risk it if it would make me feel even five percent better.

My tiny friend nodded firmly. "How do you think we are speaking right now? I wanted to give myself an edge over the Persians so I gave myself the teeniest of injections, and voilà! Of course, being able to speak has only allowed me to call them bitches to their faces, though getting to speak with you normally is quite a perk. Anyways, you must administer it into a thick muscle. Stick his ass, and then we're going to get our woman."

Cam nearly dropped the syringe. "What?"

"Our woman. Two days ago I finally found her, though she was not awake. I wasn't able to speak with her." Napoleon looked saddened, but I whooped and startled him.

"Cam, shove that in my ass right now!" I barked, excitement and adrenaline mixing with the fever, causing me to feel like I was on a serious drug trip.

Something cool and wet brushed over a small area of skin on my right butt cheek. "Definitely not what I thought I'd be doing the first time I heard you say those words to me..."

A hiss slipped through my clenched teeth as the needle pierced my skin, then warmth spread throughout my body, like the rush of water when a dam breaks.

"By the moon," Cam gasped.

"*Oui*, it is working beautifully!" Napoleon cackled maniacally, jumping up and down in excitement.

I couldn't see what was happening, but I could feel it. It was as though the infection that had been killing me was being disintegrated, wiped from existence. The lash marks that before had felt like burns just morphed into a dull ache. It was incredible. The cold was banished from my bones as I began sweating, the fever finally breaking.

On wobbly arms, I pushed myself up and sat upright. I held out my hand, and Cam gripped it, hauling me to my feet. We wore matching feral grins. The rush flooding my system now was all power—mine.

"My magic is back," I announced, rising to my full height. Fuck, it felt good.

Cam's voice was nothing but a growl, his green eyes turning nearly black as his pupils blew out with the promise of what was to come. "Well, we need to go find more of those vaccines, and then we're going to go get our family."

"*Vive la révolution!*" Napoleon cried, scampering up and resting on Cam's head.

My strength was nearly fully restored, and it had been less than two minutes. Absolutely incredible. There was a deep thirst for blood now, which wouldn't be sated until I'd had vengeance. "Death is coming to everyone who caused us harm. Fuck. Them. Up."

Bagheera woke at that moment, and a wicked snarl burst from me as we charged through the door.

Saige

Chapter Five

The doc had just left after delivering my lunch and checking my vitals. There was a small two-seat table by one of the windows, and I ate slowly while letting my gaze trail over the view. The city sprawled out in the distance; it seemed to be endless. With that many people, surely an uprising could overthrow Asrael. Then again, he was so powerful now...

He'd definitely used whatever breakthroughs he managed in his research on himself. That level of power wasn't natural.

A shadow moved over the sun, and I glanced up, seeing the body of a massive dragon soaring through the air alone. Not just any dragon. I'd recognize him anywhere—midnight black scales with molten fire surging beneath. I stood so quickly that my chair fell backward as I scrambled to the window.

"SLOANE!" I screamed, half hanging out of the castle. "SLOANE!"

My heart pounded within my chest as he slowed his flight, his large head turning to look in my direction. *He heard me. Oh gods, he heard me.* I screamed again, tears springing to my eyes as my unborn babies moved within me. Whether it was my screaming that had awoken them or Sloane being near, I didn't know. I wanted to think it was the latter.

The door to my chambers flew open, hitting the wall so hard

that a framed piece of art fell to the floor. I startled, turning my head to see who had come to tell me to be quiet. Asrael stood there, looking malicious and as smug as ever.

I looked back outside, and Sloane was closer now. I could practically see the flames rolling off of his scaled body. He was right there, and I longed to touch him. Even in his dragon form, he was mine, and I wanted nothing more than to curl up next to him and feel safe for the first time in weeks. My mouth opened just as Asrael's large hand clamped over it, effectively silencing me.

Warm breath fanned over my neck, and I whimpered. "That's quite enough noise. He's going to be here in seconds, Saige. He knows to stay away from you and he's disobeying me."

My eyes squeezed shut as Asrael ran his hand over the top of my round belly, softly caressing me. His other hand fell away from my mouth and dipped to my throat. "Quiet, witch."

The force of Sloane's wings powering through the air as he came to a stop right outside of my window sent strong gusts of wind through the space, the rhythmic whoosh of his wings loud in my ears. His mouth opened in a snarl when he saw whose arms I was in.

Making a show of it for Sloane's benefit, Asrael tilted my head to the side and ran his nose up the column of my neck. I could feel him hardening against my ass as tears slid down my face.

"Are you watching, dragon? This no longer belongs to you. This—" He moved his hands to the collar of my white nightgown and ripped it down the middle. My swollen breasts tumbled out, and I tried to cover them but it was futile. Tremors were wracking my body. Fear. Panic. Adrenaline. "All of this is mine now."

Bile burned my throat as Asrael's hands cupped my breasts, and Sloane released a growl that was a mixture of agony and fury. "I love taking what belongs to other men. Especially strong men, such as yours. I want them to see me claim you. To know they're beneath me, even when it comes to fucking and possessing their mate." His fingers pinched my nipples roughly, and I struggled to get my lungs to inflate.

Sloane was literally vibrating with rage. I could see it in the way his nostrils flared, the giant puffs of air that left him each time Asrael's fingers trailed over my skin.

'Do it, Sloane. Kill him. Please, please,' I begged in my head, even though I knew our connection wasn't working, probably due to the fucker behind me.

"Fly away, dragon. You won't like what will happen if you don't," Asrael warned, and I felt him grow behind me, his demon taking over. His tail wrapped around my thigh, and sharp teeth nipped at the skin of my shoulder.

'Sloane. Please. Get us out of here!'

I cried out as Asrael's teeth broke through my skin, causing warm blood to trickle down my chest and back. Sloane roared, and the tower shook, the entire structure vibrating from the sheer force of it.

Asrael laughed loudly, the deepness of his voice warping to sound like something from a nightmare. "Fine by me. I do enjoy an audience." His hand wrapped around my hair and he started dragging me toward the bed.

"No, no! NO! Get your hands off of me, you son of a bitch!" I cursed, I screamed, I fought. This wasn't happening to me again. My eyes watered from the sting of his hold on my hair. Fuck. He bent me over the bed, the tower now shaking even harder from Sloane's roaring. I put my arms out to catch myself, not wanting to put pressure on my stomach, and one of my hands slipped forward beneath my pillow. That was when I felt something smooth and cold—a handle.

"I hope you're watching, dragon. This won't be the last time this happens, but there's something special about the first time— the moment you know you're weaker than I am. When you realize that I will always get whatever I want. You have no power over me, beast!" Asrael slapped my bare ass with the hand that wasn't in my hair, and I growled. "Ah, the she-demon has claws after all? That will make this so much more fun."

My fingers curled around the hilt of the knife. I remembered now when the doctor was here earlier, he said he'd brought fresh pillows. Had he put this here? *Is he on my side?* There was no time to question it. Something thick and hard was pressing between my legs, and I brought the knife up, letting it slash through my hair, severing Asrael's hold on me and removing several inches of my long red hair. I couldn't care less. I twisted, bringing my leg up hard between his legs, hitting my mark. I hoped his balls split open, but I was already running and couldn't look back. I was at the window before he even hit his knees, cradling his groin.

"Catch me, baby!" I screamed, dropping the knife and jumping up onto the windowsill, which thankfully, was very low. I pushed off, flying through the air just as Sloane lifted his body, opening one of his massive claws. I'd had the good sense to rotate when I jumped so when I hit his body hard, it was with my back.

Sloane's claws tightened around me immediately, just in time to see Asrael—red-faced and fucking furious—storming to the window with his hands stretched out in front of him.

"GO!" I screamed, and Sloane shot up like a rocket. I'd never forget the look on Asrael's face, especially when I flipped him the double birds. We rose to the clouds more rapidly than I thought possible. Sloane was moving so fast; all I could do was tuck myself into a ball and protect my face from the vicious wind.

We did it. Oh my gods. We escaped.

The feeling of elation didn't last long as I thought about the other five men who were still there, all of whom held pieces of my soul within their hearts. And Khol... Gods, I didn't even know if he was alive. I refused to believe Laurie's bullshit lies.

The further we flew from the castle, the clearer my head became, and my magic began to return. It was clear that there'd been something within the castle itself blocking my magic. Out in direct sunlight again, experiencing the first sparks of power within my veins was what I'd imagine taking a hit of a powerful drug would feel like. My body sang as my affinity grew and restored my soul. I hadn't realized how much of a zombie I'd turned into over the past month.

Cupping my hands in front of me, I grew a tiny green sprout which rapidly began blooming tiny purple flowers. This was my affinity at its core. Life. The cycle of survival. There had been far too much death and destruction around me as of late, and unfortunately, I knew it wasn't over yet. Sloane and I would have to return to the castle and get our family back.

The best way to do that would be to seek out Vaeryn. Would he still be near that mountain peak? Or would he have already moved with the other dragons to fight the evil that was taking over the realm? Rain began to fall from the sky, soaking me within minutes. Not even Sloane's massive claws could've kept me dry from the monsoon that seemed to come out of nowhere.

The visibility was total shit so I didn't realize we were close to landing until the ground was ten feet from me. I gasped as Sloane used his wings to slow us, and with a gentleness a beast of his size shouldn't have been capable of, he placed me on the forest floor. I was completely nude and shivering from the sudden coolness of the wind and unrelenting rain.

I spotted a cluster of huge rocks, some of which were piled atop one another, and I took off for them. Hopefully we could squeeze within them and get some shelter from the elements. They certainly looked large enough. A snort came from behind me, but I kept moving. Another huff of warm air and Sloane's big head began nudging me the other direction, toward what appeared to be a large opening to a shallow cave. I could barely make it out with my vision, but I knew his option was much better.

"Okay, okay! I'm going!" I shouted over the rain, darting into the cave. Burrowing would have been a better word considering how small and shallow it was, but it would work until the elements improved. Spinning around, I searched for my dragon, but he wasn't there. Dread filled my stomach. Where was he? He wouldn't leave me here, I knew he wouldn't.

"Sloane?!" I screamed. The panic in my voice echoed around the burrow, but the rain was so fucking loud. I wiped the water from my face, willing myself not to cry. I was so tired of crying from fear.

Squinting out into the fog, I saw the shape of a man and I held my breath. He materialized like a phantom, moving through the mist like he'd been promised peace for his troubled soul. Our eyes clashed, and then he was running, the rain cascading down his naked flesh. I was moving for him, a sob in my throat and tears on my cheeks. I no longer felt the cold. All I felt was the need to touch him. My mate. My fierce, broken man.

Sloane and I collided, just as we always had. His arms wrapped around me, crushing me to his bare chest, and I squeezed him just as fiercely. His shoulders shook and my chest heaved as we broke together, wrapped around one another, finding the strength we'd been missing all of these weeks within each other.

He pulled back and held my face between his hands, staring down at me, his eyes moving all over, checking me for injuries. I was fine; the bite on my neck from Asrael was already sealed thanks to my healing abilities, but I knew he needed to see for himself. His gaze was frantic with the need to be sure, and when he was positive that I was safe, the urgency changed into something else entirely.

His body seemed to vibrate with desire, his pupils dilating as his lids drooped to half-mast. I pressed up on my tiptoes and wound an arm around his neck, pulling his lips down onto mine. I sighed into his mouth. It was like coming home. Large hands skated down my sides and he bent, breaking our kiss and burying his face into my neck, licking and sucking. I squealed when he swept me into his arms, wrapping an arm around his neck as he cradled me. Using my free hand, I gripped his jaw, taking his mouth again with a wildness I wasn't sure I'd ever felt.

The adrenaline of the escape. Being free from captivity. Just being in his arms again... Fuck. I needed all my men, but right here, in this moment, it was simply me and Sloane. The kitten and the dragon. The asshole and the sweetheart. The mage and the witch. Man and woman. And I needed him.

Sloane somehow got us back into the burrow and promptly laid me on my back. He spotted a brush pile a little ways from us and ignited it, the heat immediately warming my cool skin and the air around us. I found my legs parting, falling apart, welcoming my mate inside my body. He leaned over me, propping himself up with one forearm and using the other to line himself up.

We both moaned at the sensation of how fucking perfectly we fit together. My body was dripping with my need for him, and he delivered. Our eyes remained locked the entire time, every thrust, every sound of pleasure—it wasn't enough to feel, to hear. No, we needed to *see* it. See it down to the very fucking depths of our souls. Who we were at our cores and how we were made for each other.

My fingernails scored and scratched, encouraging Sloane deeper. Harder. My hips tried to meet his but my round stomach made it a bit difficult. I needed him deeper, and as though he read my mind, he pulled out and rolled me onto my side, settling in behind me. He lifted my left leg, holding me firmly just below the knee before thrusting up into me, hitting that place where I desperately needed him. I cried out, snaking my left arm back and grasping his ass.

Each clench of his muscles against my palm only served to drive me higher, and I turned my head, seeking his lips. We kissed just like we fucked. Wild. Deep. Frantic. My shaking thighs gave my pending orgasm away before I felt it building. My pussy clenched around his thickening cock and we fell over the edge together. Sloane all but roared his pleasure as we shook together, his cock sliding in and out, in and out, until the delicious swelling halted further movement and we lay there, locked together, panting.

"I need you, Saige. I'll always fucking need you." He kissed my shoulder, his breath fanning over my skin and causing goosebumps to erupt. "In the darkness, you're my sunshine. You're the sun at dawn, chasing the shadows from my wicked soul. I love you, and I'm so sorry, kitten." A tear fell and skated down my shoulder.

"Sloane," I breathed. "I've been so scared. Worried for you, for what he might do... Every part of my being ached to be near you. I'm not me without you. You have nothing to apologize for, baby. What happened was not your fault."

His large palm was gripping my hip; I sensed there was something he wanted to ask, so I waited. He lifted his hand, and I saw it tremble above my belly.

"May I?" he whispered so softly I almost didn't hear him. I took his hand and placed it on the swell of my stomach, my heart soaring at the way his breathing hitched as he felt my pregnant belly for the first time in over a month. "My gods, you're the most beautiful woman in creation. How are you mine?"

Just then, the babies began moving at the same time. Little punches and kicks, letting us know they were there. Still a part of us. Sloane's eyes were wide as he glanced at me, and they glittered with emotion.

"Our girls," he murmured in awe, and I smiled.

"Ours."

Bram

Chapter Six

I was a fool.

A fucking fool who led his family here to their destruction. Even if I made it out of here alive, I doubted they'd want anything to do with me. I'd fucked everything up. I should have known that Asrael would've already made his move. I'd played right into his hands.

The worst part? I didn't remember shit. And nobody would tell me a bloody thing. I remembered arriving in the throne room and a fight breaking out. Clearly, I'd been knocked out rather quickly, and when I woke, I was in this very room, the same one I'd been in for weeks. Better than a cell in the dungeon, but the problem was that my mind was a fucking dungeon at this point. I was my own jailer, my thoughts my punishment.

Where is Goldie? I snarled and my claws elongated. I hadn't been in my raw demon form much in years, but since being here, it seemed he liked to make appearances more often than not.

"Fuck!" I shouted when my claw snagged on the progress I'd made. Ever so carefully, I unhooked my nail from the delicate multi-colored yarn and focused on my breathing. I was nearly done with this one. What then?

The door creaked as it opened, but I remained dedicated to my task. I didn't give a shit who was showing up now. There were only a handful of people I wanted to see, and my nose told me it wasn't any of them. I refused to give the enemy the satisfaction of getting any sort of reaction from me, even if it was just acknowledgement of their presence.

"Never took you for a domesticated demon, nephew."

"Never took you for a bitch ass overthrowing motherfucker, uncle. Oh wait, yes. Yes I did," I fired back without a glance in his direction, resuming my work.

Asrael actually laughed. I did not. He stayed on the other side of the room, fixing himself a drink at the minibar. "Drink?"

"Make it a triple," I replied, looping the yarn. I couldn't make a move on him. Without access to my magic now, I'd be killed by the guards posted outside, if Asrael himself didn't do it first. Just because I could shift into my demon form didn't mean a whole lot. Without my power, I couldn't open a portal, jump, conjure, or any of my other abilities. And after what I'd witnessed in the throne room, for the first time he was stronger than I was. We'd always been evenly matched, but whatever mad scientist shit he'd been dabbling in had altered him. He was stronger than any creature I'd ever seen.

I glanced at him, his movements a bit jerky, and his hair askew. His typical photoshoot-ready appearance wasn't here at the moment, and I wondered why. I figured I'd be finding out soon enough though. In all of my time here, he'd only visited once, and that had been during my recovery. I didn't recall anything that was discussed, only that he had been there. I'd come to a lot of conclusions during my isolation—since I had all the time in the world to think—but I also had a few loyal guards who had fed me information here and there. Unfortunately, none of them knew the status of my family so I had to garner whatever information I could.

He approached me slowly as he carried our drinks, walking stiffly—like someone had kicked him in the dick. Hopefully, that's what had happened. Fucker. When he got close enough, I reached down and pressed the button on the side of the chair, sending the footrest up and causing him to have to step back quickly, our drinks nearly sloshing over the rims of the glasses.

If I had to entertain this bastard, I may as well be comfortable in my recliner with my feet propped up.

"You're a child," he sneered. "You look fucking ridiculous. What are you wearing? Where did you get a fuzzy pink robe with"—he leaned in to get a closer look—"are those *snails*?"

"I'm the rightful heir to this kingdom. I can wear whatever I want, regardless of what imposter sits his ass on my throne."

Asrael growled at the thought of there being royalists within these walls, but there were. And there always would be. I was curious how long my uncle had been parading as my father. In the last few years of his life especially, there had been more and more changes in my father's behavior and personality. Hell, Asrael had likely been drugging him.

"It's not my fault they love me so much more than you." I kept my eyes on my work, counting my stitches and ignoring the traitor. Holding my project up, I inspected the pattern, making sure everything looked even. It did. Satisfied, I continued, "I'd suggest cutting back on the killing and rampages. It doesn't really inspire—"

I was cut off when one of the glasses shattered against the wall just behind my head. Calmly, I set my supplies into the basket next to me on the small end table, not wanting to risk them being destroyed.

"I've had enough of your mouth, nephew!" Asrael boomed, pushing back the hair that had fallen into his eyes.

Slowly, I stood. My robe had come undone but I didn't bother closing it as I stretched my arms over my head, groaning dramatically. "I have an excellent solution for that, seeing as how I've seen enough of your face. How about you let me leave or you can get the fuck out of my room?"

His tail flicked in warning, and my own returning the posturing. Despite knowing what the outcome of a fight with him would be, the demon within me wouldn't back down from an outright challenge from another male. The way he was puffing up his chest, his lip curling over his teeth... We were getting dangerously close to a fight.

"I came here to offer you a deal, and yet you insult me. You know as well as I, your father was not fit to be king. He didn't have the fucking backbone for it—I do. I'm going to fix everything he destroyed!"

We circled one another, my body vibrating with the desire to rip his damn horns from his head and stab him with them, preferably in the eyes. "I haven't heard a deal yet. Get to the fucking point."

"Yield to me. Renounce your claim to the crown and publicly show your support for my reign. I will let you leave Besmet— exiled, of course—to live the rest of your days as you see fit. Far away from me and far away from this realm."

"And my family?" I questioned, wondering where he was going with this.

He chuckled darkly. "Your family?" he spat. "I'm the only family you have left, boy."

"You know exactly who I'm talking about. The family I chose, the family that chose me. The family I'd do anything for. That is not, nor will ever be, you," I hissed and my fingers curled, my claws pressing against my palms.

"You'd all leave. Never to return."

"And how do I know they're alive right now? That they're safe? Have they been treated with the same courtesy I have been shown?"

He smirked. "You know they haven't. Most have been held in the dungeons. It's war, nephew. You're too fucking soft for this world. You have to do what needs to be done in times like these."

"Where is my mate?" I bit out, clenching my jaw hard enough that I thought for certain I'd crack a molar.

He shrugged. Fucking shrugged! Rage poured through me like white-hot magma rushing down the slope of a volcano.

"That's the thing. You and those mages would be given a pass to leave, but not her. I'm not entirely cruel. I would, of course, sever the bonds that connect you to her and her to you. Same for each of them. She belongs here, for eternity. It is her fated destiny!"

I pounced. Pounced like a starved, rabid beast. We hit the ground in a clash of snarls, growls, and intent to maim. My hand found his throat at the same moment his tightened around mine. He'd flipped us so I was sprawled out on the ground, but that didn't mean he had the advantage. In seconds, we could rip each other's throats out and be done with it.

"It's the only way," he choked out, eyes bugging.

It was at that moment that I smelled it. Fire, damp earth, hard steel and that little dash of sunshine sprinkled with vanilla. Her. Goldie. On him... On his fucking hand that was blocking the air from my very lungs. The thought of her skin beneath his palms... My eyes dropped down and I saw a glint of red. Slowly, I plucked the lone strand of hair from Asrael's shoulder and stared at it. My woman's hair was on this piece of shit's clothes and her scent was on his skin. Fury became a living being within my flesh, as thoughts—of potential situations that could've led to this hair and her gods damned scent on him—flashed through my brain at high speed.

My head flew up and smashed into his face, catching him off guard. "I'm going to rip your fucking hands off! How DARE you touch what's mine!" I grabbed one of his arms, prying it away from his shattered nose and snapping it backward. The crunch and snap of bone and tendon sang to the demon within me. I would cut every inch of flesh from his body that carried her scent, for he did not deserve the gods damned honor of wearing her perfume!

Without warning, I flew back, grunting as I slammed into the wall. Every muscle in my body raged and fought against the invisible magic that was holding me. Asrael staggered around, snarling over his massacred wrist. I would've felt a pang of accomplishment had I detached it completely. Instead, I mostly just felt dissatisfied and murderous.

His eyes flared with the heat of a dragon's fire, and I roared in outrage as he snapped his wrist back into the proper place. The psychopath barely winced! That hand still smelled of my woman. It would haunt me for the rest of my existence.

"I take it you refuse to accept my offer." The skin around his jagged wound began sealing itself as he healed at a speed that should have been impossible.

I spat at him. "Suck my fucking cock."

"I can't say I'm surprised. Unfortunately, nephew, there is no going forward from this. Your story ends tomorrow at dawn. Execution via beheading. It will be public, as you'll be made an example of. Anyone in the castle who feels loyal to you will know it is futile to continue backing a prince who didn't live long enough to sit on the throne." He strode to the door and I still tried to break free, to end his reign of fucking terror. And to rip those hands off. I'd have them, one way or another.

"You may take some solace in the fact that you won't be going out to meet your fate alone. There's a good chance you'll be seeing some of your... family." He snarled the word, and my stomach clenched with unease. "It should be quite the event." Asrael stepped through the door and called out his farewell, telling me to sleep well. What a fucking asshole. The door slammed and bolted at the same moment I was released from my binds.

My mind was like a runaway train with how thoughts flew by at high speed, images and memories. Dawn. I had maybe twelve hours. I needed to use them wisely. A wave of calm came over me. There wasn't much I could do from within my prison, but I could finish my project. It was the least I could do and at least then I would have given something, regardless how small.

I settled into my recliner and picked up my knitting needles, losing myself to my purpose. Three gifts. Four letters. I'd used my time wisely. Khol had always taught me that nothing was over until it was over. I wasn't giving up; I was merely preparing.

If anyone had a chance of getting out of a situation like this, it would be the wild woman I loved and the men who loved her. I kept a cautious level of hope, not enough to be dangerous. Just enough to keep going.

Sloane

Chapter Seven

I woke to find myself curled around Red. Her sweet skin was warm and flushed from both the heat of my body and the fire that was still crackling. Her wild red hair was sprawled out over my arm, her face tucked against my chest. I carefully pushed some of the wayward strands off of her cheek. I wasn't the kind of asshole who thought women should only have long hair. I was the kind of asshole who didn't want my woman to have to change anything about her appearance just because of some other motherfucker. If *she* wanted to cut her hair, then it should be her choice—not because she needed to escape some psychotic rapist.

Soft puffs of breath tickled my hair, and I took the moment to kiss the top of her head. For the love of Saturn, I'd nearly lost her. *Again.* This madness had to stop. I remembered every godsforsaken moment in that throne room. Seeing Faris crushed beneath that chandelier, hearing Kai's cries of pain. I'd been ready to jump into the fray, literally. Fucking Asrael had frozen me in midair as I aimed for the throat of a guard who was about to make a move for Fischer. I was forced to watch as each of my brothers fell, and Khol. Gods. That blow had to have been fatal.

The worst though, the fucking worst of it, the part that

haunted my every moment—whether I was awake or not—had been watching the way Red completely broke before my eyes. The betrayal of her mother, yet again. The way she'd reached for me, looking for safety, and I'd failed her. It was as though I was nothing more than a puppet, with Asrael holding my strings.

Then the bleeding. The fear I'd felt when she gazed upon her bloodied palms had been so visceral, so consuming, that I couldn't breathe. And nobody was helping her. Not at first. I'd raged in my head, completely helpless, my entire being shaking with a primal force unlike anything I'd ever encountered.

"I can hear your mind working from here, Sloaney," Red murmured, her voice husky from sleep.

I tightened my hold on her, no longer needing to be concerned with waking her up. "There's a lot to think about," I whispered against her head. "How did you sleep, baby? Are you sore?"

"Just the normal aches and pains that come with this"—she waved her hand over her belly—"monstrosity."

I hummed as I allowed myself to caress her new shape. "It's crazy to me that there are two babies in here. Right now. What will they be like?"

She laughed, and I felt movement beneath my palm. A foot, most likely. "It *is* crazy. I got so much bigger while I was in that coma. I thought I had stretch marks before, but this is like… a whole different level. Plus, right after I woke up, I pissed myself."

My eyes widened at that. "Like… full-blown golden shower?"

"No, you idiot," she huffed, pushing herself into a sitting position so she could glare at me. "It was just a bit. One of these babies jabbed me right in the bladder and it was game over."

I had to roll my lips inward to stifle the laugh threatening to slip out. She really might've hurt me if I so much as smiled at her predicament. "My poor kitten," I cooed, moving to sit now. I needed her in my arms. "C'mere, Miss Peabody." She gasped in outrage, but was quickly tamed as I arranged her between my legs and started rubbing her back. "You're so gorgeous like this," I whispered into her neck. "Naked, in a cave, pregnant with my babies…"

Her head fell back to rest against my shoulder and she gazed up at me. "You're different."

I frowned. "How?"

"Softer, somehow. Less guarded. Like you're fully here with me, and happy about becoming a father." She linked her fingers with mine. "I was worried you wouldn't want this."

Oh hell. I freed one of my hands and tucked some hair behind her ear. "I can understand that. A year ago? No, I wouldn't have wanted any of this. When we first met? Nope. I was an insufferable dickhead and I regret so much about my behavior in the beginning, baby. I hurt you and my brothers. I thought that was the worst part, you know? Being cast out of my family for the first time in my life." Her eyes were boring into me, like missiles heading right for my soul.

"I realize now that wasn't the worst part. I think this is—knowing that my actions have placed so much doubt in your mind about me. About my dedication to our family."

"Sloane," she interrupted, twisting around slowly to face me.

I sighed, running a hand through my hair. "No, baby. I was such an asshole. I was scared of the changes, scared of what you being a part of us would mean. But I've never been happier in my entire fucking life—despite the current life or death situation. The only thing I'm worried about is fucking my kids up the way my dad fucked me up. What if they hate me?"

There it was. My ultimate fear.

She gave me a sad smile and shook her head, disagreeing. "You're a proud man. You've been through a lot. They'll adore you, just like I do."

Her face blurred, and I dropped my gaze, not wanting her to see me cry. Swallowing the lump in my throat, I willed my emotions to get the fuck under control. "Will you forgive me, Red? Can you ever trust me again?"

"You're a stupid idiot," she declared firmly, before pulling our foreheads together. "I've already forgiven you. A long time ago." Relief sang through me. "Gods, I more than trust you. I love you so damn much."

Oh.

"I don't deserve you," I confessed before taking her mouth with mine. Maybe I didn't deserve her, but she was right—she was mine. And I was hers. I was never letting go. We kissed like it was the last thing we'd ever do, like there was an urgency to stake a claim on the other.

With a sigh, she leaned back and stared at me. "What happened to you when you were taken? I want to know everything."

"It's kind of a long story…"

"Good thing we have some time while I conjure us up some clothes and essentials," she replied. "Help me up?" I hopped up and pulled her to her feet, tossing up how to begin.

"After the fight in the throne room, I was taken to some sort of holding pen a few miles away from the castle. Asrael has some serious power. I don't know how he does it, but he's able to take magic away from whoever he pleases. That's why I wasn't able to help you, baby."

She frowned, wrapping her arms around my waist. "It wasn't your fault. He took my magic away while I was there too. He's scary, Sloane. Nobody should have that much power." Hearing her reassurances, I felt the tension of guilt leave my shoulders. "Tell me what happened next," she urged.

I stepped out of her hold, feeling the need to move while I explained. "There were hundreds of dragons there, and I learned there were several of these facilities spread out now across the capital and the outskirts. The wards were reinforced by mages and demonic magic. If any of us wandered too close to the perimeter, we were given one hell of an electric shock that knocked some dragons out for hours at a time.

"After the first couple of days, and being shocked repeatedly in my attempts to break free, a group of male dragons approached me. They'd sensed my grief and panic. I'd been so focused on escape that I hadn't even tried to communicate with the others, and even if they'd been trying to communicate with me, I had been too far gone to hear it.

"It was then that this huge male dragon approached me…" I let my mind take me back to that day; it had been the turning point for me. It was very likely I would've killed myself, or others, had I been stuck in there for a long period of time.

'Brother, you must stop this.'

I panted heavily, coming back to reality after being knocked out again. Who said that?

'I did. Open your eyes.'

Slowly, my eyes opened, and I tried to recoil from the small group of males surrounding me. These were dragons that were working with Asrael; they couldn't be trusted.

The largest male of the group, who was bright orange, snorted.

'If you truly believe that any of us are here of our own free will, then you've been shocked by that magical fence a few too many times,' *he rumbled, glaring down at me. His voice reminded me of Vaeryn. I hoped he was still on that mountain, evading capture and rallying a defense.*

'Who are you?' *I asked, slowly pushing myself to my feet. I wavered, the lightheaded sensation seeming to come out of nowhere, and a dragon with deep crimson scales stepped up beside me, allowing me to lean against him for stability.* 'Thank you,' *I said to him, and he nodded.*

'We are the dragons of old. We've spent many decades in captivity, and we're desperate to defeat Asrael and reclaim our lives for our own. My name is Emrys—and you are?'

Feeling a bit steadier on my legs, I pushed myself away from the dragon at my side. 'My name is Sloane. I only recently developed the ability to shift into this form. My family, my brothers, and my mate, they're being held captive at the castle. If they're still...' *I let the sentence hang. I couldn't finish it. Shock rippled through the group, several of the dragons shaking their heads.*

A slightly smaller dragon stepped forward. His green scales caught the sun, shimmering gloriously. 'You speak of a mate?'

My hackles raised as my eyes narrowed on him. A threat? A competitor?

'I mean no harm, nor disrespect.' *The green dragon stepped back a few paces, and the relief I felt was immediate.* 'Finding a mate is a dream for most of us. I was merely curious.'

'She is mine,' *I hissed, snaking my tongue out.*

The dragons shared glances between themselves as I sank my claws into the earth beneath me. Flashes of her rounded belly, the blood on her palms, tears streaking her pretty face, all of it assaulted my mind. A mournful sound—a cross between a wail and a growl—escaped my mouth.

My body began to shake from the onslaught of memories, and I was growing more and more agitated with each passing second. 'It'll be an act of the stars themselves if I don't raze this fucking city to the ground the moment I'm free of these wards,' *I snarled.*

Emrys approached me cautiously. 'Breathe, brother. This is a miracle for our race. We're merely curious.' *I huffed, still feeling protective, and smoke spilled from my nose in warning. Emrys switched his line of questioning.* 'So you not only have a mate, but you are able to shift from man to dragon as well?'

'Normally, yes. Asrael's done something to me to block the ability though,' *I grumbled. My temper was running at an all-time high. I was agitated, and my thoughts were unmanageable. It was fucking chaos and I. Hated. Chaos.*

'Your mate,' *he said carefully, slowly.* 'You have bred her, yes?'

Every male in the vicinity gasped; some shouted out in shock and some in glee.

I. Needed. Her. Now.

'How do you know?' *I bit out.*

'A male dragon is not to be separated from his mate. We are built to protect and provide for our mate during the course of her pregnancy. To part a male from his mate is abhorrent! It is torture of the cruelest variety!' *Emrys bellowed, and the answering roars of the other males could've been heard all the way in the human realm.*

'I think... I think I'm dying without her,' *I admitted, suddenly just so fucking tired.*

'It will feel that way. Which is why it is barbaric. The false king will pay for this with blood—I promise you that, brother. We've not had a natural mating occur in centuries. Times are changing,' *he murmured.*

Then I remembered what Red had told us about Vaeryn's reaction. He'd called her his queen. Would these dragons feel the same? Would they risk their lives to ensure her safety?

'It was foretold. A prophecy.'

The silence that followed my words lasted for what seemed like forever, eventually giving way to whispers of 'the queen.'

'Your mate is the prophesied one?' *Emrys asked, his voice full of awe.*

'She is,' *I replied, pride rushing through me.*

'BROTHERS!' *he barked, gaining the attention of every dragon within our holding pen.* 'THE PROPHECY HAS COME TO PASS!' *Cheers and roars exploded through the grassy field as dragons of all colors and sizes moved closer to hear more. Hope bloomed in the field, as potent as a field of wildflowers, leaving no beast untouched.*

'Where is our queen?' *someone called out and was joined with similar questions.*

'Who is she?'

'How do you know?'

Emrys settled the crowd and gestured to me. 'This dragon is her mate. I shall allow him to field further questions as I am incredibly curious, myself.'

I sighed, straightening myself and rising to my full height. I fucking hated public speaking. Actually, I hated public anything. Especially anything with people. Or in this case, dragons. I loved getting to defer any sort of situation like this to Kai and Cam—they were much better suited to winning crowds over. I was just a dickhead who'd somehow gotten lucky enough to win the love of a woman who had never asked me to be anyone different—but she made me want to be. I'd do this for her, for us—our family.

'What Emrys says is true. It has been an eventful journey to this point, to say the least. I'm one of six mates, though I never feel that way when I'm with her. She has a way of making me feel like the only man on earth when she looks at me.' *I paused, needing to compose myself. As I swallowed down the growing lump in my throat, I could hear voices speaking about how lucky I was. About how finding a woman with that kind of heart was rare. I knew all of that. There was no way that Saige did though. She was confident, yeah... but I didn't think she would ever truly understand how special she was.*

I'd make sure she knew.

'Her name is Saige Wildes; she is a green witch and a demon. For months, we have been battling Asrael—both directly and indirectly—along with Saige's mother, Laurie Wildes. Both of them have plotted and schemed, and Laurie actually murdered one of the queen's mates!' *I let my voice carry, wanting everyone to hear as I described the vile things Laurie and Asrael had done.*

Cries of outrage rang out at the mention of what Laurie had done to Fischer. 'Your queen brought him back from the dead! Her power is unmatched, and those who have wronged her should be afraid!'

'Where is the queen, brother?'

My head dipped. 'I'm not sure. When we arrived, it was to warn King Thane. We'd discovered the dragons Asrael held captive in the human realm were gone; we assumed he was going to make a move for the throne. We got here too late and were ambushed. I don't know where my family is, or if they're safe.' *Murmurs broke out amongst the crowd.* 'The last I saw of my mate, she was bleeding heavily... from between her legs.'

My heart cracked at the memory, and it seemed the same for every scaled beast in attendance. They sensed my pain, my anguish, and they matched it. I may have been without my family, but I wasn't alone.

Emrys approached me, bumping his forehead to mine in solidarity. 'We shall have our vengeance. But your bond, what does it tell you?' *Emrys asked.*

'What do you mean?'

'Ah. You haven't been a dragon long—it makes sense you wouldn't yet know what we're capable of. When a dragon takes a mate, a bond is formed, linking you together. The same goes for our hatchlings. We're bonded to our families. Through the bond, you can sense them, their life force. I can't speak for your mate brothers, but the queen, and your child—they are certainly alive,' *the large orange dragon explained, bumping me with his snout.*

'How do you know? You're not bonded to them,' *I retorted, feeling a weird sense of jealousy at the way he was speaking of them, as though he knew something I didn't.*

Several dragons snorted at my words, some laughing. 'If they were to leave this life, the pain that would befall you would be debilitating. You are sad right now, yes. But you are not a dragon who has lost a mate or child to death. As far as how I know such things? I am very old, and we have our own tales and history.'

I processed his words. Alive. They were alive. I wished at that moment I had the same bond with the other men, so I could know without a doubt if they were still breathing.

As though he sensed my thoughts, Emrys leaned in. 'We dragons mate in groups as well. Binding your circle will strengthen each of you, including your connection to one another. The power you wield now would amplify to the power of your other six bonded, combined.'

'How the hell don't we know about that?' *A circle binding?*

If I'd ever doubted that dragons could smile, the mystery was put firmly to rest at the flash of Emrys' rows of teeth as he grinned.

'We're full of secrets, queen's mate. Our traditions and culture have been all but forgotten, many of which are regarded as nothing more than myths. Tall tales that fathers whisper to their young before sleep carries them away for the night. Tell me, are we the first dragons you've met?'

'Actually, no.' *I thought of the massive navy dragon we'd met weeks ago on a mountaintop.* 'I met a dragon by the name of Vaeryn.'

You could've heard a pin drop.

'What did you just say?' *Emrys whispered, his eyes large.*

'Vaeryn. He's the one who called Saige the queen, the fated one. We were to meet up with him before everything went to shit,' *I explained.*

'I cannot believe my fucking ears. Vaeryn is my brother by blood. I haven't seen him in so long,' *Emrys' voice softened, his eyes unfocused as he stared at me.*

'Your brother? That's incredible. He's doing well, from what I could tell. I didn't get any other information though,' *I confessed with regret. These dragons had been through fucking hell for so long. I vowed right then and there that I'd do whatever I could to reunite Emrys and Vaeryn.*

'Thank you for this information—I can't tell you how much it means to me. Knowing there are still free dragons out there and that my brother is amongst them.' *He turned to the crowd.* 'MY BROTHER, VAERYN, IS ALIVE! AND FREE!'

Roars exploded through the valley, and a rhythmic sound started up, growing in volume. Casting a wide glance around, I saw each dragon thumping his tail against the ground. The beat was one they knew well and it reminded me of a drumline, each dragon knowing which beat to follow.

'We know the truth of what Asrael has done. He tried to curse the dragons with the aid of black magic, attempting to seal our fate through the blood and tears of OUR OWN KIND!'

The music grew. The ground beneath my feet shook with the force of it.

'For years, he poisoned the water supply of his own people. You see, he played the long game. By doing so, he was permitted leave of this realm by his brother, the king, to search for suitable options to ensure the demon race. That was Asrael's plan all along. He was never concerned with the fertility problem since it was his own poisoning that caused it! When we refused him an alliance, he was driven mad with rage. He concocted a plan.

'Being unable to control our minds, he found something he was able to control. Our forms.'

My brow lifted at that. 'Your forms?'

'Certainly you did not believe you were the only one capable of walking as a man?' *Emrys winked as my mouth fell open.*

'You're all shifters,' *I gasped.* 'But why would he want you in your dragon forms? Wouldn't it be easier to control you at two hundred pounds versus two tons?'

'Two forty.'

'What?'

'Two hundred and forty pounds was my weight. Solid as the stone walls lining the perimeter of the castle.' *He lifted his chin and puffed his chest out, making me chuckle.*

'Apologies. You're clearly quite the specimen, Emrys.'

'You have no idea!' *a dragon shouted, and the group started ribbing Emrys for his apparently attractive human form.*

This was amazing. And they'd been stuck in these forms for centuries? There was something building here, a lightness that was sweeping through the crowd, and I realized it was possibility. Merely the possibility of things changing.

'How many of these enclosures does he have?'

'At least five.'

Five. And there were at least one hundred dragons in here. That meant, at minimum, there were five hundred dragons who had been mistreated, held captive, separated from their families... All we needed to do was figure out how to break the hold Asrael wielded on them.

Red's voice broke me from my trance, bringing me back to the present. "So how did you get out of the holding pen?"

I laughed. "They bullied me. That was the plan we concocted. It was clear Asrael had some intended use for me, so we tried to test that theory. If I was in danger of being harmed, he'd likely have me pulled out of there. And that's what happened."

She hummed and continued her soft touches. "And how did you break from Asrael's hold then? To be able to disobey him like you did?"

"I'm not entirely sure, to be honest." My fingers twirled in her shorter hair as I gazed up at the ceiling of the burrow. Thick, gnarled tree roots were twisted together, holding the ground above us up. "In the past few weeks, I've been working on separating myself from those memories I have from the lab. Some of the dragons were able to help me talk through things, and I felt like I made some real progress. I must have. I was able to fly away with you..."

She brushed the hair off my face and I closed my eyes, surprised how much I was enjoying the feeling of her doting on me. "I'm so proud of you. We might have a real chance now. To get the others, to get rid of Asrael and Laurie... I don't think I'll be able to rest until they're dead." Her green eyes burned into mine. "Does that make me evil?"

I scoffed at her words. "There isn't an evil bone in your body, kitten. And you're going to be a mother. Of course you want safety for your family. So, no... it doesn't make you evil or bad. It makes you a living being who craves stability and safety. I promise I'll do everything in my power to make sure you get it."

Her lips met mine, soft pecks and little licks of her tongue as she coaxed me into letting her in my mouth. The feverish fucking of last night was far away now as we lazily kissed each other, as though we had all the time in the world and there was nothing wrong.

But there was plenty wrong and I couldn't stay here with her, not without thinking of my brothers.

I broke our kiss, giving her a stern look when she tried pouting. "That shit might work on Cam, but it's not gonna get you anywhere with me." Her mouth fell open in shock, and I laughed like hell. "Come on, Red. We need to get moving. It's time to go find Vaeryn."

Saige

Chapter Eight

Thankfully, I was able to conjure some clean clothes. Sloane didn't need any yet, since he was currently soaring through the clouds with me firmly clenched in his claw. I'd flown the first part, just to stretch my wings after not using them for so long, and while it felt great, I was panting like a dog after a minute. Pregnancy was not conducive to physical activity, especially for someone like me who usually had no interest in such things anyway.

So I happily crawled into Sloane's massive claw and held on tight. I was so fucking proud of him. He'd grown so much since we first met, and it seemed that with his father finally being dead, he was able to fully step into the role of the man he wanted to be, instead of letting the shadow of his father loom over his head. His time with the dragons also seemed to have boosted his confidence in both himself and his place within our family.

When he'd spoken earlier about them, his face had lit up and I could tell he'd made new friends. I didn't think Sloane had ever really had any friends outside of Fischer, Kai, and Cam. Hopefully, I'd get the chance to meet those dragons soon and thank them personally for all of their help.

We had allies. We just needed to figure out a way to free them, and then all of Asrael's hard work would crumble. You can't build a kingdom on a shaky foundation and not anticipate a landslide. Everything Asrael had done since the beginning had been wrong. He wasn't capable of keeping his narcissistic tendencies hidden long enough to build lasting, trustworthy relationships with people. He'd rather rule by using fear and terror versus winning the people over with love and respect.

I truly believed that if we could free the dragons and other prisoners he had in the castle, we could create an uprising, and Asrael would never be an issue again. I'd take great pleasure from watching him being taken down by those he felt he could control and torture. The ones he felt were beneath him all this time. The only thing that would make it sweeter would be if Laurie was there at the same time.

We dipped through the clouds, seeing the familiar mountain range coming into view in the distance. My belly dipped with butterflies—which, let's face it, were probably gas, because these girls were making me gassy as hell. It felt like the first minute we were flying, I was propelled half by the power of my wings and half by the power of ripping ass. I was so thankful Sloane had flown ahead so I could fart in peace. I kind of hoped it was just due to something I'd eaten, because I'd never hear the end of it from the guys if this became the norm.

The guys. The thought of being reunited with them had my skin tingling with anticipation and my pulse pounding like a drum. I couldn't wait to get my hands on them; I doubted I'd ever let them go. Not after this.

We landed a moment later, and Sloane shifted smoothly, standing naked as a jaybird and peering out over the landscape. I conjured some clothes for him and tossed them at the back of his head, earning me a scoff and an 'are you serious right now' expression.

"Well? You can't be parading around here naked!"

"Actually, I think this is one of the only places nobody would bat an eye over a man walking around naked," he argued, lifting a brow and stepping into the boxer briefs.

I huffed. "Yeah well, there might be females around here."

"I still don't think they would care—" He glanced up at me before a slow smile took over his face. "Oh. I see. My woman doesn't want any other women seeing me. Is that it? You're jealous?"

I laughed, waving him off like he was being ridiculous. His eyes narrowed and he pushed the boxers back down, letting his long, hard cock spring up and slap his belly.

"Well, if you're not jealous then I'll just go ahead and—"

He didn't get to finish his sentence because I launched myself at him. I slapped his dick and pulled his boxers back up over it, then shoved a finger in his face. "This is mine. No other female will be seeing it in this lifetime or the next. Understand?"

His pupils dilated and glowed orange as we stared at each other. "Did you just slap my dick? That really happened just now?"

I pushed up on my tiptoes and put my nose against his. "And I'll slap it off if I ever find out another female saw it! I don't care if you're taking a piss and a rogue dragon is hiding in the bushes!" Damn, I was getting so pissed at the thought of this hypothetical dick viewing. Probably partly due to the hormones... But that was my dick!

"Fuck, you're sexy when you're jealous," Sloane growled, leaning down and burying his face into my neck. His hot breath trailed up to my ear, and I shivered. "You have no reason to be. You're the only woman who can handle me, Red."

I sank my hands into his hair and guided our mouths together. Now that I knew I had him back, I couldn't keep my hands to myself. Reluctantly, I slowed our frantic make out session and broke away, breathing heavily. "Enough of that for now. More later," I panted. "Let's go find Vaeryn and get our guys back."

Sloane nodded his agreement, and I started walking in the direction from which Vaeryn had appeared last time. Footsteps came right behind me and I shouted out, without turning around. "Put those damn clothes on!" When the sounds of his steps stopped, I smiled. Freaking buttlord.

We'd been trudging along down the side of the mountain for about an hour when I had to stop. My lower back was killing me, and I was now thirsty enough to kill for water.

"You okay, Red?" Sloane moved to sit beside me on a log. As I caught my breath, we stared out at the rolling hills and the thicket of pine trees that seemed never-ending.

I nodded and snapped my fingers, securing two bottles of water for us. "Thirsty. Back hurts." I chugged my water in under a minute and Sloane handed me the remaining half of his. "I can get more. Drink it," I said, attempting to hand it back to him, but he waved me off.

"I'm fine for now, and if we can get more then it's fine. I think I should fly up and check if I can see anything that might point to where Vaeryn could be. And if not him, then other dragons." He stood and began removing his clothing, throwing glances to the sky as he stripped.

"What should I do?" I didn't want to just sit my ass here and wait around. Time was wasting.

"I would really like it if you would eat something. And maybe drink some more water? You'll probably need to pee, right? That's pretty much all I know about pregnant women. They pee. A lot. And eat weird food," he added as an afterthought, and I laughed at how put off he was at not knowing all about something for once.

"Okay. Come back down in twenty minutes or I'm coming up after you. I'll get some food for you too. Be safe," I cautioned, suddenly not liking the idea of being separated even for a moment.

Sloane sensed my sudden distress and was quickly at my side, his arms wrapping around me tightly. "What is it?"

My throat felt tight and I had to work to get the words out. "I'm scared. I'm scared that if I let you out of my sight, I'll never see you again." My voice broke and tears spilled over. I was scooped up and placed firmly on his lap, our bond soothing me in a way that only my mates could provide.

Sloane kissed my forehead. "I know, baby. It's been a really rough time since we met... but we have to keep going. We're so close now to being done with this nightmare, and then we can live our lives the way we want to. Just hang in there with me a little bit longer, okay?" His thumbs brushed the tears from my cheeks, and I nodded, sniffling like a baby.

"I just feel like something bad is coming. Or is about to. I can't place it, but ever since we landed here on this mountain, I've felt this sense of urgency. It's getting stronger. What if the guys are in trouble?" I looked into his eyes and saw my own fears mirrored there. But Sloane was a soldier. Trained for times like these—being faced with the unknown and having to keep going. It was getting harder for me to do that. I wasn't anything special...

A low growl rumbled against me, coming from deep within his chest. "Not anything special?" My eyes widened and I realized I must've spoken that part aloud. "How can you—" He paused and pinched the bridge of his nose, breathing deeply. After what felt like an eternity, he lifted his head and his gaze seared into my soul.

"You listen here and you listen good, Saige Wildes. You're everything that's special. Everything you are is special. I've been all over our realm, seen dozens of countries, millions of people, and let me tell you something. Not one of them even came close to being as special as you." His voice was deep and full of absolute sincerity. I'd almost have thought he was angry, with how intense his expression was. Stony and flushed red, his mouth a thin line.

"Yeah, we've been trained for shit like this. That doesn't make us special—that makes us experts. These are skills we learned. You, on the other hand..." His eyes trailed down to my neck, continuing to my round belly before he placed his hand there. "What you are, the *way* you are? Selfless, caring, understanding of everyone around you? The way you love with your whole being, Saige, that isn't something someone can be trained to do. Nobody can become an expert in the field of selflessness.

"But here you are, and I'm fucking enamored with you. Totally and completely blown away by your very existence. The mother of my daughter. You are special—and you're mine. Ours. Forever."

I'd never imagined I'd be sitting here, pregnant, on Sloane's lap while he poured his heart out. The fierceness with which I loved him was causing my heart to thump, spreading endorphins and serotonin straight from my brain throughout my body. He was devoted; he was mine. And gods, I was his.

"I love you," I whispered, pressing my mouth to his. He returned my kiss, as though his tongue might be able to convince me of his feelings if his words hadn't already done so.

"I love you. Now, go pee and get yourself a snack. We'll fly up when you're ready. Together." He clapped my thigh and shifted me to standing so he could get up. Before I thought twice about it, I launched myself at him and gave him a hug. The silly man was stiff as a board for all of two seconds before melting against me and hugging me back. The fact that he'd noticed my distress, helped me through it without being annoyed that I was holding up his plans, and then decided to do this together... I noticed. I was pretty sure Sloane was actually a bigger softie than he'd ever care to admit. But I saw him.

"Okay, I better go pee now. Since I stood up, it kind of hit me all at once." I stepped back and tromped off to find a tree.

"Make sure you get all of those farts out over there too!" he shouted, then laughed like hell.

I pretended I didn't hear him. But gods, yeah. I did have some to unleash on this poor tree. *If he tells the others a word of this, I swear I'll get payback.*

I FLUTTERED my wings and lowered myself right behind Sloane's big ass dragon head. I was tired—again. So he could do the heavy lifting, that was fine with me. As long as he wasn't out of my line of sight, I could handle riding him like a queen.

Scanning the expansive terrain, I suddenly spotted a glimmer of something. We weren't terribly high above the trees, but still high enough that I wondered if I'd imagined it.

'I think I saw something shiny down there,' I said to Sloane through our mental link, the one that only existed while he was in his dragon form. I squealed when he abruptly shifted to the left and began to descend. *'You could warn a girl next time!'*

'What was it? Gold? Some kind of gem?'

'I told you, I just saw a shimmer of something. Fly over there and I'll see if I spot it again.' Crazy, treasure-loving dragons... Worse than a dog hearing the word 'ball.' I focused my attention on the ground, growing more and more sure I'd imagined the whole thing.

'Anything?' Sloane rumbled. I was positive his own eagle eyes were scanning the ground like some kind of built-in treasure detectors. I wondered whether his body would beep if he spotted it.

'No. It was probably noth— OH!' We dropped so rapidly, my tits almost hit me in the face.

'Found it!' Sloane squealed. Squealed. Like a two-year-old who'd just found a dropped gummy bear covered in dust. None of that mattered. Treasure was treasure.

We landed smoothly, and Sloane scampered off to collect his findings. I trailed behind him, laughing at the way his whole body shook with excitement, like a big, scaly puppy. It was especially funny when he shifted to his human form and his ass continued to shake. There was no way he even realized he was still doing it and I wasn't about to tell him.

We were on the edge of a large lake; the water was such a vivid blue and I wished we had more time here, all of us. There really were gorgeous landscapes here in Besmet. "What is it?" I called to Sloane, approaching where he was crouched down.

"I think... I think it's yours," he replied, standing and turning toward me. My eyes dropped to the object in his hands. It was easily the most stunning crown I'd ever seen.

"Mine?" I questioned him, confused—because how would he know that?

'It is yours, my queen,' a familiar deep and raspy voice said in my head, and I smiled.

"Why are you smiling?" Sloane asked, studying me.

"Vaeryn's here," I replied, looking around for any sign of the big guy as Sloane stepped up to my side, pulling me against him. "I don't see him though. Do you?" I tilted my head up to look at my mate as his eyes darted around. His enhanced eyesight was incredibly useful in times like these.

He glanced down at me with a frown. "I don't. Are you sure you heard him?"

I nodded. "Yeah. It was when I took the crown from you and questioned it being mine. He said it was."

'Welcome back, my queen and queen's mate,' Vaeryn said, and we both spun around, searching for him. *'You won't be able to see me. You'll have to follow my instructions. We've hidden ourselves for protection. Enter the lake and swim to the bottom.'*

Sloane and I looked at each other. His expression was full of his classic skepticism. *'That's it? Nice deep dive in the midst of a war, all because a dragon that we can only hear in our heads tells us to? There's no fucking way my pregnant mate is getting in that water without some reassurance, Vaeryn!'*

I blinked. *Okay. Go on then, sexy boss man.*

'I would expect nothing less. I shall reveal myself to you. It will be

quick, so pay attention. Follow me and bring the crown, my queen. You will be safe,' Vaeryn assured us.

My fingers twined around Sloane's as we stood there, facing the lake. Ripples began to spread across the surface, and I gripped his hand tighter. I couldn't believe what I was seeing when Vaeryn's scaly head rose from the water just far enough to reveal his eyes. With a wink, he sank beneath the water once more.

'So you see, it is safe. We have much to discuss. Please, follow me.'

"Do dragons live underwater here?" I asked Sloane, trying to process everything. "He's like a big ass alligator!"

Sloane laughed and ran his hand through his shaggy hair. "I have no idea. But we're going to find out. Ready for a swim, kitten?"

'Forgive me, my queen, but there are enemy spies approaching and you must come now before you're spotted. Just swim for the bottom of the lake and you will get to where you're going,' Vaeryn urged, his tone firm.

"Let's go." Urgently, Sloane and I walked hand in hand into the water, and I was pleasantly surprised to feel that it was warm. Maybe it was a heated spring and that was why the water was so clear? With the crown clutched in one hand, I sucked in a deep breath and dove down into the heated depths. I had no idea what we were swimming for or toward, aside from the bottom. Everything was clear as day as I glanced around the underwater world.

Sloane kept pace beside me easily, and I sensed the athletic bastard was actually holding back. *How far do we have to swim down? This is a fairly deep lake.* I used to be able to swim down to twelve feet at the Emerald Lakes community pool, but that was years ago. And this was much deeper than twelve feet.

The bottom of the lake appeared to be nothing but large rocks and water plants. A school of fish swam past us, and I realized that they weren't fish at all—they were seahorses. Kind of. What the hell were those? They had seahorse tails but everything from the hips up was human-like. Similar to mermaids, but on a much smaller scale. Several of them circled Sloane and I, their big eyes curious.

'They are seasprites. They aren't dangerous. Keep swimming, just a bit further,' Vaeryn instructed.

My lungs were starting to burn with the need for air. I was close to panicking when the lake floor shimmered, revealing gorgeous crystals and enough treasure to buy a country. Sloane's hand grabbed my wrist and pulled me down, deeper through the water. My vision was darkening from the lack of air, making me wonder if this was really how I was going to die. Suddenly, my head broke through the surface of the lake unexpectedly, and I sucked in oxygen like it was the best thing I'd ever experienced.

Sloane coughed. "How?"

We were in the middle of the lake, but the water we were treading was now pale pink and we were upright again. Overhead, dragons soared through the sky against a clear blue backdrop. I couldn't help the laugh that bubbled out of my mouth.

"Did we just swim to the bottom of a lake only to surface in another one? A pink one?! Where's Vaeryn?"

"I'm here, my queen."

Glancing over my shoulder, my mouth fell open at the sight of a man, not a dragon, standing on a rocky ledge at the edge of the lake. A group of about ten other people moved up behind him, each of them carrying different things—towels, water, dry clothes. Sloane tugged my hand and we started swimming for the shore. He easily lifted himself out of the water, before reaching down for me.

I mean, he was strong, but surely there was no way he was going to lift all two hundred plus pounds of me out of a lake like I was nothing more than a— "Oof!" My feet hit solid ground as water ran down my body, and I looked at Sloane like he was Thor or some shit. The veins in his arms were defined as he ran his hands over my body, checking to ensure I wasn't harmed.

When he was satisfied, he looked at my face, which still

showed my shock at being pulled from the lake like a silly salmon. Pushing my hair out of my face, he bent in close to my ear. "The fact that you're surprised right now just tells me I haven't tossed you around the bedroom nearly enough. Once these girls are born, I'll be sure to remedy that." His tongue traced the shell of my ear, and a squeak came out of me, which had him chuckling silently. Pulling back, he tossed me a cocky ass wink and then took my hand, leading me to Vaeryn.

Vaeryn smiled when we reached him. I was about to open my mouth and make sure it was really him, because how was he a man now? But he beat me to it.

"I, Vaeryn, welcome you to the Realm of Dragons. You are safe here, my queen. We have waited a long time for your arrival." He lowered to one knee and bowed to me, followed seconds later by the rest of the people who were gathered around.

Sloane's grip tightened on my hand as we looked out among these people and this strange place we'd found ourselves in. When he nudged me with his arm, I realized I was probably supposed to say something. Anything.

I cleared my throat. "Thank you, Vaeryn, for welcoming us."

Vaeryn lifted his head and grinned, his forearms braced on his leg. He was much younger looking than I'd anticipated—I'd been expecting Gandalf vibes if I was honest. Vaeryn was ruggedly handsome, his long golden hair braided close to his scalp along the sides of his skull. The darkness of his eyes popped against the light shade of his hair, and as he pushed himself up, I had to tilt my head back to look at his face. He was bigger than Cam, which was a shock since my storm mage was the biggest man I'd ever seen.

"Come, Your Highness. We have much to discuss and little time to do so."

Sloane and I shared a fleeting glance, and we stepped forward, following Vaeryn. As we walked, we were handed towels to dry ourselves and waterskins filled with cool water. I was so thirsty, I couldn't stop myself from drinking it down like an animal with no manners. The crown was still in my hand and I felt a sense of peace, standing here in this world, with these dragons. I was safe, though I wouldn't be able to enjoy that until I had all of my mates at my side.

With renewed determination, I squared my shoulders, put the crown on my head, and strode after Vaeryn with purpose.

It was time to get my mates back, and I was willing to do whatever was necessary to make that happen.

Fischer

Chapter Nine

The pain fueled my desire for vengeance. The stolen touches and filthy words that were supposed to have been coming from a lover gave life to the monster deep within me. Everything was building, rising, reaching for an escape from the prison of my physical body with every passing moment I had to spend tied down and held in this room.

Hours left alone in the dark would be enough to cause any man to lose his fucking mind, but to do something so psychologically damaging to a man who never had his full mind in the first place? Fucking stupid.

I knew I'd heard Saige's voice yesterday. Was it yesterday? I was losing track of everything in here. My ankle had been shattered again, and I was pretty sure I'd seen bone when I finally got the nerve to glance down at it. I assumed they'd healed it again, but maybe I just didn't feel the pain anymore. It didn't matter; I didn't exist there anymore. I lived somewhere deep within the walls of my mind, asking myself the questions I'd always been too afraid to really get answers to.

Did I like killing people? Did I resent my ability as much as I claimed to, or was I pretending because that's what everyone else told me it's how they'd feel if they had my affinity? All of the people I killed had been 'bad.' At least, that's what Radical had always told us. I was nothing more than a fucking hitman. I'd always seen the reports when Johnny—no, Bram—briefed us on our assignments, but really, what information did I have for sure that all of those people deserved the things I'd done?

I laughed. I laughed so fucking loud that the sound echoed around the cell. I laughed so hard I cried. And why? Because I'd never asked. I'd never asked for proof if it wasn't provided. I just trusted in the job, our purpose. Protecting the magical community from rogues and evil supernaturals who would harm humans and magical people alike—that was what we did.

And yet, something lurked in the depths of my soul. This black vortex, which felt like it needed me to kill. It was there now, churning and twisting, hungry for death, and I was more than ready to fucking feed it.

It consumed me, this forced self-discovery. I couldn't think about the guys; it would break me. I needed to stay focused. To know what I was capable of. I suspected that the guard who tortured me was also the same guard who shapeshifted into Sloane. There were little tells. Like the way he would rub his index and middle finger against his thumb when he was thinking. Sloane never did that, but this Sloane did.

The guard would also tuck his hair behind his ear since it was the perfect douchebag length that it constantly fell forward. I'd caught "Sloane" going to put his hair behind his ear several times, but his hair wasn't long enough for that. So yeah, I was pretty positive. And I was also positive I was going to take great pleasure in ending that fucker's life.

I'd spewed so much bullshit to the fake Sloane about Saige and the guys. Information about Laurie that I wasn't exactly sure was true, but I'd bet on it. Like how she'd supposedly told me that she intended to take this kingdom for herself, that she'd never trusted Asrael and planned to get rid of him as soon as possible. I could only hope that my lies made it to the man himself and

Laurie got locked up too. I no longer cared who killed that bitch, so long as she died.

The lock on the door engaged and I sighed, wondering which one I was going to have to deal with this time. Torture or rape. Essentially they were the same thing to me at this point, though one of them brought a lot more blood and physical pain versus an absolute psychological mindfuck. The door started to open and I lifted my head, just enough to see a sliver of light spill into the room.

Sounds of a scuffle and a loud thump really caught my attention, and I was surprised when Don—the asshole guard—was tossed into my cell, knocked out cold. Maybe surprised wasn't the right word; really, it was more of a 'huh' moment. The surprise came a beat later when two men stepped into the cell and closed the door. *They're really upping their game.*

"Fischer, by the fucking moon, what have they done to you?" Fake Kai cried, rushing over to me, a low whine slipping from his open mouth.

I slowly looked at him. They had his mannerisms down—the frantic movements and anxious energy he always had at the first sign of one of his pack being harmed. "They kicked my ass," I deadpanned.

Fake Kai's brow furrowed at my response, and he tossed a look over his shoulder to Fake Cam. "Cam, get over here and help me. Fuck, look at his ankle. It's destroyed. Fish, brother, how are you even conscious right now?"

Tears were building in Fake Kai's eyes, and I focused on that. His eyelashes were so thick and the moisture seemed to build there, waiting for him to blink so it could trickle down his cheeks. "Fischer. Talk to me," he pleaded. Blink.

Ah. There they go. The physical manifestation of sadness. People shouldn't be allowed to fake sadness. Or happiness, for that matter. My entire life I'd watched people act one way, only to be harboring their true feelings within, hidden away. And for what?

In this case, deceit. To trick me into thinking that these imposters were my family. That wasn't going to happen. *I'm the mind master, not whoever is pulling the strings around here, thinking they can outsmart me.*

"He's in shock, K. Move," Fake Cam barked, and Fake Kai scrambled out of the way. My friend's face appeared inches from mine. By the sun, he looked as though he hadn't shaved in weeks. His beard was usually well-kept, but right now he looked like some sort of lumberjack hermit who'd rolled down the side of the mountain and landed right here, all up in my fucking face.

"Fischer, listen to me. We're going to get out of here, but we need to be quick. We got lucky, seeing that piece of shit shifting into Sloane right outside of this room. That's why we knocked his ass out. Asrael is making moves, and we've heard whispers of an execution at dawn," Fake Cam rambled, working on the knot in the rope that was tied tightly around my ankle. The non-fucked one.

"Execution?" That was the only thing he'd said that really intrigued me. I already knew that Sloane was a fake. My practically dead and shriveled up heart skipped a beat at the thought of it being Laurie's execution.

Fake Kai slipped behind me and started on my wrists. A moment later, the bindings fell away, as though they'd been cut. "We don't know who, but I think we better find out. Fast." He dug around in his pocket and pulled out a syringe.

"Get fucked if you think I'm letting you stab me with that," I gritted out, and Kai actually recoiled as though I'd slapped him.

"Fish, it's a healing serum. It's a gods damn miracle. Cam found me after I'd been publicly flogged." Kai dropped into a crouch, looking me dead in the eyes. "Over one hundred lashes. I almost died. Napoleon raided the pharmacy lab and stole one of these." As though he'd been waiting for an introduction, the black mouse poked his tiny head out of Cam's beard.

That couldn't be faked. Right? A Fake Napoleon? But if he was real, then... they were real. But if it turned out they weren't... I buried my face into my hands and rocked, trying to clear my mind. *Get out of my fucking head. Stop fucking with me. Get out. Get out. Get out!*

"Brother, take some deep breaths. We're not fucking with your head. This injection will heal your injuries, and then we can walk out of that door and go find our woman. Don't you want that?" Cam asked, his voice soothing and steady as Kai hopped to his feet and started fidgeting.

"Prove it," I whispered.

Kai stopped his pacing. "Prove what?"

"That. You're. Real."

Cam and Kai shared a look. "Go on, K. Prove it."

A blink later, and Kai was no longer standing before me. Instead, Bagheera prowled closer. His large head came to rest on my thigh and those yellow eyes burned into the fucking core of me. My hands were shaking so badly as I lifted them and let my fingers sink into his thick, silky fur.

"We met when we were five. I'd just moved to the street, and you, Sloane, and Kai were already friends. The three of you were watching us move into our house from across the street. You were all on your bikes. Mama B spotted you guys and made me go over to introduce myself. I remember thinking that you had the curliest hair I'd ever seen." Cam's voice was so low, I had to strain to hear him, but I was there, on that street. In that moment.

"Who's the new kid?" Kai asked as we spotted a tall blond boy carrying a box out of the moving truck that had pulled up a couple of hours ago.

Sloane shrugged, picking at the scab on his forearm. He'd told us a dog scratched him. I thought he should be more careful. It seemed like he was always getting hurt.

"Maybe he has popsicles. Let's go find out." *Kai headed for his bike and we followed. We could've walked—it was only about six houses down—but we'd all gotten new bikes recently and we rode them any chance we got. Sloane especially. He was the first of us to learn to ride without training wheels. Sometimes he rode his bike so fast I thought flames would shoot out from the tires and he'd leave us all behind.*

I wasn't supposed to know, but my parents, and Kai's, had bought Sloane's bike. I didn't see what the big deal was. Sloane stayed over at my house all the time and if he wasn't with me, he was at Kai's.

'His daddy is mean and a bad man. He's scary.'

I blinked and watched my two friends pedal away. I looked around, wondering where that voice had come from.

"Hello?" *I called out quietly, thinking I must have made that up in my mind. Kai always said I spent too much time thinking about stuff. I didn't care because all he thought about were snacks and Mario. Lifting my bike, I was about to kick off when I heard the voice again. It sounded just like me. And I realized that it was coming from inside my head.*

'Sloane's daddy hurts him. We need to protect him,' *the voice said, and I found myself nodding.*

'I'll always protect him. I love Sloane. He's one of my best friends. Forever. But... who are you?' *I asked in my mind.*

'I'm not really sure,' *he replied, and I started riding toward my friends.*

'So you're like, an imaginary friend that even I can't see? That's so cool! I always wanted one. Do you have a name?' *I was getting closer now—Kai and Sloane were already stopped, blatantly staring across the street.*

'I don't think so. What kind of person doesn't even have a name?' *he asked, sounding really sad. That made my belly hurt. I didn't like anyone being sad.*

'Don't worry,' *I told him, trying to cheer him up.* 'I know your name. Maybe you just forgot?'

He gasped. 'You know my name? What is it?'

'You're worried about Sloane, so you're a protector, right? You see things and warn me. You're like a knight. You're Faris. That's what it means, ya know. In Mom and Dad's language. It's super cool.'

'Faris,' *he whispered.* 'I love it.'

Just then I braked, coming to a stop beside Sloane. Faris had gone quiet so I settled into my observation of the new kid. He was tall and had wild blond hair that looked nicer than any girls' in my school.

"Here he comes," Kai exclaimed, practically bouncing up and down.

Sloane huffed. "Act cool."

The new kid strolled across the street, like he couldn't be bothered to move quicker. I thought Kai was going to run out and meet him halfway with how excited he was. As the kid got closer, I saw that he had green eyes, and oh my stars, he'd already lost both of his bottom teeth.

"Hi, I'm Cameron. Everyone calls me Cam," *the new kid told us, his eyes moving over each of us slowly.*

Kai couldn't take it anymore. "I'm Kaito! I'm five and a half and I'm crazy good at Super Mario Bros." *He grinned widely, and Cam returned his grin.*

"I love Mario. Check these out!" *Cam bent down and pulled his sock up, showing us a pair of Mario socks. Kai gasped, putting down his kickstand and moving in to get a better look. While he checked out the socks, I walked closer.*

"Hi, I'm Fischer. Are you in kindergarten too?"

"Yeah, my moms said Miss Greene is my new teacher. Do you know her?" *he asked, looking a bit nervous.*

"You're in our class. That's really cool," Sloane finally spoke up. "I'm Sloane. I like being outside. Hey, do you have a bike?"

Cam's face lit up. "Yeah! Let me go see if they can get it off the truck. Wanna come over? I think I have popsicles?"

The four of us grinned at each other so hard I thought our faces would get stuck like that. We followed Cam across the street, laughing and joking, like we'd been friends our whole lives.

"That was the first time I followed you somewhere. At five years old, I knew I'd follow you anywhere. Along with Kai and Sloane." My voice broke, and it was as though all of the pain I'd blocked suddenly hit my body, completely overwhelming my senses with blinding, horrible sensations. "How did we end up here?"

"Jesus," Kai swore as he shifted back into his form. My eyes were screwed shut and sweat was pouring down my face.

"Fish, I'm giving you this injection. It will give you your powers back too. All of this pain will be gone in minutes—I swear it, brother." I felt hands on my upper arm.

"DO IT!" I begged, my head pounding from the intensity of the pain. White light burst in front of my eyes, and I knew I was going to pass out. Gods, I wanted it to happen.

"Fish?" Kai said, though he sounded far away, muffled.

I grunted. Damn, I must've gotten my wish because I now was laying flat on my back on that fucking table. When I realized that's where I was, I flew up and off the damn thing, wiping at my skin. My chest heaved, and my flesh felt as though it was crawling.

Cam reached out for me but I dodged his hands. "Don't," I rasped, my eyes burning a hole in the ground. Kai whined, and I knew it was probably ripping him up inside not to grab me and hug me within an inch of my life. I just... I couldn't take anyone touching me right now.

"Okay," Cam said softly. I looked up, expecting to find pity on his face. Instead, I found the face of a man with more fury swirling within his body than was safe.

All of a sudden, I realized I was upright. I was standing. I glanced down, noticing that my ankle was now healed. And the rage, I was feeling it now. It wasn't just my own, either. I could feel Cam's anger, and despite Kai's concern for me, his fury felt just as potent.

"I can feel you both. Your emotions..." Looking around the room, I spotted *him,* the guard, lying on the floor where he'd been tossed. Slowly, so fucking slowly, my head tilted to the side as I pondered all of the things I wanted to do to him.

Kai cleared his throat. "Uh, Fish? Your eyes, man. They're black."

My lips tugged at the corner as I surveyed my victim. "Get out."

"What? What do you mean, get out?"

"Come on, K." I heard Cam moving through the small room. "Fischer has a score to settle. We'll be in the hall. We need to get moving soon though, before someone spots us."

Somehow, I managed a barely-there nod of acknowledgement that I'd heard his words and understood. *Don't take too long.* They left the room and shut the door behind them, leaving me and Don alone. When they'd knocked him out, he'd lost his shapeshifting form and reverted back to being this ugly fuck.

We'd been in this room together so many times before... Only this time, I was untied. I wasn't injured. And I had my fucking magic.

I felt like I was floating across the room, my heart thrumming steadily as I moved toward him. Not too fast, not too slow. Steady. I was about to get the kill that I desperately wanted, and I felt nothing.

The sledgehammer he'd used to shatter my ankle was propped up against the wall. How convenient. My fingers were wrapped around the smooth wooden handle within the blink of an eye, and I peered down in disgust at the scum at my feet. I really wished I had more time to fuck him up beyond belief before I killed him, but I'd need days to satisfy that fantasy and right now I only had minutes.

The weight of the sledgehammer in my hand felt so perfect. I brought my other hand up, gripping the hammer firmly now as it rested on my shoulder. Don shifted slightly, and I waited. He was waking up and I needed him to see my face before he died. Thirty seconds must've passed as he just lay there, groaning.

Alright. This wasn't working.

I let the hammer swing off my shoulder before bringing it up into a beautiful arc, throwing all of my weight behind it as I brought it down on his knee. His scream of agony was somewhat satisfying, but I was also sick of screams.

"Shut. The. Fuck. UP!" I barked, pushing my influence into his mind, effectively silencing the rapist piece of shit. Tears flowed down his face from wide, panicked eyes. I laughed when they got even wider, as he realized who had just shattered his knee. Pathetically, he tried to roll away. Ridiculous.

"There's no escape for you."

My head snapped to the door when it cracked open, barely an inch. "There's guards coming, we gotta move," Kai hissed through the door.

Sighing, I crouched down and sent my mental claws out, latching onto his psyche with ease. Then I pushed the commands.

'Take the hammer.'

His hand slid around the handle.

'You're filth. Nothing but a worthless piece of shit who isn't even worth the amount of time I'm gifting you with right now. You're a rapist. Do you know what happens to rapists? They die. Gruesomely. I don't think there's a more poetic death than a rapist—someone who puts their hands on other people, even though that person despises their touch, even though they said no—dying by those hands that just don't know when to stop.

'So here's what you're going to do. I'm going to stand up and walk out of this room. The moment the door closes, you're going to bring that sledgehammer down on your pathetic dick as hard as you can. I fucking mean it. Then, count to five and do the same thing to your free hand.

Then both your feet. Then your dick again. And again. Then your ankles and knees. As. Hard. As. You. Can.

'I swear to Jupiter, I'll know if you don't, and I'll come back in here and it'll be much, much worse. After you've shattered all of those bones, you're going to take this sledgehammer and you're going to shove the handle down your throat until you choke.

'Feel free to scream in pain—nobody will come. They'll think it's me. Isn't that funny?'

I smiled, and it was all teeth. Wicked and vicious. The guard was shaking, and the acrid scent of urine hit the air. I stood, reaching for the door.

"Get ready." My hand wrapped around the door handle. "Get set." I pulled it open and stepped through, letting the thick door slowly close. "Go!"

I slammed the door, and a thump followed by a scream met my ears, slightly muted by the thick walls. Turning, I found Cam and Kai staring at me.

Brushing my chest off, I returned their stares. "Where to next?"

Cam
Chapter Ten

We ran as quickly and as silently as possible, following Napoleon's directions. He knew where Saige was, and that was all I cared about at the moment. It was pure luck, or possibly fate, that we'd seen that guard shapeshift into Sloane and ended up finding Fischer. Thank fuck, too. I shot a cursory glance at him over my shoulder and found his face impassive. Blank. Devoid of any kind of emotion.

That might be problematic later. In the past when he'd gotten like this, there wasn't a whole lot anyone could do to bring him back out of his mind. Sloane was always the best option for that, but Sloane wasn't here. And if that guard had been pretending to be Sloane... My stomach clenched at the thought. I'd seen Fischer fuck up plenty of men—it was our job. Whatever had happened back there, that was personal. When Fish was on an assignment, he operated with almost a clinical detachment from those he interrogated. But the way his eyes had lit up when he realized that guard was at his mercy had been chilling. He'd shown more emotion in that moment than he had when we walked into his cell.

Fuck, I was just thankful we had the vaccines and that there seemed to be enough for everyone. More than enough. Earlier, after Kai and I left the infirmary, Napoleon had led us to the pharmacy lab where we stuffed our pockets full of the vaccines I'd given to Kai. He'd injected me the second we found them. Fuck, it'd felt amazing to have my magic rushing back through my veins. I'd immediately reached out in my head for Saige and the others, but nothing happened. Likely because they were still under whatever wards this castle held over their magic. And without Fischer being a part of the link, I wasn't sure it'd work anyway. Still, I had to try.

"Duck into this room, *messieurs*," Napoleon ordered, and Kai pulled open a wooden door, allowing us to stumble inside before closing it behind him. Fish gave me a 'what the fuck' look at the sound of the mouse's voice.

"New development," I told him as I scanned the dimly lit room. There were shelves of what looked to be herbs, bedding supplies, and candles. A supply room then. "Napoleon, where is she?"

Kai paced the room, and I could hear his quick intakes of breath. Scenting. Napoleon was perched on his shoulder. "Her room is next to this supply room. Or it was."

"Her scent is here," Kai confirmed, but he looked back toward Fischer and I. "But I don't sense her."

"I shall sneak to her room to see if she's there? If she's alone? When I was last here, she wasn't awake. For weeks, she did not wake. There was blood at first, you know?" Napoleon clasped his little paws over his eyes, and the three of us jerked as though we'd all been kicked.

"Blood?" I questioned at the same time Fischer surged forward and plucked Napoleon from Kai's shoulder. The small mouse squeaked, and Kai growled, reaching for his furry friend.

"What do you mean, there was blood at first? Of course we don't fucking know! I've been locked in a fucking torture chamber for what? Weeks, you said?" Fish glared at Napoleon, who promptly bit Fish's thumb, earning his release. He scampered up Fish's arm and launched his little body onto mine, scurrying up to my head.

"I have watched over our woman for all the days we have been in this place, surrounded by enemies!" Napoleon barked at Fischer, pissed as hell. "I respect you, as a fellow warrior, but I shan't be spoken to with such utter disrespect. If you'll excuse me, I shall go investigate and report back. Perhaps you should make yourself useful, mindfucker, and see if you can establish a mental connection with our woman!"

Kai's face was priceless. His mouth was hanging open, his eyes volleying back and forth between the mouse and the mage who was clearly not in his right state of mind. With a huff, Napoleon sprinted down my body, slipping through a crack in the wall. Fischer just stood there, blinking slowly.

"Hey," I said, stepping closer—but not too close. "Do you think it'll work? Have you heard her at all since we've been here?"

His dark eyes locked on me and he nodded. "Once. Recently. She said the babies were alive, she loved us, and she was going to do whatever she could to get back to us. It's, uh..." He paused and took a shaky breath, which was the first sign of the Fischer I knew coming back through the darkness. "It's the only reason I was able to endure the... the circumstances."

I nodded once. "I'm glad you had that, brother. When you needed her most, she was there for you. That's our mate, isn't it? Always knowing what we need. And now we're going to come through for her. And for our other brothers who are still unaccounted for. And for Khol. We have to stick together now, more than ever." I looked at both Fish and Kai, my veins suddenly being flooded with adrenaline. "I need vengeance for this. We all need it. Saige needs it. Are we ready to fucking get it?"

Kai's rumbling growl filled the small space, and Fischer's eyes lightened drastically.

"We have our magic. They must know by now that you two have escaped?" Fish asked us, and I smirked.

"That depends on whether Laurie has decided to confess her fuck up and face Asrael's wrath. For all I know, nobody is aware we've escaped. Right now, we have the advantage." I didn't believe for a second she would've admitted her failure. She was too close to her endgame, whatever it may be. We were hurtling toward the showdown and any fuck ups on either side would be devastating.

Kai rolled his eyes. "She'd never tell. She believes this is her kingdom."

"What was in those injections? Do you know?" Fischer held his hand out and I placed a full syringe into his palm. He held it up to the light, examining the contents.

Kai stood next to Fischer and studied the syringe. "What'd Napoleon say? Nox stone and something else?"

Fischer stiffened. "No fucking way," he whispered, bringing the syringe closer to his eyes.

"What?" I demanded, trying not to get my hopes up that this could be a win for us.

He handed back the vaccine and leaned against the supply shelf. "The night we went to the cave in the woods with the others, I saw this stone. Nox stone. It's possible that the entire boulder marking the entrance of the cave was actually Nox. There was only a small section of it showing, but it was dark, and what are the chances? But I told Saige about it, how rare it is. This can't be a coincidence. When we approached the cave, I couldn't hear any thoughts or pick up on any emotions. Everyone within the cave was shielded from me."

"I haven't even heard of anyone mentioning Nox in years. Gods, probably since the academy. It's always been more of an urban legend!" Kai started pacing again; I could almost see Bagheera's tail flicking back and forth.

If this rare stone was on Saige's property and it just so happened to appear here in Besmet... And we weren't the ones who'd supplied it...

"Laurie," I spat. "It must be how she's made herself invaluable to Asrael?"

Fischer ran a hand down his face in frustration. "Perhaps. I suspect it definitely plays a part in how she's always able to slip away from the consequences of her actions."

A squeak alerted us to Napoleon's return and we all waited for him to scurry up a shelf at our level. "She's not there. But the doctor is."

My heart fell. Of course she wasn't there. That'd be too simple, too easy. "Doctor?" I lifted a brow, and Napoleon nodded.

"This demon tended to her these past weeks. I suspect he is a loyalist to Bram's family. He always treated her with kindness. He may know where she's gone."

Kai grinned and clapped his hands together. "Well, brothers. Let's go meet the good doctor, hmm?" He strode to the door and froze, listening for sounds in the hall. Looking over his shoulder, he gave a nod. Coast was clear. We spilled out into the corridor and into Saige's room within seconds.

There was one demon in the room, whose head snapped up when the door opened and the three of us charged in. We moved in formation, immediately surrounding him, and I didn't miss the way he didn't even flinch as we closed in. Interesting.

"What can I do for you?" he asked, standing tall.

"We're here for our woman," Fischer told him, his voice deadly calm.

The male nodded. "Ah. You're her mates." A statement, not a question.

"We are. Half of them, anyway. Now, where is she?" I demanded, stepping closer. The male was just a smidge shorter than me, but he was trimmer, and still, he didn't back up.

"This room needs to be spelled against those who might seek to listen in before we speak. Allow me to do this and I'll tell you everything you need to know," the doctor negotiated, and I knew Fischer was already reading him. I wasn't sure if it was mating with Saige, bringing Bram into our family, or what exactly—but I was fucking glad he was able to use his powers on demons now.

Kai and I waited for Fish's verdict. "He's being truthful. He wants to cast a silencing spell. I suppose it's a good thing we don't need him to get that done though. I've already sent out signals that will divert anyone who attempts to walk down this hallway."

The doctor's mouth fell open at Fischer's words. "Then why did you probe my brain like that?"

Fish shrugged. "Because I fucking can. Start talking, doctor."

I clapped a hand on his shoulder and guided him to a small table before pushing him down into the chair. "What's your name, Doc?"

"Balor. I am loyal to the rightful heir of the throne, King Bram Carlisle. This includes his queen and the queen's mates. I oversaw her medical treatment during the time she spent unconscious. I did induce this condition as I felt it would be less stressful to her and the unborn babes, and I knew it would delay Asrael from being able to further his plans. This was the best course of action, I hope you understand."

"I see," I murmured. "And where is our mate now, Balor?"

For the first time since we'd entered this room, I saw a bit of panic in his eyes. Electricity sparked between my fingers, the familiar sensation comforting after so long without my powers.

"There was an escape yesterday," Balor explained, and quickly rattled off the rest of the story. "The queen, she spotted a dragon flying and called out to him from the window. It was her dragon mate. Somehow, he was able to break through Asrael's control and approached the castle. When Asrael realized this, he came here in a fit of rage."

My initial smile at the fact that she'd escaped quickly fell at the thought of that motherfucker putting his hands on her.

"How do you know all of this?" Kai demanded, slamming his hands down on the table.

"I was in the supply room next door when all of this

happened. There was an... altercation. Whatever Asrael planned to do to the queen, she fought back and prevailed. When I realized she was in danger, I ran to her room, but the door had been sealed with magic. I was unable to enter so I went to the next room and stuck my head out of the window. It was there that I saw her leap—*leap*—into the open claw of her dragon! Oh! Wait a moment." He stood and raced over to the bed. What the fuck was he doing? He threw the pillows from the mattress and grinned with triumph. "The knife is gone! She must've found it..."

"What knife?" Fischer asked, unamused with this male's theatrics.

Balor traced the room with his eyes. "Aha!" He rushed to the window. Sure as shit, there was a knife handle protruding from beneath a small bookshelf. Before he could bend down to retrieve the weapon, Kai was there, stepping on the handle. Balor looked at him in confusion.

"I don't know you. I don't trust you. You're not touching a weapon, doc," K sneered down at the demon.

"I'm the one who left this weapon beneath her pillow, you buffoon. You should be thanking me," Balor snapped, rising to his feet. "She escaped; she bested Asrael. It is all any of the loyalists can talk about!" Balor was full-on grinning now, his face glowing with pride for our mate.

Kai arrived at the same conclusion and he pounced, grabbing Balor by the collar of his shirt. "She. Is. Not. Yours," he snarled, practically nose to nose with the demon. Balor threw his hands up in a nonthreatening pose, his mouth open in shock.

"Of course she isn't! She is my patient. She is the queen. Now, get your hands off of me. I've never been so offended. She may be yours in the way of mates, but she is also hope for my people. Hope for the dragons. So I suggest you all get used to seeing looks of admiration and adoration on others' faces, because she's gods damned earned it! Besides, we have more pressing matters at hand," Balor added ominously. Kai released him, brushing down his shirt as if that would release the wrinkles he'd caused.

"Apologies," K muttered, easing himself down into a chair. Fischer was standing so still he could've been mistaken for a statue. I figured he was doing whatever mind stuff he could, getting a sense of Balor's truth.

"Where are the others?" Fish suddenly asked, his voice low and commanding. Balor turned to look at him, and I already knew I wasn't going to like whatever was going to come out of his mouth.

The demon cleared his throat. "As I said, more pressing matters. There's an execution scheduled for dawn."

Fuck. Fuck. Fuck.

"Who? Who is being executed?" My eyes closed as I let out a deep exhale. The silence in the room was fucking terrible, but I think I almost preferred that to hearing the truth of whatever Balor was about to say.

"Bram," he whispered, and I clenched my fists so tightly that my fingernails were surely drawing blood. "And Khol."

My eyes snapped open. "Khol? He's alive?"

"Aye. For now. I have been in contact with him through others who fight for the real king."

"Thank the stars," I breathed. Saige was only just getting to know her father and his death would have destroyed her. "So for now, we know Saige and Sloane are together. Somewhere. The babies are doing fine. Bram and Khol are alive, somewhere in this castle. That leaves Faris. Where is he?"

Fischer shifted, and I knew he was anxious to hear, but hell, if this was about to be news of his death... I don't think there'd be any coming back from that. Fish was already teetering too closely to the edge of oblivion.

"He is in the pit."

"What pit? What do you mean?" Fischer asked, his voice deadly and calm.

Balor ran a hand down his face. "The fighting pit. After he was healed, he was taken there. He has been... unreachable."

A fighting pit? "He's been there this entire time?" I balked, my mind already drawing conclusions just based on the name.

"Mostly. I heard that when he came to after his injuries and realized the queen wasn't with him, he lost it. Took down ten guards with his hands and teeth before being subdued. He doesn't speak. All he does is... kill."

"Fuck," Kai cursed, pushing himself up so suddenly his chair fell back and clattered to the floor. My stomach twisted as I thought of Faris, alone. The guy was scary as hell, but he also had this innocence to him; it enraged me that he was alone, probably without any idea of what had happened to any of us. He'd been taken out of the fight quickly that day so if he remembered anything, it was likely just us arriving in Besmet.

"I have my powers now. There are things I can do," Fischer said slowly, as though he was thinking as he spoke. "I can get information from those loyal to Asrael. The most pressing matter is this execution. What I need to do is attempt to reach Saige and Sloane telepathically. If we can share information with them, it will help us all. What we really need, Balor, is more bodies. More demons loyal to Bram. Also, if we can get to Faris, we can give him this injection and restore his magic. With his power, we'd be able to sway the majority of the people here to simply... walk away."

All of us focused on Balor who was nodding in agreement with Fischer's plan. "The issue is that the pit is heavily guarded. And not only that, there was word that there may be three deaths at dawn."

"Faris?" Fischer demanded, and when Balor nodded, we all leaned away as Fischer's eyes turned completely black. "Asrael will regret the day he was fucking born," he spat before spinning and storming to the bed.

"We'll make him pay. They'll all pay, brother," Kai vowed, the rumble in his chest fortifying his promise.

Fish sat on the mattress, staring at us with those endless black depths. "I'm going to contact Saige and Sloane now. I think while I'm doing that, it would be wise to come up with a game plan for how the fuck we're going to save three people from execution mere hours from now."

"We got this. Do what you need to. You're safe here," I assured him, knowing he was going to go into some kind of trance-like state where he'd be vulnerable. He nodded and lay back on the pillows, going completely still.

Sighing, I tugged at my beard. Balor cleared his throat, and I gave him a questioning look. "A couple of loyalists left hours ago to see if we could convince a wild group of demons to join us here, to fight for the true king. They don't have any love for the monarchy, but if nothing else, I know they'd consider coming just for the possibility of fucking over Asrael."

"And they're skilled in combat?" Kai asked. "Because I don't think we're getting out of this without a fight."

For the first time since I'd met Balor, I saw a glimpse of his demon lurking beneath. Excitement flashed in his eyes, and a grin that started out innocent quickly turned sinister. Balor laughed.

"Oh, they can fight. Don't worry about that."

Saige

Chapter Eleven

Sloane's hand was firm in mine as we followed Vaeryn. My gaze lifted as I took in our surroundings. I couldn't believe how beautiful it was here. Huge looming mountains broke out of the ground, climbing higher and higher until their peaks disappeared into the clouds. The mountains formed a circle surrounding the pink lake that we had surfaced in. The sand beneath my feet was warm, but not warm enough to burn, and was the color of green seaglass.

I had no idea where we were, but I knew that we were no longer in the demon realm. And I knew that somehow this place was sacred.

"Welcome, again, to our home," Vaeryn said. "We've waited for you for many years. And now here you are. Come. There are many dragons here who wish to meet you."

The smile on Sloane's face was blinding. It seemed as though, I don't know, he was finally home. This was where he belonged. These were his people. Maybe this was where he should have grown up, instead of with his monster of a father.

"I didn't know that you could shift," I said to the dragon. He chuckled over his shoulder and gave a shrug. Like it really wasn't that big of a deal.

It was a big deal though.

"We haven't been able to shift in a long time. Only recently has this changed. And this is our home. It's well protected and hidden from those who would seek to capture us or to use us for nefarious purposes. We are free creatures. Not tools made to be used for other creatures' gain." He was agitated, judging by the way he barked his last sentence.

And I understood—because had I not also been used?

Sloane sighed. "This place is amazing, Vaeryn. Thank you for the warm welcome. We are desperate to discuss what's happening at the castle with you." He paused. "However, I would feel a lot better if we could make sure that our queen could get some more water, and perhaps a warm meal. If you have something?"

Vaeryn looked sheepish, but I waved him off. He was excited to have us here and they'd already given me water. Sloane was being... attentive. I fucking loved it.

"Yes, yes, of course. We must make sure that the little princesses are well taken care of. Let me show you to my home and we can eat and discuss matters."

I nodded along, because what was I going to say? No? As we followed Vaeryn, it didn't escape my notice that nearly every dragon was staring at me. If I met one of their gazes, their eyes would immediately shift to the ground. And I didn't like that—I wasn't some ruler, some kind of dictator like Asrael. Hell. I still hadn't even accepted myself as being a queen.

Yet here I was, being revered, being looked upon like some goddess. It was baffling. All I wanted to do was gather up my men and my father, and go back to my quaint little cottage in Emerald Lakes. Seeing all of these things was life-changing, and so far out of my comfort zone that it was hard for me to enjoy it. Maybe when this was all over, we could come back here without the threat of Asrael hanging over us.

We rounded a corner, and my mouth fell open in shock as I stared up and up. All along the face of the mountain were doors and carved archways with intricate details of dragons, demons, and maidens. Everything magical was there, and it was beautiful.

I increased my pace to catch up with Vaeryn. "These are your homes?" I asked him, my voice full of wonder.

"Yes. The larger ones are so our dragon forms can enter, of course. Most of us obviously had not been able to use our human-sized homes for a while. But we are excited and grateful to be able to do so once again. Welcome to my cave," he boasted, pride heavy in his voice as he spread his arms wide.

I glanced at Sloane as we entered the cave, walking around. I was completely captivated. I had never in my life seen such a unique dwelling or even imagined that something like this could exist. The cave had been dug out, so it was surprisingly large inside; it seemed to just go deeper and deeper into the mountain. I wondered if perhaps all of the caves were connected through hallways and tunnels deeper within the cave.

Nearly everything was carved out of stone, with each surface having varying shades of color. From a smooth, off-white marble to the dark sparkle of granite, pink swirling with black—it was absolutely gorgeous. "Vaeryn," I said in awe. "Your home is beautiful."

Sloane nodded in agreement. "This is the coolest fucking thing I've ever seen in my life. We will definitely have to show everyone else this place."

I chuckled as Vaeryn puffed his chest out with pride. "You are welcome anytime. It would be a great honor to host the rest of the queen's mates. Here, I have some dry clothes for you both—you may change in my sleeping quarters."

We quickly changed out of the sopping wet clothes and Sloane helped zip up the simple cream-colored gown. It was light and comfortable, giving me plenty of breathing room. Sloane was wearing a long white tunic with long sleeves and a pair of what would probably be called breeches. He looked hot as shit in them, that's all I knew. With a knowing smirk, he led us out of the bedroom.

Vaeryn was waiting for us and smiled as he took in our clothing. "Come, the kitchen is this way." We followed Vaeryn deeper within his home. I couldn't seem to stop looking around; it was like something out of a dream, which was kind of ridiculous seeing how we were already in another realm. But this place was different. There was a magic thrumming in the air that wrapped around my body. With every breath I took, it just seemed to fill me up and fuel my soul. Even the babies had been more active since we arrived here.

Vaeryn led us to a massive stone table, which had built-in stools that rose out of the ground and had obviously been intricately carved by a master. There were already place settings on the table—I had to assume that one of the other dragons had rushed here before us to get this arranged.

As though she'd been summoned, a young woman walked into the room carrying a tray filled with different breads, meats, and cheeses. She was pretty, her hair long and golden. "Thank you," I said to her, as she met my eyes and gave me a nod.

"Your Highness, this is my niece. You'll have to forgive her, for she has not spoken since she shifted back into her human form. We suspect it may be due to the fact that she was so young when we stopped being able to shift between our dragon and human forms. She is not the only one who is having issues with speech, but as you can see, she understands what we're saying. So I believe it is just due to lack of use, and her vocal cords perhaps are just not used to their purpose."

Sloane's hand on my lower back guided me to a seat, which I gratefully took since my feet and back were killing me. He took the seat beside me, placing a comforting hand on my thigh as I looked at Vaeryn's niece.

"No worries. I'm sure that your voice will return when it's ready. A lot has changed recently," I told her, offering what I hoped was a reassuring smile, which she returned. She gave us a small curtsy before leaving the room.

Sloane and I immediately started shoving food into our mouths as though it was going to be snatched away at any moment. It tasted so fucking good. Vaeryn chuckled as he watched us, taking small bites of the meats and cheeses himself, his eyes dancing with amusement.

"Sorry," Sloane muttered around a mouthful. "It's just been a while since I've eaten a proper meal." My poor Sloane. Instinctively, I wrapped my arm around his back and nuzzled up against his shoulder. I loved the way he leaned into the contact, not flinching or leaning away as he'd done in the past. We'd all already been through so much. How much more were we going to have to take before we got the chance to live our life together in peace?

A chill worked its way up my back, and I shivered. The air within the cave was much cooler than it was outside. Vaeryn noticed this immediately and rose up, gliding through the room to procure what appeared to be a handmade blanket, which he draped over my shoulders. I smiled and thanked him.

"It does get chilly in here. We have hot springs deeper within the mountain that are excellent for warming up. If we had more time, I would love to show you. As it stands, we will likely have to revisit that idea in the future."

I sighed with disappointment. A hot spring sounded like heaven for my body right now.

"So I assume that you missed the rendezvous due to Asrael's takeover?" Vaeryn speculated, lifting a golden chalice to his mouth to take a long drink.

Sloane hummed, swallowing his own drink and placing his cup down on the stone table. "That would be correct. When we discovered that Asrael was making his move, we had to bump up our timeline. Plus, with Saige here being pregnant with twins, suddenly she began showing so much earlier than we expected.

As in, barely a hint of a bump to without a doubt pregnant in an unnaturally short space of time, and we were concerned. It's not like we could just take her to a doctor in our world, so we decided to come to this realm to warn King Thane, as well as seek medical care. Unfortunately, we walked into a trap." Sloane's shoulders tensed, and I knew just by knowing the man that he was feeling guilty over this. And that was bullshit, because any one of us could have put a stop to the plan. But really, what options had we had? None. We *had* to come here. We had to warn the people. If there was a chance of saving lives, then that was what we needed to do. Wasn't that what the prophecy was all about?

I leaned over and pressed a kiss to Sloane's cheek. I didn't want him to blame himself. He carried so much on his shoulders all the time. We were a family now, and it was time that he let that family carry some of the stress, share some of the burden. We were a team. A unit. I wouldn't stand for any one of my mates feeling like they were singularly responsible for me or the babies.

"Do not beat yourself up, Sloane." Vaeryn shot him a knowing look. "We all have our parts to play in this. We've been busy doing recon now that we're able to shift to our human forms."

"How did that happen? Shifting, I mean?" I was curious as hell, because crawling out of a pink lake and seeing Vaeryn as a man had been the last thing I'd expected.

He grinned, and I was taken aback momentarily at how gorgeous he was. Totally not Gandalf. Maybe if Gandalf was in his thirties and ripped... I felt Sloane's eyes on me, and a blush bloomed on my cheeks. *Busted.*

"Well, we have reason to believe the shifting may be a direct result of your pregnancy. It's as though the magic is being slowly restored with the fulfillment of the prophecy. We hadn't been able to shift in a very, very long time. It was actually quite ridiculous when the change came back over us. None of us made it through without hitting the ground." Vaeryn's booming laughter filled his cavern home, and I pictured the scene in my head—a male as large as this one, on wobbly legs like a newborn fawn. Hilarious.

"I wish I could've seen it," Sloane chuckled for a moment before the mood turned serious once again.

Vaeryn leaned forward, resting his elbows on the table as he looked at my mate. "I'm desperate to know, did you learn anything of the dragons? Did you find any information that could be useful in helping them obtain their freedom? You're here now, so somehow, you were able to break Asrael's hold over you. I want to know if it's possible for us to do that, for the others."

Sloane began filling Vaeryn in on everything that had transpired from the time we'd entered the throne room, to me and the other men being hauled away, to him being taken to the dragon enclosure. Meeting the other dragons, how they'd rallied together around him and helped him to create an escape plan.

Vaeryn's eyes glinted in the candlelight, which was throwing flickering shadows throughout the kitchen. I couldn't imagine all of the emotion that the old dragon must be feeling. It was still tripping me out that he was ancient but looked to be no more than forty. The dragons had been cursed for centuries, and Vaeryn was already an adult male when that had happened.

"Did you get the name of any of these dragons?" Vaeryn asked, hopeful.

Sloane grinned, his eyes dancing with mischief. "I did. Emrys quickly became my strongest ally within that pen."

Vaeryn gasped loudly. "Did you say *Emrys?*" His face drained of all color and his eyes were the widest I'd seen them yet.

"I did," Sloane confirmed, stuffing a bite of bread into his mouth.

"By the moon," Vaeryn exclaimed. "Emrys is my brother! I have not seen him in hundreds of years. Goddess... This is a miracle. How was he? Please, tell me everything."

My own eyes began to fill with tears watching Vaeryn's hand shake as he reached for his chalice once more. What were the odds that Sloane would've been held in captivity with Vaeryn's brother? As much as I liked to think that all of this was bullshit—that the stars didn't get to make decisions for us—it was looking more and more as though fate was woven like an intricate tapestry. Each one of us being a thread, pulled and pushed and connected to create a picture.

But as for what that picture would look like? We didn't get a say; we were merely along for the ride. Passengers in our own lives as we hurtled toward the ending the stars had already mapped for us. On one hand, I supposed that it should have been comforting. If you accepted that it was fate and that you had no control over where your life was heading, it would be easier to roll with the punches and not second-guess your decisions.

I continued to eat and drink as Vaeryn and Sloane discussed the dragon friends that he had made. Vaeryn's energy was rising with each passing moment, as though every small bit of information that Sloane passed on to him sparked new life within his soul.

I was so happy for him. At least one of his family members was alive and could possibly be rescued. I could only hope that the same was true for the rest of my mates.

We finished eating, and I left Vaeryn and Sloane at the table to continue their discussions. Sloane was full of questions, and Vaeryn was just as curious. I excused myself to the sitting room, which was just off from the kitchen. Sunken down into the floor, it was accessible by three steps that were carved into the stone. There was no furniture; instead, it was all beautiful blankets and pillows, with rich colors and beautiful fabrics of all textures. I had never been more comfortable in my life. The only thing that would have made it more perfect would have been having all six of my mates with me, and maybe a good book.

With my belly now full, I was starting to feel exhausted after the events of the day. And yet, I couldn't seem to close my eyes, because there was this unsettled nagging feeling within my heart. I couldn't place why I felt so on edge. Yes, the rest of my mates were being held at the castle, and I hadn't seen them since the day we'd gotten there a month ago. But this was something more.

I was worried that it was some sort of internal alarm, warning me that one—or more—of my mates was in danger. Even so, I was not used to carrying around so much extra weight. Growing two babies was a lot of work and my lower back was really starting to protest. I regretted not asking Balor about an estimated due date. It had to be soon, right? Surely I couldn't get much bigger without popping.

I snagged the largest pillow that I could find and made myself comfortable. It was a good thing I'd always been a side sleeper because if I lay on my back now, I knew I wouldn't be able to breathe. And obviously, there was no way I could lie on my stomach.

I still couldn't believe that the dragons had their own world. It was smart. It was brilliant. And it was a secret, one that Asrael had no idea about, which made me smile. I'd never forget the look on his face when I got the best of him and escaped.

'Sweetheart.'

My lungs seized. Gods, I surely must have been hallucinating because I could've sworn that I'd just heard Fischer's voice.

'Sweetheart? Are you there? Please tell me that you can hear me. Talk to me, anything.'

'Guppy?' I whispered the words in my head. My heart was racing. I couldn't hear anything over the sound of my pulse hammering in my ears. Even my hands were shaking. As I waited, I held my breath, desperately hoping that this wasn't a hallucination and that I was actually hearing the voice of my mate.

'Thank the gods... Saige. Where are you? Are you okay?' Fischer's words were rapid-fire.

'I'm with Sloane. We're okay. Are you okay? Who are you with? Are the others with you? Are you safe?' My eyes fell shut as I begged, with every inch of my soul, to please let them be okay. I'd offer myself up to any deity. Please.

Fischer paused for so long that I thought I was going to lose my mind in the silence. Maybe I already had. *'Cam and Kai are with me. The three of us are okay. Napoleon is here too.'*

I realized that I was frowning. There was something off in the way my sweet Guppy was speaking to me. And I knew, in an instant, that something terrible had happened to him. Tears began running down my face without him even saying anything more. He sounded distant, his voice flat and emotionless. He spoke the words, but there wasn't anything behind them. No feeling. Nothing. It wasn't like him to not ask about Sloane. Something was wrong.

'Guppy,' I said. *'What's wrong? I miss you so much. I love you.'* I knew he could tell I was crying, even though we were speaking telepathically.

'Don't cry, sweetheart. Please, don't cry. I miss you too. Everything will be okay. But Saige, things are happening here. Things that we can't control. We need you and Sloane to come here as soon as possible. We can arrange somewhere to meet.'

Sloane had wandered over now, clearly having heard my cries. He stared down at me with his brow furrowed. "What is it, baby? Why are you sad?" He crouched down and brushed my hair out of my face, using his thumbs to wipe away my tears.

"Fischer is talking to me," I told him, and his mouth fell open.

"Right now?" His eyes widened in disbelief, like he couldn't believe it.

"Yes, right now. He says he's with Cam and Kai, and that there are things happening at the castle that we need to go back for right away."

Sloane narrowed his eyes. "What if this is a trap?" he asked.

As much as I hated to admit it, I was wondering the same thing.

"It could be," he murmured, his expression turning serious as he thought over the information I'd just given him. "Have him bring me into the conversation. If it's really Fischer, he has the ability to do that; we know that from past experience."

I nodded. *'Guppy. Sloane is here with me now. Can you connect him with us? He wants to speak to you.'* I heard a sigh in my head, like Fischer was uncomfortable, which didn't make any sense.

'Just give me a minute,' Fish replied. I looked at Sloane, relaying Fischer's response, which was even more confusing to us. Because the Fischer we knew would have been desperate to speak with both of us.

A moment later, Fischer's voice was there again. *'Sloane, can you hear me now?'*

Sloane's face broke then, reminding me of a crumbling stone. He dropped his face into his hands, overcome with emotion. *'Jesus, Fischer. Are you okay? Are you hurt? I miss you.'*

I glanced at Sloane as we waited. He fidgeted with each passing second that there wasn't a reply.

'Fischer?' Sloane said, his voice carrying an edge to it. *'What is going on? I'm not bringing our pregnant mate back to that castle unless I know for a fact that it's you I'm speaking to right now.'*

Fischer exhaled harshly. *'I understand. I need you to know there's been a lot that's happened over the last few weeks. I'm a little off right now, but I'm working on it. I do miss you; I miss you both. The only thing that kept me going in the dark was the thought of seeing all of you again.'*

My stomach swirled with his words. Nausea and the ache in my chest increased as I thought of all the things that Fischer had already been through. What more had they done to him? How dare they harm what was mine... Rage began to build before I even processed it. I was fucking pissed.

'Cam and Kai are with you?' Sloane asked.

'They are. They're speaking right now with Balor. He was Saige's doctor while she was here. He's a loyalist to Bram.'

Bram. Oh my gods. I had done everything I could to block the thoughts of my other men, because there was nothing I could do. I needed to focus. How could I save them? How could I possibly get them out of that situation if I was being stricken down by grief and anxiety? I had done it to protect my heart and my mind. And now, having this conversation with Fischer, knowing that Kai and Cam were right there with him, it didn't escape my notice that there had been no mention of Bram or Faris. Hell, or Khol, for that matter.

'Guppy? Where is Bram? Where's Faris, and where the hell is my father?' The fear within me was battered down beneath the surging waves of anger.

'That's why we need you to return. Asrael has scheduled their executions to take place at dawn.'

'Oh my gods,' I whispered. *'Oh my gods. No.'* I was gonna throw up. I turned my body away from Sloane and heaved. Thankfully, nothing came up, but a moment later, a stone bowl was shoved under my face—just in case.

"What is going on in here?" Vaeryn's raspy voice met my ears as my shoulders shook, a sob building within my chest.

'Sweetheart,' Fischer's voice was pleading, the first real hint of the man I'd come to love. *'We're working on a plan. Nobody is going to be executed. But that is what's so urgent. There are loyalists within the castle, not just this doctor. They've also sent out word to other demons, calling for aid. I promise you. Nobody we love is going to die tomorrow morning. Mark my words.'*

'But you can't know that, Fischer. You died! You've left me before!' I could barely think with how tight my throat was. I felt like I was suffocating, and I just couldn't get air into my lungs deep enough.

"Breathe, Red. Just breathe." Sloane bundled me into his arms, pulling me tightly against his warm body. Grounding me.

'I'd never leav—'

I cut Fischer off. *'But you did!'* I shouted, and then quietly, *'You did leave me. And they could leave me too.'* What happened with Fischer wasn't his fault. The fault didn't lie with any one of us. Most days I could move along, pretending it had never happened. Other moments, like these, I was right back there in those woods behind my cottage. I could still feel Bram restraining me, warning me away from Fischer's body. He'd looked so beautifully wrong, frozen in death.

"I don't believe that for a second!" Sloane barked, snapping me out of my haze. I lifted my eyes to his as he leaned over and pulled a blanket up over me. "You listen to me, Red. Yes, we lost Fischer, but we fucking got him back. You. Brought. Him. Back. Now we know what that feels like, and we're not gonna let it happen to anyone else. We need to get those dragons out of those cages. We need to rally the troops. Everybody on this island, in this realm, anybody who can fight needs to come with us now." Sloane spoke the words out loud, but I knew that Fischer heard them as well.

'What dragons?' Fischer demanded. *'Tell me more.'*

'There are hundreds of dragons being held in different camps around the capital. They're not far from the castle. I think the furthest is maybe ten miles out. They need to be released.'

'We can do that; we can figure out a way. Are you with dragons now?'

Sloane responded because I couldn't. I was so deep in my mind, my thoughts swirling around the possibility of a life without Bram and Faris, without Khol. I couldn't stomach it. I couldn't focus on the words that were being spoken, but somehow I knew that between Vaeryn, Sloane, and Fischer, some type of an agreement or plan was made.

'Guppy, I want to talk to Cam and Kai. Please.' I needed to hear their voices, since that was all I'd be allowed for the moment.

'I can try to bring them in. Give me a minute to see if I can link our

power, because the distance is taking a lot out of me already,' Fischer replied. And so, with my hands clasped in my lap, I waited, and I waited, and I hoped beyond hope that I'd be able to hear their voices, because oh my gods, what if this was the last time? Here I was, pregnant, in another world. I couldn't take it.

'Baby girl?' Cam's deep voice rattled me to the foundation of my soul. Oh, sweet mother of moons. It was Cam, my Thunder Daddy, my protector. All I could do was cry for a moment.

'Cam,' I choked out. *'Oh my gods, Cam.'*

'Thank the stars,' he breathed, his voice cracking. *'I love you so much, baby. I can't wait to see you, to kiss you, to have my hands all over you. Fuck, baby girl. I've missed you so fucking much.'*

I blinked, releasing more tears. *'I'm scared, Cam. I'm scared of what's going to happen tomorrow. I can't handle losing them. I can't handle losing any of you. We're just getting started with our story—it can't end like this.'*

Before Cam could respond, another voice broke through. *'Where's my Cub?'* Kai demanded, his voice a growl through the link.

'I'm here, Kai! I'm right here! Oh my gods, I can feel you. I can feel the bond. Can you feel me too?' Warmth was spreading rapidly from my chest to the rest of my body, a sensation of safety and love working to smother the feelings of fear and anxiety.

'Oh, sweet Cub. I've never stopped feeling you. You're like the sun. Even when I can't see you, I can feel you. Your warmth, the way you give me life. The way you brighten everything. Fuck Sprout, I need to see you. This is fucking killing me. I need to see your belly, to see with my own eyes how beautiful our mate looks carrying our babies.'

There was something inherently heartbreaking about hearing strong men break. The way their voices cracked with pain and longing. That level of love and devotion was something that I'd never known before I met them. And I knew that nothing else would ever come close to being like this.

'Where are you, baby?' Cam asked.

'We're with Vaeryn. I want to tell you where we are, but I can't. Not until we can bring you here. Please, don't take it personally. Just know that we are safe.' I felt a little guilty about not telling them, but we had to be careful. Nobody on the wrong side could find out about this safe haven.

'Okay, little witch. I trust you. But we need to move. Now. Napoleon found vaccines that restored our powers, which seemed to be blocked here. That's how this is possible right now. We have extras, so you and Sloane can be dosed as well. And then once we get Khol, Bram, and Faris secured, we can administer it to them as well. The doctor here says the execution will take place in the courtyard at dawn. So we need to be there well in advance. Now that we've reestablished the mental link, we can stay in contact and give each other updates. That's going to be crucial.' Sloane was nodding along with Cam's words.

'I think we can have Vaeryn rally up help to get the dragons free from their enclosures,' I told them. 'The issue will be that we don't know how Asrael is controlling them. Is it just a mental game? Is he using his power? We just have to assume he'll be distracted with getting his plan together, and he's such a narcissist that he'll probably be boasting and bragging in the courtyard tomorrow in front of the demons in attendance.'

'We'll figure something out. Start preparing to return as soon as possible. Let us know when you're close and we'll make a final plan of attack then,' Cam replied, his natural ability to lead coming out strong. He sounded so sure of himself, and it never ceased to amaze me how safe he made me feel.

'Okay, we'll be there as soon as we can. Be smart. Stay safe. Stick together. Nobody goes anywhere alone. We're strongest together,' Sloane reminded everyone.

'I love you all,' I declared, hoping they could feel just how true those words were. I got three 'I love you's in return, and then the link was severed. Sloane's eyes burned into mine and he leaned down, capturing my mouth in a burning kiss that set my blood on fire.

Brushing my hair out of my face, he smirked. That classic shitty, smug as hell, Sloane smirk that I used to hate and now loved. "We're almost there, Red. The end is near, can you feel it?" He was practically vibrating with adrenaline, whether it be from the thrill of the impending confrontation or being reunited with our family—it didn't matter. I knew he'd do whatever he had to to make sure we all got out of this safe.

So would I.

"Well, Vaeryn," Sloane announced, hopping up from the pillow pile we'd been nestled into. "We have work to do, and we need to do it quickly. Let's walk and talk."

The dragon grinned, feeding off of Sloane's excitement. I watched as Sloane clapped a hand on Vaeryn's shoulder, leading him back to the table where he began filling him in on the conversation we'd just had.

I began mentally making a list of what I needed to do before we left here. Get better clothes for battle, for one. Ah fuck it, there wasn't much for me to do at all. Why couldn't I get a burst of adrenaline during a time like this? All I felt was fury toward the man who'd done nothing but try to destroy me and my life since I'd met the guys, and rage at my mother who'd turned out to be more evil than I could've ever anticipated.

"I'll gather the battle dragons," Vaeryn said to Sloane. The two of them must've had an incredibly speedy discussion because they were already heading back toward me. "Meet me at the water's edge as soon as you're able." With a nod to me, Vaeryn left us, set on his task.

"Do you need anything before we leave?" Sloane asked, crouching down before me.

"I was thinking a change of clothes—something a little more protective? Oh, and I better pee before we go."

Sloane's face turned thoughtful but before I could ask him about it, he agreed to my course of action. "Sounds like a plan. I'm going to check out Vaeryn's weapons room. How about you take a nap while we prepare?" He held his hand up to stop me from arguing. "You need your rest, Red. Meet me at the cave opening in an hour?" He was already walking away, heading to wherever this weapons room was. When I didn't respond, he spun on his heel, halfway across the room. "What's wrong?"

I waved my arms out to my sides and teetered back and forth on my ass. Realization dawned, and Sloane let out a groan. "Fucking hell, I'm such an asshole." He moved back toward me and took hold of my waiting hands, hauling me and my massive stomach up in the blink of an eye. "I'm sorry, kitten. I'm not... I mean, I didn't think about how—"

Flashing a quick smile, I wrapped my hand around the back of his neck and pulled him in for a kiss. "You are an asshole, but you're mine. And I love you. I'm not used to this either, and I didn't even think about getting back on my feet after I plopped down there into that pillowy heaven."

He laughed deeply, a sound I'd heard far too little of during the course of our relationship. "I'm just glad you didn't rip one when I yanked you up like that."

My mouth fell open and I punched him in the arm. "Keep it up, dragon man. You will pay the price!"

"I'm sure I will," he replied, his laughter returning as he walked away from me. "See you soon, Red."

Fate would have it that the first step I took resulted in a fart. Gods dammit. I froze and then sighed when no teasing came.

"I heard that!"

Son of a bitch.

Kai

Chapter Twelve

*I*t worked.

Oh my gods. It actually fucking worked. I couldn't believe it. I'd heard her clear as day. Her sweet voice had penetrated my soul, just the same way it did every single time.

"Fischer," I said. "You are a fucking badass." I was smiling so hard that my cheeks were aching, but I couldn't stop. I wouldn't stop, because *my mate, my cub,* was safe. She was alive. My future cubs were safe and alive. Sloane. My brother was alive. I hadn't felt this happy for so long.

Balor had left just before Fischer brought us into the mental link. Time was running out, and we'd sent him to gather more loyalists to bring them in on our plan. I was glad that we'd had that moment alone with just us. The conversation felt intimate, the love we had for each other transcending all space and distance.

"She sounded good, right?" Fischer asked, looking unsure.

"Yeah, brother. I mean, she's upset, rightfully so. Anybody would be. We all are. But I couldn't have asked for better, given the circumstances," Cam said, taking a seat at the small dining table by the window.

Before Balor left to go to rally his people, he'd brought back a whole serving cart, filled with different food and drinks. As soon as we ended our conversation with Saige and Sloane, we dug in. Gods, the food was so good.

I hadn't eaten much during my isolation, and I needed to fuel up to have enough energy for this battle that was surely coming our way.

Cam was deep in thought as he ate, and I knew he was playing various scenarios through his tactical brain. That was just how the man operated—it was why he was our leader. If anybody would be able to lead us in a successful mission here today, it would be Cam.

Fischer was also quiet as he ate, and the silence was starting to drive me crazy. I had never been a quiet person, not when I had so much energy. So many things to talk about, places to go, things to do. I wasn't made to sit and be left with my own thoughts. The times in my life where I'd been forced to do that, when I'd had no other options, that was when things always went bad for me. And that wasn't going to happen today.

"So, you trust Balor?" I asked, looking between my two best friends while they paused their eating and glanced at each other.

Cam snorted. "Fuck no, I don't trust Balor. The only people I trust are us—our family. We are the only ones who are in this for our survival."

Fischer nodded in agreement. "That's where I'm at too. We need the man right now, and I do think he is telling the truth about where his loyalties lie. But the only people we can be one hundred percent sure about are the seven of us and Khol. That's it."

I reached for a piece of fruit, one that I'd never seen before. But it looked good, so I took a huge bite. Juice exploded from the skin and dripped down my shirt, soaking me.

"Holy shit. What kind of fruit do they have around here?" I sputtered, wiping my face with a napkin. Cam laughed, and Fischer shook his head.

"I'll be sure to pass on those." Fish pushed the plate of fruit away from him.

I huffed. "Yeah, no shit. Let me see if I can find another shirt here somewhere." Standing, I tugged my dirty shirt over my head and tossed it on the chair. As I turned and walked through the room, I heard a sharp intake of breath. Looking back over my shoulder, I saw Fischer's face had gone as white as a ghost.

"What's wrong?" I demanded. "Is it Saige? Is she saying something to you right now?" I raced back over to the table, my heart pounding. I was scared to death of what she could possibly be telling him to garner this type of reaction.

"Your back," he growled. "What the *fuck* happened to your back, Kai?" Fish slowly rose from his chair, like an avenging angel, or maybe a devil. Either way, he was terrifying. Personally, I hadn't seen my back, so I had no idea of the extent of the damage left behind from Asrael's cruelty.

Fischer was practically vibrating as he stood there before me, his eyes piercing.

"It was Asrael," I confessed. "He kept trying to get me to shift into a dragon. When I didn't—because obviously I fucking can't —he dragged me out to the courtyard, strung me up against a post and whipped me. He wanted to 'set an example.' It nearly killed me. How bad is it?" My voice was nothing more than a whisper. I really didn't want to hear that the stain of that trauma would be marked on my body for eternity. I wanted no part of it. And yet, I had no choice.

Cam cleared his throat, drawing my focus. His gaze captured me, and his face softened. "It's bad, Kai. Don't get me wrong, it's much better than it was when I found you. But you have extensive scarring. I think whatever whip Asrael used was magically infused with something to prevent healing. He wanted to harm you. He wanted to mark you. This was personal and malicious."

"Oh." It was all I could say. I was deformed. Now every time I took my shirt off, everybody would see what had happened to me. They'd wonder, 'Did he deserve that punishment? Is he a bad man, a criminal?' That would be their first guess because men who were innocent, men who were good? They didn't bear marks like these. At least, not typically. The thought of Sprout seeing my back like this was enough to make me sick.

Pushing back from the table, Fischer and Cam both stood before me. United.

"They marked me too, brother," Fish said. "My scars aren't visible, but they're there. Promise me that tomorrow, when all of this goes down—promise me that there will be blood. Swear to me that we will have our vengeance for the wrongs committed against our family." I watched as Fischer's shoulders shook, his words a battle cry. "I am *done* asking questions. I will kill first and worry about the repercussions after. If the sun reaches its peak and those cobblestones in the courtyard aren't sparkling with a sea of red, then justice will not have been served."

Something passed between the three of us at that moment. Our bond. Tightening, strengthening, wrapping around us, pulling us tighter than ever before. We had walked through the fires of hell, and we were nearly free. Together, we would defeat our enemies and seek retribution in flesh and death.

Five quick knocks in succession on the door signaled Balor's return. As Fischer strode over to the door, Cam tossed something at me that hit me right in the chest. I pulled the soft, warm t-shirt away from my body and looked over at him.

"Put it on, K," he whispered, crossing his massive arms over his equally massive chest, which was now bare. He'd literally given me the shirt from his back because he knew—without me so much as saying a word—that I wouldn't want these people at the door to see my scars.

Without hesitating, I slipped the shirt on, and the smell of a summer storm surrounded me. I could feel my cheeks heating, overcome with emotion. Embarrassment, yeah, but also love. The love I had for our stoic leader and the way he always knew what we needed without having to be told. My mouth opened to thank him but I stopped when I felt his eyes trailing down my body, taking in the look of his larger shirt on my leaner frame. When he finally focused back on my face, he winked. *Winked.* Then he turned his attention to the door.

Balor entered, followed by five other demons—three males and two females. Introductions were made quickly. All of them claimed their devotion to Bram in the Carlisle monarchy. Their excitement about seeing the new queen taking her rightful place. Their fealty to protect our family, including our unborn children.

"I do think it would be best," Balor began, "if we were to relocate to the servants' wing. There's less of a chance of Asrael's cronies messing with us if we're in that wing. The issue is just getting there."

I looked over at my brothers as we had a silent conversation. I agreed with Balor though. Right now, we were sitting ducks—I was concerned that we'd be found out if we stayed here. Cam crossed his arms across his chest, thinking everything over, and eventually gave a small nod.

I turned back to Balor. "What do we need to do to get there?"

"I can escort you. If we move as too large of a group, we're more likely to garner attention."

Between Fischer and myself, we'd be able to sense if people were approaching, and Fischer could use his affinity to direct them the other way. The only issue with this would be, of course, if somebody had a strong enough shield in place to block his persuasion.

"I feel it is a risk we'll have to take. Not only is it safer for us there, but it has an entry that leads directly out to the courtyard. We won't find a better option for tomorrow morning," Balor explained, confident in his plan.

"Well then..." Cam scratched his rippling torso and widened his stance, his large chest flexing, as if he was just struggling to keep the beast within him on lockdown. I knew the feeling; Bagheera had not stopped his relentless pacing. He was desperate for the kill, couldn't wait to feel the collapse of our enemy's throats beneath the force of his jaws. "Lead the way, Balor. Let's do this."

THE FOUR OF us stuck close together as we made our way through the castle halls. Cam, Fish, and I refused to split up, and Balor had sent the other five demons to make their way on their own. We moved in silence. Whether that was because we didn't want to chance anybody overhearing our conversation, or because each of us was lost to our own thoughts, I couldn't say.

Napoleon was riding on my shoulder, his tiny body vibrating with excitement. Who would've thought that this tiny mouse, with an insane ego and a serious obsession with murder, would be the one who'd helped save us? I was convinced that he must have been a man in another life.

As we crept through the stone hallways, my thoughts turned to Sprout. How big would her belly be by now? I thought back to that day in the kitchen, before we left to come here and everything went off track. In a matter of hours, her stomach had gone from slightly swollen to obviously pregnant, and it had been a whole month since then. I had no doubt that she would take my breath away when I finally got to lay eyes on her.

I pushed my love toward her through our mate bond. I couldn't speak with her right now, but I needed her to know, to never doubt my devotion and my total obsession for her. My body needed to feel hers. No barriers between us. Just skin on skin, our magic thrumming. I smiled and pressed a fist against my chest as the love I had sent out to her returned to me tenfold. My beautiful mate was thinking about me too, assuring me that her feelings were the same. Our love was infinite.

Balor and Fischer were leading us when suddenly Fish's arm

snapped out to pause our progress, raising a fist the signal for us to halt. I craned my neck to listen closely, focusing on hearing whatever it was he was sensing. Murmuring conversation. Soft footsteps. Whoever was approaching was not very close, and eventually, the conversation started moving away.

After a few more seconds, Fish dropped his fist and gave a curt nod, and we were on the move once again. We dodged several more demons in our journey to the servants' wing. Thank gods that we had Fischer with us, with his mind control affinity. I was able to hear them approaching thanks to my shifter hearing, but without Fish's skills, we would've needed to find places to hide and this whole thing would have taken much longer than it needed to.

After about twenty minutes of carefully calculated walking, we reached the servants' wing, and Balor turned around with a grin on his face. We'd made it. My eyes took in the large archway and massive double wooden doors that blocked our view of the other side.

"This is it. This is where everybody in service of the castle resides. And I would say with confidence that ninety-eight percent of the demons that you will see behind this door will pledge their allegiance to the true king and queen, and the queen's mates. Let me make some introductions, and we can continue formulating a plan. Time is running out—the sun will soon rise." Balor extended his hand, wrapping it around the massive metal door handle.

Suddenly, the doors blew open with a force that had to have been magical. We all took several swift steps back. My stomach sank when I saw who was behind that blast.

"Laurie," Fischer growled, and she had the audacity to grin at him.

"Hello, Fischer. Still alive, I see." Long vines coiled around her arms like living snakes, and I saw my brother stiffen beside me as he watched those vines, the very things that had once taken him from this earth.

"Don't let her get inside your head," I barked. Grabbing Fischer by the nape of his neck, I attempted to shake him out of whatever memory he was currently lost in.

"Get out of here, Laurie." Cam's voice was low and steady. In fact, it was so steady that a chill raced down my spine, for this was when our boss was most deadly.

"Fischer and I have a bond now, boys." More of those damn vines circled around her body, swirling up and down her legs. "Don't you remember? I killed him. That created a bond between us, one that will never be broken."

Fischer snarled at her words, his entire body shaking. "The only bond I have, bitch, is the one between myself and your daughter and these men right here. I cannot *wait* to see you dead."

Laurie threw her head back in laughter. The sound was pure evil. "Fischer, Fischer, Fischer," she mocked. "I'm immune to your powers. How do you think I got so close without you knowing? There's nothing you can do to me."

"If that's the case," I growled, "then there's nothing you can do to us now, either." Her eyes widened slightly, betraying the fact that this was news to her. I smirked. "That's right. We have our powers, the same as you. So tell me—who do you think would win hand-to-hand? Because let me assure you, it would take me three steps to reach you, one second to grab your neck, and one millisecond to snap it." From the corner of my eye, I could see electricity popping from Cam's hands. I knew how badly he wanted to fry this bitch. I did too.

Laurie's eyes went from me to Cam to Fischer, and even over our shoulder, likely taking in Balor behind us. Without warning, she opened her mouth and let out a truly horrific, ear-piercing scream. We couldn't even reach out and grab her because the instinct to cover our ears was just too strong. *Is she part banshee?* I had no doubt that anybody within an even remotely close radius would have heard it. Thankfully, it didn't last long.

In fact, it cut off quite abruptly. Worried that we were busted, I lifted my eyes and dropped my hands. Laurie was sprawled out on the floor, facedown with a small pool of blood spilling out around her face. The large door that she'd been standing in front of now had five masked males standing in the archway.

"Who the fuck are you?" Cam demanded, stepping forward closer to these... What they were—demons? Mages?

"Fuck are we? Who the fuck are *you?*" the male in the middle asked, also stepping forward. His mask was all black, with blue-green stitching resembling a crude mouth and crosses for eyes. All five of them wore masks, each mask completely different.

"Holy shit,' Balor said in awe behind us. "You're here."

The group of five formed a straight line. "We are. Tell me, when does the party start?"

Balor looked up and down the hall, checking our surroundings. He shook his head. "Not here. Let's find a safe place to speak. Follow me. Leave her."

"I'm not leaving this bitch anywhere. I think we should kill her now and be done with it," Fish snarled, glancing at Cam and I.

I could see where he was coming from, obviously. Why she'd be better off dead, eliminating her as a threat permanently, but it felt like a betrayal to my mate. Killing her mother without her explicit approval.

"Fish, I agree. I want her dead, but I also want our mate to be able to look us in the eye for the rest of our lives. Killing Laurie could change how she sees us." I glanced over at Cam to see what he thought.

His eyes darted between me, Fish, and Laurie's crumpled body. "FUCK!" he gritted out in frustration, his hands running through his hair. He knew I was right. Deep down, so did Fish. Revenge wasn't worth the cost of our mate's trust.

"Fine, she comes with us." Fischer bent down, wrapped his hand around Laurie's ankle and began pulling her behind him like a piece of meat, blood smearing across the floor, leaving a morbid trail.

"That's fucked up," one of the men mused, this one wearing a gas mask. "I like it."

We all followed Balor into what I had to assume was a meeting room. Fish dropped Laurie in the corner, and my eyes landed on her slumped body. I had no idea if she was alive or dead, but I found myself hoping for the latter because at least then she'd be out of our hair. And we wouldn't have to worry about her devious schemes or the way she always managed to fuck our lives up.

We all sat down at a huge conference table, each of us dropping into a chair. The five men sat across from us in various postures, from legs kicked up on the table, slumping back in their chairs, to sitting ramrod straight. The vibe of this crew, whoever they were, was chaos. Sinister energy surrounded them, as though darkness itself would cower away just to escape being near them.

The man in the middle of the group spoke first, the one with crosses for eyes. "We were invited here and told that today was the day."

"We were promised today would be the reckoning," another spoke up, this one with a black pig mask.

"And it will be," Balor replied, drumming his fingertips on the tabletop.

"Who are you?" I asked them. I needed to know. Fischer shifted in his chair beside me, and I glanced at him from the corner of my eye. It was likely he already knew who they were, whether from some kind of prior knowledge or the fact that he'd used his affinity to figure it out.

"You might have heard of us," the man wearing a black

masquerade mask taunted, his hair holding streaks of silver around his temples.

"You *probably have* heard of us," the one with the gas mask sang out, dropping his massive axe onto the table with a clang.

A chill pulsed through my veins because suddenly I knew exactly who these men were. I found myself laughing, and all five of them soon joined in. It was ridiculous. I was laughing so hard that tears were running down my face. "I know who you are," I said, finally regaining control of my emotions.

"Say it then," the fifth male—the one wearing a skull mask—challenged. "Say our name."

"The Exiled," I replied, smiling back at them.

Faris

Chapter Thirteen

This was my punishment. This was what happened to people who failed their families. The wind blew my hair around my head, and I laughed. Because how was there wind in somebody's psyche?

I had been confused at first, of course. The last thing I remembered was entering the throne room. We'd come here to warn Bram's father—as a team, a family, a unit—of the danger that was lurking, and about the dragons. The only thing I knew for certain was that I had failed. I had been thrown in some kind of purgatory where I needed to prove myself. I wouldn't be worthy of them until I could prove it.

I had no idea how long I'd been here. The sand beneath my bare feet had turned red long ago. And yet, the people continued to come. Why? Why did they keep coming after me? They should have known by now that nobody was going to leave this pit alive.

They had done something to my powers as well. I was still able to grow fangs, but my speed was dramatically diminished, and forget about any sort of mental capabilities. That's why I was convinced this was a test.

I had to admit, I was a little taken aback at the fact that my Firefly would have allowed this to happen. I thought she knew how much I loved her, how much I needed to be with her. And I wanted to be angry at the fact that they'd put me here in this prison, forcing me to kill, though the killing didn't bother me so much. It was the isolation. I'd spent nearly all of my life being isolated.

This was bullshit. There wasn't even mac and cheese here. If this was what needed to happen though, so that they knew they could trust me, then I would have to accept that.

Not long after I got here, a few guards had tried to speak to me. That was strange, because in all of my time in Fischer's mind, there had never been any other entities. So why now? What was this place? Where the fuck was I? The questions they'd asked me had mostly been who was I? Where did I come from? How did I get a body? Was I really Fischer Bahri's twin? Of course I never replied. I wasn't a little snitch. No, I knew I couldn't, because then I would have failed the test, and passing this test was the only thing that would reunite me with my family. So no matter what they did to me, no matter what they thought they were forcing me to do, it made no difference to me. I wouldn't break.

I felt the air behind me shift, and I knew that my opponent had gotten to his feet once more. Dear gods, why wouldn't the fucker just stop? I'd kicked him down a hundred times already.

After killing as many men as I had, I was getting bored. So quite frankly, I'd started seeing how long I could drag it out. If it took me five hours to kill someone, would they throw someone else in there? Try to make it more interesting? Perhaps make me kill quicker, so as not to risk injury to myself? The answer to all of that was yes. Yes, they would. Did it matter in the end? No, it did not. Because just like I wasn't a snitch, I also wasn't a little bitch. Fighting came naturally to me, as though I was born to do this.

The big idiot at my back thought it would be a smart idea to rush me from behind, like some kind of fucking supernatural linebacker. Joke was on him though, because I was too fast for his fat ass. I stepped aside at the last minute and sharply drove my elbow right into the back of his head, smashing his large body to the sand.

There were so many ways to kill men, and I was so bored. So fucking bored. I found myself grinning at the grunt that escaped the guy as he got a face full of sand. He rolled over—attempting to quickly pop back up and come at me again, no doubt. I was so tired of this dance.

As he rolled, I decided to give him a little bit of a boost and so I kicked him in the face, forcing his body into a rotation that landed him on his back. He snarled at me. Where were this guy's fucking manners? You think you're helping somebody, the next thing you know they're growling at you like a beast. Life was too short to be rude to people.

"I was just trying to give you a boost, man. There's no need to look at me like that."

"Oh, fuck you."

I slapped a hand over my heart. "You are just completely uncouth. You know, the last man I fought who showed me disrespect—and refused to *learn* how to be respectful—got his head kicked off. Literally. Did you know that was possible? I had no idea. But you know," I said, circling around him as he got himself into a sitting position, "it's really boring down here. And by my count, I think you're number fifty. I got bored of traditional killing by number five, I think. So I've learned a lot while I've been here. You can kick a man's head off if you have enough power. I can break their arms off and beat them to death with them, and if I stomp hard enough, I could completely rupture your nut sack. Isn't that crazy? You see, that's not what killed that last guy though. No, what killed him was when I popped his eyes out and poked my thumbs into his brain."

I paused, taking a moment to recall that particular death. It had been fucking disgusting. I shook my hands, remembering the way they'd been coated with... stuff.

After I'd inspected my hands carefully, accepting that they

were still clean, I ran them through my hair and stretched backward, getting an awesome crack from my spine. Number Fifty was just staring at me. *He's probably jealous. I'd be jealous too, if I was staring at me.* His gaze had a hint of judgy to it that I really didn't appreciate, and I narrowed my eyes, suspecting he wasn't taking my killing skills seriously. I guess he had a point—but *only* with the eyeball thing because yes, anyone could do that. However, the head kicking was next-level murder city, and I refused to believe otherwise.

"Okay, Number Fifty." I sighed, pinching my nose. "You're right. That last one really wasn't too special since anyone could pull that off."

His mouth opened and closed like a fish. A big, grumpy, demon fish. Not cute in the slightest, like some fish were. I gave him a couple of minutes to respond. Okay, maybe more like half a minute. After what was actually probably only four seconds, I started talking again. Number Fishty had his shot and he was too slow.

"So I'm kind of thinking that with you being lucky Number Fishty, perhaps this will break my curse of imprisonment. You could be the key to my freedom. How do you want to die, big man? I'll let you pick—dealer's choice. Well, I guess I'm the dealer. So that doesn't really make sense? But yeah, you can pick. Just try to make it interesting."

The demon sneered at me. "Did you say Fishty?" I frowned, opening my mouth to respond that yes, of course I did, but he threw his hands in the air. "You're fucking crazy. You're never getting out of here—that's the whole point of the pit. You never leave. The only escape is death."

I found myself rolling my eyes. "Of course that's what they *want* you to think. But I'm smarter than that." I tapped my index finger against my forehead. "My brain is much smarter than yours is, clearly." The man stared at me like he didn't believe my words, and that kind of pissed me off because I wasn't a liar either. I decided I would let him stand up because I felt bad for him—not because I was going to kill him, but because the man was clearly an idiot. He couldn't take me down if he tried, and he had tried. He'd been trying for four hours.

"I heard you were one of the queen's mates," he snarled, as I let him get to his feet. "Well, not the real queen. But that's what everyone is saying. How the hell did you end up in her harem?"

"The fuck did you just say to me?" My body froze; I was as still as a statue. Hell, I don't even think my lungs were working at that moment.

"You know, the queen? The prophesied one. I heard she's curvy and has a big juicy ass."

I glanced around me, because seriously, was this really happening right now? Was this male, who was already marked for death, honestly standing here and saying nice things about my fucking woman? Because yeah, she does have a big juicy ass! I didn't like him talking about it though. I was about to let him know that, but he let out a mocking laugh, which pissed me off even more.

"That's probably why she needs six men. If her ass is that big, I can only imagine how fat her cunt must be. Question is, the fuck does she need you for? You're stuck here with me, with the other degenerates. This is all you'll ever be—a killing machine."

Red bled into my vision. Dark crimson. Oh yes, this male would die. He would die by my hands and he would regret ever speaking such filth against my mate. My beautiful, gorgeous, pregnant mate.

"You're wrong," I whispered. "She has the tightest cunt in all the land. I want to live there. It's where I belong. My face between her thighs, my cock in her cunt, her ass in my face, all of the possible sexuals you can think of—that's what I live for with that woman. You couldn't handle a woman like her if you tried. And now, Number Fishty, I'm officially bored, and also like seven point eight percent pissed off. I offered you a choice and you chose to talk shit, so it's my decision now."

I swear to the gods, I blinked once and as my surroundings came back into focus, there was only a leg. A hairy, beefy-looking leg. *Where the hell's the rest of Number Fishty?*

I spun in a circle, only to discover that he was scattered throughout the arena. An arm here, a head over there. Oh look, that looked like a small, deflated water balloon. I must have stomped his nut sack. I'd told him it looked like a sad, empty balloon, and here was the proof! I was many things, but never a liar. A surge of pride burst through my veins at the sight.

Yes. Number Fishty was a good omen. I wasn't sure how I knew, but I was getting the fuck out of here. Soon. I backed up against the arena wall and slowly slid down, my legs stretched out in front of me. In the meantime, I supposed I could just sit here and either wait for the next man I was supposed to kill, or I could use my time wisely and focus on all the ways I was going to absolutely devour Firefly's body the moment I got my hands on her again.

Saige

Chapter Fourteen

We moved through the air, an army of dragons.

The only way in and out of the dragon realm was through the lake. Vaeryn said that long ago there had been other avenues, but when the dragons started disappearing they locked their world down, to protect themselves. It had been less than two hours since we'd decided on this course of action, and we sped toward Naryian, racing for the castle. There wasn't much time left before sunrise. Vaeryn had told us about a small town on the outskirts of the capital. That was where we would land and where the dragons would shift forms.

Rage was still the driving emotion in my heart. Magic simmered, as though my whole body was being held at a low heat. The blood within me bubbled both with anger and the desire to harm any who would dare come at me and mine. I had no idea what this day would bring. In the end, all I could hope for was that I would be reunited with *my* family, *my* men and *my* father.

My thoughts strayed to Khol. I wondered how bad his injury was. I'd seen it happen—the long blade had pierced his skin through his stomach and shot out of his back. I'd thought for certain he was dead. As furious as I was, there was also an undercurrent of fear rippling through me. Fear of loss, fear of abandonment—in the end, they were kind of the same thing.

Even as a woman who'd been abandoned by her mother at a young age, I was still able to love, and I had found the greatest love imaginable. I held it so tightly, because I knew what it felt like not to have it. I knew what it felt like to be separated from a mate by death. I couldn't lose any of them.

I thought about Gran. I was curious how she was, knowing she was probably driving herself insane wondering the same thing about me. If there'd been a way to reach her, I would have already done so. But I didn't want to risk that she would convince Rick to come. They'd also been through enough, and they deserved their happy ending together.

When I was a little girl, Gran and I used to spend nearly all of our days out in the garden where she taught me all of the plant names and their properties. Things that they were good for. It had become our special time, together in the garden sanctuary when I was there with only her. I never thought about Laurie. Why she didn't want me, why she was often short-tempered and cruel. Not just to me, but also to Gran.

Even as a young girl, I'd found solace in the earth. Each time my fingers and my hands disappeared into the nutrient-rich soil of my property, I knew peace. I desperately tried to cling to that notion now. Gran had always told me that anger was never the way. Anger caused people to do stupid things, things that they would normally not have done. But today, like this? This was a day that was anything but normal. I felt on some level that I needed to become *something else*. The air swirled around me as I clung onto Sloane's massive claws. I'd braided my hair before we left, and I was thankful for that now.

We began our descent near the small town. There was a large forest close by that would make excellent coverage. My heart began pounding like a war drum as I watched the rapidly approaching ground. As we closed in, I opened up my mind and forced my presence through the mental link.

'Fischer?' I called out. *'Are you there?'*

A second later, his smooth voice came through. *'I'm here, sweetheart. Where are you? What's happening?'*

'Don't worry. We're just descending into the town now. The forest is on the outskirts. We have a little over fifty dragons in our party. Our plan is that they will break off into five teams and work through the land, scouting for the captive dragons and releasing them from their prisons.'

'That's great, sweetheart. We are in the servants' wing. There is an exit that leads directly to the courtyard. We have eyes on it at all times, but there's been no movement yet. Balor has proved to be an incredible ally, and we have approximately one hundred loyalists here with us who will fight. I have no doubt there are more, and once the fighting breaks out, they will come to our aid.'

'That's a relief,' I told him. *'So what is the plan exactly?'*

He paused. *'We're going to infiltrate the crowd and be scattered throughout, hiding in plain sight. Asrael will likely put on a big production to fuel his narcissistic traits. If we can time this right, ideally the freed dragons and Vaeryn's army will arrive to create a distraction, and that's when we'll strike.'*

I couldn't believe this was happening. *'Guppy, did you imagine when you first met me that this was where you would be led, that you would actually die and be reborn only to find yourself here in another realm, surrounded by enemies?'* I could almost picture his eyes burning into mine. I wished on every star in the sky that I would be able to feel the heat of his gaze again.

'No, I didn't see this coming. I didn't see you coming. You freed me, Saige. You loved me, even when I didn't love myself. So whatever I've gone through, whatever we *have gone through to get to this point today, I would gladly do it one hundred times over. Especially if it means an eternity with you.'* Tears gathered in my eyes. His words spoke like a prayer, a promise. There was nothing but truth between us.

'I love you, Guppy,' I whispered, *'and I miss you so much.'* Sloane hit the ground much softer than one would think a huge dragon would be capable of, and I wiped the tears from my cheeks. *'We're on the ground now. I'll check back in as soon as I have more information. I'll see you soon, my love.'*

'Stay safe, sweetheart. I love you.'

The connection severed, and I carefully extracted myself from Sloane's claws. As the other dragons landed, they all began shifting into their human forms. Each dragon had carried a large pack on their back filled with supplies, and they immediately began putting on battle armor and different sorts of chain mail, and gathering weapons.

Warm breath hit my neck, and my eyes fluttered. "How are you, Red?" Sloane murmured, pressing his warm lips against my throat.

"I'm ready for this day to be over." I turned my head to the side, finding his mouth. He kissed me deeply, with purpose and feeling. Feelings that not so long ago, he hadn't even thought himself capable of. His tongue swirled against mine, coaxing me and soothing me as he silently declared his love. His large palm cupped my cheek and the other palm rested against the swell of my pregnant belly. I melted against him. I needed this connection.

"I found something for you. I need to give it to you before we leave." He lifted a brow, and my curiosity was piqued.

"Lead the way, dragon man." I smiled as we walked through the group of dragons who were hastily getting dressed and arming themselves. I filled Sloane in on my discussion with Fischer, and he nodded approvingly at the progress they'd made. Fish had sounded better this time, more like himself, but I was still concerned. Wrapping my hand around Sloane's arm, I stopped him.

"Did you think Fischer sounded strange earlier?" I bit the inside of my cheek, giving my anxiety an outlet.

Sloane's mouth turned down as a grimace flashed over his handsome face. So I wasn't the only one who'd noticed then. "Red, I think we all sound strange right now. Since we got here, we've each been on our own sort of journey, right?" His blue eyes pierced me, forcing my head to nod. "None of us are getting out of this unscathed. Each one of us has gone through a transformation. Mine started the minute you flashed me those big green eyes as I stood outside of The Pig by the moving van. It's been heaven and hell, baby."

He was right. Everything he said made perfect sense, and I gave him a small smile, trying to draw his strength into myself. "You've thought about this a lot from the sounds of it," I mumbled, my fingers playing with the hem of my shirt.

"I had a lot of time to think. When I was in that enclosure with Emrys and the others, they helped me in a way that I hadn't realized I needed. By talking." He let out a humorless laugh. "The very thing I've always despised. I spent weeks talking with those males, getting everything out of my system, and it helped. I can look at your face now without seeing the memories of what I saw in that lab. I've learned how to accept that I am worthy of love and capable of giving it. So, yeah, I've thought about it a lot, and I can't wait for this day to end so you can make that pretty portal and we can get the fuck out of here."

I shook my head sadly. "You know it won't be that simple. We won't be able to just leave. The realm is in a civil war and even if Asrael is defeated today, Bram is the true king. Do you think he will just walk away from his people? These dragons, they believe I am their queen. How are we supposed to just leave?" My chest was growing tighter as the weight of the situation really slammed down on my shoulders. I filled my lungs deeply and exhaled a shaky breath.

"You can open a portal and come and go as you please. These babies could come at any moment, and I want you somewhere safe. Don't you want to deliver them in our realm? The people here will understand." Sloane leaned down and pressed his lips to mine. "Today, when we are victorious, I will be taking you back to Emerald Lakes so you can rest. You have six mates, baby. Let us handle the politics."

Let them handle the politics? My mind either rewarded me or tortured me with a vision of me lying in my bedroom at home, two little bundles tucked against me as we slept. "Okay," I whispered. "I'll let you all take care of me."

One dark brow quirked up. "Oh, you'll let us, hmm? How will you manage?" I slapped him playfully on the chest; it was the least he deserved for that mocking tone. "Come with me, I want to show you this." He took my hand, leading me over to where Vaeryn was strapping a belt full of weapons to his hips.

"Ahh, Sloane." Vaeryn greeted my mate, then straightened to his full height as I stepped around Sloane to reveal myself. "Your Highness, how was your journey? I trust you are well?"

"I am, thank you," I replied. "I spoke with Fischer. You met him on the mountain. Do you remember?" Vaeryn nodded, and I fought a blush as I remembered what had happened on that mountain between the three of us before Vaeryn had arrived. "My mates have gathered allies within the walls of the castle and they are ready. Our mission is to free the dragons, creating a distraction. That's when we'll attack."

Vaeryn's face glowed as a wide smile broke across his mouth. "I cannot wait!" A loud, full-bellied laugh boomed from him, and I found myself chuckling, his happiness contagious. "I have waited centuries for this. I can almost smell the blood from here." We laughed, but I knew he was deadly serious. These dragons had waited a very long time for their revenge. Now it was here and nothing was going to hold them back.

"Do you have it, Vaeryn?" Sloane asked, wringing his hands together.

Our dragon friend glanced at my mate, a look of confusion abruptly morphing into glee. "Oh, yes, yes, of course I do. One moment." Vaeryn turned around and walked over to his large pack on the ground, retrieving a package that was wrapped in plain brown paper. He beamed as he walked back over to us, his chest puffed out with pride. "Here we are." He handed the package to Sloane and my mate dipped his head in thanks.

"Give us five minutes, Vaeryn." The dragon leader nodded, and Sloane pulled me by my hand, leading me a little further into the forest, just far enough to have some semblance of privacy.

"What are we doing?" I asked, my head craning as I looked back to see if we were missing anything in the camp.

"One of the seamstresses back in the dragon realm made this for you, using her dragon magic. I gave her the specifications on what I wanted and this was what she came up with. I need you to be safe today, Saige. Not just for your sake but for mine. For my brothers and for these little girls right here." He held the large package out to me, and my hands trembled as I took it from him. It looked like it should have weighed more than it did. "Go on," he urged. "Open it."

My fingers tore through the brown paper and pieces of it fell to the forest floor. I sucked in a breath as I got the first glimpse of the bodice within. "Sloane," I breathed. "It's beautiful." I lifted my eyes to his, amused when I found his face quickly turning pink. It gave him a boyish charm that I wasn't used to seeing, and I loved it.

Returning my focus to the gift, I sank down on a fallen log and rested the package on my thighs. The material was similar to leather, only stronger, which was interesting because you would have thought that would have made it heavier. That wasn't the case.

This gown had an empire waist—perfect for a big pregnant belly. The entire thing was coated in something similar to chain mail, only on a smaller scale—similar to a strong mesh. On top of that were breathtaking gems sewn along the bottom of the bust. The thread that had been used to sew this magnificent gown together glinted gold, and I knew it was the real thing. There were embroidered vines winding their way all over the fabric.

As I lifted the gown, the skirt fell to the floor and long sleeves tumbled from behind, made of the same light mesh that covered the gown. The color was a deep pine green, and with the golden accents and shimmer of diamonds, it was the most beautiful thing I had ever seen.

"It's gorgeous," I said in awe to my mate, as he stared down at me.

"It'll be even better once it's on you." He smirked. "Let me help you put it on." I nodded and stood, turning my back to him. I let his deft fingers slide my zipper down my back. The cool air of the forest slipped against my spine, causing goosebumps to erupt across my flesh.

Sloane let his wicked hands trail down my skin. "Are you cold?"

"No. Seems like these days I'm always running so much hotter than I'm used to. The cool air actually feels amazing."

He chuckled. "Well then, let's get you out of these clothes." Within moments, the fabric I had been wearing was pooled at my feet. I stood there, naked as the day I was born. "I wish we had more time," he whispered in my ear. I felt my core throb with his words.

"Soon," I told him, spinning around to look into his face. "You designed this?"

"Yeah, I did." His hand found the back of his neck, a gesture I'd started to associate with him feeling a bit embarrassed. It was cute. "I had this vision of you storming through that courtyard, taking back what had been stolen from you. All I could think was that such a warrior needed a fitting gown. Plus, this one has been reinforced with magic, and only the strongest of materials has been used to ensure your safety against any sort of weapon. This mesh right here"—he pointed to the bodice—"is stronger than a three-inch shield of steel. Isn't that amazing? It's also impervious to flames and electricity."

Launching myself at him, I felt him grunt as our bodies collided and the air was forced from his lungs. Giggling, I wrapped my arms around his neck, kissing his face.

"Who knew you were so sweet?" I teased.

"Don't push it now, kitten. It's been a long time since I was able to dominate anyone. In fact, I've never gotten that chance with you. Can't wait to make that happen." My heart squeezed at his words. I'd seen dominant Sloane before with Fischer all of those months ago in my garden. It was still one of the hottest things I've ever seen in my life. I couldn't wait to see how it felt to be on the receiving end of his orders, though something told me that he wouldn't appreciate my stubbornness in the same way Cam did. That was a game between us. No. Sloane Sullivan would work for my complete obedience. I looked forward to it.

"Don't look at me like that," he murmured, his thumb tracing the full bottom lip of my mouth.

"Like what?" I stared up at him.

"Like you want me to bend you over that log and fuck your brains out." *Oh, moon maidens. Don't picture him railing you like a woodland nymph, Saige. Stay strong.*

"Fine," I acquiesced and lifted my chin, my little pep talk helping me regain my wits. "Help me get this gown on because the longer I'm standing here naked, pressed against you, the more I want to feel you inside of me." *Shit! That's not what I wanted to say. Filthy, filthy witch demon. That's what I am.*

Sloane groaned at my words. "You're wicked. After all of this is over, I want you to show me just how much. Arms up, kitten." I obeyed, lifting my arms to the sky as he slid the gown over my head. The dress fit me like a dream and felt light and breathable. The fact that it was made to protect me and designed by a man who loved me made it all that more precious.

"How does it look?" I spun in a circle, feeling his eyes on me.

"Gods, you're a vision in that dress. A true queen. It's perfect. Come. Vaeryn is desperate to see you in it, and I want to show you off. I want all of these males here to see what is mine, and what will never be theirs. They can pledge their allegiance to you. They can love you in the way a village loves a queen, but they will never know what it feels like to breathe in your scent with their face between your thighs. They will never know how amazing it is to watch you being taken by your other mates. They will never see your body—this perfectly curvy, soft, gorgeous body. For any male that would try would meet a quick death."

I blinked slowly, taking in his words. Being in the demon realm, and subsequently, the dragon realm had really brought Sloane out of his shell. He wasn't holding back anymore. He had accepted the animal within him, and so had I.

"Let's do this." I stood tall, looking him in the eye. "I'm ready."

Bram

Chapter Fifteen

My hand trembled as I signed the final letter that I needed to write. Rising from my chair, I carried everything over to the bed and meticulously folded up the two blankets that I had knitted. One green and one purple—for my daughters, the sweet little girls who I may never get the chance to meet. At least this was one gift I was able to give them by my own hand. My time was up.

Just as I placed everything in a pile, the door to my chambers blew open and five guards spilled into my room.

"Gentlemen," I greeted them.

"It is time, my lord," one of them said to me.

I took a deep breath as my fingertips trailed over the smooth, intricate details of the blankets. I wondered how precious they would look wrapped up in these.

Gathering my bundle, I straightened my spine, as prepared as I was ever going to be walking to my death. "Lead the way," I told the guards. One of them stepped forward to bind my hands together, though I was allowed to keep the blankets clutched in my arms. All of them looked solemn, and I wondered who they were loyal to.

Keeping my head high, I strode through the halls. Surprisingly, there were very few demons out and about; the ones I did see were staff, mostly servants and maids.

As I passed one older female, our eyes met, and I saw a tear fall from her eye and trickle down her rosy cheek. With the guards all looking forward, she lifted her fist and clapped it over her heart. I winked at her and gave her a cheeky grin. That small gesture had given me a little bit of strength, and strength was exactly what I needed today.

All too soon, we arrived in the courtyard. The sky was still dark, but I knew that wouldn't be the case for long—maybe an hour. I had one hour, then my life would cease. Though I certainly wasn't going to just waltz to whatever implement of death Asrael had planned for me.

If I died though, my bond with Goldie would be no more. I was grateful for that small mercy. She would grieve me, but it wouldn't tear her apart. Wherever she was, I hoped that she wouldn't witness my death. She had already seen enough in her short twenty-eight years and she didn't need this memory staining our love story.

She was strong, and I knew that even if I was gone, the other men who loved her would keep her safe. They'd love her, tend to her every need, and they would be excellent fathers to our children. Strangely enough, the thing that did give me pause was when a pair of big brown eyes flashed in my mind, with a playful smile and a glint of sharp fangs. Faris was the one I was most worried about. In such a short time, he had bonded with me—I was his anchor, his lighthouse in this storm. This storm was dangerous and my light was about to be snuffed out. How would he fare in my absence?

I was guided over to a wooden platform in the center of the courtyard. "You may sit here, my lord."

All that was left now was to wait. I sank down on the edge of the wooden platform, tightly holding my bundle in my arms. It was awkward with my hands bound together, but I wanted to hold these gifts close to me as long as I possibly could. Waiting was torture, but in this case, I never wanted to reach the end of the timeline.

The sound of a scuffle suddenly drew my eyes to the corner, where a door was open. "You're a disgrace to your kingdom and your true queen!" a familiar voice seethed. "You should be bloody ashamed of yourselves. Look at you! Nothing but fucking *puppets!*" Khol's hands were bound behind his back, but that didn't stop him from trying to cause harm in any way he could.

"When I get free, I'm going to rip your fucking throat out! Then I'm going to stomp on it and shove it in this guy's mouth. That's a promise. Do you know who I am? Do you know how I earned my nickname? Khol the Merciless—or as the rumor mill likes to say, Khol the Cold. Either way, just know that I fucking earned that name and it's been a long time since I let the lid off that fucking monster."

I didn't miss the way the guards cast nervous glances at one another. Shit, he was terrifying. They escorted him over, and as he got closer, he realized that I was sitting there watching. Our eyes collided and I saw the ticking of his jaw and the way his chest heaved. Something like relief flashed over his eyes, but it was gone in a matter of milliseconds.

"You're to sit here and wait until the king tells us what to do with you," a guard informed Khol, guiding him to take a seat.

"Fuck the king," Khol growled. "He's no king of mine. He's an imposter, a joke." Nevertheless, he allowed himself to be forced down onto the platform. The guards walked away, each of them moving to a different entry point. Our powers had been neutralized. We couldn't fly out of here. Finding our way out was going to be very difficult, if not impossible.

"Well," Khol whispered harshly. "You just gonna fucking sit there?"

"For now, yeah," I replied.

He shook his head at me incredulously before nodding down toward the stack of blankets in my arms. "What's that?"

"Just something I made," I replied, hugging them tighter to me.

"Just something you made?" he demanded. "What is this? Some kind of goodbye gift? What, you're just going to give up? You're just gonna let yourself be killed here today? Ripped away from the family that you always desperately wanted? I thought you loved my daughter!"

My hackles raised at his tone and what he was implying. My head snapped over to him. "Are you delusional, Khol? Don't speak to me about things that you have no idea about."

He laughed. "No idea, huh? All I see right here is a man who's accepted his fate. Who's just waiting here for death like a little bitch."

I shook my head, grinding my molars together. "You have no idea. Do not mistake my calmness for defeat. There is nothing wrong with a man preparing for the unthinkable. I had a lot of time on my hands lately, and this is what I did with it. If something happens to me today, I want my daughters to know that in my last hours I worked on this, for them, in case I'm not able to provide them with physical affection. At least these blankets can provide them with warmth, and I hope they'll feel as safe within them as they would nestled within my arms." My vision clouded as tears built, and I cast a look over at Khol to see the same expression on his face.

"I'm sorry, son," Khol said quietly. "I shouldn't have said those things. My mind is a mess and I'm on edge."

I gave a brief nod of acknowledgement. "What we need today is a miracle. In case that miracle doesn't come…" I trailed off, my eyes sweeping across the courtyard.

"I understand," he replied.

I adjusted the bundle in my arms, allowing him to see the letters within. "If you make it out and I don't, can you make sure these get to the right people?"

Khol's eyes danced between my face and the envelopes, his jaw clenching. It was impossible to miss, even with the beard he'd grown. "I give you my word. If the opposite happens and I'm struck down, promise me you'll tell them about me? That I loved them with an unrivaled fierceness. All they need to do to feel my love is look to the night sky and search out the brightest star. As for my wild one, tell her I'm so proud of her and that the greatest accomplishment of my life was being her father."

Fuck. My throat was so tight that I couldn't swallow or speak, so I gave a firm nod. We were quiet for a moment, the weight of the conversation and the implications of what carrying out those promises to each other would mean sitting heavily on our shoulders.

Finally, I regained a little of my composure, clearing my throat. "I'm honestly surprised that you're alive. I kind of figured that they would have let you die or killed you quietly by now."

Khol shrugged. "Yeah, me too. But you know the sick fuck loves his grand displays of power. So of course he would want to use me as a public tool to enforce his iron fist. He makes me sick." Khol angled his body slightly so he could look at me directly. "I want to tell you a story. It won't take long, and I just need you to listen. Can you do that?"

"A story?"

"Yes, now just listen, Bram. Years ago, when I was still working with Asrael against the resistance, there was a scene similar to this. We'd invaded a neighboring town and captured two of the high-ranking members in the resistance, seeking to make an example of them. We needed to show all of the other people what would happen if they continued this foolish quest to break free from the kingdom. Over the course of several days, we had our orders—which came from Asrael, of course. We were to strike down any who opposed. He believed that fear was the best way to rule people, so that's what we did in the days leading up to the execution, but something interesting happened. Instead of the people falling in line, they merely pretended—they just went along with it for the sake of survival. You see, all they needed was a moment. One point in time that they could make their move, and little did we know, we were about to serve that moment on a golden platter."

The air stilled around me as I took in his words, the way his eyes pierced into my soul, the way his hands gripped his knees.

His leg bounced and fire danced in his eyes. "Do you know what happened next?" Khol asked me in a low voice, not expecting an answer, though I had an idea. "An uprising, to our surprise. On the day of the execution, we were gathered much like this. Two men were led to the center of the group. They were sentenced to be hanged, drawn, and quartered."

"Fucking hell," I breathed, unable to keep quiet at the thought of such barbarism.

"It's a truly horrific way to die, but Asrael was beaming. Excitement rolled off of him in waves. Anyway, as we began securing each noose around the males' necks to begin the first part of their execution, Asrael started addressing the crowd. It was his typical display of ego. It's all he ever cares about—being in power, being the strongest, and feeling like he's above everybody else." I was hanging onto every word Khol was weaving, practically seeing the scene before my eyes.

"That's when I saw her. A woman materialized as she broke from the crowd. I'll never forget the look on her face, almost as if she was in a daze as she approached. You see, the two males we were about to kill were her mates. Her long hair fell free and down her back; it was the color of a nearly ripe strawberry. She moved like a phantom, and Asrael didn't notice her at first, but I did. I wanted to see what she would do. From somewhere, maybe within the folds of her skirt, she produced a knife. I'd barely seen the glint of silver before she launched it through the air with amazing speed. Her aim was slightly off, as it hit Asrael in his shoulder. But the moment the blade made contact with his body, the crowd erupted.

"When Asrael realized who it was that had cost this whole plan of his to go off the rails, it was like he had tunnel vision only for her. He walked down from the platform and yanked the knife from his shoulder. The woman stood tall, waving off help from others in the crowd, not wanting them to assist her. She sneered at him and he called her awful names. Their weapons were slicing through the air, clanging together as she blocked him time and time again. Then she made one wrong move, and the knife that she'd hurled at her enemy to save her mates sank into her belly. He dragged that blade up, causing maximum damage. Her mouth opened in shock as blood began running over her lips. Asrael just laughed, spitting on her as he pulled out the blade. He pushed her down onto the ground, as if she was nothing more than an annoying little bug that he needed to put an end to. He didn't spare her a second glance, turning and diving into the fray, killing any who crossed his path.

"I found myself moving toward the woman. As I knelt down beside her, I knew there was no hope for her. At this point, she had already lost too much blood and her face was whiter than a sheet of parchment. Her eyes already had that dull look—you know the one, where someone is floating between the veil, the other side coming into focus and this side fading. A little awareness returned as she gasped for air, and her eyes lifted to my face so slowly, as she struggled to hang on.

"The question that was burning me alive left my lips without permission. I asked her why? Why would she do such a stupid thing? My mind couldn't comprehend such an act of stupidity.

And through labored breaths, she told me, 'Because there is no me without them. This will have all been worth it if they make it out alive. Are they alive?' Her declaration hit me with the force of a speeding dragon, and I fell onto my ass and watched two tears fall from the same eye, one for each of her mates.

"I scanned the crowd, which was more like a mob at this point, and spotted the two males who had been marked for death. They fought back to back. True warriors. Not realizing that their mate was laying twenty feet away, gasping for her last breaths. I found myself reaching for her hand.

"I wasn't familiar with these feelings, you see. It was all so foreign. I didn't like the way it made me feel—as though I was the enemy. So I held her cool hand and told her 'They're alive. You did well. You're a warrior, and today you saved your loves. Sleep now, wild one.' Her mouth morphed into a smile. She sighed happily, and that was the last breath she took. I couldn't bear to see how her men would react when they found her body. So like a true coward, I left. But you know what? I see her face often in my mind, and I always thought if I was ever blessed to have a daughter one day, I hoped that she would be like that woman. Brave and unafraid to love with her whole heart.

"Saige reminds me of this woman. Wild, free. Do you understand what I'm telling you? Bram, history often repeats itself. Not everything is what it seems. Sometimes we need to take a closer look. To realize the truth."

My heart hammered as I considered Khol's words. I let his story flow through my mind and I could almost picture it. That horrible scene, that poor woman, knowing what was to come, and yet she refused to accept it. Death was not to be the fate of her men that day. She took their fate and turned it into her own.

Was he trying to say that Goldie was going to sacrifice herself for my life? No, I'd never let that happen. I glanced over at him and saw the way he was taking in the courtyard. I'd seen that look several times before on his face—the man was plotting. My eyes found their way to each of the guards and I noticed that they, too, looked like they were plotting.

"You can't demand loyalty, Bram. That's not how this works. Loyalty is earned and given to those who deserve it. You never know how small a gesture can impact somebody's life. Every time you're kind and understanding, that matters. That is something that Asrael never learned, and he never will."

"What's going on here, Khol? What the hell is happening? Because I can't help but feel that I am missing something important." I spoke harshly, but my heart was frantically pounding in my chest. I didn't want to get my hopes up. "Where is she? Have you heard anything?" My tone was demanding, but gods damn I needed some fucking answers, not riddles.

Khol's leg continued to bounce. It was all I could focus on now. "All I know," he said slowly, "is that she's alive. She's far from here, as she should be."

My eyes fell shut as I tipped my head back to the sky. "Thank you."

She was alive and she wasn't here, which meant she was far from Asrael's evil grip. She needed to stay as far away from here as possible. I desperately hoped that she opened the portal the first chance she got and ran. I felt relief flood my body, picturing her safe in Emerald Lakes with her gran.

"How do you know this?" I asked Khol, once I regained the use of my voice.

"As I said, loyalty is something that's earned, and I have done my time."

"And the others?" I asked, holding my breath. "What about the rest of them?"

"From what I've heard, everyone is alive. Their whereabouts? That's another story. I believe Saige is with the dragon." My heart sank because she hadn't left. Well, that had been a nice little daydream while it lasted. "The other original three are together, and they've been working on something."

I was frustrated that Khol was still speaking in riddles, and while I was well-versed in coded messages, now that he'd opened the lid on speaking about them, I needed to know.

"What about Faris? What about him?" Khol visibly swallowed, and I got a sick feeling in my stomach. "What? Tell me... What do you know?"

"Listen, Bram. We aren't the only ones marked for death today. There's a third. I don't know what shape he's in, but I've heard it's not pretty. When he's brought out here, you need to control yourself. Do you understand me? You need to stay calm and trust that the stars will see us through."

My hands clenched into fists. What had they done to Baby Fang? He was so innocent and pure. The thought of him alone with these monsters who were capable of literally anything was enough to wake up my demon.

I barely had time to process what Khol had said when the large double doors before us swung open. Ten guards escorted a man toward the platform. He was dressed in rags that were covered in blood. His entire body was red, and he thrashed like a wild animal, growling and snarling, snapping his teeth.

"What the fuck..." I whispered. I noticed Khol was now still as a statue beside me, his knee no longer bouncing to a silent beat.

"I did what you wanted!" the bloodied man shouted. "I killed fifty of them. Fifty! I didn't even bat an eye. What more could you possibly need for me to prove myself? I'm worthy of my family. You can't do this to me. You can't keep me trapped here forever. Do you hear me? I will kill you so brutally that ten generations down your pathetic line will know my name!"

"Faris," I choked out. "Oh my gods. Is that you?"

The man stopped thrashing at the sound of my voice, his wild black eyes locked on me. I couldn't believe the way he looked. His features had become gaunt, his cheekbones sunken in, giving him an even fiercer complexion than usual. He looked every bit the monster that he was not.

Warm liquid dripped from my face. I hadn't even realized that I'd started crying. It felt as though time stopped in that moment as we stared at each other. Two broken men, separated from our family, from our woman, and from each other.

Faris's chest heaved and his eyes trailed down my body, noting my bound hands. He took in the blankets before shifting his eyes and recognizing Khol. An unreadable expression crossed his face, and I had no idea what to expect from him. He'd always been a loose cannon but this was not the same man as before.

Suddenly, his laughter pierced the air. It was deep and genuine. He clutched his stomach as he laughed and laughed. Nudging the guard he'd just threatened to savagely murder, he smiled at him.

"I told you. I fucking *told you* fifty was the lucky number! Look here, it's Bram. He's kind of like my boyfriend, only more than that. Does that make sense? Never mind." He shook his head, bringing his focus back to me.

I couldn't breathe. *Is he seriously laughing at a time like this?*

He was led over to the platform and pushed down by one of the guards. "Take a fucking seat. We'll be getting started soon anyway." He was all smiles as he sat down in between myself and Khol. The guards went to work securing him to the wooden planks beneath us. I suppose they were more concerned with him doing something irrational.

I was starting to think maybe they should have been concerned about all of us. It was looking as though we'd been underestimated, and that was their fuck up. Once the guards had properly secured Faris and seemed assured that he wasn't going anywhere, they moved off to stand alongside the wall.

Faris looked at me, swung his head the other direction and looked at Khol, then looked back at me. "What a fucking mindfuck, am I right? Where the hell have you guys been? Did they make you kill people too? How many did you get?"

All I could do was stare. I couldn't even speak.

"Faris, do you understand what's happening here?" Khol asked gently.

"We're here to be executed as soon as the sun comes up," Faris replied, without skipping a beat, looking at Khol like he was asking dumb questions.

"I need you to focus," Khol told him, his tone conveying the importance of the situation.

Faris scoffed. "I don't believe that they have a man or a woman within these walls who could kill me. I have spent my days wisely. You see, I can kill a man in seven seconds. That was my best time anyway." He cleared his throat. "I understand why you guys did what you did, okay? I let you down and I had to be punished and fight my way out. Yeah, I was a little upset at first, but now I understand. Is this like my final test? I break us out of here and then I get to be a part of the family? Where's everyone else?" He stared at me with his huge brown eyes piercing me, splintering my heart.

"Fuck, Faris. We didn't do anything to you. Don't you remember anything that happened?" He shook his head slowly, and I groaned. "We walked into a trap. When we got here, Asrael and his guards took us down. They've separated all of us for close to a month. I don't know where the others are, or what they've been through. Asrael offered me an opportunity. If I publicly renounced my claim to the throne and showed my support for him, he would let us walk away, but not Saige. He wants to keep her. I told him to go fuck himself, after I smashed his nose."

Faris sat there, frozen. He didn't even blink. I wished I could reach out, give him a hug, something, some kind of contact.

"Talk to me, Faris. By the moon, are you okay?"

"So you mean to tell me that this wasn't a test?" he asked, his voice wavering slightly.

"Gods, no," I replied, holding eye contact with him. "We would never do that to you. You're a part of us, Faris. We love you."

"Holy shit." He shook his head. His brown curls bounced with the movement. "Why did they make me kill all those people?"

"Who knows why Asrael does anything?" Khol muttered.

"If I had to guess, I would say he was studying you. You probably stirred up his curiosity. He had to have been surprised when Fischer walked into the throne room, let alone an identical version of a man who was supposed to be dead."

"This whole time, I thought I was being punished, that I needed to show that I was worthy. Now you're telling me that I wasted a whole month in that sandpit filled with blood, when I could have been escaping? Firefly was in danger, and I didn't know? I can't even process this right now." Faris hung his head, staring blankly at the ground.

"Hey, look at me." He made no effort to follow my command. "Look at me," I demanded more sternly. Slowly, he obeyed. "This entire situation was out of our control. Not one of us is to blame for anything that's happened while we've been here. We each did what needed to be done—that's all that matters. We survived. We're here now, and we're not fucking leaving without our woman. Are you with me, Baby Fang?"

Faris held my eye contact. I watched his tongue snake out of his mouth as he ran the tip of it over one of his fangs, the glint of the barbell in his tongue catching on the faint light from the torches surrounding us.

"Of course I'm with you. It's the only place I want to be," he declared.

I nodded. "Good. That's good."

"Listen," Kohl murmured to both of us. "You need to stay alert. I don't have any more information than that. Be ready for anything. I believe in the stars and their path for each one of us, but I refuse to believe that our journey ends here today."

Hope bloomed within me as I sat there with my father-in-law and my... boyfriend? Faris had called me his boyfriend earlier; I didn't think I misheard that. Is that what I was to him? It didn't feel like the right word, but that was only because it wasn't strong enough. Label or not, the two men beside me renewed my strength, and I found myself excited for the first time in weeks. I couldn't wait to see how this all played out.

Cam

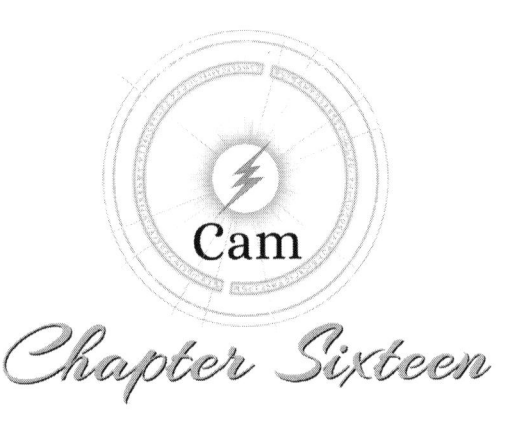

Chapter Sixteen

My eyes narrowed slightly as I stared at the men. No, not men—demons. The demons across the table from me and my guys. I couldn't believe that the Exiled were actually here. They were notorious in the human realm. Last year, we'd been sent on an assignment to spy on them, just to see what they were up to. They weren't wearing masks back then, so I wondered if they were simply trying to hide their identities or if this was a new gang thing for them.

Of course, now that I knew more about who Khol Larsen actually was, I was curious what the true purpose of that mission had been. We were only in Port Black for about a week and as far as I knew, they hadn't realized that we were there.

Kai was grinning at the males across from us, and I knew it was because with their extra strength and power behind us, we just might be able to turn the tables today and do the unthinkable.

In the end, it was Fischer who spoke before I got the chance. "I thought they called you the Exiled because you know, you've been exiled," he deadpanned.

An eerie silence settled over our group as each side of the table took in the other side. They all still wore their masks—which I found strange—with most of them completely covering their faces. It was hard to tell what their current mood was. Without being able to read facial expressions, it really put a damper on the conversation.

The man in the middle, who had crosses for eyes, leaned back in his chair, like he was the true king here. I had to admit, he certainly had an air of importance to him. He didn't look at Fischer. I could tell because his head hadn't moved. He was staring me straight on. Now was not the time for some alpha macho posturing bullshit.

"Well," he finally said, crossing his arms in front of him and leaning forward on the table. "That's a long story. One that, unfortunately, we just don't have time for right now. Let's just say our isolation has now ended. That's all that matters."

I found myself running my fingers through my beard as I perused our new allies. "Actually," I started, "what matters here—the *only* thing that matters here—is our mate. That's number one."

The pig mask demon shook his head, letting out a disbelieving huff. "It always comes down to girls, doesn't it?" His voice was unlike any other demons that I'd heard. While I would consider most of the demon race to have accents that reminded me of British or Irish, his was more Russian, very harsh and to the point. That was when I knew exactly who I was speaking to.

"Not just a girl," Fischer cut in, his hands clenched into fists. I knew that Fischer and Kai would also know the man by his accent. This was The Carver. His real name, Misha. He had earned his nickname through many bloody kills; he was an expert with a knife, or any blade really. His skills were legendary—as was his complete lack of humanity.

"That's fine." Another man shrugged, the one who wore the masquerade mask that just covered his eyes. You could tell he was older by the silver glint in his dark hair, mostly around his temples. Rhodes, I realized, the oldest of the crew. He was maybe ten or fifteen years older than his gang partners and often seen as the more responsible one of the group. I'd heard tales of people who'd made the mistake of thinking that responsibility was equal to softness. Rhodes was always quick to correct that misconception.

"We're here because our interests align with yours. We want to see Asrael destroyed today, and I think that all of our goals will lead us to the same destination," the man in the middle added.

Suddenly, I knew who this one was too. Of course. *Of course he would be sitting in the middle.* He was known as their ringleader, Ashland. He was known for tempting people, making deals with them. From what I knew, he had a bit of an addiction with gambling. Only with him, it usually wasn't with money. No, he actually preferred the highest stakes a person could offer—their life.

That would mean that the remaining two men were the twins, Talon and Felix. These two made the twin girls from The Shining look like little lambs. Their bodies always moved to a strange beat that only they could hear. They couldn't fit in if they tried. From what I'd studied about them in their files, they also had a tendency to be wildly inappropriate, often misreading situations. Or maybe it wasn't even that they were misreading them, it was that they just didn't give a shit. They often laughed at inappropriate times, smiled when a smile was the completely wrong reaction. Felix didn't wear a mask. He wore face paint—white paint with deep black circles around his eyes, the features of a skull painted boldly. His twin, Talon, wore a gas mask and liked to carry an axe.

All five of these demons were completely unhinged, and in my opinion, certifiably insane. I had mixed feelings about their presence here. It was clear they had their own agenda, their own goals. I just hoped that they realized the moment they hindered our plans was the moment they would pay.

"What are you thinking about so hard over there, big man?" Felix asked, taunting me.

I ran my tongue over the backs of my teeth, staring at them. "Look, we need your help. This entire fucking realm needs your help. We need to come up with a plan that gets everybody what they want, and we need to stick to it."

Ashland straightened up in his chair. "Is this the same kind of plan like the one last year, where you and your team snuck into our city to spy on us?" His head tilted, studying our reactions as the air grew tense.

"No, it's not," Kai growled. All five of the Exiled turned their attention, in perfect synchronicity, from me to Kai. "That was for our job. This is for our life. There is absolutely nothing similar. Every man has his limits, how far he's willing to go in the name of his work. I can tell you honestly that for me and the other five men who are bound to our beautiful mate, there is no limit on how far we're willing to go."

Balor stood, suddenly sensing their tension. "Alright, everyone needs to get ahold of themselves. Everyone in this room is on the same side. You wouldn't be here right now if that wasn't the case. We don't have time for this." He crossed his arms over his chest and glared at us, like we were a bunch of unruly punks and not trained assassins who could kill him before he blinked. *The man has balls.*

"Alright then. Balor's right," Rhodes agreed. "We have more important things to discuss than your less than professional ability to sneak around without being detected." His eyes glinted. I could see he wanted to rile me up, but I wasn't going to fall to his level.

Before any of us could respond, Fischer held up a hand, immediately gaining all of our focus. "It's Saige," he said quickly, standing and walking over to the other side of the room. I didn't blame him. I wouldn't want to be distracted by us either.

"Why the masks?" Kai asked, straight to the point. "You didn't have them last year."

Felix chuckled. "Because they're cool as shit." He held his

hands up in a motion that was like he was speaking to a moron. Kai actually laughed, and I swallowed a chuckle myself.

"So everyone here is aware that Asrael has dragons that he either captured or created locked in enclosures around the outskirts of the city?" I asked, letting my gaze fall on each member across the table from me.

Ashland chuckled. "Oh, we're aware." My shock must've shown on my face because he smugly added, "That's right. We've known about this for a while, and in addition to keeping tabs on our city, we've been working on our own little project." He looked over, giving a sharp nod to Talon.

The fire red-haired demon stood from his chair. Reaching into his pocket, he retrieved a small canister. "We've created this." Though I couldn't see his mouth, I could hear the wicked grin on his face.

"What's that?" Kai asked curiously, leaning closer to get a better look.

"This is a vapor. Essentially what it does is free a person from being under the persuasion of anyone else," Rhodes explained.

"Why have you created such a thing?" I inquired curiously. It was definitely what we needed to be able to set the dragons free, and actually have them be of use to this fight. But I needed to know why. The Exiled would have spent time—and likely a lot of money—to create something like this. In the wrong hands, it would be a disaster. Control of power like this was used in high-security prisons for witches and mages, so if such a thing got out, it could really be scary.

Misha grunted. I knew he was a man of few words, so it surprised me when he said, "It was necessary."

"Now listen—" I started, but was quickly cut off by Ashland.

"No, you listen. We're here to help. Yes, we have our own agenda, but I can assure you that our end goals are the same. Asrael will be defeated here today. The reason why we do things has nothing to do with you, and quite frankly, it's none of your business."

I could hear the challenge in his voice and my hackles raised, though I knew that I didn't want to piss these guys off, because we really did need them. They were powerful, and not only that, they were from this realm. Their reputation was widespread and it wouldn't be beneficial to me or my family to push things with them. We didn't need to get on their bad side. Our purpose today was to eliminate our enemies, not create new ones.

Gritting my teeth, I replied, "Fine. How does it work then?"

"This little canister is enough to saturate the air in a three-acre radius," Felix boasted, clearly proud of their creation.

I frowned. "And you only have one? We have it on good authority that there are at least ten enclosures, so one can isn't going to cut it."

Rhodes waved off my worries. "Leave it to us. We'll handle it. You know what you need to know, and that is *all* you need to know."

I glanced over at Kai from the corner of my eye and found him giving me a curious look in return. He knew we needed them too; we had to take any help we could get.

Fischer strode back over and reclaimed his seat. "So," Kai asked, "is she okay? Where are they?"

Fish rubbed his temples. It was clear to see that all of the long distance telepathy was getting to him. "She's fine. Her, Sloane, and Vaeryn's dragon army are on the outskirts of the capital, in a little town about five minutes from here, flying. The plan is that they'll break off into five teams to go free the captive dragons. I told her we want it timed so that they could create a distraction during the execution, and that's when we'll strike."

"That works for us," Ashland announced, wasting no time pushing himself up on his feet. "We'll meet them at their current camp. That way, one of us could go with each team, so we can ensure the vapor is set off in the correct way."

We quickly explained to Fischer about the vapor, since he'd been speaking with Saige when we got what limited information the Exiled had been willing to give up. But still, Fish seemed excited, impressed even about this new development. Maybe even a little bit relieved.

I'm sure he was concerned that we were going to have to utilize his power in order to free people's minds from Asrael's hold. He was already struggling, so a task that large would certainly put him out of commission. Still, I knew he would've done it, because he would do anything for us.

"What are we going to do with her?" Fish asked, pointing over at the lump on the floor in the corner.

"What do you think we should do?"

"I say we kill her and get it over with. That bitch has been nothing but bad news as long as I've known her," Ashland piped up, and we all looked at him with our mouths open.

"What did you just say?" Kai found his words sooner than the rest of us.

"What? You seriously are surprised that we know who Laurie is?" Felix taunted.

"Honestly, I think there's not much we should be surprised about anymore," I muttered, shaking my head.

"You're probably right about that. They always say to expect the unexpected. But I say fuck the expected and fuck the unexpected, and fuck everyone in the ass, because the only people who matter are you and your circle. Who gives a shit what anybody else does?" Talon held his hands out wide, letting a laugh that bordered on a giggle slip out from behind his gas mask.

Jesus. These guys are fucking nuts.

"We can't kill her yet," Balor spoke up, walking over to Laurie's body and leaning down to make sure she was still breathing. "We may be able to use her to get out of a sticky situation. I'd hate to kill her now and not have her later if we need something."

"Fine, but I'm tying her up. She has more lives than a cat and I won't be blindsided by her again," Fish said, his face stern as he looked around at each one of us, daring anybody to challenge him.

Nobody did, and he walked over to a counter area that had rope sitting on it. He quickly got to work, binding Laurie's ankles together, along with her wrists. There was a steel pole, likely used as a support beam, running from floor to ceiling. He propped her into a sitting position before wrapping the remainder of the rope around her torso, securing her so that there was little chance that she would be able to escape without help.

I watched Balor as he walked over to one of the windows, pulling the curtain back slightly and taking a peek outside. "Nobody's out there yet," he told us.

My shoulders were tense—hell, my entire body was one big knot of tension. I didn't want to think about seeing Bram, Faris, or Khol up on some executioner's platform. I didn't think I could bear it. When Saige had stormed in and taken over my life, showing me a love that I would never have believed possible, I certainly hadn't expected to gain all of these feelings for the other men as well. I loved each one of them and I would always do everything in my power to keep them all safe.

"Fuck," Balor cursed. My head whipped up. "They're bringing the prince out now."

Kai, Fischer, and I all hurried over to the window to get a peek of Bram. My heart squeezed as I took in the large demon. He was carrying a stack of what looked like blankets. His face was a careful mask, void of emotion. I couldn't see any visible injuries on him, but that didn't surprise me. Being royalty had its perks, even if you were being held captive and about to be executed.

"Alright, let's get this show on the road," Ashland announced, clapping his hands. "We're going to need to move quickly."

I dropped the curtain and stepped away. I felt a hand land on my shoulder and I took a deep breath, knowing who it was without looking. "It's alright, boss." Kai's smooth voice calmed me. "This isn't all on you. We're in this together."

"I know. It's just hard seeing him like that. Let's do this." I pushed away all thoughts of injustice and sadness for my brother, Bram. "Fischer, tell them what they need to know so they can meet up with Sloane and Saige."

Fish nodded and walked over to the group of men who were practically dancing around with excitement, the adrenaline of the upcoming fight rushing through their veins, fueling their fires.

"Once we free them, we'll meet you in the courtyard. Don't worry, we'll find you. I hope you're ready to spill blood." Felix cackled, as the five of them disappeared from the room without a trace, as though they'd never been here to begin with.

A look of determination flared on Balor's face. "Let's prepare the ones here who are ready to fight. There's nothing else we can do."

"Lead the way," I told him, and the three of us fell in line behind him. This was about to be a day to remember.

Sloane

Chapter Seventeen

Red and I stood there together, my arm wrapped securely around her shoulders, and I kept her tucked in close to my body. We kept our eyes to the sky as we watched the dragons, who had become our allies, take off through the air.

We'd been startled a moment ago, as the Exiled had popped up out of nowhere, stating that they were coming along to help in the rescue mission. They'd created some kind of gas that would effectively cut Asrael's hold over every dragon that he had kept prisoner. Normally, I would have interrogated the hell out of those men. Today, I didn't have the time or the energy. Checking in and getting confirmation from Fischer was good enough.

"Do you think it'll work?" Red asked, turning her big green eyes onto my face.

"It has to," I answered, dipping down and taking her mouth in a quick kiss.

Vaeryn had gone with one of the teams, the one that would be liberating the camp Emrys was held in. He was determined to be a part of history. I had so much respect for him—he loved his people, and they adored him. I let myself gaze down at Red, and fuck, my mate looked fierce. The gown I'd designed for her was perfect in every way. It would protect her, and it also portrayed her image in a way that would be told for years and years to come.

"Aren't you scared?" She cupped my cheek, gently brushing her thumb along my cheekbone.

"Of course I am," I admitted, placing my hand atop hers. "But more than being scared, I'm excited for this to be done. I'm excited for our lives together to really begin. No matter what happens today, I'm going to do everything I can to ensure we can begin the next chapter. Together, all of us."

She nodded and pulled her bottom lip between her teeth, gnawing slightly with worry. "I know. You're right. I just wish we could fast forward a few hours, so that we know the ending. Then this anxiety that's eating me alive would be gone."

"I understand. Something tells me though, that everything that happens over the next few hours is going to be something to remember. Those dragons?" I pointed up to the sky. "They've been waiting a very long time for this call. And all the demons here who have been mistreated? They've been waiting too, for Bram. Everyone has a horse in this race. Let's just hope that we're all celebrating later today." I tracked her hands as they moved over her swollen belly, watching her face for any sign of discomfort. "How are you feeling? Is everything okay?"

"Yeah, I think I'm just really tired. It's a lot of activity and excitement for a pregnant woman," she chuckled.

"Did you drink all the water that I gave you? You have to make sure that you drink enough water. And what about food? When did you last eat?"

She playfully pushed me in the shoulder. "Yes, I drank the water and I already ate. I'm fine, but thank you for thinking of me."

Gods. This woman was going to be the death of me. She was like a little sugar-packed gumdrop; every taste I got had me craving her more. Just being near her gave my darkness a hit of sweetness. A sugar high for a monster. *Her monster.*

"Alright then, we should get moving." I brushed away the sweet thoughts and squared my shoulders. The plan was that I would fly us in a little closer to the castle. From there, we would go on foot. It was too risky to fly the whole way in, knowing that there was a chance Asrael would recognize me in my dragon form. That was a chance I wasn't willing to take, so walking it was.

I shifted and held open my large claw for Saige to carefully climb into. With a couple beats of my powerful wings, we were up in the air, heading the opposite direction to the rest of the dragon army. It was a quick flight since I could cover so much distance in such a short time. The air was cool but not uncomfortable, as we sliced through the darkness.

Landing, Saige scrambled out of my claw and began pulling out my clothing from a bag. It was a disguise of course, an outfit to match that of Asrael's guards, which the dragons had acquired on one of their recent reconnaissance missions. It was nauseating to say the least, having to wear this uniform, but I did what I had to do. Dressed as a guard, nobody would question who I was or who I was escorting, nor my presence on the castle grounds.

"Are you ready?" she asked, linking her arm through mine.

"Ready as I'll ever be."

We stepped out of the woods, onto a brick-paved street. There weren't cars here; most people chose to fly if they needed to go somewhere or used a horse. I'd suggested a horse, but Saige had promptly shut that down, stating that her cervix would fall out of her vagina right now with the amount of bouncing. The visual image of that alone had me shuddering. What would I even do if something like that happened? As much as I wanted to know if that was an actual situation I might have to deal with, I just didn't ask. It seemed even I had my limits, and a cervix falling out sounded like a fucking nightmare.

"It's dead around here," Red observed softly, and I took in the empty streets and the closed shops. It looked like these stores hadn't been opened in ages. We passed a bakery, a bookstore, all your usual shops. All of them had been boarded up, cobwebs hanging in the windows. "Maybe it was just too close to the castle. People decided to flee."

Whatever the reason was for the absence of people in this town, it worked perfectly for us to move through unnoticed. After about fifteen minutes of walking, we came to a bridge that crossed over a small, babbling creek. It wasn't guarded, which I found to be interesting since this was the way to the palace.

"Everyone's probably at the castle because of what's happening this morning," I speculated, and Saige hummed in agreement.

"You're probably right. But let's hurry, just in case. If we get there quickly, maybe we can see the guys." Her voice lifted, full of hope and longing.

As we strolled through the empty town, I started to feel that telltale drain on my magic with each step we took toward the castle. "Do you feel that?"

"Yeah, something is siphoning my power. Asrael must have wards placed. Pretty strong ones to be working from such a distance," she murmured with a frown. "I don't like being powerless."

"I shouldn't shift again until after we get those vaccines from the guys. I might have been able to break free from Asrael's mental hold, but I think the only reason I was able to shift again was because I flew far enough away. I'd rather not chance it and get stuck in that form, unless it's necessary." Which, in the end, it very well may be.

"Well then, let's get those vaccines as soon as possible." She squeezed my hand, and our pace quickened.

I was lucky. I'd gotten to spend time with her over the past day, and just being near her made me feel like the best version of myself. I knew how it felt to be isolated, so I knew exactly what the other guys must be feeling right now. Desperation. The kind so intense that all you could do was think about that person. Try to remember the feel of their hand in yours. The smell of their hair, the sounds they make in the dark. Those were all the things that kept each of us going.

The grass along the creek bank was tall and hid us well as we crept closer to the castle. An idea hit me as I trailed my fingertips over the swaying stalks, and I pulled a few pieces of the foliage, tucking them into my pocket. It was still dark, with only the sounds of the running water over the smooth stones and the gentle wind through the reeds filling the air. It should have been calming, soothing. Instead, it was the opposite. Silence meant plotting, which I knew our enemies were doing every second of every day. Being confronted with that lack of sound as the world continued to turn around us? It was unsettling, to say the least.

We came up to a high stone wall that boasted a large gate blocking the entrance. The sky had started to turn from black to a mix of purples and pinks. I held up a hand to halt Red so that I could take a peek around the corner and see what we were dealing with. I spotted two guards, just on the other side of the gate, talking in hushed voices. I looked back at Saige, holding up two fingers to let her know how many. Turning back to the guards, I cleared my throat and stepped out so that I would be visible to them.

"Who goes there?" one of them called, each of them drawing long swords.

"It's just me," I replied, acting as though I had every right to be here. I was dressed the part, after all. My hand gripped the plants within my pocket as they squinted at me, trying to make out who I was, though their shoulders relaxed when they noticed my uniform.

"What the hell are you doing out there?" one of them questioned, sheathing his sword.

"I was looking for a plant for Balor, one of the healers," I lied, the fib rolling off of my tongue with ease as I recalled the name I'd heard from Saige and Fischer.

The larger guard moved closer. "Well? Did you find it?"

"Yeah, right here." I held up the bits of the tall grass that I'd plucked as we walked through the field earlier. "Is everything still on track for this morning?" I asked as they moved closer to the gate, the smaller man lifting a large key ring to unlock it.

He shrugged. "As far as we know, yeah."

I grinned as the gate swung open. "Perfect. Should be quite the spectacle." My feet carried me through the entrance to the grounds, both guards nodding in agreement at my comment.

"Indeed. Everyone in the castle is to attend. We haven't had a public execution in decades. Come on, Joris, we need to get back to our rounds. Lock that gate up before we get our arses in trouble," the larger guard barked at the smaller one.

Excitement danced beneath my skin as Joris moved past me, taking hold of the gate. His guard buddy for the night stood next to me now, watching him. With both males focused ahead and not behind them, I pounced. My arm wrapped around the bigger guy's neck and I locked the hold with my other arm. He couldn't even get a sound out with how tightly I was squeezing.

Joris was still fiddling with the keys and whistling now as he went about his task. When the big guy I was choking went limp, I gently lowered him to the ground. He wasn't dead, just out cold. Fischer had told us there were several demons here that were loyal to Bram, and I didn't want to take out any innocents.

The sound of the keys hitting the cobblestone ground drew my attention back to Joris. The young male was standing there with his mouth open. "W-what are you doing?" he asked, slowly backing away. I took a step toward him.

"Joris," I said soothingly. Well, as soothingly as I could manage. "Listen to me. I don't want to hurt you, and your partner here is still alive, but there's somebody that needs to come in here now."

The young demon's eyes widened as his back hit the bars of the gate. "Who?" he stammered, fear clearly taking over.

"Me," Red said from behind him, earning an audible gasp as Joris spun around and came face to face with the true queen.

"Your Majesty. Oh, thank the stars." Joris immediately knelt, bowing his head in a sign of respect and fealty.

"Thank you, Joris," Saige said sweetly. "Would you mind opening the gate again and letting me in, please?" Joris tried to grab the keys but his hands were shaking so badly, it was almost comical. Finally, he managed to get his fingers around them tight enough, and he stood, opening the gate once again.

"Thank you. So I take it that you're loyal to Bram?" she asked him, and the young male nodded rapidly.

"Yes, my queen. My family has served the Carlisle family line forever. It was a great honor to be chosen as one of the guards for this castle."

I studied the boy, not trusting him completely because that would make me an idiot, but I was well-versed in being able to tell when people were being dishonest. It didn't appear that Joris was lying.

His eyes were still as round as dinner plates as he looked in wonder at Saige's swollen belly. He'd probably never seen a pregnant female, and my heart softened toward the young demon a bit. He was staring at her like she was an exotic creature—I'd bet that this young male would remember this moment for the rest of his life. This was his chance, and I knew all too well what it was like to want a chance to prove myself, to be a legend.

"Joris," I said, stepping in. Instinctively, my arm wrapped around Red's waist as I pulled her against my side. His eyes darted back and forth between us, nervously.

"But who are *you*?" he whispered, his eyes eventually settling on me.

"I'm Sloane," I replied coolly. "One of the queen's mates."

"Oh sweet gods," Joris stuttered. "This is the best day of my life. This is... I can't..."

Saige took pity on the poor guy and held up her hand. "We're pleased to meet you, Joris, and I want to thank you personally for your service to not only the kingdom, but to this realm." The poor dude looked like he was about to faint.

"The queen is right," I agreed. "However, we're kind of here secretly, and we really need to make it to the courtyard without being detected. Do you think you might be able to help us with that?" I let my stare weigh heavily so he knew how serious I was.

"Of course, it would be my honor. We might need to, um... hide him a little bit though." He pointed down at the other guard, who was still out like a light.

"Who is he loyal to?" I asked.

Joris shook his head. "Not to you."

"Huh, that's unfortunate. Why don't you and the queen get started heading toward wherever you think would be safe? I'll catch up." I dropped a kiss to the top of Saige's red hair. "I'm right behind you, kitten."

Her big green eyes bored into me. I could tell that she wanted to argue, but now was not the time. We couldn't risk leaving a guard who was under Asrael's thumb alive, especially after he'd seen us enter. She knew this as well as I did. So begrudgingly, she clamped her mouth shut and stepped out of my hold, following Joris.

As I stalked toward the unconscious demon, I surveyed my surroundings, spotting a row of full bushes. Perfect. I hooked my forearms under the dude's arms and dragged his limp and extremely heavy body to the hiding spot. Sweat was building on my forehead and I wiped it away, knowing I needed to keep going. I quickly retrieved the small, sharp blade that I had hidden in the waistband of my pants. I didn't take pleasure in killing unarmed men, but I found today that I really didn't give a shit. I didn't hesitate, dropping to one knee and slicing his throat like it was a stick of butter.

He would be the first casualty of many today, and it was best that I prepared myself for that now. I knew things were only getting started from here and it was going to get a whole lot bloodier. Wiping the knife on the man's shirt, I tucked away my blade and ran to catch up. Both Saige and the guard glanced at me from the corner of their eyes.

"Where to now?" I asked, not even acknowledging that I'd just murdered a man in cold blood.

A sound suddenly pierced the quiet. A deep, booming bass, forming a cadence.

"What the hell is that, Joris?" I barked.

The young guard's face paled quickly. "We need to hurry. It's beginning."

Saige and I shared a look, our fears silently passing between us. "Take me to my men," she demanded.

"Yes, my queen." Joris spun on his heel and took off, moving much quicker now. We dipped and ducked and snuck through corridors, all of them completely vacant.

The sound of drums bled through the stone walls, casting a malevolent beat. I knew we were getting closer as the rhythm grew louder; it felt as though my heart had synced up with the drums. Saige was breathing heavily from the quick pace we were keeping, but she refused to slow. She wouldn't stop now, knowing how close we were and what was on the line.

"Wait here," Joris said, as we met a dead end in the hallway.

There were a couple windows that were a little higher up and allowed me to peek outside. The courtyard was right there. From our vantage point, we were behind everyone, but in the predawn light, I had a straight shot to see the platform. Khol, Faris, and Bram were lined up, shoulder to shoulder, their hands bound.

"Fuck," I cursed, letting myself drop back down.

"What did you see? Tell me," my mate demanded, and I knew I couldn't lie.

"There's a platform," I started, running my hands through my hair. "Your father, Faris, and Bram are all standing up there, in the middle of a huge crowd. There are two huge demons in the back corner pounding on drums. I didn't see Asrael yet."

"So we're not too late." I wasn't sure what I'd expected from her. Maybe tears. Maybe, I don't know... screaming, raging, trying to get past me to run outside. What I hadn't expected was the look of absolute fury that now morphed her normally pleasant features.

Her eyes narrowed to slits as her brows lowered. Her mouth fell open slightly as her jaw cocked over to one side, like she was processing what I'd just explained.

"Red," I said gently, placing my arms on her shoulders. "Talk to me." I could feel tremors rippling through her body as anger flooded her senses. "Saige," I growled. "Talk to me."

Suddenly, the tremors stopped completely, and her eyebrows raised, her mouth closed, and her eyes returned to their usual state. "I'm fine," she replied calmly. "Perfectly fine. Where did Joris go?"

She was a lot of things, but fine was not one of them. Not in this moment, and certainly not after that transformation I'd just witnessed. Before I got a chance to question her further, or to really ensure that she was focused enough to go through with our plans, Joris reappeared.

"This way. Quickly," he urged, disappearing through a door.

Saige didn't wait, practically running after him, leaving me to chase after her. Fucking hell. I didn't know what was about to go down. Though even if I had known, there was nothing any of us could have done any differently.

Fischer

Chapter Eighteen

Cam, Kai, Balor, and myself spent what little time we had gathering the loyalists and going over our plan. The Exiled had left on their mission to free the dragons, and we were hopeful that we'd hear something from them soon.

Surprisingly, we had over a hundred demons, both male and female, show up to the large conference room, eager to join us and willing to do whatever we asked of them. We might just stand a chance with these larger numbers. Not all of them were the greatest fighters, but that didn't matter because we had plenty who were. The ones who weren't would be useful in helping the injured and keeping a lookout for incoming threats.

At the first pound of a booming drum, everybody paused and the mood grew solemn. It was time. I let my gaze sweep across the group. Our small army had to be strong enough—there was no other alternative.

Cam whistled, gaining the focus of everybody in the room as they waited anxiously for his instruction. "Alright. This is it. I would just like to take a moment to thank each and every one of you for being here, and embarking on this battle with us today. By being here, you're taking a stand. You're willing to sacrifice your anonymity. By standing with us today, you will be known as loyalists to Bram, and there are many risks with that. Not all of us will walk out of this with our lives. What we're fighting for—to rid your kingdom of this evil and oppression? It's worth everything. I know each of you is here because you believe that to be true."

Cam paused, scanning the crowd. "If any of you wish to go, you're free to do so." It felt as though the room as a whole held its breath. Nobody moved, and Cam nodded.

"Thank you. Remember to stay alert and watch for anything suspicious. We're going to go out that door and blend in with the crowd. Nobody will suspect anything. We'll wait for the dragons to create a distraction, and that's when we'll attack. If you're feeling scared right now? Good. Just know that's what our enemy will be feeling as he faces his end in a very short while. Take your fear and mold it, turn it into something useful. I'm sure each and every one of you is sick of feeling afraid. It's time to feel something different. It's time to take back your freedom, your magic, and your happiness. Let your determination fuel you today."

His eyes moved through the crowd. I knew he was making eye contact with as many of these demons as he possibly could. Cam was an excellent leader, and people often felt connected to him. His energy was contagious. A simple act of looking a person dead in the eye, knowing that you were going into a dangerous situation together, it created a connection. It let people know that those they were fighting for—and fighting beside—actually gave a shit. They weren't just nameless, faceless soldiers in the crowd.

"Balor." Cam raised his voice as he called out to the doctor across the room. "Open the doors."

Balor nodded and gripped the two iron handles, pulling the wide wooden doors open. Fresh air from the courtyard drifted through the doorway, giving everybody a taste. Within these walls right now, we were captured. Birds in a cage. Fish in a net.

A bear in a trap. But out there... Out there, we are going to be free.

I could see the crowd was already growing in the courtyard. So as our people started filing out, they melded right into the masses. Perfect.

Cam had come to a halt a few feet from the door, his green gaze scanning the scene. As I stepped up beside one of my oldest friends, a strange sensation of déjà vu hit me. Like we'd been here before. I suppose in many ways, we kind of had. All of the missions, yeah, but even before that. As kids, sneaking over to each other's houses, standing up to bullies together, checking out girls—and in my case, boys.

We did everything together. The four of us. All roads led us here.

"Well?" I asked Cam. "What are you thinking?" Kai stepped closer so he could hear what we were discussing.

"I'm thinking that it's time to fuck this shit up, brother." Cam smirked. It had been a long time since I'd seen that expression on his face, and despite feeling fucked up and not quite like myself, I found my own lips twisting up into a grin.

Kai bounced on the balls of his feet, shaking out his hands. "Fuck, I'm excited. I need to burn off some energy."

I snorted. "Yeah, like we couldn't tell."

'Guppy.' Saige's voice floated through my head.

"Hold on, guys." I let myself sink into my psyche. *'Are you guys here?'* I asked her, my heart picking up speed as I waited for her answer.

'Yes,' came her instant reply, and I breathed a deep sigh of relief. *'We were able to see the front of the platform when looking out of an arched window in the left wing of the castle. We're in a storage closet now around the corner.'*

'That's good, sweetheart. Alright. One of us will come to you, because we need to give you these vaccines. So just stay put for a few more minutes, and then you guys will be able to use your magic.'

She murmured her agreement, saying she'd be listening and watching for one of us. I quickly relayed our conversation to Cam and Kai.

"Who's gonna go?" Kai asked, looking between us.

"I think you should," I told him honestly. "I need to be out there. I need to be able to use my powers to assess what we're dealing with, and not only that, I'm the mental link between all of us. So I need to see what's going on firsthand."

"What do you think, Cam?" Kai asked, his eyes gleaming with hope.

"I agree—you should go, Kai. I'm the leader of this makeshift army. It wouldn't be right if I wasn't out there." Cam dipped his large hand in the pocket of his trousers and retrieved a handful of syringes, placing them carefully into Kai's upturned palm. "There's some extras, in case you need them. Go fast, Kai. After you give them these, you know where we'll be. Kiss her for me." Cam spun on his heel, and marched out the door.

"Good luck, brother," I told Kai, surprising myself when I pulled him into a hug. I still didn't like the idea of anybody touching me, but I also couldn't stand the thought that I might not get another chance if something went wrong.

Kai purred, squeezing me tightly, and patting me on the back. "We got this. Be strong." His voice didn't waver. His confidence was unbreakable.

Stepping back, we looked into each other's eyes and nodded at the same time. Then with a playful smile, Kai turned and ran. I watched as his back disappeared from sight, before turning to follow Cam.

My footfalls were heavy as I walked toward the call of the courtyard, anxious about the battle that was coming. The anticipation that was swirling in the air guided me. So many emotions calling me, pushing me, driving me. This time, I didn't push them away. I didn't try to shield myself. Whatever I was feeling, I needed to. I stopped just shy of the line separating the stone prison I'd been held in and the open air of freedom.

Steeling my spine, I stepped out, ready to do whatever it took.

We couldn't be defeated.

Victory was the only option.

Saige

Chapter Nineteen

I found myself standing within a small, windowless room that held shelves of cleaning supplies, obviously a stock closet for the maids within the castle. I'd felt Fisher's presence in my mind a few moments after we entered the room, and I called out to him. Sloane and Joris were engaged in a conversation, so I let myself focus completely on my mate who I hadn't seen in weeks. Knowing he was so close and yet I still wasn't able to see him was a cruel type of torture.

I described to him the window where we had been standing, looking out over the courtyard. Since we were just around the corner, I knew we'd have to send Joris out there to be on the lookout. When Fisher's presence faded away, I found both Sloane and Joris staring at me curiously.

"Well?" Sloane asked. "What did he say?" He knew without me even having to say that I'd just been having an internal conversation. My mouth twitched, wanting to smile despite the tense situation we were in, because we were at that point in our relationship. The point where we just vibed, instinctively knowing what the other was doing.

"One of the guys is coming here; I'm not sure who. They're bringing the vaccines! So as soon as they get here, we'll need to get that injected."

Sloane's eyebrows lifted. "Are you sure about this? What's even in this vaccine? How do we know it's safe? I don't know if I like the sound of that, Red." Sloane was spitting a million words a minute, and I swallowed my indignation because I knew he was only worried for my safety and that of the babies. Still, if I had a chance to get my magic back and use it today, to save someone, to save my *family*—wasn't that a risk I was willing to take?

I put my hand on his chest, to calm him. "Okay, let's just take a breath for a second. I don't know the answers to any of that and honestly, I understand where you're coming from. We'll have to ask them when they get here what they know about it. Can we try to stay calm and listen for footsteps? Joris?" I turned my focus to the young demon. "Do you think you can step outside the door and keep an eye out? I told Fish that we could see the platform from where we were standing, but now we're in this closet so I don't want them to accidentally miss us."

"Of course, my queen," Joris answered without hesitation. Immediately, he walked outside, and let the door swing shut.

"So they're still okay?" Sloane asked me.

"Yeah," I replied. "According to Fischer, everybody's fine. They were able to gather a group of fighters, and they're gonna mix in with the crowd. So once we get vaccinated, we can go out there too."

"Red, listen," Sloane started, but I didn't hear anything further, because suddenly I was gasping. There was a surging energy within my chest, and with each second, the feeling just got stronger and stronger.

"Kai," I whispered. I barely had time to spin around before the door was pushed open, my Alpha taking up the entire width.

"Cub, thank the gods." In two strides, Kai's body was pressed firmly against mine. He was shaking. Or maybe that was me. Or maybe it was both of us. All I could do was chant his name, hoping to the stars that he was really here, and that by speaking his name it would make him real. That I would be safe to blink my eyes and know that he wasn't going to disappear.

He felt quite a bit thinner than I remembered, and I pulled my tear-soaked cheek away from his chest to peer up at him. His eyes were shiny with his own tears as he cupped my face with his hands.

"Never again, Cub. I can never do this again. Do you understand? Every second I'm not with you is agony." I barely had a chance to process his words before his mouth was crashing against mine.

The steady beat of the drums was still audible here in our little closet, though it was hard for me to hear them over the sound of my racing heart in my ears. I moaned into Kai's kiss as his tongue brushed against mine. A reunion, and a promise.

Leaning back, I broke our kiss because I needed to look him over. I needed to see that he was actually safe, that he was unharmed. My eyes trailed down his frame, not finding any visible injury, and relief flooded my body. The worst thing about the separation had been the things I'd thought of in the dark. The way my mind would betray me, making me dream up all of these horrible, terrifying scenarios. To find him like this in one piece…

More tears slipped out. "You're okay?" I asked in disbelief.

"I am now," he replied, giving me one of his signature playful grins that never ceased to send the butterflies in my stomach into a fluttering swarm. Kai's eyes lifted over my shoulder. A genuine, full smile broke out, and I knew that he was seeing Sloane. A whine was all the warning Sloane received before Kai darted around me and pounced, taking both of them to the floor.

"Gods dammit, Kai," Sloane complained, though there was laughter in his tone. The two men embraced one another on the cold, dusty stone floor in a supply closet. How we got here, I would never know, but I knew I'd never forget this scene.

"Oh shut up, Sloaney Baloney. I know you've missed me." Without warning, Kai planted his lips full on Sloane's mouth, making my mouth drop open in shock. Sloane squirmed, but he wasn't fooling me. He wasn't actually bothered by this kiss. It only lasted a second, and Kai jumped back up, extending a hand to one of his best friends, and helping him up to his feet.

"Are you done kissing everybody now, you overgrown housecat?" Sloane asked with a huff, pretending to be indifferent.

"For now," Kai teased back. "Look, we don't have a lot of time; I just couldn't help myself. But I do have these." I watched as Kai reached into his pocket and produced two syringes.

"What are these exactly, Kai?" Sloane looked down at the vaccines as if they were going to jump up and bite him.

"We don't know much about them, and I know that's not ideal. To make a long story short, I was gravely injured." I couldn't help it—my hand flew to my mouth. Kai's eyes moved to mine as he reached for my hand, taking it into his own and bending down to press a kiss to it. "As you can see, I'm alive, and that's thanks to this right here."

"And to me," a squeaky voice called. Sloane and I looked at each other, our eyes wide.

"Who the fuck said that?" Sloane barked.

"Oh," Kai chuckled. "That would be Napoleon, and he's right. Without him, I definitely wouldn't be standing here right now. He also dosed himself, and now he can speak to all of us, bizarrely enough."

Napoleon scurried out of the pocket on Kai's chest and perched himself on his shoulder. "Good, giving credit where credit is due is basically a soldier's unwritten oath." His little black head turned from Kai and landed on me. "Saige," he said. "You're looking fierce today, like a true warrior. Where did you procure such a fashionable gown befitting a battle?"

I couldn't help it. I laughed. "I had it made for her, Mouse," Sloane piped up, taking his own credit where it was due.

"Huh," Napoleon grunted. "Well, I wasn't aware that you had an eye for such things. Here I thought that all you were good for was brooding and being a smart-mouthed dragon. It's good to know you have other talents, should the need arise."

"Napoleon, that's enough," Kai chastised, snatching the little mouse from his shoulder and holding him in his hand. "We need to focus. The vaccines are made with Nox stone. We don't really know what else is in them. But like I said, I was at death's door when Cam administered this to me, and I was completely healed and full of magic within two minutes. The same went for Fischer when we found him."

"What do you mean? He was hurt?" I questioned, wringing my hands together nervously.

Kai paused. His mouth opened and then shut abruptly as he considered his words. "We all went through different things while we were here. Let's just say it wasn't an easy time for anyone. But right now, you need to take these shots, and we need to get our fucking asses in that courtyard, because we want to be out there when Asrael starts his speech."

I could feel Sloane stiffen beside me. "And how do you know this vaccine is safe for a pregnant woman? For *our pregnant woman?* You think we should give this to her?"

Kai shrugged. "I don't know what other option we have, man. I gotta be honest, we're outnumbered at this point. If the dragons don't show, and if Asrael has more support than we thought, this whole thing is going to go up in smoke. I think we need every advantage we can get. I don't think that this is going to harm her or the babies. If anything, it's used for healing. Not to mention, even if she doesn't use her magic for offensive fighting, to deny her the ability to use it to defend herself would be plain stupid..." My Alpha looked at me and quickly added, "Unless you don't want to take it. Of course, then we can always—"

The door suddenly swung open, and we all jumped.

"Balor, what's going on?" Kai questioned, concerned.

"I realized I should come find the queen, to check her over quickly before we head out there? Is that alright with everyone?"

Balor replied, but he was looking right at me, which I appreciated.

"Hello again, Balor." I smiled, placing my hands over my stomach.

He bowed with a flourish. "It is an honor to see you again."

"So this is your doctor?" Sloane asked, stepping around the demon and sizing him up. I shook my head at his alpha male posturing.

"Yes, Sloane. He took excellent care of me and our babies. It was thanks to him there was a weapon beneath my pillow that I was able to use to escape with you."

Sloane grunted. "Thank you." A small smile tugged at my mouth at his begrudging thank you.

"You are most welcome. It is my duty and pleasure to serve the queen, her mates, and her children. This won't take but a moment—I just need to place my hands against your belly. You remember from before?"

I nodded. "Of course." My hands fell away, giving him access. Kai and Sloane were both watching eagerly, ready to hear Balor's professional opinion. He extended his palms and they began glowing softly as his magic sensed whatever he was searching for.

"Perfect. They're perfect!" he gushed, clearly pleased with his findings.

"How long does she have left? Can you estimate a due date?" Sloane asked, and Kai nodded eagerly. I held my breath. A due date. Part of the reason we'd come here was to get answers about my pregnancy and yet, I still didn't have a date or even an estimate.

Balor was focused on his task, the babies moving within me as though they sensed his presence. "No more than a week. That's my best guess."

"*A week?* Seven days?" I balked at the idea, but not for long. We had to get out to the courtyard. I'd just have to clamp my thighs together and keep these babies in until it was safe to deliver them.

Sloane looked emotionless at the news—though I suspected he might be frozen with shock—and Kai jumped for me with a wide grin. "A week, Cub. Oh gods, I can't wait to see them." He bent down and kissed my stomach. "At some point in the next seven days, little ladies, you'll finally get to meet your favorite father. I'm going to kiss you both and sniff your heads. Fair warning."

Balor cleared his throat, and Kai straightened, completely comfortable with his private discussion being overheard. I loved that about him. He was so unapologetically himself. Flaws and all.

"Is the vaccine safe for her?" Sloane stepped up against my side, linking his hand with mine as he addressed my doctor.

"Indeed, it is. This is a medical and magical breakthrough for our community. Not only for demons, but for any magically inclined creature. Asrael commissioned it, wanting to create something that would protect him from being at risk of being controlled by anyone else. This is everyone's best bet at getting out of today alive. I don't mean to be so blunt, my queen." Balor tipped his head in apology, but I waved him off.

"I'm well aware of the risks involved today. You don't need to apologize. I want the vaccine. I want to be able to help against Asrael, and keep me and the babies safe." I looked to my two mates to see if they had any objection, but they both nodded. Turning back to Balor, I smiled weakly. I was nervous even though I was trying to be brave. "Please, inject me."

I wiggled the sleeve of my dress down to reveal my upper arm, and Balor quickly administered the shot. I hissed at the slight wince, earning a low warning growl from Sloane. I gave Balor a look that I hoped said 'I'm so sorry for my overbearing mate.' Kai distracted my dragon by getting him prepped for his own little stabby stab.

"You're all set." Balor tossed the syringe into the trash and reached for the door. "I better get back out there. It truly is great to see you again."

"Thank you—for everything," I replied, meaning it with every fiber of my being. If Balor hadn't assisted with keeping me unconscious… I couldn't even think about what might've happened. With a nod, he slipped out. *Stars, please let that demon survive today.*

"It has to be injected into a dense muscle. Since your brain is pretty protected, we'll go with the upper arm," Kai joked, and Sloane rolled his eyes as he pulled up the sleeve on his shirt.

"The brain is an organ, you fool," he grumbled, earning a chuckle from me and Kai.

"Just a little poke," Kai sang out, ignoring Sloane's attempt at ruining his joke. He sank the needle into his arm and pushed down the plunger. "Alrighty then. That's that." He pulled the needle back and put the cap back on, tossing it into a trash bin in the corner.

"Can we get out there now?" I was antsy and I couldn't stay in this room for another second. I needed eyes on them, needed to see what we were up against. Plus, I really wanted to hear what kind of bullshit Asrael was going to try and spew. Both of my mates nodded, just as ready as I was.

Kai opened the door and we found Joris, waiting eagerly for instructions. "You can come with us," I told him. "Which way will lead us to the courtyard?"

"Follow me." We followed Joris, taking a couple turns before we came to a large open archway that led directly to a small garden area in the corner of the courtyard. There were already so many demons here. There was an uneasy edge to the air. People were tense. Whether that was because of the heaviness of the situation, an execution of three men, or because they were on our side and were preparing for a battle that might kill them, I wasn't sure.

Whatever the reason, the air was thick with it, and it was hard to take a full breath. I hadn't had time to find a wig or something to disguise my hair, but luckily it did look different. It was a good deal shorter than it was before I cut it off to escape Asrael. Standing here in the back, I felt safer knowing there was a chance he might not recognize me from such a distance.

It was officially dawn now, and it was at that moment that the beating of the drums sped up. They were pounding so loudly now that I could feel the bass in my toes. The crowd shifted slightly, giving me a direct line of sight to the platform, and it felt like all of the air in my lungs rushed out of me.

Khol and Faris looked terrible. It was obvious that they hadn't been held in the best of conditions. Bram, by far, looked the best, and I assumed that that was just because of his royal status. All three of them had scraggly beards and wild hair. Their hands were bound as they stood side by side. Khol's expression was absolutely murderous—I'd never seen him look like that before. I bet that was what he'd looked like back when he was a warrior for King Thane.

Bram had a mask of indifference on, even his eyes looking void of feeling. Faris was fidgeting, shifting on his feet, twisting his fingers. And was he... I looked closer. *Okay, yes. He's snapping and snarling at people. Oh moon maidens, this is not good.* I could see his fangs, which made me wonder if he had his super speed power. He must not though, because there's no way he would just be standing there if he did.

Kai and Sloane stood on either side of me, and when I heard Sloane's soft chuckle, I looked over to see a tiny flame on each of his fingertips on his left hand.

Suddenly, the drums cut off, the last powerful sounds echoing around the courtyard before they drifted off into nothingness. Silence fell across the crowd. There were two enormous doors in the back of the courtyard that were suddenly opening up, and a line of guards marched in. One of them called out, "King Asrael, King of Besmet."

And then there he was, striding through those doors, the most narcissistic, posturing psycho that I'd ever met. He was dressed impeccably in his king's regalia. Sharp, black pants with tall boots, all of which had gold trim. He wore a cape that was a deep blue with gold accents that flailed out behind him as he walked.

Everybody was starting to kneel for the king. I gritted my teeth together, realizing that I was going to have to comply. Otherwise, I would stand out and that was the last thing I needed. Kneeling as a pregnant woman should be banned. *Forcing pregnant women to kneel should be an act that would earn you severe punishment. If I were truly a queen, that would be rule number one. Fuck the patriarchy and their ability to piss wherever, and never worrying about how they'll get their big freaking asse—*

My ragey thoughts were interrupted when thankfully, my mates each gripped my waist and helped me lower myself. I hadn't had any time at all to adjust to this new body. My center of gravity was all fucked up, and I was really tired of peeing my pants a tiny bit every time I did anything physical—sneezing, coughing, laughing, walking, it didn't matter. They were just gonna have to start calling me Saige, piss pants witch. I guess it came with the territory.

Everyone in attendance sank to their knees as Asrael waltzed up to the platform like the king he pretended he was. It was nauseating to have to be down here on my knees. I never thought I would be in this position, bowing down to this evil demon who had completely fucked up my simple, perfectly normal existence. Well, I guess it wasn't actually all that simple or normal, not knowing what I knew now. That I'd been essentially tethered to Emerald Lakes by my evil ass mother. *Gods, is this rage part of being pregnant? I'm not an angry person!*

All too soon, Asrael was in front of the three men who meant so much to me. He held both hands in the air, looking every bit the pompous, narcissistic fuck that he was. He signaled, giving everybody permission to rise from their knees. Like he was a god. He was about to learn just how ungodly he was.

Sloane and Kai basically lifted me off the ground, and I didn't have any objections to that. My right knee was already smarting from the stone ground that it'd been digging into.

I was glad I'd taken the vaccine because truly, there was no way that I could let them go into this fight alone, not when I had power that was arguably stronger than anybody else's here. I wished I'd had more time to practice and fully gauge the limits of my magic. I made a promise to myself right then and there that when this was over, I wanted Khol and my mates to train me to be able to use my power to its full extent. What good was all of this magic if I didn't know how to wield it properly?

"People of Besmet, I welcome you this morning. We are all here today to bear witness to justice being meted out against these three criminals. They are traitors to the crown, and traitors will not be tolerated within my kingdom." There was a mixture of cheers and whispers that dispersed through the crowd. Asrael paused, giving the people a chance for his words to sink in. This was nothing but a production to him. He was manipulative enough to use every trick he had. "This is not the way I hoped I would begin my rule. My nephew and I could have made a great team. But he wants nothing to do with me. He would rather die than see our great realm enter its best years ever, thanks to me." This time, the booing and the jeers took over the whispering and the cheering.

The booing quickly died down, but I scanned the crowd nervously because it seemed like nearly everyone had participated in it. Hopefully, that was just all for show and we weren't really that outnumbered. Asrael began spewing more bullshit about how awesome he was, and how much of a dick Bram was. To be honest, I tuned it all out. I found I actually didn't give a shit what he had to say after all. I'd wanted to get out here, and now his voice was making me nauseous.

Trying to refocus, I couldn't help but search through the crowd, looking for Cam and Fischer, but I didn't find them anywhere. That didn't surprise me, because if I could find them, then I'm sure Asrael and his guards would be able to find them too.

The skin at the back of my neck prickled with awareness—somebody was watching me. Glancing to my right, I met a pair of cold blue eyes. His hair was light blond, and his appearance was striking, if not slightly intimidating. He was every bit as tall as Cam, but slightly leaner. His cheekbones were high on his face, leading to a prominent nose that I'm sure when he was younger, probably looked too large for his face.

Clapping broke out around us, and my eyes were still locked with this stranger. It was a strange connection. It was almost as though I knew him on some level. My eyes dropped to his hand at his hip. He was clutching something. *Is that a mask?* Before I got a chance to further evaluate that, I heard Kai mutter a curse under his breath. Just before I broke my stare with the blond demon, he winked at me, flashing a grin that was much too sinister to be confused with playful.

"What is it?" I said to Kai.

"Didn't you hear what he just said?" Sloane whispered.

"Uhhhhh," I stammered, "Um, well, no." They both gaped at me, like 'how the hell are you not listening to what this man is saying when he holds our future in his hands?!' "What did he say?"

"He said that he's going to start with Bram. The punishment is beheading."

I'd never know for sure if that was really the moment that the vaccine kicked in, or if it was simply my heart exploding within my chest, unable to take any more abuse from men who thought they could push me around and change my life without my consent. All I knew is that I was fucking done.

Instead of my knees going weak, I felt them stiffening. Instead of my hands shaking in fear at the thought of losing Bram, they clenched into fists. I wanted to scream. I wanted to fight. I didn't respond to Sloane or Kai. Instead, I turned to look up at the platform.

Two of Asrael's guards were carrying a large wooden stump. A third trailed behind them with a massive axe. The magic in my body started making its reappearance at a low simmer. The sight of that stump and that weapon quickly turned the simmer up to a slow boil. Khol and Faris were raging against their restraints, but couldn't break free; they'd been secured too tightly. A group of guards was working on releasing Bram just enough for him to walk over to where they'd unceremoniously dropped the stump. Asrael was parading around on the platform, trying to hype up the crowd. It was sickening. I could feel tiny sparks of magic at my fingertips, like little jolts of electricity, as it begged to be unleashed.

Soon, but not yet. As Bram was brought over to where the execution was to happen, Asrael stepped up before him. "Do you have any last words, nephew?" he taunted. I could see Bram's upper lip lifting at the blatant disrespect.

I knew that if he could, he would rip the other demon's head off within seconds. His magic was still being contained, and he wouldn't be free until either Asrael was dead, or one of us was able to get him a vaccine.

Bram straightened to his full height, looking every bit as devastatingly handsome as he had when I'd first met him within a dream. It felt like so long ago, when in reality, it had only been months. We'd found each other in a fantasy of our own making. A dreamscape that was, and always would be, ours.

Turning away from Asrael, Bram faced the crowd. "The only thing I would want to say today," he started, his loud voice carrying through the air, reaching everybody's ears, "is that, given the chance, I would've loved to be your king. It was what I was raised for, and I always knew that one day it would be my role. I'm here to tell you today that even if we weren't gathered together for such an exciting event..." He paused and chuckled, the crowd joining in with him. "I couldn't be your king."

The silence that descended in the courtyard was engulfing. All over, there were sharp intakes of breath, blinking eyes of disbelief, and looks of confusion as his words were processed.

"I was raised to be your king. I always thought I had no other choice, but then something changed. I met the love of my existence. My true fated mate. I know that each and every one of you understands how rare and precious that is."

My heart was seriously going to explode. I saw so many in the crowd nodding in agreement at his words. If there was something demons could agree on, it was certainly the dynamics of a mate relationship.

"Over the past month, I've given a lot of consideration to my life. If I wasn't a king, what would I be? I have no siblings, no family to speak of—aside from an uncle who's here today to murder me for no reason." One of the guards took a step forward, his hand on the hilt of his weapon. To my surprise, Asrael waved him down, motioning for him to back off. "So what would I do if I wasn't dying today? I still feel a responsibility and a love for all the demons within Besmet, and it's because of that it's become clear to me that a monarchy is no longer in the best interest of the realm."

Well, that got the people going, including some of the guards. Everybody just exploded. Yelling, cheering, crying. It was all of the things all at once, and the noise was deafening.

Asrael looked completely murderous, his jaw clenched in his face red. "That's enough!" he barked to the guards, signaling for them to grab Bram and get him in position.

"It's time for change! Fight for what you believe in!" Bram

bellowed, and I felt like I was choking on my fucking heart. I thought it was just going to break right through my ribs. My power was at a full-fledged boil now. Little bubbles of heat popping, splattering. I was at the point that if something didn't happen to break this tension, I was going to overflow.

There were no signs of the dragons yet, and I could feel my stomach sinking as Bram fought the guards. There were five of them attempting to restrain him, and when one of them kicked him hard in the back of the knee, forcing him to hit the ground, the others didn't hesitate to pull him forward, grinding his cheek into the wood.

I started moving before I even realized what I was doing. I could hear Sloane and Kai yelling at me, but it was distant, like I was underwater. I couldn't be touched. I slipped through demon after demon, moving for the platform, surprised that nobody had grabbed me to stop me. It was then that I looked down, and noticed the faint green light that was surrounding me like an aura. It pulsed with each step I took.

There was so much going on though, that either I hadn't been noticed yet, or people just didn't seem to care. They couldn't take their eyes off of what was happening on the platform. I couldn't fault them, because neither could I. Bram was locked in place, his face turned toward the crowd. His eyes lifted briefly, and that was all it took. Our gazes crashed together, like the ocean meeting the sand during a hurricane. It was violent and all-consuming. I saw his mouth. I knew he was screaming *"No,"* but I couldn't hear him, and I didn't know why he would be saying no. There was no way that I was going to let this happen.

Suddenly, a sound that I could only describe as hundreds of freight trains boomed around us, completely freezing everybody in their place as we looked around, searching for the source. Even Asrael looked momentarily distracted. A wicked smile bloomed on my face as Bram's eyes locked on mine.

The dragons were here. This was the moment we'd been waiting for.

Most of the crowd was still looking up at the sky when I saw Asrael lift the axe above his head.

Oh gods. NO.

Bram saw it as well, and his frantic, panicked eyes pinned me, spearing me right through my heart. All I saw was red, and just like that, I bubbled over. No lid could contain the force that was now swirling through me like a tornado. My hands shot out in front of me as I screamed; my wings snapped out at the same time, as did my horns and my tail. Thick vines flew from my body, finding their way to Asrael's axe. They stopped it an inch from my mate's neck. I could feel that fighting had broken out around us, but I ignored it, yanking hard on the vines and pulling the axe from Asrael's hands.

I knew I'd never forget the confusion on his face as I used my vines to snap the axe back and crash it against his forehead. Unfortunately, it wasn't the sharp end, but it was hard enough that he stumbled backward, meaning Bram was able to scramble free, the nearby guards currently distracted by the fighting.

I had never felt this much magic in my life. Maybe it was because this was life or death, or maybe the vaccine was causing it, maybe the pregnancy... Either way, I was nowhere close to being done. I had a gods damn vendetta and I was going to ensure that justice was carried out.

I sent my vines out next to Khol and Faris, who were both staring at me wide-eyed, like they were hallucinating. My vines wrapped around their binds, quickly working to untie them. The moment their ropes fell free, Faris leaped off the platform, jumping into the battle, while Khol stayed on the platform. He and Bram began to circle Asrael, their eyes promising murder.

There was so much fighting. It was chaos. Demons were falling left and right. Still and lifeless, if they were lucky. The screams of the ones who weren't would haunt me for the rest of my life. My vines became a living thing, an extension of my body. They knew what to do without being told. I was in danger, and they knew exactly how to protect me, and still, there was so much power.

Sloane stumbled beside me, and three demon guards surrounded him. My dragon was giving them one hell of a fight. The amount of blood sprayed across his outfit told me that he'd already had his fair share of kills. One of the demons managed to get a cheap shot in, as the other approached Sloane from behind with his knife raised.

A thought popped into my mind—if I was able to bring Fischer back from the dead, would I also be able to send somebody there to the other side? My magic had always been about life and growth, but that wasn't what I needed from it today. All I knew was that I couldn't lose any of my mates. Anybody who was a threat needed to be eliminated.

I flung my hand out in front of me, aiming for the man with the knife as magic surged through my fingertips. The demon froze, the knife dropping to the ground with a clatter as Sloane regained his bearings and quickly killed the other two guards. I watched in horror as the demon turned into a wilted version of himself. He was exactly like a plant, one who'd been left out in ninety-degree weather for days on end with no water. Sloane looked from the guard to me, speechless.

Now that I knew what I was capable of, I completely let loose. They were all going to regret the day that they ever thought they could take what was mine.

Kai

Chapter Twenty

Gods, I was going to need a fresh pair of underwear after this shitshow was over with. When Saige had decided to walk toward the stage, leaving Sloane and I looking at each other like a couple of idiots, we had to let her go. I mean, to follow her would have only drawn more attention, and that would have been potentially devastating for our entire plan. Then when she started glowing like a frickin' firefly, all I could do was stand there and watch, because I had no idea what was happening.

I could feel through our bond that she was furious. She was feeling protective; the need to make sure that her mates were safe was overriding all logical thinking. All hell broke loose on the platform, and I nearly pissed myself when I saw Asrael heaving that massive axe above his head.

So many things were happening at once. It was hard to know where to look, but my eyes stayed glued to that flash of steel as Asrael brought his weapon down toward Bram's neck. I wondered if this was what having a heart attack felt like, because I was pretty sure at least ten years of my life had just been shaved off.

"Good thing she took that vaccine," I heard Sloane hiss under his breath, as we watched the vines sneak out from her, wrapping around the axe before smashing it back into Asrael's head.

"Fucking hell," I gasped, amazed at the sheer power that she was possessing. Not only that, but my Sprout was not normally a violent woman. Seeing her go to these lengths to defend one of her mates was hands down the number one hottest thing I'd ever seen.

A chorus of ominous, deep roars tore through the sky, and I knew our moment had arrived. Had Saige not stepped in when she did, the dragons would have been too late. "Go," I told Sloane. "I need to get these vaccines to Khol, Bram, and Faris. Go help our girl." Sloane was already diving through the crowd before I'd even finished my sentence.

Fighting was all around me. But, thankfully, I had a pocket full of needles—something that might help win a favorable outcome for our side. I darted through the mob, weaving through arcs of blood spraying through the air, and trying to ignore the grunts and groans of injured or dying demons. I tried to block it all out, just focusing on what was ahead of me.

I intercepted Faris right as he dove from the platform. He froze, his eyes widening as he recognized me. "Holy shit," he laughed, and then abruptly ducked as a knife sailed through the air, narrowly missing his head. "Whew, that was a close one."

I shook my head, a smile on my face as I pulled him against me, giving him a quick hug. "I'm so fucking glad to see you, brother." And that was the truth. Physically, he hadn't been a part of us for very long, but he'd already weaseled his way into my heart, and I couldn't imagine our family being complete without his crazy ass.

I glanced over his shoulder, seeing an approaching guard. So I spun Faris quickly. He launched forward and ripped the demon's throat clean out, completely covering the lower half of his mouth and neck with a deep red.

"Gods, that felt good," he groaned, stretching out his neck.

"I need to talk to you," I told him, positioning my back against his for optimal visibility around us. "Listen, I'm gonna pass you a needle. I need you to pop the cap off and inject yourself with it into a dense muscle. I don't have time to answer questions. Everyone else has already taken it, except for Khol and Bram. It'll restore your magic—you'll get your speed back and your ability to do whatever creepy mind fuckery shit you do."

We moved in a circle together, fighting off enemies as I reached for his hand and slipped him the syringe.

"Is it going to hurt?" he asked with a whimper, and I turned my neck slightly, wishing I could give him a 'what the fuck' look because seriously, we didn't have time for this.

"No," I told him, "it's not going to hurt. Just hurry up and get it in you."

My fist smashed into the face of a male demon who thought he could sneak up and pull a fast one, and I could've sworn I heard Faris chuckling under his breath over my last statement. Something along the lines of, "Is that what you say to Thunder Daddy?" I couldn't even be mad though. Fucking cute ass, innocent-looking, evil little vampire boy.

"Oh my gods! That hurt, Kai. Why didn't you tell me?"

I rolled my eyes, sending another demon to the ground. "It's just a little pinch."

"Okay, it's done. But my dick kind of hurts, like still. Is that normal?"

We'd cleared all the guards that were around us, so I was finally able to turn around and face him. "Your dick?" I questioned. "Why the hell does your dick hurt?"

"Well, because of that needle," he replied, looking at me like I'd lost my mind. "You said dense muscle."

"You gave yourself the shot in your dick? In the middle of a battle? Why would you do that? Like, wh–what—" I couldn't even speak. I was done. "Your dick will be fine. Get back out there— we need to make sure Asrael doesn't escape." Casting a quick look up to the platform, I saw Bram and Khol still had him engaged in hand-to-hand, and he looked a little groggy after being smashed in the head. So I felt confident that I could put my fighting skills to use in the mob, and help keep Sprout safe.

I could see Faris' speed increasing with each passing second, and I knew that his power was being restored. He would be able to reach the others much quicker than I could. "Faris," I said, drawing his attention and trying not to cringe at the amount of both fresh and old blood covering his body. His face was nothing but red. "Take these needles and make sure that Khol and Bram each get one. Be careful." He looked down and snatched the syringes faster than I could blink. The wind around me swirled as he took off.

A huge dark shadow fell over the courtyard as the dragons blocked out the sun. The beating of their wings was so loud—they reminded me of a helicopter flying too low, but times a hundred. The way the light hit their scales made the army appear like some sort of reptilian rainbow.

"Kai!" I heard someone screaming my name. Spinning in that direction, my eyes landed on Cam who was currently fighting four demons. "Archers!" he bellowed. My eyes widened as I searched around, looking for high points in the wall. Sure enough, a row of archers was lining up, taking aim at the sky. Their thick, metal-tipped arrows were more like harpoons.

"Finally, a task befitting a warrior of my stature!" Napoleon yelled, creeping out onto my shoulder. "Get me onto that wall, *géant*." I was already running, slipping through the different battles that were raging around me.

"What the hell are you going to do up there, Napoleon?" I asked.

"Mice are incredibly destructive creatures. Though I pride myself on being above my furry brethren, it is not beneath me to go back to the ways of my ancestors, who were lesser than I. I don't have these sharp teeth for nothing. I will wreak havoc upon their weapons. They will go to draw their bow only to have the string snap."

"Okay, that's actually a really good plan... Hold on tight. I'm shifting." Bagheera was right there, ready to take the lead, bursting forth. My body transformed from a tall man to an enormous sleek black panther. We took off, running as fast as we could, but it wasn't going to be fast enough. We let out a loud roar in warning, hoping that the dragons had already spotted the archers, but reached the wall just as the first row of arrows fired into the sky. The outraged cries, growls, and other sounds of fury and pain nearly burst my eardrums.

We hit the wall with a running start, our claws easily finding traction between stones. Then we were up, face to face with an unsuspecting archer. He shrieked as our jaws closed around his thigh. Blood poured quickly into my mouth, and I knew we'd severed his femoral artery. Shaking our head roughly, we tossed him over the side of the wall.

"That's it, *géant*. You are a big scary cat. You're the only cat that I like. Mark my words, if I see those pesky Persians out here on this battlefield, this day will be their last." Napoleon sprang from our back, landing on the demon closest to us. We watched —me in horror, Bagheera in amusement—as our small mousy friend wasted no time in going straight for the demon's jugular. Those teeth were impressively destructive in a very rapid fashion. Napoleon's black fur was quickly shiny with blood, but all it seemed to do was feed into his bloodlust.

'*Get on with it, Napoleon,*' Bagheera growled, sick of his shenanigans.

We took off racing along the wall, knocking as many archers down as we could. But all too soon, the call went out and the arrows were aimed in our direction. That was all we could do up here. We dove off of the wall into a roll and sped away back into the crowd. Napoleon would have to do whatever he could. It was in his hands now, as if that wasn't fucking terrifying. Hell, for all I knew, he'd be the one being crowned king at the end of today.

The Exiled were sprinkled throughout the crowd, their masks firmly in place, hiding their identities. The twins were making excellent use of their axe and their bat. The Carver looked like he was right at home with the way he was hunched over, hacking away at someone.

A large demon was sneaking up behind Fischer, and that wasn't going to fly. We launched ourselves, landing firmly on the male's back, giving us the perfect shot at the side of his neck.

Fischer spun around just as the blood started flying. "Thanks, K," he grunted. Sweat was running down his face. It was clear he'd been wielding his power. A group of demon males suddenly fell to the ground, screaming in agony and holding their heads. Fish's eyes turned blacker than night, and at the same time, black tears began running down the screaming demons' faces.

By the stars, he just keeps getting scarier and scarier. This was probably going to give me nightmares.

'Get it together,' Bagheera snapped, drawing me back.

I shuddered. *'You're right. It's just so unnatural-looking.'*

"Alright," Fischer said, straightening up as his eyes began to lighten again. "Let's go find our people. If Faris and I can power-link, we can end this really fucking fast. Anybody who isn't with us is dying today."

The air swirled through the courtyard, thanks to the wings of the dragons above. Fischer's thick curls swayed with the movement, but all I saw was the fire in his eyes and the desire for death. He was walking the edge right now, and I couldn't help but prepare myself for the fact that he was likely going to cross it. Not just cross it, but throw himself several miles past that line.

"He's over by the platform. Let's go, brother." My dark-eyed bestie spun and marched off through the crowd.

Stars, give us strength, and please keep Fischer from going psycho today. There's enough of that going on right now.

Bram

Chapter Twenty-one

I was livid. And I was fucking terrified. I was going to turn her ass red the second I got my hands on her. What the fuck was she thinking showing up like that? With Kohl's cautionary tale still vivid in my mind, all I could think of was that history was going to repeat itself.

I was mere seconds from death when my eyes locked on hers, and gods dammit if she wasn't a vision. She was lit up like a string of lights. I'd never seen anything so captivating. Of course, I didn't miss the swell of her belly in the stunning gown that she was wearing.

If that was my last glimpse before death, then it was an amazing one. I could die knowing that she was alive and just as beautiful as ever.

Suddenly, all hell broke loose, between Goldie managing to disrupt the execution and the arrival of the dragons. As soon as we were free, Khol and I began circling around Asrael. The sight of blood pouring down his forehead gave me great satisfaction, especially knowing that it was my tiny warrior who had wounded him.

"You're fools. All of you," Asrael growled as he nervously took in the situation. The dragons were above us and all around us. Insurgents were rising up against him—against this false king who'd thought all he needed to take a kingdom was an iron fist and vicious power. He was learning the hard way that that wasn't the case.

Khol laughed deeply, taunting the outraged Asrael. "I think it's you who's the fool, Az."

"Guards!" bellowed Asrael. "Kill them all. Anyone who doesn't stand with me is against me, and they'll meet their death today." He focused in on me next. "You think you can beat me? You don't stand a chance, boy. I have power that you could only dream of."

"Yeah, I don't believe you," I replied calmly. I wanted to ruffle his feathers. I knew he'd done something unnatural to boost his power levels, but I needed to stall. The angrier he got, the more likely he would be to make mistakes. It was a distraction tactic at its finest.

With a snarl, he lunged forward, swinging that great axe. I jumped back, narrowly missing the blade that would have sliced straight across my abdomen.

"You'll have to do better than that," I mocked, rewarding his shitty effort with a smirk.

"This kingdom was always meant to be mine!" he roared, swinging the axe around in a circle as he noticed Khol moving in behind him. "You'll never take it from me. Those dragons are under my command."

"If that's true," Khol mused, keeping his eyes on this mad king, "then why are they here? You certainly didn't bring them here, did you?"

"It doesn't matter," Asrael replied. "Whether they're here, or a hundred miles from here, they're *mine*."

"You know, Asrael, I expected better from you. All those years we spent together fighting, taking over different towns, raiding and plundering. I figured you would have learned from the mistakes you made back then, but it seems you're just as stupid as ever. You should know by now that you can't force the people to bend to your will and still expect loyalty in exchange."

While Khol engaged him, I took a quick moment to look around. None of the guards were approaching the platform to come to his assistance. It was impossible to know whether that was because they were changing sides, knowing that they weren't going to be fighting a losing battle, or whether Asrael really did have less support than he imagined. Either way, I was grateful.

I heard Bagheera's roar just as arrows flew toward the sky. We were going to need to speed things up. The green glow coming from Goldie caught my eye. It seemed she was holding her own—nobody could get near her. Thank the stars for that.

"That's fine," I heard Asrael say to Khol. "We'll do this the hard way then." Asrael launched himself at my longtime friend, not releasing the hold on the axe. But Khol didn't back down, the stubborn bastard that he was.

The two demons were nothing but flashes of fists, steel, and anger. There was so much history between them, and it was coming to an end today. Finally.

"This is a plan that has been *centuries* in the making, and you think you can just come in here and fuck it all up? You're wrong," Asrael spat. "There's nothing I wouldn't do to make sure I keep my crown. Thane underestimated me. You underestimated me. Who did you think was behind the fertility problems? To put my destiny into motion, I knew I needed a way to get into the other realm, and without good reason, that idiot king would never have let me go. My brother was nothing but a worthless piece of shit."

"You cursed your own people? Threatened the future generations of our kind because you're selfish?" I couldn't believe what I was hearing right now. Asrael landed a solid kick to Khol's chest, launching him across the platform and sending him rolling off of it backwards.

Asrael spun on his heel, sneering at me. "Indeed. And who do you think they're going to respect and rejoice over when I single-handedly replace all that was lost? When our females are able to have healthy pregnancies again? When the dragons are able to do so as well? It's me who will be responsible, and it's me everybody will be thanking—because without me, they would never have had it."

I just stared at Asrael. I couldn't believe the bullshit I was hearing.

"You're wrong. Without you, they never would have had this problem to begin with! You've ruined so many lives. You're irredeemable. Nothing but an evil piece of shit who wants to wear a crown that he doesn't deserve. But not to worry, you won't have a head to place it on by the end of this day." I saw Khol's head pop up on the other side of the platform as he scrambled to climb back on.

"This is enough child's play," Asrael growled, with a knowing look in his eye that I really didn't like. Unease began to swirl in my gut, telling me that he had something up his sleeve. Of course he did. I just really didn't want to know what it was. Tilting his head up to the sky, his eyes drifted shut. His whole body began to vibrate.

"Khol!" I shouted in warning. "Get ready." At that moment, a blur appeared beside me. "Faris?"

"Hold still, demon boy." Before I could blink, a sharp pain exploded right on my dick.

"Ow! What the fuck, Faris?!" I shouted, grabbing hold of my wounded weiner.

"You'll thank me in about two minutes. I gotta go." He quickly pressed his mouth to mine. I didn't even get a second to enjoy it, before he was gone.

He was standing before Khol, the older demon giving him a dirty look. "You stab me in the dick and I will rip yours off," Khol promised fiercely.

"Fine, here, take it. It'll restore your magic." Faris handed a syringe to Khol, who drove it into his bicep, no questions asked.

My gaze didn't linger on them for long. All of my focus was back on Asrael, who was now shaking so violently, it looked like there were seven of him. Without thinking about the repercussions, I darted forward, intent on snapping his neck while he was so out of it with whatever the fuck he was doing. But the second I wrapped my hand around his neck, I was jolted back. Pain burst through my body, like I'd been electrocuted. My back hit the wooden platform and all the air in my lungs was forced out, leaving me gasping. Now staring up at the sky, I could see the multitude of colorful dragons flying overhead, with spurts and spouts of great fire raining down on different parts of the castle.

A deep, disembodied laugh boomed out throughout the courtyard. It was so loud, I felt it in my soul.

"Get up, Bram," Faris hissed from above me. He grabbed both of my hands and yanked me up, causing my head to spin.

"What the fuck is that?" I slurred, trying to regain my bearings and wondering if I was seeing things. Where Asrael had been standing was now some kind of creature. A creature that was terrifyingly unnatural. At least eight feet tall, with the form of a demon but the skin of a dragon, and long fangs and nails. Even his face had transformed, taking on more of a reptilian appearance, with slits for nostrils and slanted eyes. The wings that exploded from his back were at least twenty feet wide.

"You will never defeat me!" that deep, demonic voice yelled out to the crowd, which was now completely silent as everybody stood and stared at the abomination that was Asrael.

Cam

Chapter Twenty-Two

I couldn't believe what I was seeing. Asrael was turning into a living nightmare. A lot of the battle had ceased as everybody turned toward the platform, captivated by what they were seeing. I knew that whatever the fuck was happening, this was going to be bad.

Tilting my head to the sky, I yelled out for the dragons to land. It was time. We needed reinforcements. Rhodes and Misha were standing beside me as the dragons began to descend to the courtyard. "Are you positive that he can't control them anymore?" I demanded.

Rhodes lifted an eyebrow that was barely visible over the black mask he wore. "Yes, we're positive. All of those dragons are now free. Something Asrael will find out as soon as he tries to exert any sort of control over them."

"Well, I sure fucking hope you're right," I replied. I saw Rhodes' eyes flick over my shoulder, the movement the only warning I received at the last second. Drawing electricity to my hands, I spun around, unleashing it on a large demon who'd been seconds away from running me through with a blade.

"Thanks for the heads up," I said snarkily, as the guard began convulsing on the ground.

Misha just stood there, watching. "Well, we have to keep it

interesting. Plus, I wanted to see your powers. Fascinating. I bet that's popular with the ladies." Rhodes grinned wildly, and I rolled my eyes.

"Stay focused," I barked. "We can't afford to get distracted now. There's too much on the line."

For the most part, the battle around the courtyard had started to slow immensely. I didn't know if that was because of Asrael's distraction, or if it was because we were really winning. But for the first time since everything started this morning, I began to feel a real sense of impending victory. Group after group of dragons flew down, shifting as soon as they touched down with their feet. They were males and females, all of them warriors.

Asrael must have seen what was happening because he was pissed. An ear-piercing scream sounded just before he shouted, "What the fuck is going on? Guards, kill them all!" I imagined it was likely quite a shock seeing these massive creatures he'd held captive for years suddenly shifting into their human forms without a single problem.

Rhodes and I shared a grin, before shouting orders to separate groups of dragons. Most of them looked shell-shocked and a bit unstable on their legs, likely due to lack of use.

"Stay focused!" I yelled at a group. They nodded, acknowledging my orders.

Misha's deep voice came from behind me. "You might want to go check on your little lamb. I don't know what she's doing over there, but it doesn't look too good. Or depending on who you are, it looks really fucking good."

Eyes wild, I scanned the mob in search of Saige. The crowd began to rush toward the left of the platform, like the people there were trying to get away from something. Pushing past them and letting my electricity take care of any who tried to hurt me, my feet came to an abrupt halt as I took in the bodies, or what used to be bodies… They were unidentifiable now.

In the center of it all, was Saige. My woman.

Her body was glowing, as were her eyes. Her once long red hair was now shorter, but that wasn't the most noticeable change. When my gaze fell on her stomach, I could've dropped to my knees in relief. She was still pregnant. Perfectly pregnant, round and swollen. Her belly had gotten so much larger since I'd seen her last. Anger flared within, because I'd missed it. I'd missed the majority of her pregnancy. Had it been hell for her? Had she been mistreated in our time apart? I felt robbed. I could only imagine how she felt, how my brothers felt.

My legs carried me the remainder of the distance between us, and I found myself reaching out for her. "Little witch," I called, my voice cracking. I knew I needed to be paying closer attention to what was going on around me, but just like every time I laid eyes on her, I was fucking captivated. Pulled into her orbit with no way out, but I didn't want a way out.

She spun around where she stood, her hands out in front of her. Her magic hit my body like a freight train. The surprised wheeze that left my chest was full of pain, but it was the only sound I could make as it felt like my lungs were being squeezed.

Her eyes locked on my face, and awareness trickled in. The fierceness gave way to horror as she realized what she was doing. "Cam!" she cried. "I can't make it stop. It's too much." I could barely get a breath into my lungs. The force of her power was unlike anything I'd felt before.

"Let go," I rasped.

"Oh gods," she cried, looking at her hands as if they were betraying her. My eyes widened as I saw the masked man approach her from behind. Ashland was walking slowly, using caution as he approached.

"Saige," he said sternly. "You need to focus." Tossing a look over her shoulder to see who was speaking, she took a step away from the demon. "I'm not going to hurt you. You're hurting your mate right now; you don't want to do that. I know your magic feels out of control, but it's not. You are controlling it. It's scary, but you need to push that away. You're arguably the strongest person standing in this courtyard, and you have nothing to be scared of."

Saige was shaking her head back and forth, as my vision started to tunnel. Black bled into the corners, with white stars popping each second. I was going to pass out soon. "Help me!" she cried out. "Please, help me."

Ashland moved in closer. "It's all you, girl. You're the only one who can shut it down. Focus on my voice and take a breath." I struggled to watch as she did what he suggested. Her breaths were choppy, verging on hysterical, but she tried. "That's good," Ashland's deep voice praised. "You're doing great. Now, you need to release Cam and focus this power where it belongs."

My girl nodded her head, her breaths coming slower now. Just when I thought I was going to be lost, her magic receded and I was released. Air had never tasted as good as in that moment, and my knees hit the ground as I sucked in great gulping breaths.

"Cam! Oh gods!" she screamed, rushing over to me, joining me on the ground. Her tiny hands were rubbing all over my body, checking me for injuries. It was like she couldn't believe I was actually here. "I'm so sorry," she cried, huge tears leaking from her pretty green eyes.

"Baby girl, I'm so fucking glad to see you." My hand wrapped around the back of her neck as I pulled her in and pressed my mouth to hers. Every fucking problem in the world ceased to exist in that moment. The way her soft lips melded to mine, the slight salty taste of her tears coating them as I snaked my tongue out and sank it into her mouth. Gods, I would never get enough of this woman. I wasn't sure what I'd ever done to deserve her love but I was fucking grateful for it.

She whimpered into my mouth, still upset by what had just happened. I brought my hands to her face. Breaking the kiss, I rested my forehead on hers. "It's not your fault. I'm fine. You're fine. We'll be okay. Fuck, baby, I love you so much. Do you hear me?"

"Yes. Yes, I hear you. My gods, Cam, I missed you so much. I love you." Before either of us could say another word, the sound of multiple bodies hitting the ground echoed all around us.

Whipping my gaze over to the platform, I saw Asrael had his hands extended, having clearly just exerted some sort of power. My guess was that he was taking out anybody who wasn't directly under his control. The Exiled were still standing, along with all of our family, and the dragon shifters. I saw Balor moving around the platform, injecting fallen guards and soldiers. This wasn't over yet, and we would still need any help we could get—if not to fight, then to help with the wounded.

"Come on, baby. We gotta get up." I pushed myself to my feet and scooped my woman up off the cold stone ground. My hand protectively fell to her belly, and my eyes widened as I felt movement within, sharp jabs and kicks. My girls. Fuck. Emotion was threatening to seize me, and I had to stuff it down because we needed to end this.

"Thanks for the help, Big Daddy," Saige whispered, a small smile on her mouth.

"Well," I said, "I figured this belly isn't good for getting up off the ground. It's a good thing you have such a big strong man here to take care of you." It was totally not something I would ever normally say, but it had the effect I intended when she giggled.

A flash of red caught my eye over the top of my little witch's head, and I caught sight of someone who had no fucking business being out here right now. In fact, she had no fucking business breathing air. With my eyes locked on her, I wasn't going to let her out of my sight. Laurie causing issues today was the last fucking thing that we needed, and I wouldn't hesitate to slit her throat this time.

"Come over here, baby," I told Saige, wrapping my arm around her waist and hastily walking her over to the walkway that ran along the side of the castle. It was covered, and thanks to some strategically placed potted plants, she would be mostly hidden.

"What are you doing?" she asked. "You want me to hide?"

"I want you to be safe," I replied, guiding her in. "Just wait right here for a minute. There's something I need to go check on. This is all coming to an end very soon, and I need to know that you're okay. Please stay here, Saige," I begged, using her real name. "I can't bear to lose you." Emotions were warring in her big eyes as she stared up at me. "It's not a weakness to be safe, baby girl. You're strong and capable. After today, nobody will ever question that again, but things happen all the time that are out of our control. Things you don't see coming until it's too late. Please do this for me."

"Okay," she whispered. "I'll stay here, but I swear to gods, Cam, the second I see any of you in trouble, all bets are off. I'm not losing anyone today either. No one is going to take you from me."

I pressed a quick kiss to her mouth. "Thank you," I whispered. Stepping away was the hardest thing that I'd done in my life, but it had to happen. I wasn't going to let Laurie do whatever it was she had planned, because I knew that bitch always had plans.

I just hoped that I'd be able to catch her before she got the chance.

Faris

Chapter Twenty-three

It had turned out to be a really good thing that I'd had all that practice over the last month with killing little bitches. I was unstoppable now. Every time one of their round faces popped up, ready to scramble onto the platform, my foot was there like I was playing kickball in the Olympics, and damn was I talented. My magic was back at full power and I was fast as fuck. The speed that I could now kick and punch and run was just so exhilarating. Plus, it made the blood splatter so much farther than anything I'd seen in the last four weeks. And in such pretty patterns too. It was really impressive.

My fist sailed into the face of a particularly hideous guard. Blood, teeth, and sweat flew off of his face, and I wondered for a moment if maybe I should pursue some type of passionate hobby work in the art of splatter painting. It wouldn't have to all be done in blood. I mean, I could really fuck up some paint tubes, and just throw them at a canvas—boom, art.

I wonder what Firefly would think about that. Speaking of my woman... Damn, she was looking good today. I really wanted to make her come while I had my hands on that big belly. I'd let her sit right on my cock. She'd have to lean back a little bit to accommodate, but that was fine because our demon prince could stand right behind her, supporting her so her arms didn't get tired.

She'd just bounce to her little pregnant heart's content. Yeah, I would definitely enjoy that.

I would still try to knock her up every time. I mean, the fact that she was already pregnant twice over, it really, uh… it hadn't done anything to diminish my desire, and the thought of filling her up and knowing that my seed had taken root within her body? It was just as hot, though it didn't matter that biologically the babies weren't mine, because they were mine in every other sense of the word.

Mine. Ours.

I'd already decided that their first meal was going to be mac and cheese. I just wasn't sure how that would go over with everybody else, since they were very opinionated on my diet for some reason. When really, it was none of their business to begin with. That was fine. I could be sneaky. It would be the girls and Papa Faris, having our little tea parties, and mac and cheese lunch. I would be their favorite. They could have little cups of tea or juice or water, then I would have a little teacup of their Mommy or Daddy Bram's blood. I could see it now. Nothing but good days ahead.

Khol and Bram were kicking ass. We were like a special ops unit, and I was loving it. They kept trading barbs and insults with Asrael. I wasn't really listening since I was too busy saving the day and killing people. I just wanted this to be over with. I couldn't wait to tell Firefly about Number Fishty. I knew she would be really proud of me for my accomplishments.

A pained grunt caught my attention, and I spun around fast, my eyes darting around wildly for the source of that sound. When my eyes landed on Bram, and I saw three huge scratches across his chest with blood pouring out, something in me snapped. A sound that was pure beast, completely primal, exploded from my chest as I launched myself across the wooden platform like a frickin' lion.

My hands hit the ground and my feet came right after as I

used my legs to launch myself, colliding with Asrael before he even saw me coming. By the stars, it was like hitting a wall of steel. It definitely knocked me a little dumb for a second as I bounced off of his ridiculously hard body.

"Fuck," I groaned. My eyes widened a second before Asrael's fists came down. I quickly rolled to the right, avoiding a smash that would have completely destroyed my pretty face. His hits kept coming, and I was rolling around along the ground looking like a fish out of water. I was beginning to sense a theme for all this fish business.

Speaking of which, where the fuck was my brother? We needed to team up and take all these fuckers out. He was probably off standing in a corner with black eyes, looking around like a creepy ass nightmare mage. I was gonna have to have a talk with him. Yeah, he was strong and he had all these powers, but so did everybody else. That didn't mean you got to stand in the corner and look like a creep. We had business to take care of. Pain exploded through my shoulder as I moved a second too late, and Asrael's iron fist collided with my arm.

"Faris!" Bram grabbed hold of me by my uninjured arm, dragging me back away from Asrael as Khol jumped in to distract him. "What the hell are you doing?!" he barked, getting in my face.

"He hurt you," I said, like it should have been obvious what I was doing.

"Well, he hurt you too, you fool! You can't just do stuff like that," he said, exasperated. My fingertips trailed across the open wounds on his chest while I watched him struggle with his emotions. He was also sporting a hell of a black eye, and it just made him look all the sexier to me. Gods, I couldn't wait for this battle to be over. I was hornier than hell. The need to fuck and be fucked was so strong right now that it was nearly killing me.

"Faris," Bram whisper-shouted. "Why are you hard right now?!" I chanced a look down, and oh yeah, hard as a rock. Full mast. Land ho, mateys. There was no sinking this Titanic. "You're calling it the Titanic now?"

"Nooo," I said sheepishly. *Oh shit, did I say that out loud?* "Don't worry about my dick right now. It's your problem for later. Let's end this." I sank my fangs into my wrist, shredding the skin relatively painlessly. Bram stood there sputtering, like he'd never seen me do such a thing before—which was ridiculous because this is exactly the type of thing that I lived for. "Here," I told him, shoving my wrist up to his mouth. "Suck it."

He opened his mouth, probably to berate me or I don't know, yell at me. Whatever bossy demon things he liked to spew my way. We didn't have time for that, so I did us both a favor and just shoved my wrist right in his mouth.

My blood could heal him right now, which was exactly what we needed. I didn't like the look of wounds on his body that I hadn't put there myself. It was like another man marking what was mine. That couldn't stand. Hmmm. With my anger renewed, I took my arm away, satisfied that the wounds were already starting to close on his chest. I turned my attention back to Asrael.

"I'm gonna fucking kill this asshole. Anyone touches you again, they die. Do you understand? Anyone."

"Baby Fang, stop." Bram grabbed my arm to halt my very near attempt to pounce on Asrael's head from behind like a cat. "We need to be smart about this. Thank you for healing me, by the way. Why don't you go check on the others real quick and see if anybody else needs help? You have a gift—you should use it."

With my jaw clenched tightly, I darted my eyes between Asrael and Khol battling, to my big red-headed demon lover, to another demon who was scrambling to administer vaccines to other demons. I found it interesting though, that he wasn't administering them to anybody's dicks. Porn was really giving me some weird recommendations. First the pregnant lady stuff and now this. Never mind. I needed to focus.

"Okay, you're right. I'll go heal people, but I swear to the stars, if he touches you again... I'm going to rip his eyeballs out, I'm going to juggle them, and then I'm going to ping-pong those motherfuckers into another dimension."

"Alright, psycho. Go." Bram gave me a small smile, and I nearly swooned like a heartsick little goose. Here we were in the midst of a real battle. I'd already killed fifty other demons over the course of the last month, and now, here today I'd put down another ten.

Bram loved fighting just as much as I did. I could see the bloodlust in his eyes when he drank my blood. Oh boy.

"Okay, bye," I said quickly before I could do something epically fucked up like just steal the man and have my wicked way with him. Sprinting across the platform, I used my legs to push myself off and flip, effectively landing like a human bowling ball, knocking out five demons. Thankfully, I avoided their horns. Those might've hurt.

Throwing my head back, I released the battle cry. "Long live King Bram!" I dipped and weaved through our enemies, kicking kneecaps and taking ball shots, and punching people in the throat. It was my life's calling to be an assassin like this.

I wondered if this is what it felt like to be a hornet. You got them pissed off, then didn't even see them coming, and wham! A world of pain. At least they had it coming. I smiled maniacally as cheers of "Long live King Bram!" resounded around me, getting louder and louder.

Asrael was pissed. I could hear him screaming and carrying on like a big ugly dragon demon baby. I'd had enough of his shit. Maybe if I could get him pissed off enough, he'd get distracted and then we'd have a chance. Yeah, that's exactly what I was gonna do.

Throwing my head back once more, I decided to really up my game this time. "Asrael's a bitch!" It took a minute, but soon everyone took up that battle cry, and I knew it was working. Asrael was practically throwing a temper tantrum up there now.

I focused my attention on finding wounded after that, getting them healed up and back on their feet. This wasn't over yet, but hopefully, it would be soon and the casualties would be limited.

I was both the Grim Reaper and an angel of life.

Saige

Chapter Twenty-Four

Cam was already swallowed up by the crowd. I could still feel the lingering sensation of his lips against mine, his hands on me. Cam was my rock. He just had this way about him, of grounding me while still making me feel like I could fly. It was like he wanted to protect me, wanted to make sure I was safe, but he also made me feel capable of doing all that for myself. It was one of the things I loved most about him.

All around me, there were bodies lying with pools of blood around them. Some of the guards and demons who had joined our side were still groaning in pain, while others were completely still. I briefly wondered if I'd be able to heal them, and then I thought about Cam's face when he'd begged me to stay put. So that was what I did. It was agony, knowing that maybe I could help but I was choosing not to. I didn't want to be that kind of person.

My eyes scanned the courtyard once more, and I caught sight of Balor near the platform, injecting people to give them a leg-up over Asrael's power.

Khol, Bram, several guards, and a few people from the servants' wing were making progress in their fight against him. But still, he wasn't going down. He was not an easy enemy to defeat, and I suspected that was because he was wielding some sort of power that was either diminishing the effects of other people's magic or maybe strengthening his own. Possibly even providing some sort of forcefield around himself. Whatever it was, he was still looking incredibly strong while our army was starting to show signs of exhaustion.

Vaeryn and his dragons were making excellent work going after the archers who remained along the stone wall. There was another man fighting alongside Vaeryn now who looked strikingly similar to him. His brother then. Good, I was glad they'd found each other. All kinds of people had come together today for this. Including whoever these creepy dudes were wearing the masks. They were particularly violent, and I was thankful that they were on our side, because gods... the excitement they seemed to get out of killing just didn't seem natural. I couldn't even stand to watch, to be honest.

A scuffle on the platform had me turning my attention there again. Balor had gotten in the way of another fight and either tripped or been knocked down. I watched as he fell, and panic rose in my veins. I hoped that he wasn't gravely injured—he was the only one here who'd shown me any kindness while I'd been imprisoned. Without him, who knew what would have become of me and my girls? Without Balor, I doubted that we would've had the army that we had today.

I stepped out from my hiding spot before I could even realize what was happening. I watched in slow motion as the vaccine he'd been gripping in his hand flew out and rolled a few times before coming to a stop. Balor didn't get up. He wasn't moving.

I'd already made my mind up to help him as I stormed my way closer. As I moved through the melee, the hair on the back of my neck began to prickle. I felt my palms getting slick. Something wasn't right.

Our eyes collided at the exact same moment. Laurie was crawling on her hands and knees, remaining undetected from the men who were fighting above her. Slowly, her eyes looked over to where the needle was laying that Balor had dropped and then they came back to focus on me.

Oh, hell no.

Surging forward, it was a race to see who would get there first. I didn't know why she wanted that vaccine, but I didn't want her to have anything that she wanted ever again. I didn't care if it was two-ply toilet paper—she wasn't having it. My fingers closed around the barrel of the syringe, and she screeched in my face.

"Give it to me, you ungrateful little bitch." She tried to snatch my wrist, but I was too quick.

"I don't know why you want this, but you can fucking forget about it, you evil cunt." The words flew from my mouth like fire. I was done with this sad excuse of a woman. Honestly, I didn't know if she even possessed a shred of humanity anymore.

I used to assume that she harbored some type of feeling toward me, whether it was friendship or you know, just not wishing ill on somebody because they're related to you. Her feelings toward me had never been motherly, but I'd accepted that a long time ago. She'd had me when she was young. She wasn't prepared.

But knowing what I knew now, that changed everything. She deliberately got pregnant with me. She deliberately broke my father's heart. She deliberately fucked up my childhood by letting me think that I didn't have a father who wanted me, and letting me know for sure that I had a mother who couldn't be bothered with me.

The vile creature who was staring at me with the hatred of a million souls didn't feel anything about me at all. She wasn't even seeing me in this moment. Her jealousy, her ego, her desire for power—that was all she cared about, and that was all it would ever be. It would never ever stop. Her gaze dipped to my stomach, and I snarled, the sound terrifying enough to get the attention of those around us. If she thought she was going to get her hands on my children… Fuck no. I'd do whatever I had to do to ensure that never happened. She'd abandoned me, and gods only knew what she'd done to my sister.

Laurie let out a wicked laugh at my words. "So," she taunted with a sneer, "the good little witch has fangs after all. I always knew you were nothing but a fake. Everyone's always so happy to see your smiling face. You're always so eager to help everybody. Everybody just loves you, don't they? They don't know what's really inside you, because for every bit of happiness and kindness that lives within you, I live in you also. It's about damn time that you show your true colors."

Laurie's hand raised almost faster than I could track it, but I was able to throw my own arms up at the last second, causing her vine attack to collide with my own. She was definitely strong, and it wasn't a natural magic. It felt dirty and tainted, synthetic. I didn't know what she and Asrael had been up to, but whatever it was, it wasn't supposed to exist. Still, even as pissed off as she was and with as much power as she was aiming my way, I was *more* pissed and I was *more* powerful. It was about time that I showed her what I was really capable of.

"I don't know why you want this, but you're never getting it, Laurie. I will do everything in my power to make sure that anything you want, you'll never get. Your days of making demands are over."

She screeched and launched herself toward me, her face transforming into something horrific. Her teeth sharpened into needle-point fangs, while her jaw began to distend as if she was going to take a bite out of my body.

"What the fuck are you?" I squeaked as I dove out of the way. Thankfully, I was able to remain on my feet. The last thing I needed was to go down and accidentally hit my belly.

I saw Cam prowling behind her. When my eyes caught on his, I could see his anger surging. I swallowed thickly, knowing he was probably pretty pissed that I'd left my hiding spot, but there was no time to fight about it now. Laurie must have sensed the danger lurking behind her because she spun quickly, launching another attack. Thick vines—ones equipped with thorns for maximum damage—exploded from her hands. Cam was ready though. Electricity crackled in his palms as he sent a blast her way, hitting her square in the chest. She flew back with a shriek, hitting the platform hard.

"Asrael!" Laurie screamed as she rolled and hopped to her feet, quicker than I would have expected after the hit she'd just taken. "We need to go. Come on. It's over." I was surprised at her abrupt change in plans until I saw what she must have seen when she stood up.

The battle was over. The only people still fighting were us. It was Asrael and Laurie versus us on the platform. She'd realized there was no way they were going to win. She was like a cockroach. Always knowing when to run, when to escape, to ensure that she survived over everybody else.

Asrael snarled and a blast of bright fire flew from his mouth. I watched in frozen horror as it slammed right into Bram and Khol at the same time.

"No!" I screamed, taking a step toward them at the same time as Laurie moved toward me.

"Saige, no. Look out!" Cam yelled just in time for me to shift my gaze away from Bram and Khol, only to find Laurie inches away from me. She pulled back her fist and punched me right in the face.

Holy fucking shit, that hurt. A cry left my mouth, despite me trying to hold it in. I hated giving Laurie the satisfaction of knowing how much she'd harmed me. I returned her punch with one of my own, nailing her right in the windpipe. I took great joy in watching her gasping for air, and I wondered if—and hoped— she felt a little bit of what my Guppy had felt when she took the life from him.

A vine wrapped around my wrist, and she dragged me across

the wooden beams. Cam was right there, firing electricity at her. Blast after blast, thunder exploding in the sky, but she was untouchable. There was something protecting her.

"Give me that fucking needle," she snarled.

I felt like I was having a complete out-of-body experience. The sounds of my men yelling and fighting Asrael, the smell of fire in the air, the humidity of a storm rolling, and the roar of a panther. Everything slowed. All I could hear through that was the whooshing of my heartbeat in my ears as Laurie's evil face grew closer and closer. I felt my girls kicking and moving wildly within my stomach like they were trying to help me get away from this evil bitch, and then I heard it.

'A witch, a mix of green and red, save a race before they're dead. Change, rise, manifest. A soul so pure. You almost pass the test. Many for the price of three. Hurry, witch. What will it be? In royal red, your strength renewed. Hurry, witch, or all are doomed.'

A prophecy. Another prophecy. Most of the lines were from the previous ones with subtle changes, but suddenly, I knew exactly what I needed to do. In a rush, I uncapped the syringe, watching as Laurie's eyes grew wide, realization dawning. She knew what I was planning, and oh, she was pissed.

I watched as my gown magically turned from deep green to royal red. This was the moment. Everything had led to right now. Without a second thought, I sank the needle into the exposed skin in my forearm and pushed the plunger down. The serum hit my bloodstream like a jolt of pure energy. I couldn't hear any longer—at least, not the sounds of the world around me. All I could hear were whispers of the past, the voices of my men.

Kai's voice drifting through my ear, telling me how much he loved my shirt the first day we met in the store, how it cheered him up. Fischer telling me that I should never have to sacrifice who I was as a person to be worthy of someone's love. Cam assuring me that he would protect me no matter what, that I was precious to him. Bram promising that I would be his, even before

I knew what we were to each other. Faris, my sweet Faris, the way he told me how he wanted to fill me with babies and how he always wanted to please me. And Sloane, my broken dragon, confessing his devotion and love for me. All of their whispered words and sounds that we'd made together flooded my mind as I began to float above everybody else.

Asrael was staring at me in shock and anger, but I didn't care. Whatever it was that was happening—this was destiny. I could feel it in my bones. This was a moment that needed to happen. It was predetermined, and I knew with absolute certainty that no matter the choices I'd made before, we still would have ended up here.

It was fate.

I watched as Fischer moved beneath me, stalking his way toward his victim. She hadn't seen him yet, but oh, this was going to be a reckoning. Asrael was still distracted by me, allowing the Exiled, Vaeryn, his brother, Sloane, Faris, Kai, Cam, Bram, and Khol to all attack at once. I sent out a wave of power just before they reached him, effectively decimating any type of magical shield that he was using, and doing the same for Laurie.

Fischer's eyes were black, and Laurie was scrambling backward, having finally seen her death. Guppy held his hand out, holding her in place. His mouth was moving but I couldn't hear the words. Laurie thrashed back and forth, grabbing her head in agony, and I knew that his magic was deep within her brain.

I watched as Laurie's own magic turned against her with the influence of Fischer's power invading her mind. Vines crawled out from her body and quickly found their way around her neck. They tightened, and her legs kicked, while her fingers frantically tried to wedge themselves between her skin and the vines that were suffocating her. Fischer stood there with his arms crossed, as he stared down at the woman who had inflicted the same type of death upon him.

It was poetic justice, and I was glad that he was getting this moment. He may be the one who would get the credit for killing her, but gods knew this was a win for all of us. I watched as the life slowly left her body, her eyes wide, like she couldn't believe that she'd been bested. I just felt pure relief; I didn't have to worry about her any longer. She would never harm my children or my men ever again.

With Laurie dealt with, my eyes drifted over to the fight with Asrael. It wasn't much of a fight anymore. Blood was pouring out of him at an incredibly fast rate. Knives, blades, and swords stuck out of his body like he was a pin cushion. His knees finally hit the ground, and he was swallowed up by the crowd of angry men.

Magic surged, swirling through me like a cyclone. If I thought the power I'd had before had been monumental, it was nothing compared to this. A burst fired out, forcing my head back to the sky, my arms outstretched, and everything went white.

"Where am I?" I demanded, looking around. It was in some type of void. Everything was white here. Just nothing but never-ending blankness. No people. No sound. "Hello?"

"Hello, child. You're here." They appeared from the nothingness like apparitions, their makeup as gaudy as ever.

"Where are we?" I asked the two seer women who had been a part of this from the beginning. Their tinkling laughter flooded the space.

"We are neither here nor there," Roberta replied.

Matilda made her way toward me, taking my hands into hers. "You've done it, Saige. You fulfilled the prophecy."

I just blinked. "What do you mean? It's over then? Is it really over?" I could hear my voice cracking with emotion.

"Yes, my child. It is over. The stars are happy and impressed by you and your mates, your tenacity, and the fact that throughout all of this, you never lost who you are at your core. Selfless, pure, kind, and generous. You didn't know what was going to happen when you made the decision that you made, but you decided to trust in your fate."

I could feel tears running down my face. I couldn't believe that it was finally over. "What happens now? Am I alive?"

Both women laughed. "Yes, you are alive. As for what happens now... What do you want?"

What do I want? What a question. It had been so long since I'd really given that any thought because the last several months had been all about survival. Getting from point A to point B in one piece, outsmarting enemies who knew more than I did, and now, I was supposed to know what I wanted?

"Say the first thing that comes to mind. You know what it is," Matilda encouraged me, squeezing my hands.

"I want forever... with them," I replied.

"Then forever it shall be," the two women replied in perfect sync.

Suddenly, I was rushing through the white void, like I was being sucked through a vacuum. Matilda and Roberta were gone, and I found myself with my feet firmly planted on the platform once again. Asrael's body was slumped on the ground, his head fifteen feet in the opposite direction. Everybody was staring at me, and I began to shake, the adrenaline and aftereffects of the battle taking hold of me. My men didn't hesitate. They ran for me, and I collapsed into their arms with a cry.

"It's over. It's really over." Someone was shushing me gently, while another ran their hand through my hair, soft lips pressed against my throat, and a warm body found its way against my back. *This is exactly what I want.* "We did it. We really did it."

I laughed, even as the tears just kept falling. I let them wash away the taint of evil and trauma. It felt cleansing, purging this darkness from my soul, and as I stood there, the sounds of applause and cheering started up, growing louder and louder.

"Long live the queen!"

Oh, my moon maidens. I was no queen, but I was too freaking tired to argue.

Sloane

Chapter Twenty-Five

"Gods, I don't think I will ever get used to that feeling," I cursed as I stumbled forward, bracing myself on the back of a chair. "Where are we?" Bram had jumped us somewhere within the castle, and while I was grateful that we didn't have to walk as we were all exhausted, I still didn't like that sensation of hurtling through space and time.

"These are the king's quarters," Bram announced. "It's large enough for all of us to sleep here. Since I figure that is what we'd all prefer?" He looked around the room questioningly.

"Yes please," Saige sighed. "I need all of you in my line of sight for the rest of my life after all of this."

"How do you feel, baby?" Cam stepped up beside her, tugging her against his large body.

"Like this isn't real. Like everything that happened was a joke, and any second Asrael's gonna come take you away from me again." She believed that to be true; I could tell by the panic in her eyes.

"That's not going to happen, sweetheart," Fischer piped up from the wall he was leaning against. We all looked like hell, battered and bruised. Though we were already healing, largely in part thanks to Faris' power.

I cleared my throat, drawing everyone's focus. "We got some

news just before the battle started." I paused and raised a brow at Red, letting her decide if she wanted to be the one to share what Balor had told us. She smiled, giving me a small nod to continue.

"Well, don't keep us in suspense, brother," Cam grumbled.

I found myself grinning widely. "We have less than a week until we're officially fathers."

"A week?" Bram gasped, looking to Red for confirmation. Seeing her smile and watery eyes, his knees hit the floor, his fist pressed tightly over his heart. I walked over and gripped his shoulder, giving it a reassuring squeeze.

"Less than a week?" Fischer piped up, his tone both curious and shocked. "As in… it could happen any time?"

"This is amazing!" Faris darted over to our woman and held his hand up. "High five, little mama."

Saige laughed, and it sounded so carefree. It had been a long time since I'd seen her like that.

"Why do you keep doing that?" Faris asked curiously.

I glanced around to see who he was talking to, but found everyone looking at me. Cam was smirking. Dickhead. My curiosity won out, though I had no idea where this was going.

"Doing what?"

"Showing your teeth and like, moving your face upward." Faris gestured with his hands over his face dramatically.

I blinked. *Who is this creature anyway? Where do the things that come out of his mouth come from?*

"You mean smiling?" Cam snorted, covering his mouth with his fist as his bare torso shook with silent laughter.

"Faris!" Red hissed.

He threw his hands up. "What? He looks weird."

"No, he doesn't, Baby Fang. He looks happy," Bram said, rising back to his feet and slinging his arm over my shoulders. Faris tracked the motion, and I wound my arm around Bram's waist, giving me the perfect angle to flip the bird at that little shit. Which I did. He saw it too, lifting his own middle finger to his mouth and piercing the pad of it on a sharp fang. The conversation continued around us as we glared at each other.

That crazy fucker let the blood well just enough to start dripping down his finger. He brought it to his mouth, painting his lips red, flipping me off the entire time. Puckering his bloodied lips, he kissed his finger, then blew the kiss at me and snapped his teeth a few times for good measure.

I didn't appreciate his antics… At least, that's what I tried to tell myself, despite the fact that every damn time he acted up, it caused my balls to ache and my dick to twitch. *Look away, Sloane. Look away.*

Red's voice had turned strained and emotional. "I just… I'm so happy that we'll all be together when we become parents. I missed you all so much, and I feel like even just the thought of what could've happened will give me nightmares for the rest of my life." Her lower lip quivered, and it damn near broke my black heart in two.

"Come here, Cub," Kai purred as he took a seat on the chair. "Come sit on my lap. It's been too long since I've held you against me." Cam walked her over and deposited her into Kai's lap, who didn't waste any time nuzzling his face into her neck, taking great heaving breaths of her scent. The two of them shivered at the contact. It felt like we all just were desperate for each other. We needed to feel connected again, because if we were together, nothing could hurt us.

Directly after the battle, Khol had immediately told us to get out of there and go get some rest. Thankfully, Balor's injuries from the battle were able to be healed, and he'd stayed behind to help Khol. The young guard, Joris, had also survived, though he would have a gnarly scar from his hairline down the right side of his face for the rest of his life.

The Exiled didn't stick around after Asrael hit the deck. They claimed they had no desire to participate in any sort of government rebuilding, that their job was done. We were grateful to them, of course. They still gave me the creeps with those masks, but their power was unmatched, as was their level of fucking craziness.

There were already discussions going on about a celebratory ball the following evening to celebrate our victory and the return of health to the realm. So that gave us a little over twenty-four hours for some rest and whatever else we decided to get up to.

Faris glided through the room, plopping himself down on the floor between Saige's legs, resting his head against her inner thigh. Her hands immediately sank into his hair, his eyes fluttering shut at the contact. My own eyes trailed across the room to a man that I hadn't seen in far too long. I knew he was looking at me, because I could feel it. I'd always be able to feel Fischer. His attention ignited my blood every fucking time. When his honey oak eyes collided with mine, magic pulsed between us.

In three steps I was before him, towering over him just slightly. "Hey, pretty boy. I missed you." I lifted my hand to his face, wanting to feel the smoothness of his cheek beneath my thumb. He flinched away, and hurt ricocheted through me. "What is it?" I asked, confused.

"I—" he started, and shook his head like he was trying to banish whatever thoughts were tormenting him. "I'm sorry. Sloane, I–I just went through some stuff, and... Fuck." He dragged his hands down his face, his expression pained.

"Whatever it is, we'll figure it out. We always do." I tried to reassure him, and also put my own feelings on the backburner. I was pretty sure that whatever had happened wasn't something I'd done. And yet, the fact that he didn't want my touch, that he didn't crave it as much as I did... It stung a lot. "Do you want to talk about it?" I asked. Even I could hear the pain in my voice. I hated that.

His eyes searched my face. "Can I just hug you first maybe?"

"Gods, Fischer, you don't even have to ask." I opened my arms and welcomed him in. He was stiff at first, slowly wrapping his arms around my waist, but then I felt his cheek press against my chest. He was trembling in my arms, and I wanted nothing more in that moment than to know who had hurt him and what they had done so that I could make them fucking pay for it. This was not the reunion that we were owed.

"It's okay, baby. It's okay," I whispered as I rubbed his back.

"You smell like you," Fischer murmured. "It really is you, isn't it?" Dread settled in my stomach, and suddenly I had an inkling of what he'd possibly gone through.

"Yeah, Fish. It's me. Nobody's going to hurt you. I love you." He lifted his head from my chest all too soon and I missed the warmth of his body. His eyes were glimmering with unshed tears.

"They did things... Well, one guard in particular did things to me." He took a deep breath and my heart hammered within my chest. I was desperate to know what had happened to him, and at the same time I didn't know if I was ready to hear it.

"What did he do?" I asked softly.

"He raped me... repeatedly. As you," Fischer confessed, and it felt like the ground was falling away from beneath me.

"No." It was the only word that made sense at that moment.

"Yeah. Yes. I knew, *I knew* it wasn't you. I know it now, and I knew it then. But just seeing you here now, feeling you touch me... Everything feels fucked up. I need to be sure it's you."

I nodded. "I understand. I'll do whatever you need. I'm so fucking sorry, Fischer. Please tell me that person is dead, because if they're not, you're gonna have to give me an hour to go paint the walls red."

"Don't worry about that," he replied bitterly. "He's definitely dead, though I didn't get to give him the death he deserved."

We stared at each other for several moments. Our relationship had been a wild one. What started out of necessity had morphed into something so much more. We grounded each other, supported each other. We were definitely in love with each other.

"Smelling you helps," he murmured. "He didn't smell like you."

"No, I imagine he didn't, because you know the real me, Fischer. I would never take anything from you without consent. I want you, always. But I want you to want me in return. Do you know what I mean?"

"I do know." He paused, searching my face once again. He brought his hands up to my chest, slowly exploring the feel of my shoulders, down to my pecs. The feel of his hands on my body was nirvana.

"What can I do? Tell me how to help you. I'll do anything," I begged.

"Kiss me," he rasped, and I pulled back, shocked at the request.

"Are you sure? I want you to be certain, so that when my lips are on yours, you'll know that it's me kissing you. And one day, when our bodies come together again, I will leave no doubt in your mind that it's me that's making love to you. So if you want me to kiss you, I fucking will. I just want you to be sure."

Pink bloomed on Fischer's bronze cheeks. I loved when he blushed for me. He was so pretty. "Remind me, Sloane. Remind me how good we are together, and never let me go."

"Never," I growled, wrapping my arm around his neck and pulling him in against me. Our lips brushed in the softest caress, like a feather, barely dusting over the smooth bare skin. A tease and a tickle, ramping up the desire for more. A small whimper escaped his mouth and landed in mine, which I swallowed eagerly. With more intention, I let myself sink into the kiss, gently swiping my tongue against the seam of his mouth. It was a question. *'Is this okay? Will you let me in?'*

When his mouth opened and his warm tongue slid against mine, I got his answer. *'Yes. I'll let you in. Just take care of me.'* And that was something that he never had to doubt—I would always take care of him. I would always take care of everybody in this room, because the truth of the matter was, I loved them all in different ways. They were all mine, and I was theirs.

Fischer's hands moved to my face as he deepened our kiss. My head swam from the euphoria of this sensation that I thought had been lost. It was a fucking rush. I wasn't sure how long I stood there, kissing him, worshipping his mouth with mine. With a groan, he eventually leaned back and bit his bottom lip. He never looked sexier than when he did that. He knew what it did to me.

"Are you okay?" My voice was like speaking through glass, raspy as hell.

"I love you, Sloane. Thank you."

"Okay, everyone needs to stop making out long enough for showers," Red pleaded, and I glanced over my shoulder to see Kai licking his way down the column of her neck. Faris had lifted her full skirt and was eyeing a rather prominent blue vein that I could see from across the room. Cam and Bram were eyeing those three like they were a platter of appetizers they couldn't wait to get a taste of.

"It's been too long, Cub," Kai groaned, shaking his head.

"I know, and I agree, trust me… But I can't tell you the last time I had a shower, and I really want to wash the battle from my body before anything else happens," Saige demanded sweetly, pushing herself up slowly and awkwardly from Kai's lap.

Bram crossed the room with huge strides, helping her up. "My Goldie girl," he whispered, pulling her against him. "I have the perfect idea."

She looked up at him through hooded eyes, and he gave her a knowing look. "Oh. *Oh yes.* That is a perfect idea."

"What is?" Cam asked, pouring himself a drink from the bar.

"Bram has a huge bathroom that has a hot pool in it. It'll be big enough for everyone. Oh, I can't wait to get in it. Take me there now, demon man," Red begged dramatically, lifting the back of her hand to her forehead like she might faint.

"So dramatic, sweetheart," Fish murmured as he prowled her way. I took in the way she shivered when his hands came to rest on her shoulders. My dick definitely appreciated the sight of her squeezed between Bram and Fischer. Adrenaline was still running high—I was horny as hell. I'd already fought and I needed to fuck. Soon.

If Fischer wasn't ready for that yet, I would respect what he needed. I'd been the victim of shapeshifting headgames before, and recovering from that was very much a personal journey. The way everyone was eyeing Red though? I wasn't the only one feeling the primal urge to mark and claim.

Clapping loudly, I broke the trance. "Can we move this to the bath? I'm ready to get clean."

Bram's eyes burned into mine as he flashed a feral grin my way. "Everyone gather around and hold on tight."

I placed a hand on his shoulder, and my curse of "Motherfuck—" was cut off as we were pulled into the abyss. *I hate that shit.*

Saige

Chapter Twenty-Six

Warm water lapped against my neck as I floated in the heated pool. My body was burning under the intense gazes of my men, who were all eyeing me hungrily. I wanted them. All of them. A hand landed on my bare hip and I was tugged backward, causing my legs to sink as I was pulled against someone's chest. The sensation of a rock hard cock pressed between my ass cheeks had my belly clenching low.

"Little Cub," Kai purred in my ear. "I missed you, and I swear if I don't get to touch that sweet pussy and breathe in your sweet scent in the next ten seconds, I'm going to lose my fucking mind."

My eyes rolled back in my head as his hand slid lower, between my legs. The slickness that he found there had his purr getting louder.

"How does she feel, brother?" Cam rumbled, his eyes blazing with heat. I moaned as Kai's teeth nipped my neck.

"She feels like ours. Don't you, Cub? You want us to show you? Do you need us to remind you how good it is to be ours? Stars, I missed this sweet cunt."

"Kai," I gasped, as he slid two fingers deep within me.

"What's he doing to you, Firefly?" My eyes flicked to Faris. I found him sitting on the side of the pool, stroking his length methodically.

"He's touching me," I whimpered.

"Yeah?" Bram asked. "Where? Where is he touching you? Does it feel good, Goldie? Maybe you want all of us to touch you at the same time, hmm?"

"Please," I begged, as Kai rocked his hips against my ass.

"Please what, little witch?" Cam taunted, stepping in front of me.

"Make me come. Please." I moaned again as Kai's thumb began circling my clit, my head falling back on his shoulder where his lips easily found my neck. I squealed as a delicious pain burst through my nipples. Cam was toying with me now, and I eagerly wrapped my legs around his waist, desperate to have as much contact as possible.

"I want to eat this pussy, baby. Do you want that? You want to feel my tongue fucking you? Lapping you up? Put your legs on my shoulders. I want to eat what's mine." I cried out at the loss of Kai's fingers and his skilled thumb. But my disappointment didn't last long as Cam sank down into the water, easing my thighs over his shoulders and burying his face into my center. My back arched as his tongue lapped at me like a man possessed.

"That's right, boss. Eat that pussy." Kai encouraged Cam with his filthy words, and fuck if he didn't rise to the bait.

"Fuck, that is so hot," I heard Sloane groan. My head tilted to the side, seeking him out, and I found him sitting near Faris. The two of them had their eyes locked on the show as they fucked their fists.

"Guppy?" I questioned, looking for my sweet mage.

"Right here, sweetheart," he replied, his smooth voice coming from somewhere behind my head.

"Come kiss me," I begged. "Please, Guppy." And then there he was, just as Cam speared me on his tongue, and I cried out in ecstasy. Fischer leaned down, taking my mouth in a harsh kiss. Kai's hands slid down my back toward my ass as he began moving me onto Cam's face. The two of them set the pace and I just floated there, being completely ravished. Pleasure built quickly with each roll of my hips. I mounted that peak faster and faster until my orgasm crashed over me like a tsunami hitting the shore, much like the waves of the pool were lapping against the stone walls around us. I heard several growls echoing around the bathroom cavern. I knew we were just getting started, but holy fuck.

Cam licked up my center, getting as much of my slickness as he could. "I'll never get enough, baby. You taste like heaven." I squirmed away, my clit suddenly hypersensitive.

"Bring her over here," Bram ordered, his voice full of authority, and excitement filled my body as I wondered what he had planned. He was now sitting beside Faris, Sloane still beside them, all three of their rock hard cocks at full attention with their feet dangling in the water. My mouth watered. How did I get so lucky? Six beautiful men and they were all mine.

"Where do you want her?" Kai asked, as we glided through the shallow water.

"Right between my legs would be great," Bram replied, a dirty smirk on his face. I detached myself from Kai, and moved through the water at my own leisurely pace, staring up into the golden eyes of my demon prince. Well, I guess he was a king now, wasn't he?

"You want to feel my mouth, Bram?" I pulled myself up, bracing my palms against his thighs. His large hand cupped my cheek as he stared down at me. The thing about Bram that had captivated me from our very first meeting was his intensity. He was so sure of himself all the time. He knew exactly what he wanted, and he wasn't afraid to say it, or just take it for that matter. It was such a turn-on.

"I want everything, Goldie. Your mouth, your ass, your tits, and your cunt. All of it. But for now, your mouth will do." He guided my face down toward the crown of his glistening cock. I opened my mouth eagerly, desperate to taste him. His flavor hit my tongue like a shot of heroin to my veins. Jesus, he was all masculine beauty. He groaned as I slurped him down.

"Fuck," he hissed as he nudged the back of my throat. I reached up to cup his balls, so full and tight. I couldn't wait for him to spill his cum all over me; the demon within me wanted all of it right now. Wanted it on my skin. In my mouth. Wanted to smell like him so that every female in this realm would know this male belonged to me.

"You fought like a fucking queen today, Goldie. But by the stars, you suck this cock like a goddess." Hands trailed down my spine, and I lifted my ass up, eager for any sort of attention. I needed to feel our connection.

"Can I touch you, sweetheart?" Guppy asked. His hands paused just above my ass.

I popped Bram out of my mouth and glanced back. "Of course you can. I want you to. I need you, Guppy. Touch me, lick me, fuck me. I'm yours." His eyes looked almost pained for a moment. Before I could ask him what was wrong, I felt his hands moving down my hips and a finger gliding through my cheeks.

Bram turned my head back to him, easing my mouth back over his length. I swirled my tongue, eager to please him. The groans that left his mouth spurred me on, while the feel of soft lips down my spine had a shiver erupting through me.

"Fuck, I missed you, Goldie," Bram breathed. The lust in the air was becoming so thick, it was almost like I could see it swirling around us, holding us captive in this pool, prisoners to each other's bodies. Bram leaned back, bracing himself on his palms, his beautiful abdomen on full display.

"Baby Fang," he grunted. "Come here." My eyes flicked over to Faris, who was staring at my mouth around Bram with unbridled want. In a flash, he was standing right beside us.

"What do you want, you big demon?" Faris flirted, his erection proud as he placed his hands on his hips and stared down at Bram.

"I want to try something," Bram confessed. Oh, my gods. Was he going to suck his dick? *If he sucks his dick right now, I think I'm going to die.* Literally. I'd made it through a battle with pure evil, but the idea of my big ginger demon getting his mouth fucked by my blood mage? I was certainly going to die of dehydration. A whimper left my mouth before I'd even realized, and my two mates' eyes were on me in a flash.

"What do you think, Firefly? Do you think I should try whatever Bram has in mind?" Faris' voice was raspy and full of seduction. I nodded eagerly, and was met with several deep chuckles from my other mates.

"You really are a dirty little witch, aren't you?" Cam asked. His hand was beneath the surface of the water. I could tell by the way his arm muscles were clenching that he was stroking himself.

"Please," I begged, the words mumbled since my mouth was currently stuffed full.

"Please, what, Princess? You want me to touch Faris? Do you want to watch me taste him while you taste me?" Bram lifted a brow in challenge, and yep, I was officially dying. Two fingers slid into my cunt, and I jerked, taken by surprise.

"It's just me, sweetheart," Guppy whispered behind me as he swirled his fingers deep within my body.

Bram's eyes raked down Faris' body, before pausing at his dick. He licked his lips. "I've missed this cock. I never thought I'd fantasize about something like this..."

"You're not the only one," Cam replied smoothly, though I noticed his eyes briefly flick over to Kai. Fucking hell, these men. Where did they come from? Some kind of delicious passion pit forged in hell—I wanted them to drag me there, keep me captive.

"It's not that hard to get addicted to the sight of a man with your cock in his mouth," Sloane rumbled. He was sitting close to Bram and had a front row seat. Faris reached down, leisurely pumping himself. I caught sight of a glistening bead on the tip of his cock. He was already weeping with arousal. "Faris," Sloane's deep voice continued. "Put your cock in his mouth. Let him suck you off."

I watched, continuing to bob my head up and down at a slow pace as Faris glared at Sloane, his fangs slowly elongating. He stepped forward, a foot on either side of Bram, who was still propped up on his hands, right at the perfect height.

"Lay back, Bram," I whispered, keeping my lips in contact with the crown of his cock. "If you lay back, then I can watch." I was dying to see how this was going to go down.

"Filthy witch," Kai praised me, gliding through the water, bending down to grip my chin and kiss me deeply. He didn't care that I had just been licking another man's dick. He wanted me no matter what. I heard Cam grunt as Kai swirled his tongue in my mouth, and I knew Kai had to be getting a taste of my demon.

He turned my head back toward Bram and Faris. My demon was now flat on his back and Faris was slowly lowering himself down to his knees. Cam was suddenly on my other side as he leaned close to my ear, whispering, "Keep your eyes on them, baby girl. I want to see how much you enjoy watching them."

"Oh, gods," I moaned. My eyes widened as Bram's large hands moved up the back of Faris' thighs, urging him to lean over his head. The first swipe of Bram's tongue against Faris' cock had both of my men groaning. Faris hissed as he fed the length of his thick, fat dick into Bram's eager mouth.

A thumb suddenly circled my clit, and I moaned even louder. *"Fuck."*

Sloane chuckled. "You like that?" My eyes glanced over to see that *he* clearly liked it a lot, judging by his impressive erection.

"Holy cocksucking demon prince motherfuck—" Faris bellowed, as Bram's knuckles turned white as he gripped his thighs hard. His hands slid up, gripping Faris' ass, pulling him deeper into his mouth, urging him to fuck.

"That's right, Faris. Fuck his face." Sloane's deep voice hit me right in my core. My orgasm came out of nowhere, barreling through me as my body rippled around Fischer's thick, talented fingers.

Cam fisted my hair roughly, pulling my head back and forcing my face up to stare into his green eyes. "You are so fucking sexy when you come. I dreamt of you every night while we were apart, baby girl. Tell me, did you dream of my big dick filling you up?"

"Jesus," Kai groaned at Cam's words. My eyes widened when Cam's other hand reached across my body. He roughly grabbed hold of Kai, the same way he was holding me, and he pulled us both against him at the same time. First kissing me, then turning his attention to our Alpha who was practically whining with need. I panted—I couldn't help it. I was so close. I could see their tongues battling one another. Their hard, wet bodies pressed up against each other. Oh my gods, it was all too much.

"Sexy fuckers," I whispered, earning a chuckle from Fischer as he lowered his mouth to my neck and began nipping the skin there gently.

"Bram! You naughty demon!" Faris shouted. We all looked over to see Bram's middle finger circling Faris' ass. "I'm going to blow down your throat, Bram. If you don't want it, you need to stop right now." Bram released an unholy snarl, slamming Faris' cock all the way down his throat as his middle finger gently breached his hole. His tail snaked up, wrapping around Faris' tight balls. *Oh. Oh my moons.* I watched as Bram's throat worked, swallowing down every drop that Faris fed him. My body felt like it was on fire. I had to get out of the water or I was going to burn up.

"Get me out," I begged no one in particular, and suddenly I was pulled through the water and deposited carefully on the side of the pool. I would normally have felt self-conscious right now. I was the largest I had ever been. At this point, my stomach was so swollen that I couldn't even see my legs or my knees sitting here.

"Are you okay, kitten?" Sloane asked, reaching out and running the backs of his fingers down my arm.

"Hell yes, I'm okay!" I grinned at him. "Just so fucking hot all the time. You can't expect me to watch you guys swallowing each other's dicks and not expect me to catch on fire."

Kai threw his head back and laughed. "So I shouldn't suck Daddy's cock then?" he teased, and I didn't miss the way Cam's eyes flared.

"Oh no, you definitely should. You should absolutely do that. If you want to, I mean. I would like it if you, you know, did that with Cam..." I was rambling. I locked my fingers together over my stomach to keep myself from adding hand gestures along with the babbling.

Kai shot me a cheeky wink before turning to Cam. "Get over here, Thunder Daddy. Our little witch wants you to get your dick sucked." Cam growled as he moved through the water like a fucking water god. His long hair fell in wet waves down his chest and water dripped from his beard. His tattoos seemed to sparkle in the lighting.

He practically tossed Kai up onto the platform around the pool before climbing out of the water himself. They were both harder than stone, fully erect. An absolute vision of masculinity.

Kai dropped to his knees, his hand wrapped around Cam. The glint of piercings caught my eye, and I found my own mouth watering. It had been too long since I'd tasted him as well.

"Come over here, closer."

Kai smirked as he scooted over toward me at the edge of the pool. Cam now stood between us as we leaned in together, each of us running our tongue from his base to tip. Oh, this was hot.

"Let's blow Daddy's mind, Cub," Kai teased, smiling as he placed open-mouthed kisses up the length of Cam's erection. I nodded eagerly, wanting to do exactly that. We worked together, taking turns sucking on the head of Cam's cock, running our tongues down over the bumps of his piercings, and when Kai dropped his head lower and began sucking on Cam's balls, I thought we were all going to die of a heart attack right there.

I could feel the tightening of Cam's cock and knew he was seconds from blowing. "Fuck me," he groaned, his jaw clenched. "Fucking take it." His body shuddered as Kai and I waited cheek-to-cheek for him to spray us with his cum, and boy did he come and come. Thick ropes of his hot load landed on both of our faces, and I heard the sounds of all of my mates orgasming with him. I reached down and gripped Kai, giving him a few strong pulls before I felt his desire coming to a head. His tongue snaked out, and I watched him lick Cam's cum from his lip, and a second later he came in my hand, hard.

"Holy fuck," Fischer gasped.

"You can say that again, brother," Faris rumbled.

"Can I have a nap now?" I was suddenly fucking exhausted. What the hell was I thinking, having a seven-way after a damn battle? It seems I was still Saige, peen witch and snake tamer. At least they were fucking each other now too—that would give me a little bit of a break. Problem was, even just the thought of them fucking each other got me aroused.

Everyone slipped back into the water to get cleaned up. Tiredness was creeping in quickly now. The excitement was over, and our bonds had been satisfied.

"I'll go make sure that our sleeping arrangements are taken care of," Bram announced, exiting the pool and heading for the towel rack.

"We'll all be together, right?" I hated the thought of being apart from any of them so soon. Guppy was suddenly beside me, lacing his fingers with mine.

"Don't worry, baby," he told me, sensing my distress. "None of us are going to take our eyes off of you for a very long time."

"Okay. Good. That's good." I was relieved. The threat had been eliminated, but the memory of everything that Asrael and Laurie had put us through would always be there. I hated that even in death, they still held that power over our minds.

The guys were all drying themselves off, with huge towels

that were really more like freaking blankets. I assumed they needed towels made for demon-sized males here. Guppy went to move past me and I reached out, grabbing his hand. His honey oak eyes searched my face questioningly.

"Are you two coming?" Faris asked, as he tied the towel up around his head.

My eyes stayed locked on Guppy as I answered Faris. "We'll catch up."

"Don't be long, Goldie. You need your rest." The others gathered around Bram. Sloane threw a lingering look at the two of us, and my eyes bounced to Fischer just in time to see him drop his gaze to the water. Whatever was going on, I knew I needed to find out in private.

"We'll be right behind you guys. Go warm up the bed for me?" I asked hopefully. Gods, a warm bed with a whole pile of blankets and pillows sounded so damn good.

"You got it, Sprout. One warmed up bed, coming right up!" Kai grinned down at me, and blew me a kiss.

"Link hands," Bram ordered the other guys, holding out his own. They formed a circle, and then they were gone.

I spun around and gazed at my sweet mage. His curls were thick and wild, thanks to the humidity of the room, but his eyes were sad. So very sad.

"What happened, Guppy?"

Fischer

Chapter Twenty-seven

All I could do was stand there and stare at her concerned face. It shouldn't have surprised me in the least that she knew something was off with me. She shivered, and I took her hand, leading her back to the warmth of the pool. Giving myself time to think of how to answer that question.

"What happened, Guppy?" How could I even begin to tell her what had happened to me? I still felt broken and dirty. I knew what had happened wasn't my fault. I was a fucking victim. Gods, the word alone made me sick. I didn't want to be a victim.

"Sweetheart," I started, but no more words would come. I could see that her eyes were turning glassy with unshed tears, and I just couldn't handle it. "Please don't cry for me… We're all safe and we're back together, and that's what matters."

She shook her head. "That's not all that matters, and you know it. Do you know what happened to me? The day that I escaped with Sloane?"

"No," I replied. Staring down into the water, I wished that it could wash away the stain on my soul.

"Asrael almost raped me, Guppy."

It felt like my lungs had seized up in my chest as my eyes snapped up to hers. "What?" I growled. I moved through the water and took her into my arms. "I'm so sorry, sweetheart. Are you alright?"

Her arms wrapped around my waist, the pressure of her pregnant belly pressing against my own stomach. Her body had changed so much, yet she was still by far the most beautiful creature I'd ever seen. Pregnancy agreed with her. She looked like some kind of fertility goddess.

"I'm glad he's dead," she murmured against my chest. "I kicked him in the dick really hard."

"Good," I replied. "It's the least the fucker deserved. How do you feel now, though, with everything?" Maybe she was telling me this, because on some level, she knew that I had been through something similar.

Her big green eyes gazed at me, hitting me right in the heart. "I feel like I'm free."

Relief was rolling off of her in waves, but there was also that undercurrent of concern for me. Even after everything that she'd been through, she still put everyone else at the top of her list. It's who she was at her core—a loving and understanding woman with the heart of gold. She'd given me so much, and I needed to be honest with her now. Truth be told, I was terrified that she would look at me differently now, but I had to trust in us, in our relationship.

"Why didn't you want to touch me earlier?" she whispered.

I inhaled deeply through my nose. "It's not that I didn't want to. And I did touch you. You felt perfect. Your gorgeous body wrapped around my fingers, like it should be."

"But?" She lifted a brow, knowing there was more. She wasn't going to let me off easily.

"But I didn't know that I could do it," I replied honestly. Her brow furrowed. "When I was held prisoner here, I was tortured daily."

"Oh gods." Her hands flew to her mouth.

"They wanted information from me. They wanted to know

about Faris and how it was that he existed. I refused to break, so they tried harder." I pinched my nose with my fingers; my breathing was already becoming more choppy. "I'm not sure how long I'd been locked away by then; everything was blurring at that point. So it had to have been a considerable amount of time. Anyway, the demon who had been interrogating me was particularly sadistic. I was strapped to a chair, and Sloane appeared. I was thrilled—excited, you know? Finally, he was alive and he was with me, and we were going to get the fuck out of there." Saige's face was whiter than a ghost as she processed my words. "I figured out pretty quickly though, that it wasn't actually Sloane. But he kept coming back, over and over."

"No." She shook her head so violently that water flew off the tips of her shortened hair. "Guppy, no."

"I know, sweetheart," I said softly, as tears began to fall from both our eyes. It felt like my throat was closing over, and I was positive that the weight of my own emotions was going to crush me. My. Own. Emotions. Not the weight of everyone else's—no. These were all mine. Another effect of having my own mind and body completely to myself. I didn't have Faris there anymore to buffer, to take on some of the turmoil.

Suddenly, Saige was surging through the water, heading for the ledge of the pool. *Oh fuck. She's leaving me. Is she as disgusted with me as I am?* My own curiosity didn't let me keep my mouth shut, and my voice cracked as I asked, "What are you doing?"

She looked back at me over her shoulder, and my eyes widened. Her green eyes were glowing gold. *What the fuck?* "I'm going to kill them. All of them." A shriek of frustration left her as she lifted her trembling hands to her hair, tugging it. "I want to take your pain. I wish I could grasp those memories with my hands and destroy them."

I shook my head sadly. "I know that feeling, sweetheart. I've wanted to do it for so many people. If there were a way for me to do it to myself, I would. I don't know how to get myself back to what I was before."

I might not ever be able to handle anybody's touch again. Being in the pool, behind her, having control of the situation... My desire for her had been overwhelming. I'd needed to touch her, to make her body ripple around my fingers. However, the thought of her touching me, or any of the guys touching me—especially Sloane... Fuck.

"They tried to break me. They tried so fucking hard." My head dipped, and I wondered for the hundredth time—why wasn't I strong enough? Fucking hell, I was so ashamed, but I had to tell her. She needed to know the man I was before wasn't the same man standing here now. "I think they succeeded, Saige. I think they broke me."

Growling, she shook her head. "No. You're not broken." I couldn't look away from her golden eyes that were flashing with so much emotion. Anger, fear, sadness, protectiveness, love.

"I don't want to be. I don't want to cringe every time one of you goes to touch me," I whispered as the water moved gently around our legs.

"Guppy, I want to feel your heartbeat." She lifted her palm in question.

It's just Saige, my mate, the mother of my unborn children. I'm safe. I'm safe. I repeated those words as I nodded. Slowly, she reached out, almost as though I was a cornered animal that might bite her at any moment. Her fingertips connected with my chest, and I sucked in a breath. Fire raced through me, our connection flaring, reminding me that this right here? It was everything.

"You're not broken," she repeated, flattening her palm right over my thundering heart. "You're bruised and battered. You're strong, and one of the best men I've ever known. Any time you feel anything less than *mine*, I'll be here to remind you."

My hand was suddenly squeezing hers and my other was

pressed over her heart. Our eyes locked and a magnetic force seemed to hold me there. I couldn't have looked away if I tried.

"I think I can take them, Gup. Everything in me is demanding I take this trauma from you. Please, let me try? I love you, no matter what... But if I can take them away, for good, do you want that? I won't try it without your consent, Guppy."

"Why do you think you can?" I asked, genuinely curious.

"I took two of those shots. I think... I think I took on your affinities," she breathed, her eyes wide and still locked on mine.

"Can you read my emotions?"

She nodded. "I couldn't before I touched you, but I can now. You're disgusted and ashamed, but you're also hopeful. Hopeful that I can do this for you?"

Not taking my gaze from hers, I dropped to my knees. "Please help me, sweetheart. I'm begging you. I can't— I can't—"

"I know, baby. I know it hurts. Give it to me," she murmured, running her hands through my hair. Green and gold wisps of color began to circle the two of us, her eyes searching mine and then there, I felt her presence. It went against every fiber of my being, all my training, to let her into my head. But I did.

I watched as black, tainted memories in the form of fog began to wrap up her arms. I began to panic, not wanting those vile images in her brain. *Oh gods, what have I done?* Just as the fog began to creep up her neck, her eyes flashed black and the fog dissipated, the sounds of my past screams echoing around us until the very last bit of it lifted.

We slumped together, breathing heavily, holding each other tightly. "How do you feel?" Saige asked, wiping the moisture from my cheeks.

"Like I have the best woman in all the realms. Whatever you did, it worked. I don't know what you took from me, but I'm so fucking glad you did. Never tell me, Saige. Promise me? Whatever version of me that was just here with you—I don't ever want to be that man. That man was dead inside."

"My Guppy," she whispered, her eyes brimming with tears.

"My whole fucking world." I hauled her against me, taking her mouth with a fevered desire that she gave me right back. That was Saige. Anything we threw her way, she threw right back, usually harder. Fucking perfect.

"I love you," she breathed, nibbling on my bottom lip. "You sure you're okay? That was pretty intense."

My hands couldn't stop touching her skin, seeking contact wherever they could. "I'm more than okay. I missed you so much."

She pressed a quick kiss to my lips, before rising to her feet with a determined look, her eyes glowing gold again. "I have something I need to go do though."

"Wait, what?"

She stepped from the water, and the moment her foot connected with the stone floor, everything shook. A small tremor at first. Then, the intensity increased, with her wings, tail, and horns exploding from her body as her anger built.

"Sweetheart," I said gently, walking slowly in her direction. Her tail flicked, and the fury within her was so potent, it was nearly choking me. The ground rocked as she took a step away from me. "Shit. *Shit.*" I sped through the water, desperate to stop her. Her magic was roaring, and it was the perfect recipe for a disaster.

Saige's low growl reverberated through the room, as the sound bounced off the cavernous walls. The hair on the nape of my neck lifted at the animalistic noise. Without warning, her wings snapped out wide to their full size and vines exploded from everywhere. They crept down the walls and seemed to slither out of the damn pool. Fuuuuck.

'Guys, you need to get back here immediately. Right the fuck NOW!' I barked, opening the mental connection to the other five men who would be able to help tame her. My eyes widened as I watched the vines start to trail after her like snakes.

I hopped from the pool and followed, not letting her out of my sight. The air around me became charged, and the sound of a pop—followed by cursing—let me know the others had arrived.

"What the fuck is she doing?" Bram demanded, rushing to my side. The six of us were trailing behind her now, the ground still shaking. Nothing was being knocked over yet or falling from the walls, so I'd take that as a good thing.

"She wanted to talk about what happened while we were apart, so I told her. Or I started to... and she lost it. Her fucking eyes are glowing! She said she was going to kill them all, but I thought she'd calmed down. She seems to have taken on our affinities, thanks to that extra shot she took during the battle—she actually managed to remove some memories from me. Then this started, and I don't know what's happening."

"Firefly," Faris called out, and the vines paused in place, twisting around each other like living beings. "Firefly, we need you. Come see your mates, let us hold you." We held our breath as she turned slowly to face us.

"She feels threatened, feels her family is threatened. Female dragons—especially pregnant ones close to giving birth—aren't known for their patience or forgiveness when it comes to their mates and children," Bram explained, keeping a wary eye on her. "I'm sure the injections amplified everything, too."

"By the moon," Kai whispered, a deep purr rumbling from his chest. Saige's glowing eyes flashed over to Kai when she heard the sound. "Cub. You look beautiful." Kai blinked and his eyes transformed, closely matching our woman's.

Her chest heaved as she stared at Kai, and a sound that I'd only ever heard from him before slowly escaped her. It was a rumbling, relaxing sound—a purr.

"Jesus," Cam whispered in awe. "She's a shifter now?"

The shaking finally ceased and the vines began to slink away, disappearing up the walls and out of sight. We all stood there like fucking fools, staring at our mate. She looked every bit the epitome of a fertility goddess. Her large breasts were swollen, matching her belly, as she stood proudly, baring herself to us. Red lines had popped up along her hips and stomach at some point in our time apart. Her body had stretched and reformed itself to prepare to birth two babies.

"I... I need..." she whimpered, her eyes fading back to green as we swarmed her.

"Whatever you need, baby girl, we've got you," Cam promised.

Sloane wrapped his arms around her from behind. "What's wrong, kitten? Do you need to lie down?" My heart clenched at the sight of him holding her, his large hands spread over her belly. It was the most beautiful thing I'd ever seen.

A flash of sudden pain had me doubling over, this painful pressure in my abdomen hitting me like a sledgehammer.

"What the hell, brother?" Faris was beside me in an instant, encouraging me to speak. But I couldn't.

What fresh fuckery is this?

I got my hands on my knees, and lifted my head in time to see Saige mirroring my position as we panted together. Horror dawned as we both realized at the same moment what was happening.

"What can we do, Goldie? Please, for the love of fuck, can someone tell me what to do here?!" Bram barked, as he paced a few steps and turned to pace back.

"You need to get Balor," I grunted, and every one of my brothers turned to look at me.

Kai ran his hand up Saige's arm soothingly. "What? Why?"

"Find Balor," our woman gritted out. "Tell him to pack a bag because I'm going home."

Silence. Utter silence.

"Oh gods. Okay. He seemed like a pretty cool guy. He's got this whole sophisticated thing going for him and I really dig that, but I just don't think he's the right fit for our harem." Faris crossed his arms and glanced around at us. "I'm willing to put it to a vote. All in favor, say aye."

"What do you mean, you're going home?" Bram asked, ignoring Faris completely.

"I mean..." She paused and took a deep breath. Her eyes met mine, and I felt the squeezing again, like a big rubber band around my waist. Sweet merciful fates. "Someone better get me to my own damn house right this instant and bring me my damn doctor, because I'm in labor."

The contraction built, and I grimaced. Why in the hell was I being affected like this? Was I going to experience what vaginal birth felt like through my dick? *No, no. I can't do it.*

"Oh. Yeah. Okay, the babies are coming..." Bram mumbled, as he stared off into space. "I'll just go— Balor. Yeah..." He stumbled a few steps before vanishing to find the doctor.

"Sweetheart, your magic—what's going on with your magic?" She'd been powerful before, but the display I'd just witnessed had been next level.

Her eyes flickered, green flashing to gold. "I'm still going to kill those fuckers. Just as soon as I get these babies out. It's killing time!"

"Little witch, please sit down over here. Come on. Bram will be back soon." Cam wrapped his arm around her waist and directed her to a long bench that was cut from stone. He draped a large towel around her, securing it beneath her arms.

Sloane was hovering while Kai and Faris seemed unable to keep themselves still. "Red, talk to us about the magic. Are you okay? It's probably from that fucking vaccine," he gritted out.

The tightening was coming on again. Fucking hell.

"I'm fine!" she snapped, leaning back against the wall and closing her eyes. "Where the fuck is Balor?!"

As if on cue, Bram and Balor both appeared out of thin air, the doc rushing to her side and taking her hand. "Tell me everything."

"Tell you everything?" Kai scoffed. "She's in fucking labor, man! Do something!"

Balor released a deep chuckle. "And what do you propose I do? There is only so much a doctor can do. Every woman's labor runs at their own pace. This could go quickly or it could be days."

"Days?" Saige all but groaned at that revelation when Balor nodded, confirming she'd heard right.

"She wants to go home, man. To her house. What do you advise?" Cam demanded, running his hands through his hair.

Balor paused for a moment, thinking. "I think the queen should be fine to deliver wherever she feels safest and most comfortable. I will prepare my medical bag and meet you in the king's quarters in fifteen minutes." Then he vanished.

"Firefly," Faris whispered, dropping down next to her and trailing his fingers down her hair. "I love you."

She gave a weak, but genuine smile. "I love you, Viper."

My stomach began to cramp, and I watched as her face turned from happy to a grimace. "Get me home. Now!" She moaned in pain, and everyone sprang into action. We all gathered around her so that Bram could jump us out of there to grab some clothes and prepare to meet up with Balor.

Sloane's gaze met mine, and his look of sheer terror nearly stole my breath. Reaching out, I laced our fingers together and felt some of the fear drain as he stared at our linked hands. Slowly, his eyes returned to my face, and I smiled.

"We're about to become fathers," I whispered, my words just for him.

"I can't believe this is happening. Like, it's really happening, Fish. I'm fucking terrified."

I laughed. "The man who knows no fear is scared of a couple tiny baby girls?"

He gave me a scowl. "I may not know anything about babies... or girls, for that matter. But something tells me that these two will be most dangerous at their tiniest. That's when they'll make me their slave for life."

"Well." I squeezed his hand. "You'll have five other 'slaves' to commiserate with. We'll all be under their spell soon enough."

Bram stepped up to the circle, completing it. "Plan is to get dressed and the moment Balor arrives, I'll open the portal and we'll go. When I retrieved Balor, I sent word to Khol so I think he'll be waiting for us." He inhaled deeply. "Right then. Here we go."

The room spun away and we landed back in Bram's massive bedroom. Kai and Faris hustled to grab Saige something to wear and a loud knock pounded on the door. "Where is my daughter?!" Khol boomed, his knocking sounding more like full body slams.

"Fuck's sake," Sloane cursed, disappearing from our room to answer the door.

"Here, Cub. This should be comfortable. I know how you love nightgowns," Kai spoke sweetly, slipping a soft cotton nightdress over her head. She'd tucked her wings and tail away so it easily fell over her body.

She smiled. "Thank you, Kai." My adrenaline kept spiking through me while I moved through the room, gathering up clothes to wear.

Khol barged into the room, and I covered my dick. "Are you out of your mind? She was just naked two seconds ago!"

He didn't even glance my way as he charged to the bed, dropping to his knees and taking her hand. "Wild one. I was told it's time. Is it?"

"Yeah, it's time." She smiled wide and Khol sucked in a harsh breath, dropping his face to his hand. I still couldn't get a read on his emotions, but I didn't need to have my magic to do that. This man was proud. He loved his daughter fiercely. He was, in this moment, complete.

Saige's eyes glistened as Khol stayed kneeling before her. "I'm so proud of you, my brave daughter. The stars truly blessed me the day they gifted me you." He stood and took a step back, but Saige rose from her seat on the bed and threw her arms around him. Khol's eyes were wide as dinner plates but his entire posture quickly melted into contentment. I was sure I wasn't the only one who saw the lone tear that slipped down his cheek.

"I love you, Dad," Saige proclaimed, and he released her, pulling back to look at her face. All of us were shamelessly watching our mate have this moment with her father.

"What did you say?" Khol gasped, and I sucked in air as a bolt of pure happiness radiated from him. It was the first time I'd ever picked up on anything from him, and it was overwhelming. Saige was feeling loved and protected by her father, and he was beyond happy. They were staring at each other in a way that made it hard to believe they'd only known each other for a few short months.

"I said I love you," she repeated with a sniffle.

Khol's bottom lip trembled. "After that."

She beamed at him. "Dad. I said, I love you, Dad."

Khol's mouth opened to speak, but nothing came out. Saige hugged him again, giving him time to get ahold of himself. "I love you so much, my wild girl. You're beautiful, brave, and strong. Thank you for letting me earn your love and trust. I'm going to stay here in Besmet and set things up. Vaeryn and Emrys have agreed to help. If anything changes, I'll send word. Have someone come tell me when the babies arrive? I'll come for a quick visit."

We were ready to go. Balor would be here any moment.

"What do you want me to tell Miranda?" Saige asked, lifting a brow.

Khol grinned. "Tell her what I wish to say to her isn't appropriate for my daughter's ears."

"Oh gods, gross." Saige gagged, and we all laughed just as Balor popped into the room.

"Tell her and Annie that I miss them both, and I'll see them very soon." He kissed her forehead and ushered her over to us before meeting each of our eyes. "Take care of my daughter and my granddaughters. I've never met a more loyal group of men in my existence and I am happy to call each of you family. Safe travels. Enjoy this moment."

He didn't have to say why he wanted us to enjoy it. We all knew it was because it had been stolen from him. Not only had he missed the birth of his baby, he'd missed her entire childhood. As I looked around at my brothers, I knew there wasn't a chance in hell that any of us would ever take this for granted. Bram cast his palm out against the spacious stone wall and the portal burst into existence. Saige took the lead, stepping before our group and glancing back over her shoulder.

"It's time to go back to Emerald Lakes. I'm going home."

With a smile on her face, she disappeared and we followed.

We'd always follow.

Bram

Chapter Twenty-eight

"Listen to me, you fancy-dicked, knotted-up, breeder stallion sons of bitches!" Goldie growled as another contraction passed, allowing her to breathe air into her lungs. She'd used each chance for breath wisely, cursing all of us, but mainly Sloane and I for putting her in this condition.

"You think I'm a fancy stallion?" I puffed my chest out, pleased with that compliment.

"It's... not... a compliment!" She threw herself back against her pillows, huffing a breath of irritation.

Balor had given her some medication and used some of his healing magic to lessen her pain, but my mate was exhausted. When he'd predicted her labor could last days, he wasn't wrong. It had been over twenty-four hours now. He'd assured us that the girls were in an optimal position for a safe, natural delivery, but with each passing hour, we were all growing more anxious. Fischer had needed to go sit in the fucking woods twelve hours ago because if he was in the same room as her, it debilitated him.

Turns out Balor was a demon of many talents, and was able to place some kind of physical block on Fish's ability to actually feel her pain, but it wasn't enough. Between Goldie crying and screaming, Kai's relentless whining and pacing, Sloane's nervous scowling, Cam's helicopter daddying, Faris' ridiculous questions and my own excitement.... It was too much for our empath to handle.

We opted to all leave the room for an hour at a time so Fish could have time with her alone. She told him she didn't want him going through the mental torture of it, but he said the real torture was sitting alone in the woods and not getting to be a part of the birth. We were to call him inside when it was time for the delivery.

"This is taking too long. I don't think this is normal. Where is that damn demon? Balor?!" Kai roared, storming out of the bedroom that had been turned into a makeshift delivery room. Faris slipped in past him, proudly carrying a large loaf of bread and a jar of grape jelly.

Goldie's narrowed eyes tracked him with the precision of a serial killer, and I was starting to get concerned for each of our lives if these babies didn't come soon. We were all watching as he sat everything down on the pink loveseat before rushing from the room again, muttering curses.

"What the hell is he doing?" Sloane asked, arms crossed.

Faris flew back into the room before anyone could respond. Not that we had answers. Faris did whatever he wanted. He proudly placed a six slice toaster on top of her dresser and plugged it in. Balor and Kai returned, the doctor assuring the shifter that yes, this was actually normal. Especially for a first-time mom. It was going to take some time for her body to get to where it needed to be for delivery. Kai didn't want to hear it though, and Cam grabbed the back of his neck just in time to stop him from tearing into Balor.

The sound of the toaster lever being slammed down brought the focus back to Faris.

"Hungry, are ya?" Balor inquired, opening up his bag of supplies.

Faris' face screwed up in disgust. "Like I'd ever eat this shit. This is for my Firefly. As you will soon see, she's become quite...

ferocious. Bette told me in the kitchen that she suffers from hanger. A disease easily cured by snacking."

"Gonna... kick... his cute ass..." Goldie panted. Sloane ran a hand down his face and groaned. Faris narrowed his eyes at Sloane, and I took that as my cue to intervene.

"Baby Fang," I murmured, walking up to him and smiling in an attempt to diffuse the tension. "That was nice of you. Where'd you get a toaster this size anyway?"

He smiled widely at my interest and started rattling off the specifications of this supersize toaster. "I thought it'd be good because you know, we have a supersize family." His eyes widened. "I probably should buy another one. We'll have two more to feed soon. I won't stand for breakfast fights over the toaster usage. That doesn't seem like a healthy environment. Plus, I read that babies really like toast and stuff. They had strawberry jelly too, and it kind of looked like blood so I thought maybe I would like it?"

I couldn't believe my ears. He'd tried jelly? Of all the foods? "Well? Did you like it?"

A full body shiver overtook him and he shook his head. "Fuck no. It's all... jelly-like and jiggly. One tiny lick was all I needed to know it wasn't for me. How does anyone eat food like that? Fucking psychos." He was so serious I couldn't help the full belly laugh that escaped me. "I knew you'd agree with me. I never saw myself being sexually involved with a demon who has a loose butthole, but here we are."

He clapped me on the shoulder and sauntered off to the bed. "What the fuck?" I cursed and glanced over to Sloane, Kai, and Cam. All three of them were shaking with laughter, trying to be quiet. I stormed over to them. "My butthole is not loose. Keep laughing, fuckers. One day, we'll have a tightest butthole competition, and I guarantee you that I will win. It will be a whole event!"

They laughed harder, and Kai grinned. "Did you hear that, guys? He wants to have a *hole* event."

"Oh, I heard. I bet there'll be some tight competition." Sloane smirked at me.

I leaned down and whispered, "Okay, you shits. Laugh all you want... but mark my words, I will win by a wide margin. There'll be no stretching the truth then!" I flipped them all off and stormed away to their roaring laughter.

Dropping down beside my queen, I took her hand in mine, and she smiled up at me. Her face was flushed and shiny from the work she'd been putting in over the last day. "You're gorgeous, Goldie."

"Ha. You're funny, Bram. What were you guys laughing about?" Her eyes briefly fluttered shut as Balor palpated her belly, his hands glowing softly as he worked his magic.

"Nothing, princess. They're all just jealous of my superior physique." I tossed a scathing look over at the laughing fools.

"How's she doing, doc?" Cam asked, composing himself as he joined us at the bedside.

Balor removed his hands and smiled down at Goldie. "Perfect. Everything is perfect. Can you have Bette bring up the supplies we prepared for delivery? I need someone to fetch a stack of clean towels and it would be best to get Fischer in here." Every male in the room was surrounding the bed in the blink of an eye, except for Faris who leaped to his feet and took off, yelling about his brother.

"What? It's time? Finally?" Goldie practically whimpered.

"Yes, my queen. Your body is ready. Have you been feeling an urge to push?"

My beautiful mate paused. "Uh... well, I've been feeling like my butt was going to fall out or something during the last few contractions..."

My wide eyes flicked across the bed to Cam, Kai, and Sloane, who were all mirroring my stunned expression. If I wasn't mistaken, big Thunder Daddy was looking quite pale.

Balor chuckled. "That sounds about right."

"Oh gods, here comes another—" Goldie's breath was stolen as a strong contraction took over her entire body. Fischer, Faris, and Bette appeared just as it waned. Fish had a stack of towels which he promptly delivered to the bedside. Faris and Bette set a basket full of herbs, crystals, and who knows what else on a table that we'd set up for this purpose.

"Sweetheart." Fish dropped down beside her and stroked her cheek. "You're almost there, okay? The pain will be over soon."

Another contraction hit and she let out a terrible scream. I couldn't take hearing her in so much pain. Gods, I wished I could just take this agony from her.

"She should get on her hands and knees," Bette declared, bustling over with a bundle of dried herbs that she arranged in a tin tray and lit aflame. "It was the only way I was able to deliver, and it was how she was also brought into the world. It's a good position."

Bette knew that Laurie was dead, though the specifics hadn't been discussed yet. Too much had been going on to get into the nitty-gritty of everything. Rick, Hunter, and Randy Roger were hanging out together in Bette's cottage to give us all privacy right now. Much to everyone's surprise, Goldie's sister, who was supposed to be here, wasn't. Hunter assured us she was safe, but there was a story there. Unfortunately, none of us had the time right now to worry about it.

"Do you think you'd prefer that? We can help you flip," Balor offered.

"Gods, yes. I can't lay on my back anymore. Help me, please help me," she begged, her eyes pleading with each of her mates. A thin sheet was over her legs and she'd lost the nightgown a long time ago, saying a sports bra was more comfortable.

"Okay, baby. Come on, let's get you comfortable," Cam

soothed, pulling her sheet away. Together, we helped her get into a better position and she groaned in relief as she let her belly touch the mattress, allowing her to stretch her back out.

She was bare from the waist down already, and Balor instructed her to face the side of the bed and let her feet hang over the edge of the opposite side. This would allow him to catch the babies.

Her arms were shaking so badly I didn't see how she'd be able to hold herself up, but she did. Our woman was so strong. Bette took a small glass jar from her basket and dipped her fingers into the contents, a clear liquid. She trailed her fingers down Goldie's forehead, over her nose and lips while murmuring some kind of incantation.

"Sweet child, I am so proud. You're about to find out what it means to love fully. There is no comparison. It's how I love you. May the stars bless you and guide you through safely to motherhood," Bette whispered, wiping away the rogue tears from her face. "Enjoy this moment with your mates. I will return soon to meet your sweet girls."

Goldie reached out with one hand and gripped Bette's tightly. "I can't. It hurts, Gran. Oh gods, it hurts!"

"You can and you will, Saige Wildes. You're the strongest being in this room. Focus now, feel the comfort of your mates, the presence of the stars, and push those babies out," Bette told her sternly. Shit, I didn't even have babies to push out and I felt myself give a test push.

Goldie nodded, releasing her hold on her grandmother. "I love you, Gran."

The older witch smiled. "I know. I'll see you soon." She turned to look at each of us. "Take care of her and send word as soon as you're able. I'll be at my cottage with the others." With that, she left the room.

"Oh fuuuuuck!" Goldie screamed, dropping her head to the bed to stifle her cries.

Balor moved behind her, assessing. "Push, my queen. Push through the pain. You can do this."

A slice of toast sailed through the air, followed by another, and another. "What the fuck are you doing now, you lunatic?!" Sloane barked.

Faris growled, continuing to throw bread around. "It's all burnt. Ruined. I need an untoaster. This is garbage!"

"Fuck the toast, Faris! Get your ass over here!" Goldie yelled, snapping him out of his panic.

He rushed over and took her hand. "I'm sorry. I'm nervous," he muttered. Goldie didn't respond, as another wave of pain quickly hit.

I climbed up on the bed, and ran my hand up and down her back. "You got this, Goldie. My tiny warrior. Push, princess. Keep pushing."

"Ahhh, I've been cursed!" she shrieked into the blankets.

"Red, you're almost there. Come on, you got this. We're right here with you." Sloane's voice was serious, but it seemed to give her what she needed at that moment.

"Push, push, push! That's it. Here comes the first one," Balor announced, and I felt as though my heart was going to explode from my chest.

With an animalistic scream, Goldie gave it her all. I watched in disbelief as Balor held up a tiny, wiggly baby with a red face and very red hair. "A beautiful little girl."

She slumped over onto her side, panting wildly. "I did it?"

"You did it, Cub. Gods, you did it." Kai dropped a kiss to her head, and Cam came over with a cool, damp cloth to wipe her face.

"Who is cutting the cord?" Balor glanced around and chuckled when the group of us froze. "Ah, come on now. It's a little cut."

"Kai," Goldie said, smiling at our Alpha while Faris and

Fischer sandwiched her between them, each holding one of her hands.

Kai's gaze snapped to hers, his mouth dropping open. "Yeah? Really?"

I couldn't help but laugh as he started bouncing on his toes with excitement. Kai suddenly glanced at me, and his face fell. "Oh, I... I mean, Bram, you should do it."

"What? Why?"

"I just thought because she's got the same hair and you're her—"

I shook my head slowly at first and then more firmly. "I'm her what? Father?" I looked at my family, all of us together and alive, sharing this moment. "Regardless of who sired this baby, or any of the others the stars bless us with, I vow to love every single child created in this family as my own. This little princess, she's not just mine. She's ours. Please, Kai." I clapped his shoulder. "Cut the cord, brother."

"Couldn't have said it better myself," Cam agreed, his voice tight with emotion.

"I'm so excited!" Kai bounded, quite literally, to the end of the bed, and Balor explained what he needed to do.

"You were perfect, sweetheart. I love you so much," Fish whispered to Goldie, kissing her cheek.

Faris watched in awe as Kai cut the cord, and I suddenly noticed a scattering of toast crumbs through his hair. "Absolutely amazing, Firefly. Thank you for giving us such a gift."

Balor carefully carried the baby over to the table. "Let me clean her up. Rest for a moment, my queen."

Little wails were bouncing around the room and with a lingering look at my tiny warrior, I walked over to join Balor. I needed to see my daughter's face up close.

"Shh, little princess. We'll get you to your daddy in just a moment. Your mama still has some work to do," Balor cooed as he wiped her down. He glanced at me over his shoulder. "Take your shirt off, Your Majesty. Babies need skin-to-skin."

Tears blurred my vision as I all but ripped my damn shirt off. "Where should I— I mean, do I need to—" Fuck, I couldn't even form a sentence. I'd never held a baby before.

"Have a seat there, on the loveseat."

"Okay, yeah." I ran to the damn thing. Balor had her loosely wrapped in a soft cream-colored blanket, which I'd be replacing with the one I'd made as soon as possible. The bundle in his arms was so damn small. So fragile.

I looked over to the bed and found Goldie staring at me with love, before her face crumpled, morphing into an expression of extreme pain. "Oh gods, I need to push!"

Balor quickly guided the baby into my arms, with her body against my chest. He carefully tucked the blanket over her, before rushing back to my mate. The others were helping Saige back into position when I heard the tiniest little coo I'd ever heard. My heart melted into a puddle before I even laid eyes on her face.

Like a magnet, our eyes connected as soon as I looked down, and I had to stifle the sob that was sitting in my throat. Chubby red cheeks, big hazel eyes with gold flecks, and a wild mess of red hair. "Sweet girl," I whispered, running my hand over the top of her head. Gods, I'd never felt anything so soft. My face was wet, my heart was full, and my soul was singing with happiness. This moment was one I'd thought I'd never get. The time spent as a prisoner, the moment my knees had hit that wooden floor and I'd been forced down, Asrael swinging that massive axe... A ragged sob took me by surprise as I stared at my perfect daughter.

I'd lived a long time already. Demons were raised rougher than humans or any who lived in this realm. Death for us was simply the next phase. A new beginning. The disappointment and heartbreak that I'd felt in what I thought were my final seconds— knowing that I'd never get to make love to my mate again or wake to her wrapped snugly around my body, that I'd miss not only the birth of my children, but the honor of knowing what kind of women they'd grow up to be... I was positive I'd never felt something so utterly devastating in my life.

But here I was, with my family, holding one baby and about to meet the next. She wiggled within the blanket, breaking my train of thought and pulling me back to the moment, which was exactly where I wanted to be. I didn't want to miss anything. She freed one arm and quickly brought it to her mouth. Clumsily, she tried to get her little fist into her open mouth and I gently helped guide her. The moment her fist hit her mouth, she started sucking and chomping like a wild little monster, and I found myself chuckling deeply.

"You'll get to eat soon, little piglet. For now, you get to spend some time with your Papa. Come here," I whispered, rearranging her so that more of her bare skin was pressed up against my chest. She started thrashing like the little monster I was quickly learning she was, and I yelped when I felt a deep suck on my nipple. Raising her higher, I helped her get her fist in her mouth again. "I know you're hungry, but Papa doesn't have anything for you. These chest raisins are merely for visual appreciation. By the stars though, you might take your mother's right off with that force."

"Push, little witch! You're almost done." Cam's voice pulled me from my baby-induced fog.

"Oh gods, it hurts. It hurts so bad!"

"Balor!" Fischer barked. "What's happening?"

The room exploded when Balor lifted his hands and we found them covered in dark blood. My Goldie was sobbing as she continued trying to deliver the other baby.

"This baby is bigger than the first. I'll give you five minutes to deliver her or I'm going to have to take her to surgery at the palace." He placed his hand on her belly. "The baby is still doing fine, but I'm getting concerned with the amount of blood loss here. There's been some internal tearing."

"What do you mean? *What does that even mean?!*" Faris demanded.

"It means that her body has been through a lot, and it's taken its toll. After delivery, I'll have to do some stitching..."

Goldie groaned. "No. I can do this. I can do—" Another scream.

"Come, brothers. Everyone touch her. We're going to lend her our power and hopefully, it will give her enough strength." Sloane leaned down to her, brushing her wet hair back from her face. "You're doing so good, baby."

I walked as carefully as possible, not wanting to fuck up and drop the baby. Fischer's eyes never left the little red head that was peeking out of the blanket against my chest as I sat down and reached out with my left hand, wrapping it around Goldie's fist that was tangled in the blankets.

"Alright, my queen. Give me one more big push, let your mates' magic fill your reserves and strengthen your body. She's right here—she's ready to meet you," Balor instructed, as all of our hands lit up with our magic. Goldie's own body took on a green glow and then a rainbow of color engulfed her body.

"Now! Push like hell!"

The scream that left her was gut-wrenching. My beautiful, exhausted, warrior woman. I begged whoever would listen to let this be it. *She's done enough now. Let this be enough.*

A new screech pierced the air, and we all looked in amazement at the chunky dark-haired baby who was wailing her little butt off.

"You did it, Sprout! Holy shit, you did it!" Kai cried, tears streaming down his face. His smile was probably the widest I'd ever seen it.

"One more push, then you're really done. You have two beautiful daughters, my queen. Cam, come here and hold this underneath her, like this." Balor motioned to an honest to gods bucket. *Since when did this become a barnyard?!*

"What? What is that for?" Cam stepped next to Balor, who was cleaning off the still wailing baby as best he could.

"The afterbirth. Now, who is cutting the cord?" He looked around and landed on Sloane. "Would you like the honors?"

Sloane took a deep breath. "Faris?"

My Baby Fang startled at the sound of his name. "Yeah?"

"Would you? Cut the cord?"

Faris' mouth fell open. "Really?" His entire face lit up, and it was one of the most beautiful things I'd ever seen.

"Yeah. I want you to be the one," Sloane replied, blinking rapidly, and I caught the look of adoration it earned him from Fischer.

"Why?" Faris narrowed his eyes in suspicion.

"Because, I don't want you missing out on anything anymore." The grumpy mage shifted on his feet awkwardly as Faris stared at him, before speeding over and wrapping Sloane in a bear hug, lifting him a few inches off the ground.

"Thank you!" He put Sloane back on the ground and was beside Balor in a flash. "What do I do? Do I use my teeth?"

"I think we'll just use these surgical scissors, if it's all the same to you," Balor replied in his dry tone that had me chuckling. He handed Faris the scissors, pointing out where to cut.

"Neither of them will feel this?" Faris asked, concerned.

"Nope, not at all. Just cut right here and then we can get her cleaned up."

Faris grinned as he cut the cord, and then Balor whisked the baby over to the table. "Just keep that bucket right there, Cam. The placenta will be coming any moment now."

I could see sweat beading Cam's brow. "There's a lot of blood, Balor."

Goldie groaned, her teeth clenched. "Pushing now."

"Sweet gods in the sky," Cam choked out, and I couldn't help the booming laugh that left me.

"Hey, Kai, you better help him out," Sloane called, from his position over by Balor and Faris.

Kai joined Cam, and his expression was one I'd never, ever forget. Eyes wide in horror, mouth open in shock. "By the stars," he breathed.

A plopping, squelching sound signaled the true end. It was what happened next that would go down as the greatest thing I'd ever witnessed.

"That is… the most disgusting— I… Oh no." Cam leaned over and threw up next to the bucket holding the placenta.

"No, Cam. No, I'm a sympathy puker. Don't do this!" Kai shouted, covering his eyes and ears with his hands. Cam stood and wiped his mouth, his face void of any color.

"Did you just vomit?!" Goldie screeched into the blanket, going to roll onto her side, not realizing the two idiots behind her hadn't moved the bucket yet. As she moved, the entire thing tipped and the placenta splashed out onto Cam and Kai's feet.

"Fucking hell!" Sloane shouted, watching the entire thing with shock.

"It's like… a big, bloody pancake thing," Fischer noted, unhelpfully. Cam grunted something, and his eyes rolled back in his head. "Fuck, he's going down!"

Faris was behind him in a flash, holding Cam up just enough to soften his fall. "Yep. He's out cold," Baby Fang observed casually. "Was it the puke or the placenta, do ya think?"

Saige

Chapter Twenty-nine

They say you can't fathom the amount of love a mother has for her children until you become one yourself. I understood now.

My firstborn was the smaller of the two and the fussiest, but only when she was hungry. Which, coincidentally, seemed to be all the time. She was always munching on her tiny hands, being very dramatic with her loud chomping and sucking. Bram had taken to calling her his little monster.

It was actually Cam who'd come up with her name. The two of them had formed a fast bond, and when she really got to wailing, Cam would immediately drop whatever he was doing and take her into his arms. It was like magic how she always settled for him.

Two days after their birth, we still hadn't decided on names, and my little red-haired girl was screaming the house down. Cam plucked her from my arms and came back a half hour later, telling us about sitting on the back patio with her—the morning sun had broken through the clouds, and the rays bathed them in light. When he returned with her, she was snoring softly, and he told us all, "She's my little sunray. Helia. Her name is Helia."

It was the perfect name.

Helia and her sister were already so different from each other.

My chunky babe loved to nap, and she wasn't picky about who held her, so long as someone was. She had thick, dark hair that was already beginning to curl. Her eyes were icy, just like her father's—and the first time she scowled, it was like looking at a mini-Sloane. It took a few more days before we settled on a name for her.

Fischer and I were lying in bed, both girls between us, as we talked quietly about anything and everything. So far, the memories of his trauma hadn't returned, and I hoped they never did. The extra magic I'd gained from that second shot didn't seem to be available to me at all times, not like my own green magic. I think my body had just known what my mate needed from me that day in the pool, and that was that.

Guppy sometimes got a little confused by the blank gaps, but he never asked for clarification on anything. It seemed he really did want to keep those weeks of his life as a closed book. Sloane, Cam, and Kai had all agreed to keep it to themselves, though my sweet mage had been vague at best about his torture. I was just so fucking thankful that he was happy again.

And so, as we lay there together, he trailed his fingers through the baby's dark, messy hair. "I've never known such peace," he confessed. "When I look at her, seeing these little curls, it feels like she has a part of me."

"Of course she does. I think parts of all of us are with them. What is it about her specifically that makes you feel that way?"

He paused, thinking. "I think it's because I've been having this identity crisis. Originally, I thought it was because Faris and I split, but I've realized it goes much deeper. My whole life, from the moment I first heard Faris..." He shook his head, his curls bouncing with the movement. "Anyway, when I look at this little one, I know who I am. I'm her father. And this might just be the first time in my life that I haven't had to dig deep within myself, to figure out if it's really how I feel. Ya know? I'm her dad, and I know I'm going to be an amazing one to these two. My sweet Salem."

Faris walked in at that moment with Sloane, both of them catching the end of our conversation. "Salem is perfect, brother."

"What does it mean?" Sloane asked, curling himself behind Fish's body and pulling both him and Salem closer.

"In my family's language, it means safe, secure, complete. Or peace. I feel all of those things when I look at her."

I smiled. "Salem. I love it, Gup."

Snuggled back into the pillows later, I had my two girls tandem nursing, thanks to creative use of pillows. At first, I'd been terrified my huge boobs would smother them, especially about a day after delivery when my milk had rushed in like a dam breaking. For days, Faris hasn't stopped staring at my tits. He was absolutely mesmerized by my "skills." I was still trying to figure out where his obsession for making toast came from, and if I had to choke down one more slice, I might scream. He'd been so sweet and attentive though; I just couldn't find it in my heart to tell him I needed to eat more than one food item.

The past two weeks had been spent doing a lot of random sleeping, slathering myself in nipple cream, spraying my lady bits with a squeeze bottle—that I was convinced was crafted by the gods themselves—and cuddling my girls. All of my men stepped up, and I didn't have to change a single diaper. I wasn't sure Sloane was going to brave it again though. I couldn't even think about what happened without snorting with laughter. Fischer had been showing him the proper way to wipe Helia, and when Sloane lifted her by the ankles, a loud gurgling sound had everyone freezing. I'd watched in horror as a stream—a freaking stream—of watery poop flew out and landed on the wall.

Sloane had released her ankles in a hurry, and all but fell

backward in an attempt to get away. Fischer and I had laughed so hard we cried. It was glorious. That was nearly a week ago.

Cam had been almost scared to touch them at first, not trusting that his hands—which were bigger than half their bodies—wouldn't be too rough. I reminded him that while he could use his hands for destruction, he always handled me with care unless otherwise requested. That caused his eyes to flare with heat, and I then had to point out that it would be a while before we resumed any of those activities.

My delivery hadn't been the easiest, but thankfully, my body healed the wounds within and I didn't require stitches or further repair. Balor had stayed for a couple of days to monitor me and the girls, but he cleared us and took off back to Besmet, anxious to help with what they were working on there.

I didn't know if it was normal or not, but I'd barely left the sanctuary of my room. I felt like a mama bear in hibernation and I simply didn't want to leave. I had everything I needed right here.

I hadn't let anyone visit either. Not my dad, not Rick, not Roger, not Miranda. Nobody except Gran and my mates. Even then, sometimes I just wanted to be left alone. I could stay right here in this bubble of safety. I knew Napoleon had been sneaking in while we slept because I'd always find little flowers on the nightstand, and Bagheera got to lay at the bottom of the bed some nights. His deep purrs were like a lullaby to the girls and myself.

A knock on the door had me sinking deeper into the pillows. "Saige?" Gran called out, cracking the door and peeking in. "May I come in?"

"Yeah," I answered softly, not wanting to wake my milk-drunk princesses. I finagled my boobs back into my nursing bra, making sure the nursing pads were in place. I'd soaked through so many things that I made sure to keep up with them. Bram called them "Mommy Tassels" which Kai thought was the best fucking thing he'd ever heard.

Gran approached me slowly, a soft smile on her face as she stared down at the two sleeping beauties. "Gods, they really are something, aren't they?"

I grinned. "They are. They really are."

"Do you want to bring them outside for a bit this afternoon? We can sit on the patio and soak up the late summer sun?"

"Oh." My fingers absentmindedly trailed over the intricate patterns on Salem's blanket. Bram had knitted two of the softest and prettiest baby blankets I'd ever seen. Who knew my demon could create something so delicate? Helia's blanket was a combination of greens and soft creamy whites, while Salem's was more deep purples and soft blues. I wasn't sure how he'd done it, but the border of each blanket was a mixture of flowers and leaves. In the middle of each, he'd woven an intricate circle using the colors of our individual magics. I'd bawled like a baby when he'd got them out a few days after the girls were born. Come to think of it, I'd been doing that more often than not lately. Crying over everything.

Glancing up at Gran, I shook my head. "I don't think that's a good idea. I mean, it looks pretty hot outside."

"Okay. Why don't you let a couple of the guys take over for you for an hour and you can join me then?" Gran asked, but I shook my head.

"They might need me. Plus, I'm feeling pretty tired, Gran. I think I'll just take a nap now, if that's okay?" My eyes were burning with tears for some reason. I couldn't look at her. If I did, the tears would fall and that was the last thing I needed. Gods, it pissed me off that I even felt like crying at such a happy time.

"Saige," she whispered, her voice cracking.

I forced the lump in my throat down. "Yeah?"

"Talk to me, child. Everyone's worried. What's going on in your head?"

Ugh. The last thing I wanted to do was talk. I didn't want to talk to anyone. Even if I wanted to, where would I even start? It would be fine—I'd get through this and everything would go back to normal.

"Why would everyone be worried? That's ridiculous."

Gran sighed. "You really want to play this like that?" I didn't respond. "Hm, well, let's see. It's been sixteen days since the girls were born, and you haven't left this room. Not once. It was relayed to me that you've taken three showers during that time, and during all three, you had to have someone holding the babies in the bathroom so you could see them. You're not sleeping. The last time anyone else held one of them was three days ago, Saige. Three. Days."

I reared back as though she'd slapped me. "That's absurd. It hasn't been three days. Cam was holding Helia last night!"

Gran smiled sadly. "No, child. That was three nights ago. You're losing track of time due to exhaustion, and I think you should speak with Balor about getting some help."

"Help? To sleep?" I was getting irritated. A tiny part of me knew I was being irrational, but there was no stopping the swirling anger, causing me to be defensive.

"If that's what you feel would be helpful. I certainly think it would be a start. I'm worried about you," Gran said softly, her voice strained as she rubbed her hands together.

I shook my head. "You don't need to be. My body is completely healed now. I'm just adjusting to this crazy schedule."

Gran stared at me, searching for something. "Okay, honey. Well, since the girls are asleep now, how about a nice warm bath? You can soak and relax. I'll sit here and look after them while they sleep."

My heart began racing. Why was that happening? "What if they need me?"

Gran took my hand in hers. "They will always need you, child. You're their mother. But you have needs also. Taking a bath and letting their great-grandma watch their pretty sleeping faces for half an hour doesn't mean you're not being a good mom. Trust me, you'll feel better after a nice hot bath."

In theory, it did sound nice. Maybe just a quick one. Like ten minutes. And I could keep the bathroom door open so I'd hear if they needed me.

"Okay," I sighed. "I'll go take a bath." Gran smiled widely as she stood, and I passed Salem over to her. Shimmying across the bed, I placed Helia carefully down in the middle, making sure there were no pillows or blankets anywhere near her face. "Helia usually only sleeps for short spurts and then she's up and demanding to eat. Oh, and Salem has to keep these little mitten things on her hands because she flails around and—"

"I got it, Saige. Leave me to enjoy my grandma time. It's been quite a while since I've been around any precious babies." She was speaking to me, but her entire focus was on Salem's perfect face. Gran sat on the bed and stuffed the nursing pillow around her waist to help gently cradle my sweet girl. She wasn't paying attention to me at all.

I slowly dug out a fresh nightgown and nursing bra. Kai had bought me seven of them and spent a small fortune. They were really comfortable though, and I remembered how I'd cried like a baby when he gave me the shopping bag full of bras, tanks, and even a couple of nursing nightgowns.

Glancing over, I saw Gran's lips moving as she talked softly to my daughter. The tears in her eyes glistened as the afternoon sun moved through the clouds and broke through the windows of my room. My throat felt as though I'd swallowed a ball and my chest felt too tight, but I didn't want to worry Gran. I forced myself to the bathroom and left the door cracked as I ran the water.

Slowly, as though my limbs weighed a hundred pounds each, I stripped out of my clothes and caught my reflection in the mirror. *Oh my gods.* Dark, nearly black circles ringed my eyes. My hair was wild. Beyond wild. Completely unkempt, greasy, and tangled. I felt something run down my stomach.

"Oh lovely," I muttered, realizing that I'd started leaking. My stomach was so soft and squishy, it could've been mistaken for a stress ball. I looked nothing like myself. I felt nothing like myself, either.

I turned from the offensive mirror, feeling hollow and numb. Sighing, I stepped into the bath. A groan slipped free as I slid down, leaving only my head and knees exposed. The warmth surrounded me like a blanket, and I had to admit it felt damn nice. My shoulders and neck were starting to take a beating with the awkward positions of holding the girls and feeding them. Breastfeeding was practically an Olympic sport.

My eyes drifted shut and I focused on my breathing. In and out. Nice and slow. I'd wash my hair in a few minutes.

Jerking, I flung water out of the bath and all over Kai, who was kneeling beside the tub, looking at me with concern. "Sorry," I mumbled. "Didn't mean to get you wet. I must've dozed off." The water was cold.

The babies.

Kai's hand flew out to keep me from standing. "They're fine, Cub. Still sleeping. Let me wash you, hmm?" He reached over and pulled the plug, and the water began rapidly decreasing. I shivered, goosebumps making themselves present over every inch of my skin. Replacing the plug, Kai turned the water on to a nice warm temperature, before grabbing a washcloth and some of my fancy coconut and vanilla body wash.

As I hugged my knees, he began gently washing me, starting at my shoulders and moving around to my back. Once he was satisfied, he motioned for me to lift my leg. He was being so quiet and attentive. I wiped my face quickly, hoping he hadn't seen me crying. What did I have to cry about? Nothing. I gritted my teeth as I mentally battered myself for being ungrateful.

Kai picked up a cup and began wetting my hair. I tilted my head back and closed my eyes. If they were closed, they couldn't fucking betray me.

"Cub, I'm worried," he whispered. The snap of the shampoo bottle was loud in the small bathroom, but I kept my eyes shut.

"Why?"

He sighed. Not in annoyance, more like exasperation. "You're depressed, Sprout. I've never seen you like this. I know that some sadness is normal after giving birth, but I think this is more extreme than the normal "baby blues."

"Depressed?" I brought my brows together as he worked the shampoo through my filthy hair. "I'm not depressed, Kai. I'm just sleepy. It's been a lot lately, you know?"

"It has been. Which just adds to everything else. You've been through so much over the past several months. We all have, and we're definitely not feeling like ourselves yet... and we didn't even go through pregnancy and birth."

His words made sense. They resonated, and were logical. On some level, I knew that. The problem was, my brain was telling me that by not being able to handle it, I was weak. That I didn't deserve the babies I'd been blessed with by the stars. Why would they ever show me favor again, if I couldn't even find it in myself to be happy at such a joyful time?

"I'm... I think I just need to get like three hours of uninterrupted sleep and then I'll be back to normal."

"Sprout. We have all been trying to make sure you get more than three hours of sleep. Nobody is normal with three hours of sleep. Now, I know we need to be reasonable since you're nursing, but you literally have six men who are desperate to help you in any way we can. Please don't shut us out. Not now. Tilt your head back."

I did as he asked, and he began rinsing the shampoo from my hair. "Is that what you think I'm doing? Shutting you out?" I whispered, scared to hear the answer.

"Aren't you?"

"No! I mean... No. I just... if the girls aren't near me, how will I be able to see their chests rising and falling? Sometimes I need to be able to see that. If they're not with me, I can't and if I can't see that then they might not be safe, Kai. I can't..."

The door creaked, and I opened my eyes to see Cam walk in, his eyes surveying the scene. He lifted them to mine and looked directly into my damn soul. Oh no. Kai was working conditioner through my tangles, and I felt my bottom lip wobble. I was going to lose it. How did Cam get me to drop my barriers every damn time?

"Baby," he rumbled, his voice deep and soothing. Too soothing. He lowered his large body to the floor and took my hands in his. Kai stood and turned to the vanity, looking for my comb. "Whatever's going on, we can get through it. The way you're feeling? It's not permanent. But we"—he gestured between the three of us—"we are forever."

Oh hell. A sob barreled out of me with so much force, it felt like I was having an exorcism. "This... isn't... me!" I gasped between huge, choking breaths. My entire body was shaking. Every emotion, every fear, it was coming out now. *Oh my gods.* I couldn't breathe.

Hands were on me, lifting me out of the water, and a soft towel was wrapped around my body as Cam pulled me onto his lap. Kai scooted up on my other side, tossing his legs over Cam's thighs so the two of them were completely surrounding me. I cried, and cried.

"Oh, baby... This is killing me," Cam murmured. "I want to make it better. Tell me how to make it better."

"I don't know!" I shouted against his chest. "I don't know what's wrong with me!"

Kai whimpered as he ran his hands down my back. "Breathe, Cub. Just breathe."

"I'm just so tired and scared," I whispered, feeling my body deflating.

Cam stiffened. "What are you scared of?"

I laughed without humor. "What aren't I afraid of? I have two gorgeous newborns who are perfect. I love them so much it hurts to look at them sometimes. I've nearly lost each of you to death or kidnapping, or something, over the course of our relationship. That broke me every time. I try to sleep and every time I close my eyes, I think I hear a noise—someone coming to steal my babies. Or if I don't hear noise, I think they're not breathing. I. Can't. Sleep. If I sleep, something could happen."

I glanced between my two mates, their expressions a mixture of pain and shock. It was all coming out now and I couldn't stop.

"I didn't get to adjust to any of this. I always wanted children, but I thought it would be in the future. I don't regret anything, but it all happened so fast! Every time I had a moment to wrap my head around things, something new would happen. I was in a coma for a month! Most women get nine months to be pregnant; I feel like I had three damn days. None of which I got to spend focused on the girls because I was so worried and stressed, wondering if I did survive, was I going to be a single mother? You all could've died!"

There wasn't enough air. I couldn't breathe. My eyes widened as my chest tightened up tighter than a fist.

"Baby, breathe. Breathe for me. We're here, we're safe. You're safe."

"In and out, in and out, Sprout. Feel your chest expanding, you're breathing. You're okay. We've got you."

They held me while I cried, my pain finally breaking free. Everything I'd bottled up since I met them, all of the stress and huge life-changing events, things I'd never had time to process because we were trying to make it out of everything alive... I was finally cracking. When I eventually spoke, my voice cracked, too.

"It feels like I'm swimming in a sea of sadness without a life jacket. Like, I'm trying very hard to stay above water… but sometimes it would be easier to stop kicking because I'm just so tired. But I'm scared to sink."

Slowly, Kai began brushing my hair with a wide tooth comb, working the conditioner through that was still in there. "You might feel like you need to sink or swim. That's black or white thinking. You're forgetting you have a third option."

I looked back at my shifter, confused. "What do you mean?"

Kai leaned in and wiped my wet cheek, pressing a kiss to my forehead. "Float. There's nothing wrong with biding your time and resting. Just float for a while, Cub. You can do this for yourself—you're strong enough, you're capable. You don't always have to, though. Some days, everything will feel like it's too much. But if your head ever dips below the surface, I will drag you back up. We all will. We're your damn life jackets."

My chin trembled as Kai trailed his thumb across my mouth. "Alpha." It was a whimper, a cry, a plea. Leaning back against his chest, I pulled his mouth to mine. His kisses were sweet, just like him. "Thank you," I mumbled against his lips.

"Let me finish brushing your hair. I need to take care of your needs right now or Bagheera is going to riot," Kai said with a wink. I looked away, giving him full access to my hair again, sniffling and wiping my eyes.

"K is right. You're not alone, and I know it doesn't matter what I say," Cam started, and I lifted my eyes to his. They were bloodshot and wet from emotion. "Your hormones are a huge factor in this, too." He shook his head, coming to terms with something as he exhaled deeply. "I'm done letting you struggle alone. There's no need, little witch. I gave you space because I thought that's what you needed. I was wrong, and I'm sorry."

I opened my mouth to argue, but he lifted a hand, making me pause.

"You've trusted me to get us this far, and I need you to trust me now to take care of you. Do you?" he demanded, his face serious as ever.

"Of course I do," I replied, dropping my head. His hand lifted my chin, bringing my eyes back to his.

"Good. Then here's what we're going to do. Kai is going to finish combing and washing your hair, then he's going to slather you in that cocoa butter you *think* you need for your stretch marks." He rolled his eyes playfully but the look in his eyes dared me to challenge him on it. I didn't, and he leaned in close to my ear. "You're the sexiest woman I've ever laid eyes on, baby girl." My breath hitched as he pulled away and continued laying out his plans. "You'll put on fresh clothes and brush your teeth."

Hmm. That sounded nice in theory, but it also sounded exhausting. Like everything lately. "Then what?"

Cam held my face between his massive hands, his thumbs stroking my cheekbones. The love between us enveloped me, our connection reminding me how much I loved this man. Before he got the chance to respond, Kai swiped my hair off of my neck and placed a soft kiss there.

"Let's just go slow, Cub. My Alpha instincts are screaming at me to pamper you, to tend to your needs. Will you let me?" Kai's breath fanned over my skin as he spoke, and the intensity of Cam's gaze combined with Kai's tenderness had me feeling like I might crumple into a ball of nothingness.

"The babies are okay?" I hadn't heard them, but that incessant nagging in my head made it impossible for me not to ask. Kai returned to combing my hair, and the soothing sensations were making my eyelids heavy.

"Yes, baby. They're with their other daddies right now, getting some snuggles and love. Bram had to go to Besmet this morning but he should be back anytime now," Cam replied, letting his hands fall from my face to my hands.

"Besmet? And nobody told me?" *Ouch.* That stung.

Kai paused his brushing and turned my head to face him. "We

tried to, Sprout. I tried earlier to talk to you and you didn't seem interested. In fact, I don't think you said more than three words to me. Then we sent Fischer in to see you. He said you were staring out of the window the entire time."

Fuck. Oh gods... I vaguely remembered them coming into the room earlier, but for the life of me, I couldn't recall anything they'd said. It was just... blank.

"I'm sorry," I breathed. "I'm so sorry."

"Hey, none of that now. I've been where you are now, Sprout. Not exactly the same circumstances, but those feelings you're talking about—I understand. You have nothing to be sorry about, no matter how much you feel like you do. The only reason I told you about what happened earlier is because I want you to understand why we're so concerned for you. We love you more than anything. Sometimes it takes hearing what others are seeing for us to realize we've been blind to our own behavior."

"I knew I was feeling off, but I thought— I mean, I am really tired. That's true." I looked between my two men. I didn't know why, but I needed them to believe that I hadn't realized it was so bad. That I was so bad...

"We know, little witch. And some sleep will have you feeling better. We're going to get you through this. After everything you've done for us, please let us do this for you." Cam stood up, holding a hand out for me to take. It was a lifeline. If I was going to get back to myself, I needed to take it. I could stay isolated and continue to drift further from the woman I was and the woman I wanted to be, or I could be brave and accept help. I clasped my hand in his, and he smiled softly, pulling me to my feet. "I'm just going to head downstairs and make sure the soup Faris made earlier is fit for eating."

"*Faris* was cooking?" *What in the name of...*

"He's been restless, and driving Sloane up the fucking wall. I kind of took him under my culinary wing, so to speak," Kai explained sheepishly. "It's been... Well, to put it lightly, it's been a gods damn experience."

"Nightmare," Cam coughed into his fist.

I snorted with laughter. "As long as he's moved away from toast, I'll consider it a win."

"He's not happy, but we hid the toaster." My mouth fell open, and Cam winced. "What? He was going through enough bread to feed a fucking army, and it always ended up getting fed to the birds anyway. He was fixated on the damn thing."

Kai scoffed. "That, and Napoleon has been stress eating. I found a HOARD of toast crusts in one of my old boots! I thought they were croutons because they were so stale, but it all made sense when that fat little mouse scurried around the corner with a whole slice of bread in his mouth!"

I couldn't stop the laugh that exploded from me as I envisioned what Kai was explaining. "Oh gods," I wheezed, trying to get some air into my lungs, my belly aching with laughter.

"There's my Cub," Kai crooned, smiling wide.

Cam brushed his ass off and headed for the door. "I'll just be downstairs. Come down when you're done?" He shifted on his feet, staring intently at me. I nodded. I'd follow him anywhere. With that, he left us.

"Alright, Sprout. Let's get you cleaned up and then we'll figure out all the rest, okay?" Kai grunted as I surged forward and wound my arms tightly around his waist. The purring started right away, soothing me. It did the job, too. I felt myself calming. He was my Alpha and he'd always take care of me.

I'D BEEN SCRUBBED and massaged in the shower. My skin felt raw, but in a good way. Like I'd shed away something dark that had been plaguing me, slowly infecting my mind and consuming me. It was a small step, but taking a shower, letting Kai shave my legs and clean me—it was everything I'd needed. The man even combed and used the blow dryer on my hair afterward. I felt cherished, and like a woman who was deeply loved.

"Ready?" he asked, extending his hand.

I swallowed. This was ridiculous. This was my cottage, my home. It wasn't a big deal to actually leave my room, but damn if my heart wasn't racing. I reached for him. My love, my mate. Together, we descended the stairs and I could already hear the low timbre of conversation coming from the living room. I hoped Bram was back.

When I reached the living room, my mouth fell open. My eyes couldn't move fast enough as I took in the space that had been completely transformed.

"What is this?" I whispered.

The couch had been pushed back into a corner of the room, the other furniture pushed out of the way. The center of the room had a huge bed and around it, soft white tulle draped from the ceiling over the entire thing, enclosing it. Pillows and blankets were arranged neatly, and I felt my feet carrying me closer.

Tears blurred my vision as I ran my fingers over the canopy.

"Do you like it?" Bram rumbled, startling me from my haze. I searched the room, finally finding him standing tall next to Sloane.

"You made me... a nest?"

Bram was in front of me so quickly, his amber eyes pinning me to the spot. "*We* made you a nest, Goldie." He lifted his hand and slid it through my hair. "It was a recommendation from an elder in Besmet. It's been so long since we've had any births there, but he remembered his mother speaking about a friend of hers who was suffering after delivery. Much like you are. Her mates made her a family nest, not knowing what else to do. It soothed her, and greatly helped with her worries and depression."

I processed his words and let my gaze take in more of what

they'd done. When had they done all this? It must've taken a lot of work. There were soft robes and fuzzy socks laid over the end of the bed, just waiting for me to use them.

"This is... This is so thoughtful," I said quietly, trying to keep it together. It was hard to do when you had the best six men in creation doing stuff like this.

"I'm sorry I didn't think of it sooner, Goldie. Please forgive me," Bram pleaded, and the guilt in his eyes was clear as day.

I shook my head. "No, no. You don't do that. You did nothing to be sorry about." That was the last thing I wanted—for them to blame themselves over this.

Faris came into the room, carrying a tray piled high with food and a big ass smile on his handsome face. "I apologize, Firefly. I know how much you love my toast, but it appears the toaster grew legs and ran away." He narrowed his eyes, looking suspiciously at each of my other mates.

"Aww, man," I whined, pretending to be upset. A snort came from behind me, and I shot Guppy a glare that quickly dropped away when I saw him in the recliner with a baby in each arm. I'd never seen anything more appealing than these big, dangerous, scary ass males holding their pretty babies. Gah.

"Come sit by me and eat some food, Red," Sloane ordered. He'd tried to make it sound like a request but we both knew it wasn't. His jaw ticked as I approached him where he'd made himself comfortable on the sectional in the corner of the room.

"Here?" I pointed at the spot next to him, and he grumbled something that was impossible to decipher. Guess that was a yes.

As I went to lower myself down, his hands landed on my hips and he guided me onto his lap, my back to his front. He buried his face against my shoulder and took several shuddering breaths, nearly wrecking me all over again. My mates were hurting. I thought I'd been on my own, but that couldn't be further from the truth.

Everyone else crept over, joining us on the couch. It was quiet, but not awkward. I knew I needed to be honest with them about how I'd been feeling, but the thought of going over all of that again sounded like hell.

Sensing my predicament, Guppy spoke up just as I opened my mouth. "Cam filled us in, sweetheart. We don't need to talk about any of that tonight. We just want to be near you, okay?"

Relieved, I nodded. I was too emotional to speak.

"Alright, Sloane, release our woman so she can eat. The little piglets are going to be up any time, and I want to make sure she eats first for once," Cam said, leaning back against the couch and propping his ankle on his knee. Reluctantly, Sloane slid me off of his lap, but kept me tucked closely next to him.

Faris grinned as he placed the dinner tray over my legs. I took in the food options, and holy shit. I felt like I was in the movie *Elf*. Things that had no business being together were piled up in some kind of sick food orgy. Tortilla chips and peanut butter. Taco shells filled with marshmallows and drizzled with—I took a closer look—mustard?

"Viper... I uh, my stomach is a little off right now. Someone mentioned soup earlier? Do you have any of that?"

"Ah... no," he replied, dragging out the end of the word no.

"What do you mean no?" Kai jumped up, heading for the kitchen. "We had a whole pot!"

Faris shrugged. "There was a mishap. Let's just say soup is off the menu."

Fuck. I was hungry but I couldn't eat this. The food before me reminded me of when Miranda and I had played truth or dare as kids, usually daring someone to eat or drink some crazy concoction.

The sound of the doorbell had everyone freezing, looking at the babies to see if they'd wake, but they just kept snoozing.

"Are we expecting someone?" Guppy whispered. Cam winked at me, then pushed himself up and left the room to get the door.

"Faris! Where the hell is that soup pot? The entire thing is gone!" Kai growled from the kitchen.

Sloane sighed. "Where's the soup, Faris?"

The mischievous mage rolled his eyes, and I felt Sloane stiffen next to me. He hated when anyone rolled their eyes at him, but I suspected it probably really got him going when Faris did it.

Cam came back into the room carrying bags of Chinese food, and I groaned. A full-on, 'there's a wild beast within me who needs that food immediately' kind of groan. "You are a god. Someone grab plates and shit. I'm about to devour this."

And I did. I ate more than I had in two weeks and felt as though I would burst. Afterward, I fed the babies before crawling into the huge bed, loving the nest feel. It was beyond cozy and warm, the blankets smelled of my mates, and I felt safe and loved.

Bram climbed in next to me, with Faris on my other side. "Sleep, Goldie. We'll wake you when you're needed."

I nodded, my eyes too heavy to remain open. As sleep rushed in, I relaxed against the softness of the bed. Soft touches and quiet murmurs were my lullaby.

"I love you all," I whispered, unsure if anyone heard it. But as I fell into the open arms of slumber, the feel of soft lips against my forehead soothed me, and the many declarations of love swirled around me just like the embrace of their arms.

"We love you so much, Goldie. Rest now, my queen."

And I did.

Saige

Epilogue

Four Weeks Later

I stretched like a cat as I came to, nestled deep within my blankets. Damn, that had been a good sleep. I wiggled down into the nest, my eyes still shut.

The girls were six weeks old today. How was that even possible? Time was moving faster now than it ever had before and I was scared to blink.

I suddenly realized that it was quiet. Too quiet. My eyes flew open and I pushed myself up, looking around the room and finding it empty. *Strange.* The smell of bacon drifted in, so I listened closer and heard faint movement from the kitchen. Okay, bathroom first, then delicious bacon.

A few minutes later, I padded into the kitchen, finding Gran dancing around as she fried up bacon and pancakes. "Oh good! You're up. I can put on my jams now." She shouted at Alexa to "Play my fuck around and find out playlist," and I gasped.

"Your *what* playlist?"

She tossed her head back and cackled like the lunatic she was. "Here, have some coffee."

I sighed deeply as she handed me a large mug with stupid

snail peens all over it. Bram and his creations... "Where is everyone? It's too quiet."

"Your men took the girlies to the park for a walk. They wanted to let you sleep in. How are you feeling?" Gran glanced at me, attempting to be casual, but I knew she was still worried about me.

My index finger followed the rim of the mug. "I'm feeling a lot better, Gran. Really. The therapy is helping and the medication is really kicking in now. I still get overwhelmed, but I think that's just a normal part of motherhood."

After my breakdown last month, I'd decided to seek treatment. It wasn't an immediate cure, and I wasn't crazy about taking antidepressants, but my brain wasn't working like it should have been. I didn't want to miss moments with my family just because I was terrified of bad things happening, nor did I want to live in my room for the rest of my life. That wasn't fair to my mates or my daughters.

My therapist had actually been recommended by Balor. He'd found me a female demon who was able to shed some light on things I'd been experiencing, explaining how they were caused by my demon side. Like the urge to keep everyone close, to nest, to feel secure, especially after birth. That first night I'd slept in the nest, I was out cold for ten hours. Nobody woke me, instead using the little bit of breastmilk I'd pumped to feed the girls during the night.

While I'd felt like a whole new woman when I woke up, my tits were as big and hard as bowling balls. I'd leaked through my nursing pads, bra, and nightgown, and the moment I got those wet clothes off, milk had started spraying like a freaking sprinkler. I had to pump and nurse to get all of it out. The look of horror on Sloane's face as I sat there like a human fountain would live in my head for the rest of my life.

Thankfully, everyone understood that in the future if I needed to catch up on sleep, that I'd make sure I was well and truly empty beforehand, and someone would wake me just to check on the boob situation after four or five hours. Of course, my kinky little Viper offered to 'take the edge off' without waking me. I thought Sloane was going to throw up.

We hadn't had sex yet. I was slowly coming around to the idea of it. I'd started noticing again the way Cam's shirts stretched across his wide shoulders, and how his tattoos flexed with his arm muscles. The other morning, I'd seen Kai—shirtless and wearing a tiny, tight ass pair of shorts—doing yoga in the garden. I'd definitely been noticing them.

"You seem more like yourself," Gran commented, interrupting my thoughts.

"I feel more like myself. Finally."

She sat a plate of food down in front of me before taking a seat herself. "Do you remember when I told you the story of after I gave birth? I went through the same thing. I wish I'd gotten help like you did. It was just... Back then, you didn't talk about mental health problems. And I was so deep in my grief with missing Rick that I didn't know which end was up. I'm proud of you."

"Thank you, Gran." I reached for her hand. "I was just so worried that if I didn't do everything, be a part of every moment, that I'd be like *her*." I didn't need to say who. We both knew. It was something I'd been working through with my therapist. In order to be the mother I wanted to be, I had to make sure I was taking care of—at the very least—my basic needs as a person. Eating, showering, sleeping. She was right. Even on days where showering was exhausting, I pushed myself to do it because I always felt a tiny bit more like myself when I got out.

We ate together in silence for a few minutes, just enjoying each other's company. "Have you heard anything more about Fern?"

Gran's fork paused halfway to her mouth, and she sighed. "Just the same. She's being held in a WISP holding center until a more permanent facility can be arranged."

Hunter had shown up a few days after his expected return to Emerald Lakes without Fern. Apparently, Fern had tried to make a run for it and Hunter tracked her down once more. Only this time, she'd used her magic on him. It went wrong. Very wrong. A few people were seriously injured—one of them was still in a coma—and it was her fault. She'd nearly killed Hunter in the process too.

Her power was strong but untrained, thanks to the shitty area she'd grown up in and the lack of support from responsible adults. She'd never learned anything about restraint, and according to Hunter, she was a very angry young woman. Gran had offered up the spare room in my cottage to him, and Hunt had lived at my place while we were all away in Besmet. He'd insisted on moving out once we returned, saying we needed the family time together. Apparently, he'd found a place downtown, above Dinner Thyme.

Since Asrael was dead, Montague Industries had been shut down, the truth of his evil work finally coming to light. All of Asrael's work was confiscated by WISP, and so many children had been recovered. Each new article I saw on it never ceased to make me smile. Khol had hired Hunter straight away, more than impressed with his resume and skill set. Hunter now led one of the rescue teams for the missing kids, and seemed to really enjoy his new line of work.

My temples throbbed as I thought about this sister that I'd never known. She wasn't allowed visitors yet, but I really wanted to meet her. I didn't know what WISP had in store for her—if she'd be sentenced to jail time or if they'd try to put her in some kind of mandated magic course. It was anyone's guess.

"Maybe if the guys get Kai's project up and off the ground soon enough, she could be transferred there..." It was something I'd thought about ever since they started planning this new training facility seriously. Khol had offered to fund the entire project, adding it as a new division of the Radical company. Since my mates needed a new type of job to be close to home, they'd all seemed surprisingly excited about the idea of being trainers and teachers at this new location.

The warehouse they'd been pretending to be interested in when they first blew into town was part of the purchase, but there also was a massive old stone school building about half a mile down the road that had come up for sale. Now they were eyeing that as well, to convert into dormitories. It was pretty exciting, though I was also getting curious because twice in the past month, Sloane and Fischer had gone to this warehouse to check it out.

Last week, they'd been getting ready to leave, slipping on their riding gear and grabbing their backpacks, when I heard Sloane ask Guppy about his flame butt plug. I'd walked right into a fucking wall. One of these days, I was going to show up there and see exactly what it was they got up to. Just the thought made my blood pump and my thighs clench. My body had been off-limits since having the babies, but damn, I really was starting to feel the desire returning.

"Wouldn't that be great? We could really get to know Fern then, and be a part of her progress," Gran mused, and I smiled. I really did hope that Fern would eventually want a relationship with us.

I didn't get a chance to respond because Gran's phone rang, ending our conversation about my estranged sister. She answered, listening intently to whatever was being said, then her mouth fell open.

"Oh, I don't know if I can make that work. An hour?" She paused, listening. "One second." Gran lowered the phone to her chest, covering the mouthpiece. "Saige, you know how I put the apartment up for rent again?"

I nodded. It had been empty for a few weeks now, Miranda having bought a new place for herself and Annie. Kohl was there when he wasn't in Besmet, but from what my bestie had told me, he was usually at their place almost every night.

"Well, I have a tenant who wants to see it, but their schedule is very busy. There was an opening in their schedule and they can be there in an hour. I have an appointment today for my full body wax so I—"

I held my hand up. "I'll go. Just, please, don't tell me anything more about that."

"Great!" She beamed and returned to the call. "My granddaughter will meet you there in an hour. Yep. Okay, perfect. Let me know what you think." She disconnected the call and went back to eating. "Thanks. You're a lifesaver. Rick and I are going to do a little Vegas trip and I want to be smooth as a whistle to receive his meat missile."

"Okay, I'm out! Enjoy your wax! BYE!" I practically ran from the room and up the stairs. Right. I needed to hurry up, shower, and get to The Pig.

WELL, *wearing regular clothes after having a baby is a bunch of bullshit.* I squeezed into a pair of black yoga pants which was as close to regular clothes as I was getting, and one of my store t-shirts. This one was black, with The Pig logo and white lettering that read *I beg your garden?* Tossing on my backpack, I texted the group chat, letting the guys know where I was heading. I slipped into my old faithful leopard print flats and pushed through the screen door.

"Son of a bee sting," I cursed, noting that the cars were gone. Six weeks ago, I'd pushed out two whole ass people from my vajingle, and now they'd only left me my bicycle. *Stars, have mercy.* I hadn't ridden my bike in so long, which I was quickly reminded of when my thighs started burning. Oh, I was going to kick some ass. What used to take me five minutes now took me ten, and I was huffing and puffing like the big bad wolf.

I dug around in my bag for the keys to the shop, desperately trying to catch my breath. Gran, Rick, Frank, and Arlo had been running the store and doing a fantastic job while I was in Besmet and then recovering from having the girls.

As I placed the large skeleton key into the lock, I caught my reflection in the large glass window on the door. My face was fuller, my hair shorter, my stomach softer and rounder... but my eyes, they were no longer the eyes of a woman who'd lived her entire life in this small, quirky town. They were the eyes of a queen—though we were working on getting Besmet established with a democratic type of government. These were the eyes of a woman who had lost so much and gained even more.

Twisting the key, I swung the door open and stepped inside, the dated hardwood floors creaking beneath my shoes. The scents of sage, rosemary, wood, and patchouli slammed my senses, and I smiled wide. Damn, I'd missed my shop. It looked just the same, smelled the same. For the first time since having the girls, I felt the urge to come back and work.

Checking my watch, I saw there was only a minute until this tenant was due to arrive. Fuck. I could feel how sticky my face felt, and I darted around the bar, looking for some tissues to clean myself up. *Where the hell are they?* I pulled open the drawer where I usually stored extra boxes, finding it empty. *Fuck!*

I crouched down and rooted around on the deep shelves beneath the bar top. The doorbell jingled, startling me. "Just a second!" I shouted, finally spotting the damn tissues. I swiped the box and hopped up, a shriek leaving my mouth when Kai's face was right there. An inch from mine. "Oh. My. STARS!" I clasped my hand to my heart as it tried to escape my ribcage.

Kai laughed, deep and rich. "Sorry, didn't mean to scare you." The doorbell jingled again, and I looked over to see... Cam?

"What are you guys doing here? Can you wait in the back or

something? There's a—" Cam held his finger to my mouth, a grin forming on his own.

"We heard there's an apartment for rent?" He lifted a brow as he stared down at me.

My eyes darted around. "Nnn—" I started to say no slowly, but then I realized this was probably some kind of kinky role-playing situation, and oh my moon maidens, I was here for that. So my "Nnn" turned into a "Nnnyessss?" which had both of my mates cracking up.

Suddenly, the rest of my mates came through the door, all of them crowding around me. *Oh shit yes.* I felt like I was in a live action porno, ready for all the dicking. Each one of them looked like they wanted to snack on me like I was corn on the cob. Though maybe not quite that... teethy.

Then I realized they were missing two very small, very important people. "Where are the babies?"

"With Bette," Sloane replied, eyeing my thighs.

"Oh," I squeaked. "But she's not taking them to her waxing appointment, right?"

"For the love of Saturn," Guppy cried, as all of them covered their ears.

I blinked. "Ohhh. There is no appointment, is there? Soooo, you guys are the new tenants?" I waggled my eyebrows. "Perfect," I purred, stepping up and grabbing hold of Cam's shirt, dragging his big, tall body down to me. "I gotta tell you all, I've been... missing you. I didn't expect such an elaborate plan to, you know, get my toes wet again." I winked, and instead of the looks of lust I was expecting, they all looked confused. No matter. They wouldn't be confused for long.

"The apartment is upstairs, but I'll show you the interior entrance through here. It's just out the... back door." I winked and spun on my heel, grabbing the hem of my shirt and ripping it off, tossing it over my shoulder.

"Fuck," Bram cursed. "Goldie—"

"Come on, boys," I called in my best 'come fuck me' voice, my hands reaching for the snaps of my bra.

"Baby, wait!" Cam shouted as I tossed my bra, and the back door I was facing was flung open. I stumbled back as literally every person I knew filled the small hallway. Gran, Rick, Khol, Miranda, the Seers, Randy Roger, Frank and Arlo...

"Oh my gods!" I shrieked, diving behind a shelf to hide my bare tits. Someone was firing off little popper things filled with streamers, and I stared on in horror, flicking my focus from this parade of people to my mates—some of whom would be dead soon, because they were laughing their asses off.

"Child, why in the name of the stars are your boobs out right now? Is this some kind of demon custom, Bram?" Gran demanded of my mate. "We don't typically do topless proposals... At least, not in public settings." She batted her eyelashes at Rick, indicating that she'd like to do something topless with him.

Kai tossed me my bra and shirt, and I quickly shimmied them back on, before my mind drifted to what she'd said. "Proposal?!"

"You ruined the surprise, Bette!" Randy Roger scolded, tsking.

"Well, how was I supposed to know it'd turned into a game of free the boobies?"

"ENOUGH!" Sloane barked, and everyone quieted down. I stared with wide eyes as all six of my mates dropped to one knee.

Oh my gods. What a sight.

"Saige Wildes," Guppy said, loud enough for everyone to hear.

"We thought it would be appropriate to do this at the place where you first bewitched us," Kai piped up, propping his elbow on his knee and his chin on his fist, his smile broad and all for me.

"I might not have particularly liked you at first," Sloane muttered, and everyone laughed loudly, making him blush. "But you did bewitch me, nonetheless."

"Who would've thought that the woman who, honest to gods, thought she was going to drive my Harley with zero experience and make me ride on the back would have all six of us so completely in love?" Cam teased, and I couldn't hold back the tears.

Bram snorted. "Well, I could've told ya, mate. She iron-plated a man's tenders to wear as a necklace." My demon smiled wickedly, much like he had when I'd told him that lie the first time. I'd told him time and time again it wasn't true, but it turned him on so I'd stopped trying to get him to accept it.

"And you helped me figure out how to live a real life. Plus, you give me cool shit like pom-pom pens, furry notebooks, and fuzzy socks," Faris sighed in a totally loving voice.

"Don't get me started on the babies you gave us," Fischer piped up, and my dad and Miranda walked over to the guys, handing Helia to Faris and Salem to Kai.

Cam smiled gently. "What we want to know, little witch, is if you'll be ours forever? Will you bind yourself to us in a ceremony in front of those we love and care about?"

Sloane reached into his pocket and produced a small black box, flipping it open to reveal the most unique, gorgeous ring I'd ever seen. In the center, a Nox stone had been shaped into a crescent moon. The band was thin, consisting of seven strands of some type of metal, but each piece was a different color. The colors of our different magics were twined together, completely wrapped up, each color connecting with the others, just like us.

"Yes," I said, my voice shaking. "Yes!"

Cheering exploded around us, and people set off more exploding streamers. My mates were up off their knees, kissing me, hugging me, and declaring their love. Bram plucked the ring from the box, sliding it on my finger. I smiled as I looked down at it, loving the way it sparkled in the light.

Music started playing, drinks flowed, and a celebration went on for hours.

Later that evening, I snuck upstairs to the apartment, feeling nostalgic. It felt like so long ago that I'd shown them this place. We'd been through so much together.

Discovering each other in itself was a miracle. We'd survived the betrayals—whether they were caused by each other or someone outside of our circle. Not only did we survive, we got revenge against those who had harmed us. Our destinies were tied to each other.

The door slammed, and I heard a stampede of feet on the stairs. My mates, racing to get to me. Always finding me.

I was eternally theirs.

The End.

For now....

FIRST THINGS FIRST! Want to discuss the book? Check out the spoiler group here. https://www.facebook.com/groups/themagicofeternity

AFTERWORD

Damn.

One year later, five books in total, a whole series and my life has been changed forever.

This book was hard to write. Not because it wasn't flowing, but because I knew the faster I wrote it, the sooner it'd be done. I wasn't ready to say goodbye.

These characters got under my skin from the very first moment Saige popped into my head back in April 2020. I wanted to create relatable, likeable and memorable characters that would stay with readers long after they finished each book, the same way they stayed with me throughout the day. It's fascinating how real they feel, how something can happen and I'll be like oh my gods, that's totally something Bram would say, or Cam would do, etc.

Emerald Lakes is a fictional town that will always be real in my heart. It's been my escape, my safe haven, my break from reality. I'm really going to miss it. I hope that you found someone within these pages who resonated with you.

There are some things that went unanswered in this final book, and that was on purpose. I have a few spin-offs planned,

AFTERWORD

the first of which is Demons in My Bed - The Demons of Port Black series. Those psycho, hard ass, mask wearing demon gang you met just now? Say their name.

The Exiled.

They will be the male main characters in the Port Black series and Palmer, who you met in The Magic of Revenge (Hunter's best friend) is the female lead. I did have a pre-order up for this, but I had to cancel it due to time restrictions. So keep an eye out for updates!

My next book release is Lost in Sleepy Hollow.

For all of you who have stuck by me through this series, I thank you. To the readers out there who left reviews on each and every book, thank you! It means so much. To the friends I've made across the different social media platforms, especially in The Misfits reader group on Facebook - your posts and comments give me life and keep me going down this crazy path.

To the fabulous bookstagrammers and booktokers, thank you for promoting my stories and being so wonderful. Your videos and posts crack me up.

Cassie Hurst, my content and development editor, you were one of my very first readers and you've cheered me on the entire past year. Thanks for all the late night plotting phone calls and for helping me navigate this story and these characters.

Polly Nichols, one of my best friends and my kick ass proof-reader, seriously couldn't do all of this without you. From your thirst comments to the way you're quick to jump in and pick me up every damn time someone so much as looks at me funny... you're a true gem of a person and I love you. Yes, Faris is still keeping the restraining order, this changes nothing between you.

Raewyn Ash, my sweet editor who I know I nearly killed with this book. Thank you for taking my manuscript and making it shine without changing my voice. You're one of the hardest working people I've ever known and your work ethic is top notch.

AFTERWORD

Cat, Jess, Rebecca! The trio of wild women who came into my life and have made it so much better. I couldn't get half of the things done as I do without you three. Your professionalism and dedication to being my personal assistants shows with everything you do. Thank you.

To my ARC and Weenie Wagoneers! YOU GUYS ROCK!!! I appreciate you guys so much, taking time from your lives to share stuff about Emerald Lakes on your social media and to read my stuff before release day... I am so grateful.

Emerald Lakes PD. Stacy, Taylor, Robin, Elizabeth, Jess, Polly, Reb, Cat and Nikki. My squad. The group I'd pick to do anything with because at least I know we'd have a damn fun time doing it. So lucky to have friends like you.

Author besties Maya Nicole, Rory Miles, and Kathryn Moon. Thanks for sharing your knowledge and being a sounding board for all kinds of stuff. Self-publishing isn't easy, but it's a lot more manageable when you have great friends.

Bridget and Jake Bordeaux, the super narrators who took my book TO A WHOLE OTHER LEVEL! If you haven't checked out the audiobooks yet, what are you waiting for?! Seriously, thank you, I couldn't have picked a better pair for these stories.

To you, the reader... thank you. For the reviews, for loving these characters. Without you, I wouldn't have the success I've had in the past year.

Last but not least, thank you to my family. My husband and children, who I work hard for to make our dreams come true. My extended family for believing in and supporting me. I love you all.

So yeah, it's been a year. I can't wait to see where the next year takes us.

LOST IN SLEEPY HOLLOW

The riders, they come at night.

Are you ready for something scarily sexy?

Sleepy Hollow was supposed to be a legend. It became my reality.

After a botched spell, I find myself stuck in an old stone well. I'm terrified and injured, until the handsome and flirtatious Gideon hears my calls for help and I'm rescued. Realization hits me as fast as the sugar crash at the end of a trick or treat haul. I'm not in Wisteria. And it sure as hell isn't 2021.

Most of the people are welcoming, accepting me as a part of the town. Then there's Father Jude, who despises me at first glance. Magistrate Lucian; who is suspicious of my sudden arrival, and Headmaster Bodie who can't seem to stop staring at me. October is suddenly filled with mystery, murder, and mayhem. Just like that, my favorite season becomes a true nightmare.

My name is Hattie Van Tassel and I'm lost in Sleepy Hollow, a town that's righteous beneath the sun and absolutely depraved beneath the moon.

Lost in Sleepy Hollow is a full length spooky why choose romance that features themes that may be disturbing to some readers. Strong language, violence, sexual situations and MM content included. Reader discretion is advised.

Pre-order here! books2read.com/sleepyhollow

ALSO BY BRITT ANDREWS

Check out my website for new releases and updates!
https://www.brittandrewsauthor.com/

The Emerald Lakes Series:
-The Magic of Discovery
- The Magic of Betrayal
- The Magic of Revenge
-The Magic of Destiny
-The Magic of Eternity

Diamond Dreams With Maya Nicole:
-Catching Kalen

Lost In Sleepy Hollow

Printed in Great Britain
by Amazon